MEANT FOR NOW

ALLISON SPEKA

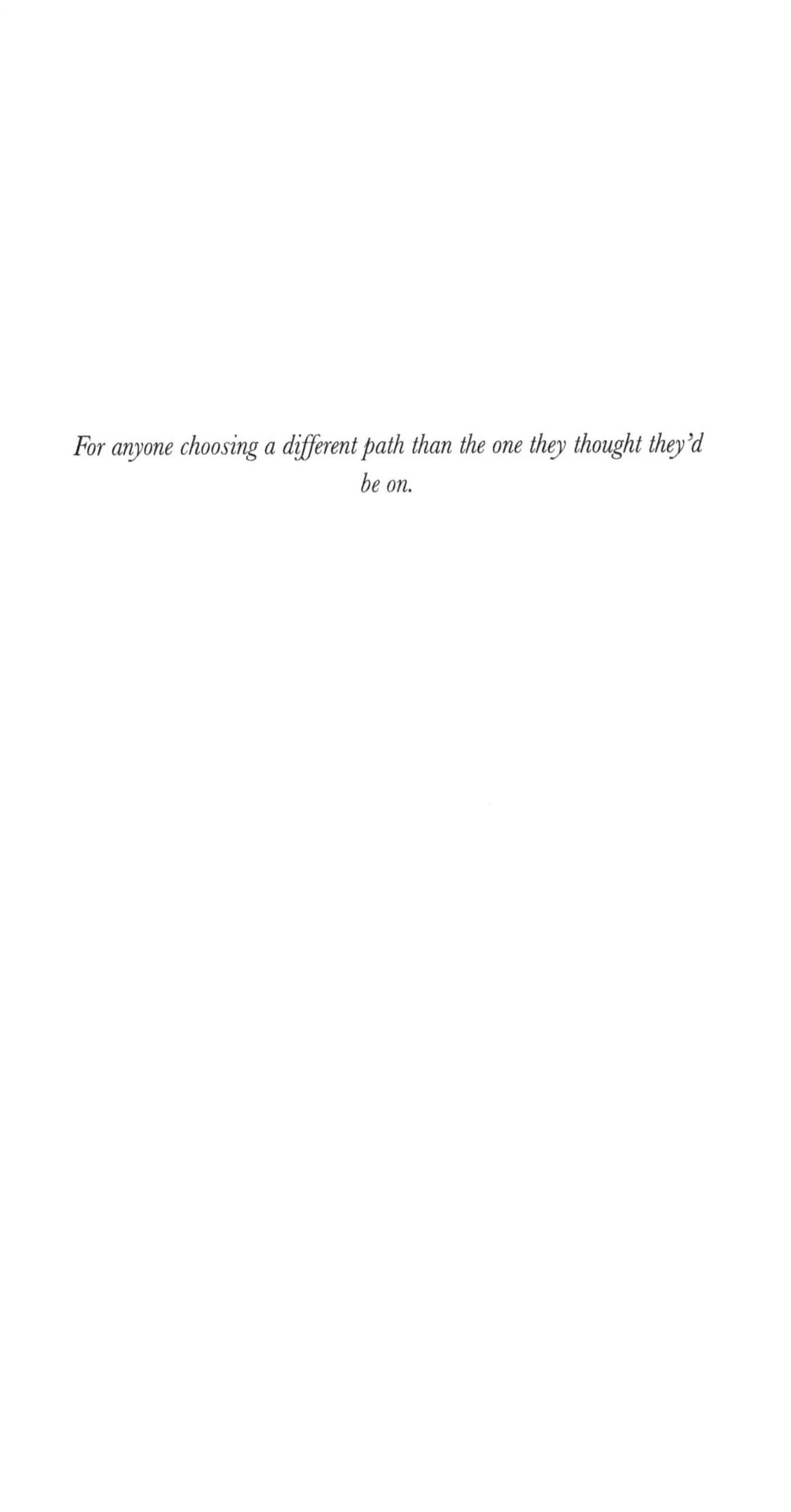

For anyone choosing a different path than the one they thought they'd be on.

Meant for Now

ONE

Frankie

"Fired? Fired! Can you believe it?" I knocked back one of the tequila shots the bartender had set in front of us. The burning sensation coated my throat and I welcomed the sting. The shot glass hit the table with a loud clank before I brought the lime wedge to my lips and sucked.

"I mean, it was a shock at first, but considering this is the fiftieth time you've brought it up, I'm starting to believe it," my older sister Mattie muttered from the barstool next to mine. "And technically you got laid off, not fired."

"What's the difference?" I demanded, snatching her shot and knocking it back too. "It's all just an excuse to get rid of me. *Me!* I've done everything for that company. I've been there for years. And to just lay me off on a random Thursday without even giving me a chance to say goodbye?" Tears pricked at my eyes, but I had already sobbed over this enough in the past twenty-four hours. I refused to be reduced to a shriveling mess of a human.

Mattie lightly placed her hand on my shoulder. "Frankie, it's going to be alright. You're the most qualified, driven person I know. You'll find another job. This is a slight detour in the grand scheme of things."

Her words danced around in my brain. Maybe it was the buzz, but they didn't quite hit their intended target. The din in the bar faded to background noise as I tried to focus on the conversation at hand.

I was fully prepared to spend a few more days wallowing before I accepted this turn my life had unexpectedly taken. And what better place to wallow than in the company of my only sister? As soon as I'd stepped out of my former office in downtown Atlanta, clutching a box of my belongings and still feeling shell-shocked, I had stumbled over to a bench across the street and looked up flights on my phone. I had to get away. Spending some time with my sister in the small town she'd moved to a few years ago had sounded like the exact getaway I needed.

Key Ridge, Colorado had one main street, a handful of hotels, a ski resort, and a population of just over one thousand people. But when I got off the plane a few hours ago and Mattie picked me up, I was surprised to find the streets practically bustling. We'd even had to wait to get a seat at the bar we'd been holed up in for the past two hours.

"Spring break," she'd explained, like that was supposed to mean something to me. We'd both grown up in Florida before I'd moved to Atlanta after college. Spring break to me meant lazy days on a beach and sun-kissed skin. But apparently in Colorado, spring break was prime time for skiing and snowboarding. Which explained the feet of white fluff piled up alongside the sidewalks.

When I'd decided to fly here on a whim, I hadn't exactly pictured this much snow in mid-March. But Mattie had informed me there was at least a month left before the ski season officially ended, and Mother Nature had blessed them with way more snow this year than the past few. Funny—I didn't realize more snow was a blessing, but you'd have thought it was a miracle with how excited my sister was describing it.

"Twenty-eight and unemployed," I groaned, resting my forehead in my hands. "I never thought it'd come to this."

"You're being dramatic," Mattie unhelpfully pointed out.

"I can be dramatic if I want to be. It's my life."

"It's a job, not your life." Mattie waved the bartender over to order another drink, purposefully ignoring the scowl that had creeped onto my face.

My career *was* my life. Or at least it had been up until yesterday. I'd been scaling the corporate ladder of that company ever since I graduated from college. It defined me, and I was more than okay with that. It thrilled me when people asked me what I did for a living and I could tell them I was the Director of Marketing at a thriving real estate company.

Now I was nothing.

"Did you tell Mom and Dad yet?" Mattie asked.

I scoffed. "When would I have had time to tell them? When I was sobbing on my drive home after my boss broke the news to me? When I was packing to come visit you? Or did you want me to call them from the plane? Where I was such a whimpering mess that the gentleman sitting next to me asked if he could switch seats."

"He did not," Mattie said.

"He did too. He picked a seat next to a crying baby—*a baby*, Mattie. He thought that would be a more peaceful flight than being in my vicinity."

Mattie completely ignored my hysterics. "They're about to leave for that month-long cruise in Australia. You should really call them while they still have service."

"I'll call them when I have a new job," I said.

"Who knows how long that will take?" Mattie argued. "You're just going to lie to them?"

"I thought you said I'd find a new one in no time." I narrowed my eyes at her, throwing her words back in her face.

An elbow bumped my back and I turned around to glare at the culprit.

"Excuse you," I said to the older woman getting settled onto the barstool next to mine.

"Sorry." She looked at me with apologetic eyes.

"You're fine." Mattie leaned forward and offered the woman a smile. "My sister is having an off day." With that, she tugged at my arm and glared at me. "Can you not be so on edge right now? You almost ripped that poor lady's head off."

"She bumped me," I grumbled.

"It's a crowded bar." Mattie's eyes flicked to the ceiling in a silent plea for patience.

The grizzly-looking bartender showed up at that exact moment and set down another margarita in front of Mattie. She took a small sip before pushing it in my direction.

"Can we get an order of fries, too, Dave? She needs to soak this up."

The bartender gave Mattie a small nod and punched something into the handheld device he carried around.

"I'm fine," I argued, even though I was a complete lightweight and the two shots of tequila had already gone straight to my head. But if losing your job wasn't a good occasion to get a little tanked, then what was? "And sorry I'm not in a hurry to tell Mom and Dad my life is over."

"I don't think there are any acting scouts in Key Ridge so you can lay off the melodramatic monologue." Mattie shot me a look, and irritation bubbled in my gut—the kind that only a sister could cause.

"No," I fired back stubbornly. "When that asshole ex of yours cheated on you and you thought your life was falling apart, I didn't call *you* dramatic."

She rolled her eyes. "Um, yeah you did. And you heavily implied I needed to move on. You're probably half the reason I ended up in Key Ridge to begin with."

She had a point there. Perhaps tough love ran in our family.

I took another sip of the margarita, attempting to quell the adrenaline that somehow raged inside of me. Exhaustion should have stepped in by now, but I was wound up tighter than a toy top. Apparently, I did not handle change well.

Trying to distract myself, I regarded the small, divey bar. When I told Mattie I needed a drink as soon as I exited the airport, she'd taken us here. It was the only place open right now.

The bar had sticky floors, old pool tables with ripped felt, and dartboards that currently held the interest of a small group of men who let out excited cheers every five minutes or so.

"I still can't believe you live in a town like this," I said, glancing back at my sister.

The Mattie who had picked me up at the airport today in her olive-green puffy jacket, beanie, and boots was a far cry from the Floridian sister I'd always known. The one who preferred to wear flip-flops well into the winter months and thought she'd freeze in fifty degrees. I had only visited her here once—for her wedding to her husband Giles—but that had been in the summer.

"You sure Giles won't mind me crashing?" I asked again. I had sprung this visit on them, after all, and I hadn't bought a return ticket yet. I'm sure an open-ended visit from his sister-in-law wasn't the most exciting news for the guy. We got along well enough, but he was a quiet one. Probably preferred his alone time.

Mattie waved off my concern. "It'll be fine. Our basement is completely redone and has a full guest bedroom and bathroom. It'll be like your own little apartment."

"And I won't overstay my welcome," I promised. Even though I had no idea how long I'd be staying, it felt like the right thing to say. Besides, it was more of a promise to me than to her. I'd figure out this whole mess soon. Maybe I had been thrown for a loop, but I was still me.

Responsible. Driven. Not afraid of a challenge.

This was only a tiny little setback. Microscopic even.

The bartender returned and set a plate down in front of us. The scent wafting from the fried, salty goodness was utterly mouthwatering. Without hesitation, I stuffed a few fries into my mouth and moaned.

"I know you're still in mourning, but this is actually going to be so great." Mattie clapped her hands, then daintily took one fry while I continued shoveling them into my mouth by the handful. "We can spend time together, I can show you around town—oh, and you can help out at the lodge too!"

The lodge being the Key Ridge Ski Lodge—the one Mattie had originally come to town to work at. The same one owned by her husband's family.

I wrinkled my nose. "You're going to extort me for free labor while I'm visiting?"

She shrugged. "It'll be fun."

I thought about fighting her on this, but it actually didn't sound *that* bad. I'd been punching away at my corporate job for years at this point—sitting in my cubicle from eight to five every day, often even staying later to finish something. That was the only life I'd known. Getting a taste of something different could be a welcome distraction.

"Mattie!"

My thoughts were interrupted by a pretty brunette with a very pregnant belly. She smiled and waved as she walked from the front of the bar over to us. Mattie stood from her stool and embraced her tightly.

"Erin, oh my God. What are you doing here? I thought you were already on the road."

"We're all packed up and ready to go. Johnny is in the car. I figured you'd be at the lodge so I stopped in to say goodbye, but Bev said you'd be here."

"Ugh, I'm going to miss you." Tears welled in Mattie's eyes.

"Denver isn't that far," Erin said, going in for another hug. "We'll be back for the Fourth of July."

Mattie nodded before looking back at me as if just remembering I was still here. "Frankie, you remember my friend Erin from the wedding. She's married to Giles's cousin, Johnny."

"Right, of course." I waved, the reminder effectively jogging my memory.

"And of course I remember you!" Erin exclaimed. "I was in awe of the color-coded itinerary you handed out to all the guests."

"Oh, um, yeah. I'm a pretty organized person." That was an understatement. That color-coded itinerary was nothing compared to the binder I'd put together for Mattie. She had begged me not to plan her entire wedding, but I hadn't listened. Growing up, everyone had always joked that I had the older sister energy. Not that Mattie was a mess by any means; we were actually quite similar in a lot of ways. It was just that I'd never met a situation I didn't want to take charge of. That had caused us to butt heads quite a bit growing up, but Mattie had slowly learned to just let things go when it came to me. If I wanted to plan something, she no longer fought me tooth and nail on it.

When she had moved to Key Ridge, I'd been shocked. She'd had a nice little career of her own in Florida, and our lives were relatively parallel to each other. She'd originally come down here through her last job, but when she'd dropped everything to move here because she'd fallen in love with the town—in addition to some local ex-professional snowboarder —I had thought she'd lost her mind.

But now she had this whole life. She was happy and settled. And here I was, the lost and aimless one.

Mattie and Erin continued their drawn-out goodbye. From what I'd gathered, Erin and her husband were moving to Denver for a job opportunity for him. It was more stable and safer than what he'd been doing—odd jobs around town, including teaching private snowboarding lessons for the Key Ridge Ski Lodge.

Seeing Erin and Mattie give each other one last hug left a lump in my throat. It was a stark reminder that my sister had created this whole family here. Even though I had lived in Atlanta for years—owned a condo, had roommates, the whole thing—I hardly had any acquaintances outside of work, let alone real friends.

Erin waved goodbye and left the bar.

Just as Mattie turned back to me, her phone vibrated on the wooden bar top, almost sending it over the edge. She snatched it and pressed the answer button before holding it to her ear.

"What's up, Bev?" she asked. Bev was Giles's aunt and owned the lodge with him. I remembered that much at least.

Lines formed between Mattie's brows as she listened to whatever Bev was saying on the other end. "Did you check the storage room? I could have sworn I put the extra sheets there." She paused before letting out a sigh. "Alright, no worries. I'm still at The Ridge. I'll swing by before I head home."

Mattie hung up and slid off her barstool.

"Speaking of Erin and Johnny leaving, I've got to run to the lodge. Giles has a friend coming into town to take over the private snowboarding lessons for the rest of the season. He's staying in the studio above Bev's garage and she's rushing around trying to get the room ready before he gets in tonight."

"Okay," I said, sticking another few fries in my mouth.

Mattie slipped on her coat and pulled the zipper up all the way to her neck. "You coming?"

I gestured to my full plate of fries and barely sipped margarita. "Um, clearly not."

"Seriously?" she asked, pulling on her mittens.

Instead of responding, I took a slurp of my drink.

Mattie pinched her lips together and gave a disapproving shake of her head. "Fine, whatever. But I'm going to be at least an hour."

"Have fun."

She turned to leave before whipping around. "You're really going to stay here alone?"

"What better way to commiserate than with myself?" My attempt at a joke fell flat and Mattie's eyes instantly softened. "I'll be okay," I insisted. "I remember the way back to your house. I'll finish these and head out."

"You have the address?" she asked.

Wow, either she was really worried about me, or seriously underestimating me.

"Yes, I have your address. And my phone. Plus, you live like two blocks away. Pretty sure I can find my way back."

"Says the person who got lost walking back to her own

dorm room freshman year of college and had to call the police," Mattie said.

My smile froze in place. "That was one time," I said through clenched teeth.

Mattie laughed, tossing her wild light-brown hair back in the process. "Call me if you have any issues."

"I'll be fine," I insisted.

Mattie turned to address the bartender—Dave, was it? "She's having a bit of a mental breakdown at the moment," she said. "Please don't let her drink too much." With that, she walked away from us and headed toward the exit.

I scowled at her back, before turning back to Dave. "Am not," I said, picking up another fry. Then I offered, "I got fired."

Dave had already returned his attention back to the drink he was making. "I'm no babysitter," he said.

"Then can I have one more drink?" I asked, batting my eyelashes innocently.

Dave chuckled and eyed the margarita still in front of me. Then, he slid a full glass toward me that looked suspiciously like straight soda water. Part of me wanted to object, but the more rational side of my brain recognized that I was plenty buzzed. The headache already threatening to make an appearance in the morning was thankful for this.

"Any plans while you're in town?" Dave asked as he pulled the taps. Amber liquid flowed into the beer glasses he held.

"Umm..." I pursed my lips. In reality, I hadn't spent a single minute thinking about what I wanted to do with my newfound freedom, or my time in Key Ridge for that matter. I had been thinking one singular thought when I'd bought that plane ticket—escape. "I don't know, I guess."

"Well, Key Ridge is a pretty magical place. I hope you find

what you're looking for here," he said, before he walked away to serve the beers.

I frowned and took another large sip of my drink. Little did he know, the only thing that I was looking for was a new job that would get me out of this town as quickly as possible.

Now left alone to my own thoughts, I started making a mental to-do list. Update my résumé. Sign up for job-searching sites. Rerecord my voicemail so it sounded more professional. Let my roommates know I would be out of town for an indefinite amount of time.

I groaned thinking about the girls that I lived with. I owned my condo, and being the financially responsible person that I was, I had always rented out my spare bedrooms to cover the mortgage. I wasn't close with the girls that lived there now. I knew them from work, but we weren't friends by any stretch of the imagination. Aside from the occasional happy hours and work talk, I knew nothing about them. But now, after all this, I never wanted to face them again. Their sympathetic eyes as they'd pout and tell me how sorry they were. Ugh, I couldn't take it. I already felt pathetic enough.

I slurped down the remainder of my margarita and rested my cheek in my hand.

The front door opening caught my attention, but only because of the guy who'd just stepped inside. He was tall—definitely over six feet. His shaggy dark hair was tucked into a beanie and it poked out in a careless way that still somehow looked perfect. I couldn't describe his face as anything other than boyishly charming. Like he had a permanent twinkle in his eye or something like that. The stranger brushed off a few snowflakes from his tan jacket. I knew I should turn around so that he wouldn't catch me staring, but I was completely taken with his face. I found myself wondering what his smile looked like. But when he looked up, our eyes met for only a second before I jerked my gaze forward.

The last thing I needed was some random local thinking I was sending out some flirtatious vibe. I had way more important things to think about aside from how a man was perceiving me. No matter how attractive he was.

Even though I'd already told myself that I didn't care, I still found my fingers frantically brushing through the ends of my messy, wavy hair, attempting to tame it. I froze when I felt a presence looming over the empty barstool next to mine.

"This seat taken?"

TWO

Oliver

"Hey, I just got in."

"Nice," Giles said on the other end of the phone. "Did you stop by The Ridge?"

"I'm here." I looked up at the worn wooden sign. The bar was right off Main Street and Giles had already told me it would be the only place open this late to grab something to eat.

"Get some food, and by the time you're done, the apartment should be all set up for you. I just got off the phone with Mattie and she said she's finishing it up now. If she's gone when you get there, it's above the garage of the address I gave you, and my Aunt Bev left a key under the welcome mat."

I smiled at that. Leaving a key under the mat? How small-town cliché. Key Ridge was just as charming as I remembered it being. I'd only been once, a few years back, but the memory of my time here had always stuck out to me. The streets were quaint, the people were nice, plus it was a stone's throw away from some of the best snowboarding and hiking Colorado had to offer.

It was quite the drive from Denver, so I hadn't had the chance to make it out here in ages, but I was psyched to be here for the rest of the ski season.

"Thanks again for hooking it up, man. I'm excited to be here." I cradled my phone between the side of my face and my shoulder as I patted my coat pocket to double-check I hadn't left my wallet back in my car parked around the corner.

"No, seriously, Ollie, thank you for coming. Johnny leaving was unexpected and it's tough to find snowboard instructors late-season like this. And you know how it's been lately. Bookings at the lodge are crazy, and of course, everyone wants a private lesson."

"I'm your guy," I said.

"Hey, I've got to run, Mattie's calling me. But why don't you stop by tomorrow for breakfast and then we can head to the hill together? I'll show you around."

"Sounds good. I'll see you then."

I hung up and slipped my phone back into my pocket. Giles and I had known each other for years. I was only nineteen when I'd first moved out to Colorado, and I'd decided to enter a few local snowboarding competitions. Giles was a pro at the time and had all these incredible sponsorships and awards. He was a bit of a loner, but he showed me the ropes. We hadn't seen too much of each other after I decided competitions weren't for me, but we'd stayed in touch and had met up to board a few times over the years.

It had taken me by surprise when he offered me this job. Even though it was already late in the season, I had still jumped at the opportunity to move out here for a bit. I needed a taste of something different. My life in Denver had gotten a little monotonous lately, and this was exactly what I needed.

The smell of a well-used deep fryer and stale beer hit my

nostrils the moment I stepped into the bar. The space was dark and tight, but in true small-town fashion, managed to cram in everything.

I made my way over to the bar before resting my arms on the top and leaning forward to get the attention of the sole bartender.

The man with a graying beard nodded in my direction before heading over. "What are you having?" he asked.

"Hey, man. Can I get a burger and fries to go?"

"Kitchen is pretty backed up. That group just put in a big order." He pointed to five older guys cluttered around a dart-board. "Might be closer to twenty minutes."

"Not a problem," I said with a smile. "I got nowhere to be."

He nodded. "Coming right up. Anything to drink while you wait?"

"Sure, give me whatever's on draft."

I tapped my fingers against the bar and looked to my left. A girl was perched on a barstool a few down from where I stood. She was by herself. Just as I was about to look away, she looked up and made brief eye contact with me before ripping her gaze away.

Shit, she was pretty. A long mane of golden-brown waves framed her round face with pink, heart-shaped lips and almond eyes that I desperately wanted to get a closer look at.

Key Ridge was off to a promising start.

The bartender passed me my beer. I thanked him and handed over some cash before sliding down so that I was on the barstool next to my new dream girl. Shyness and I didn't know each other, and making a beeline for the first cute girl I spotted in this town was exactly my style.

I took a long pull of my beer before setting it down. "This seat taken?" I asked, already occupying it.

Her whole body stiffened before she slowly turned in her seat. Her light-blue eyes widened when they met mine. "Nope."

I grinned at her. "I couldn't help but notice you staring a second ago."

That simple statement caused her wide eyes to narrow. "I wasn't staring."

Her voice was velvet.

I pretended to frown in contemplation and drew my eyebrows together. "Really? I could have sworn we made eye contact."

"I was looking around the bar. Briefly meeting someone's gaze accidently does *not* count as staring," she argued. The briskness of her words screamed uptight—something I typically steered far away from. But the little lines that had formed between her brows were cute, and I had nothing else going on anyway.

"Really? Because it felt like an intentional look to me. And if it was accidental, why look away so guiltily?" I asked.

"I looked away when you looked up because I wasn't trying to stare into the eyes of some random guy I don't know."

Something about her irritation sparked joy inside me. I leaned an arm against the bar, drawing myself closer to her. "For the record, looking away that quickly just makes it seem like you were caught."

She continued to lock eyes with me before finally looking to the ceiling and letting out a drawn-out sigh. "Fine. Maybe I glanced over for a second."

My grin widened. "Is that so?"

"Don't let it go to your ego," she said.

"I love to be stared at. And my ego is already unmanageable, so don't let that stop you."

Her scowl wavered as the corner of her lips turned upward. Just like that, I knew I had her on the hook. She might not want to admit it, but she liked me. Charming women was one of my few talents in life.

"Is that right?" she countered. Her irritated tone now sounded a hell of a lot more like flirting and I was living for it.

Her eyes roamed over my face in an excited, familiar way. I knew what this was. She was attracted to me. Despite the drained glass and empty plate in front of her, she wanted to linger so she could talk to me more. I'd have to do my best not to disappoint her.

"You live around here?" I asked. She didn't seem like a local. The coat hanging off her barstool was too thin and her haircut looked expensive. The kind you could only get in some fancy salon in a city.

"Nope." She shuddered at the thought. "I just got into town. I'm staying with my sister."

I mentally gave myself a pat on the back for reading her right.

"You here for the weekend or something?"

Her lips curved down as she eyed the empty glass in front of her. "Or something."

I desperately wanted to wipe the new forlorn expression clean off her face.

"Isn't that a coincidence. I just got into town too."

"Huh?" She shifted in her seat so we faced each other. "That's surprising. You seem like a local."

"And why is that?" I countered, although I knew with my thick flannel jacket and messy, beanie-clad hair, I probably looked every bit the local.

She didn't shy away from me, though. Instead, she shrugged. "You've got that whole, I-could-build-a-log-cabin-with-my-bare-hands vibe."

That made me toss back my head with a laugh. "Are you saying I look like a lumberjack?"

"You *are* wearing plaid," she pointed out.

I took another sip of my beer, pleased with myself that her almost-smile had returned. "What's your name?" I finally asked.

"Frankie."

"Frankie," I repeated, not positive I'd heard her right.

"Yes, why?" Defensiveness coated her words, making me chuckle.

"No reason. It's just an interesting name."

"It's short for Frances," she said haughtily. "I was named after my grandmother."

"And Fran or Franny didn't suit you?"

She shook her head. Despite her best efforts, her smile kept creeping wider. "Everyone used to call her Fran. When I was a baby, my parents decided I would be Frankie, and I've been Frankie ever since." She shifted in her seat so she could evaluate me better. "And what's your name? Better be a good one if you're giving me attitude about mine."

"Oliver," I told her. "Or Ollie. I'll answer to both."

She pretended to mull it over in her mind for a bit before finally nodding. "I like it."

"Thank God." I wiped my brow. "Would have been a pain to change it after all these years."

That got a small laugh out of her. It was short and soft before she cleared her throat and bit her lip. I wanted to thump my chest in triumph that I'd finally gotten a chuckle out of the girl. Frankie very much gave off the impression that she needed more laughter in her life. Everything about her read as tense and on edge.

If this was her attempt at flirting, I'd hate to see how she'd act if she genuinely didn't like me.

"So, Frankie, what brings you into town. Skiing? Snowboarding? Just a visit with your sister?"

She snorted. "You wouldn't catch me dead skiing or snowboarding."

I clutched my heart and winced as if she'd inflicted some sort of irreparable damage on me.

Her eyebrows shot up. "What? Are you big on those things?"

Was I big on those things? I wanted to laugh. My entire life revolved around extreme sports. It was the sole reason I moved to Colorado in the first place. "I just came over here from Denver to be a snowboard instructor."

Frankie gave a knowing smirk. "Of course you did."

Her words should have rubbed me the wrong way. They came across as elitist, and I couldn't help but get the feeling she might be looking down on me in some way. But it didn't bother me. I liked who I was and how I chose to live my life. My brother, Nathan, said I'd never grow up. Maybe that was the case, but what was so wrong with my lifestyle? I loved things the way they were. I didn't want to weigh myself down with the unnecessary burdens of the world.

I folded my hands in front of me and waited for Frankie to continue. When she didn't, I pressed, "What *are* you here for, then?"

She sighed and squeezed her eyes shut, as if whatever she was about to say was physically difficult for her to talk about. "I got fired." It came out as a whisper.

"Fired, huh? You do a crappy job or something?"

That caused her scowl to return, like I knew it would. Man, she was fun to mess with.

"I did a fantastic job, for your information." She tried to infuse venom into her words, but she just sounded defeated. "I gave everything to that company. I was the best person on my team, and they knew it. I was the only one willing to stay late and I never missed a deadline." She exhaled sharply. "But they didn't care. In the end, I was just a number to them. An expendable person they could dump like a piece of garbage so they could improve their numbers."

She looked genuinely upset by this. No—*heartbroken*. This was more than being worried about money or something like that. She actually cared. I couldn't even imagine loving a job that much.

"I'm sorry," I said, with as much sincerity as I could muster. Just because I didn't understand the corporate grind, didn't mean I couldn't see that she was in pain over this. "That sounds tough."

Frankie clenched and unclenched her hands. "I was shocked when it happened. I just stood there like an idiot when my boss told me. I didn't even register it at first. I asked him if he was ready for our Q1 presentation." She sniffled, and I hoped she wouldn't cry. Getting deep didn't exactly make me comfortable. I was the fun, carefree guy. Not the guy you stayed up late with and told all your secrets to.

"Look, I know we don't know each other, and I know I have no idea what your job was or what it entailed, but they sound like assholes. Idiot assholes," I said.

She didn't meet my eyes, but she smiled at that. "He was kind of an asshole."

"See? Didn't that make you feel better to say?"

"A little," she admitted.

"And now you can take some time off," I continued. "Travel. Do something different. It'll be like a blessing in disguise."

She gave a sharp laugh at that. "Take some time off? No way. I already started working on my résumé on the flight over here. I'll be applying to jobs as soon as I wake up in the morning. The job market sucks right now, so it might take me a while to find something. Looking for a job is even more work than actually working."

Uptight. I knew it. This girl was in one of the most beautiful mountain towns in the world and she didn't care at all. She could have been anywhere right now—in some bland high rise in a faceless city, or cooped up at a desk in the back of a musty library. Her surroundings were nothing because all she cared about was her career. I'd never related to anyone less. She'd come to Key Ridge to plan her next step. I'd come here because I *never* planned my next step. Giles had only asked me a few weeks ago, and I'd come here on impulse. I had no idea what would come after and that was fine by me.

"Sounds like you got it all figured out," I said.

Frankie pressed her mouth into a thin line. "What's that supposed to mean?"

I shrugged. "That you've got your plan for your life and that's that. You're inflexible, rigid." Her mouth parted to protest, but I continued. "You're completely fine busting your ass at a nine-to-five to make someone else rich who doesn't give a shit about you. You have this nice little routine that you're dying to get back to. I get it, I do. I might not agree, but I know a lot of people can't handle instability."

"There's nothing wrong with wanting stability," she argued.

"Sure, I guess." I knew my words were getting under her skin and I relished it. "Some people don't have an adventurous bone in their body, and that's okay."

Now she looked offended. "I came here, didn't I? I dropped everything and got on a flight without a second thought."

I dipped my chin and gave her a pitying look. "And what are you going to do now that you're here? Sit in front of a computer screen and find the next job to suck your soul away."

"Burger and fries." The bartender interrupted us to hand me a brown paper bag with grease soaking the bottom.

"Well, Frankie. It was lovely to meet you, but I have a date with this burger and my couch to get to."

"I can be adventurous." She was still arguing with me as she slid off her barstool and put on her way-too-thin coat. I wanted to point out that she shouldn't be walking anywhere in that. She'd likely get sick or something. But I bit my tongue. I was already pushing boundaries with her, and an over-bearing comment like that might push a girl like Frankie to her limit.

"Whatever you say," I said.

"You just met me. You don't know me," she huffed as she followed me to the front of the bar and out the door.

I turned to look at her and she came to a crashing halt, almost running right into my chest. "I might not *know* you, know you. But I know you."

The moonlight lit up the street outside. Frankie looked even more beautiful out here than under the harsh neon glow of the bar lights.

"What does that even mean?" She let out a frustrated sigh.

Even though she was incredibly irritated with me right now, I still felt tempted to ask her back to my place—a place I hadn't even been yet. Frankie was stunning. Tense and easily bothered, sure, but stunning, nonetheless. I had to drag my gaze away from her pout.

She must have caught the shift in my eyes because she traced her lips with her tongue. Damn. That wasn't fair.

Who was I kidding? Frankie wasn't the type of girl to proposition for a one-night stand or anything of that nature. She looked like she overthought everything. Probably had to go home and make a pros and cons list before she made even the smallest of decisions.

But still, I did see a flicker of something in her eyes. Lust? Intrigue? Maybe it was just frustration. I couldn't quite place it, but the way she seemed to forget we were still arguing as she lingered by my side said everything I needed to know.

We stood outside, wordless, for what felt like a while but surely was only seconds. The cold evening air was far more bitter than it had been in Denver, and I fought the urge to reach out and put an arm around Frankie and her insufficient coat.

"Look, I'm a straight shooter. Sorry if I offended you," I offered. "Can I walk you home or something?"

"I'm fine. My sister lives right around the corner." Her voice was softer than it had been only minutes ago.

"Alright, then," I said, disappointed this was where we'd be leaving things.

Warm air trickled from her pink lips, and I found myself unable to take my eyes off of them.

"You're right," she whispered, taking me by surprise. "I'm not adventurous."

I lifted an eyebrow. "Look, I shouldn't have—"

"You know what's something I would never do?" she continued.

"What?" I breathed, our bodies drawing closer together as if they were magnetized.

"Kiss a random stranger outside a bar who I'll never see again." Her voice shook, but her eyes were determined.

The bag of food in my hands and the warmth of my new apartment were completely forgotten. Suddenly, I was thinking of nothing else except what she might taste like.

"Is that something you're looking to cross off your bucket list tonight?" I asked huskily.

She nodded, her eyes searching mine. She tilted her head up and her mouth looked like an offering. I leaned toward her instinctively, our eyes locked. I saw the open invitation in them and eagerly bent the rest of the way down until my lips brushed hers. They were warm and soft. The slight shiver that ran through her as soon as I touched her made me ravenous for more.

For someone so uptight, her lips tasted reckless.

I pressed into her, my mouth moving over hers as I lightly nipped her bottom lip. She tilted her head, parting her mouth and letting her tongue dance against mine. I lifted my free hand to cup her soft cheek before moving it to her hair and tangling my fingers in it.

The kiss was sweet and hot all at once. I'd had my share of meaningless makeouts in my life, but none had hit me quite as hard as this one. Maybe it was the fresh start in a new town. Maybe it was that everything about Frankie was still a puzzle to me. Whatever it was, I welcomed it.

She nibbled on my bottom lip before pulling away. I tried to lightly tug her back in with my hand, but she moved her face out of my grasp.

"Come home with me?" I asked, desperate for more.

She laughed breathlessly and opened her eyes. "I've got to get back to my sister's."

"Please?" I offered her my best charming smile. Somehow, I knew it was fruitless. I couldn't change her mind, but I wanted to. "We don't have to do anything—although more of this would be amazing. We can just talk. Or you can have some of my fries." I held up the forgotten bag at my side. They must be getting cold, but I couldn't have cared less. I'd happily let them freeze if it meant standing out here for a few more minutes with Frankie locked beneath my gaze.

But to my dismay, Frankie patted my chest and stepped

away from me. Her absence left me cold, but I let her go without argument.

"I've got to get going. This was fun though." She had already turned away from me. Just like that, whatever magical moment that had transpired between us had completely passed. She turned back around to point at me. "Think about this moment next time you call some woman you've just met in a bar rigid and unadventurous."

"I don't think I used those exact words," I called.

When she kept walking, I tried again.

"Can I get your number?" I asked, even though she was already a quarter of the way down the block.

"No offense, Oliver, but I don't think we have all that much in common," she called back.

My heart raced with adrenaline. "I would beg to disagree. I think we have a lot in common. Like how much we both enjoyed that kiss."

"Goodnight," was all she said before turning a corner and walking out of sight.

"Maybe I'll see you around," I called after her.

But she was gone.

"Damn," I breathed, rubbing my hand over my mouth.

That was a hell of a welcome.

THREE

Frankie

"Rise and shine!"

To my absolute horror, sunlight infiltrated the room and seared my eyelids. I threw the quilt over my head and groaned. For being a basement guest bedroom, there was entirely too much natural light for my liking.

"Get out," I said weakly.

Mattie chuckled. The edge of the bed dipped down as she plopped down on it. "Giles is making breakfast. Come join us. There's lots of coffee."

"You couldn't bribe me to move for all the coffee in the world."

My head was ringing. I had woken up in the middle of the night and pounded a glass of water and two ibuprofens. It was helping a little but not enough.

"You should have left with me last night."

I moved the quilt down to peek out at my sister. She was already dressed in a maroon sweater and dark jeans. Something about her being so put together right now irked me. It was like this mild hangover was a reminder of how pathetic my current predicament was.

"Are you really trying to lecture me at" —I glanced at the digital alarm clock from the nineties placed on the bedside table— "seven-thirteen in the morning?"

Mattie laid down next to me and looked up at the ceiling. "No. But you'd be feeling better right now if you'd listened to me."

"Whatever," I said, sitting up and reaching for the water bottle I'd set on the nightstand. My mouth tasted and felt like sand.

"How was the rest of the night?" she asked. "I was surprised when I beat you home. I almost called to check on you, but then I heard the basement door slam right as I was getting ready for bed."

I rubbed my temple. Thankfully, the headache was already dissipating.

"It was exactly what I needed to get my mind off of things," I said, my thoughts drifting to Oliver. He definitely *had* helped get my mind off things. He had been just as infuriatingly annoying as he'd been attractive. And a good kisser to boot.

"I'm glad it helped," Mattie said.

Her look of sympathy made me want to curl up into a ball. I wasn't the type of person people pitied. I'd been the top of my class, always popular, financially secure, thriving in my career. People always envied me. They didn't feel sorry for me.

"I kissed a guy last night," I said, wanting to change the look on my sister's face to one of interest instead of sympathy.

Her eyes widened as she sat back up. "What? Who?"

I shrugged. "I don't know. Just some guy. He came into the bar right as I was leaving."

"What was his name?" she asked. "Maybe I know him."

I threw the covers off and got out of bed. "I doubt it. He said he literally just got into town."

Mattie's face wrinkled. "You made out with some random guy? A stranger? That's not like you at all."

"That was kind of the point," I said, rifling through the top drawer and pulling out a fresh T-shirt. I was the type of person who had to immediately unpack their suitcase upon arrival at a destination. It didn't matter how short or long the trip was. I couldn't stand living out of a messy suitcase.

"Was he cute?" Mattie sounded both impressed and disturbed at the same time.

"Obviously." I pulled the T-shirt on before throwing on a pair of sweats over the tiny shorts I typically slept in. The rat's nest on top of my head would have to wait until after breakfast. The pounding in my brain had nearly subsided, but it now demanded coffee in order to go away completely.

"What did he look like? Do you like him?"

"Mattie." I looked at my sister exasperatedly. "I don't even know him. We flirted for like two seconds before he started being kind of rude. He tried to call me out for being uptight or something." I stretched overhead before rubbing my eyes. "But he had a cute face and I was little tipsy. End of story. He seemed like some sort of drifter or something. Not even close to my type."

"What *is* your type again?" Mattie asked, tapping her chin. "Neurotic douchebag who would sell your soul for a promotion at work?"

I snorted and threw a pillow at my sister's face. She caught it easily.

"That was one guy," I said, holding up a finger.

She was referring to the coworker I had slept with ages ago. She'd met him while visiting me for a long weekend. We'd all gone out on a Friday night and he'd talked her ear off about how indispensable he was to our company. We hadn't lasted much longer after that. It was hard not to be grossed out by him after seeing him through the unforgiving lens of my sister.

"It's all I have to go off of." She winced as if remembering how physically painful her interaction with that guy had been.

"My last boyfriend was nice. You would have liked him," I said, remembering Thomas. He was a sweetheart, but not very career driven. It had worked for a bit, but he'd gotten fed up with my schedule.

"Too bad you only dated for like two months, and I never got the chance to meet him."

I chewed the inside of my cheek. "It was three."

"Whatever. Same difference."

"I need coffee if we're going to discuss my love life this early in the morning." I threw open the door to the guest bedroom and walked out into the finished basement. Mattie had moved into Giles's house when they started dating. It was this quaint little bungalow. The bedrooms were all upstairs, but he'd finished the basement off years ago to add a guest bedroom, bathroom, and a small sitting area. It was honestly perfect. I could stay here for a bit and not be right on top of my sister due to the two floors of separation.

Mattie scrambled off the bed and followed me. "Tell me more about the guy from last night. Did you get his number? I really don't think you're in a position to be turning down anyone right now."

I shot her a dirty look before trudging up the wooden stairs. "Why would I get his number? It's not like I'm going to date him or something."

"Not date. Flirt. Hook up. Have you no imagination?"

I threw open the door to the main floor. "That sounds like a distraction. I need to focus on perfecting my résumé and getting interviews," I said, walking into the short hallway that led to the door to the backyard. Immediately to the left was the opening for the kitchen, where voices spilled out.

"And you can't get laid while you're at it?" Mattie asked as we both stepped into the kitchen.

I froze as soon as I saw him. Mattie's husband, Giles, stood there with a cup of coffee—but he wasn't alone. Leaning against the counter, wearing a gray sweatshirt, a beanie, and a smirk, was Oliver.

Shit.

Not only did I look like absolute crap while he looked completely perfect, he had *definitely* overheard Mattie.

"Um." Giles gave us both a raised brow look. "Morning?"

I turned to Mattie and whispered in her ear, "That's the guy."

When I pulled away, she had a confused look in her eyes before a lightbulb went off. She glanced at Oliver then back at me, giving a small nod of approval.

"Morning," she said loudly, sweeping into the kitchen and wrapping an arm around her husband. "I was just telling Frankie that she needs to have some fun while she's here."

I tipped my head back and groaned. "And I was just telling your nosy wife that I don't have time."

"You have nothing except time." Mattie reached into a cupboard and pulled out two mugs before handing me one.

"Thanks for that," I said flatly, taking the mug.

"Mattie, this is Oliver. Ollie, this is my wife, Mattie." Giles pointed the spatula he was using to scramble some eggs between the two of them.

"Thanks again for all the hospitality." Oliver reached out to shake Mattie's hand. "And it's good to finally meet you. Giles says great things."

Mattie squeezed Giles's shoulder. "I would hope so. But

seriously, thank you so much for coming. We never thought we'd find an advanced instructor to replace Johnny this late in the season."

"Happy to be here," Oliver said.

"And this is Mattie's sister, Frankie. She's staying with us for…well, I guess I don't know exactly how long." Giles sounded a bit worried about the idea of an open-ended visit.

"Frankie, huh?" Oliver stroked his chin, assessing me.

"Don't worry, I'm not moving in or anything," I said to Giles, ignoring Oliver and moving straight for the coffee machine.

I could feel Oliver's eyes on me as I filled my mug from the carafe. When I met his gaze, he still wore a smug smile, clearly waiting for me to say something.

"Um, can I talk to you over there?" I asked, pointing through the small dining room to the living room.

"Me?" Oliver pointed at his chest.

"Him?" Giles looked between the two of us.

"Yep."

"Sure." Oliver pushed himself off the counter and led the way into the other room.

As soon as we stepped into the living room, he spun around. Damn it, he looked good. Even better than I remembered from last night. The dim bar lights and my tequila haze had not done him justice at all.

"Look," I started.

"Nice hair." He surprised me by grabbing a piece of hair by my face and twisting it between his fingers.

I blanched before raising my own hand to my head. I could feel the frizziness of my messy bun. Any attempt to smooth it down would be pointless.

"Sorry we can't all look perfect in the morning," I mumbled.

"You think I look perfect?" he teased. Why did he have to be so obnoxiously endearing?

I took a sip of coffee to distract myself. "Okay," I started again, but he still interrupted me.

"Is this the part where you ask me not to tell anyone what happened last night?" he asked.

"What?"

"You know. The part where you're embarrassed by what happened last night and you don't want anyone to know we made out so you ask me to keep it a secret. But of course, we'll inevitably slip up and everyone will find out anyway."

"I told Mattie like the second I saw you," I said flatly.

His forehead creased. "Oh."

I let out a small laugh. "Did you think this was one of those movies where the main characters can't communicate and cause all this unnecessary drama?"

He tilted his head, still smiling. "Maybe. Sounds like fun."

My grin spread across my face. Oliver might not be the kind of guy I could see myself with, but he was amusing. I'd give him that.

"All I was going to say was that I wasn't exactly acting like myself last night. I'm sorry for—"

He held up a hand. "Let me stop you right there, because you have absolutely nothing to be sorry for."

I tipped my head back and resisted groaning. "Fine. Sorry was the wrong word. I'm just trying to say that last night was out of character for me."

"You mean you don't typically go around kissing strangers you just met outside a bar? I'm shocked."

Something about the know-it-all way he said it, eyes staring right into mine, made me want to kiss him all over again to prove him wrong.

"Exactly," I said instead.

"What sort of person are you then?" he probed.

I took another exaggerated sip of my coffee, staring at him over the lip of my mug. "The kind that doesn't like to get into the gory details of my psyche before eight in the morning."

"Got it." Oliver snapped his fingers. "I'll wait until the evening."

"That's not what I meant." I narrowed my eyes. "All I'm trying to say is that you shouldn't expect it to happen again."

He stroked his chin at that and pretended to look thoughtful. Then he leaned in so his face was only inches from mine. "What if I beg?"

A small gasp escaped my lips. But before I could regain my composure and give him a response, Giles entered the room behind us.

"Breakfast is ready," he said, giving us both a quizzical look. "Do you two know each other or something?"

"No," I said at the same time Oliver said, "Yes."

Giles furrowed his brow and looked to Mattie, who had stepped into the room behind him.

"They just met," she clarified. "At the bar last night."

"Oh, small world," Giles said, still assessing the two of us. My brother-in-law wasn't exactly the warmest and cuddliest of people, but we got along okay. He was more of a loner than anything. We'd hardly had a conversation alone since he and Mattie started dating. I knew she secretly hoped that my being here would spark a friendship between the two of us. I wasn't opposed to the idea. I just simply didn't know if I had the time.

"Did someone say breakfast was ready?" I asked, dying to change the subject and get away from the curious nature of Oliver's stare.

"It's on the table," Mattie said, shooting me a devilish grin.

"After you," Oliver said, placing his hand on my lower back and motioning toward the kitchen. He seemed to be reveling in every moment of my discomfort, and it drove me nuts.

I stepped away from his touch and moved into the dining room before sitting down for breakfast. Oliver took the seat across from me and winked before digging in.

I did my best to ignore his stolen glances throughout the meal and focus on my food.

So much for never seeing this guy again.

And so much for a kiss without consequences.

FOUR

Frankie

THE SMALL WOODEN CABIN WAS LIGHTER THAN I EXPECTED AS I picked it up to examine it before setting it down with the rest of the small trinkets. The store smelled of pine and vanilla, which I had to imagine was due to the large assortment of candles in the back corner.

"What about this for Mom?" Mattie held up a pink-checkered sweater that did look exactly like something our mother would wear, except for one fact.

"Are you forgetting she lives in Florida?"

Mattie thrust the sweater into my hands. "Are you forgetting they're taking another Alaskan cruise in a few months? Feel it. Isn't it soft?"

The texture was indeed plush and luxurious. I fought the desire to bring it up to my cheek and nuzzle against it.

"I'm getting it," Mattie insisted. "And I'm buying you this green one." She held up an oversized cable-knit sweater that I'd been admiring when we first walked into the boutique.

"You don't have to do that," I protested, but she was

already moving toward the checkout counter with the sweaters and a few additional items in hand.

Mattie had taken the day off today and insisted on showing me around Key Ridge. So far, that had entailed eating breakfast at her favorite diner, then she took me over to the small reservoir at the edge of town. The surface of the water was frozen and littered with cars and tents. She'd insisted it was fully solid, but I still couldn't imagine feeling confident enough in nature to drive a car out to the middle of a lake. We'd walked around the outskirts of the reservoir before heading back to Main Street.

Now she was dragging me into every shop in town for a little retail therapy.

My mood had recovered a bit since arriving in Key Ridge a few days ago. While cheery might be too extreme of a word, I had at least stopped outright sulking. Mostly.

The job pool wasn't great. So far, I'd only received rejections, but I was holding out hope. My résumé was good—I knew it was. Someone would see that and give me a call. They had to.

"There's a crystal shop next door." Mattie looped her arm through mine and led me back outside. She handed me the bag since she was already holding a few in her other hand. Even though this retail therapy was supposed to be for me, Mattie was doing most of the spending. I was financially responsible, and my savings were great. But not dropping money on clothes and random little trinkets was exactly how I'd be able to keep it great, especially when I had no idea when my next paycheck would be coming in.

"Crystals?" I shot her a puzzled look.

"Right. Like energy and manifestation and all that jazz." She wiggled her fingers.

I raised an eyebrow. "You don't believe in all that, do you?"

"It's fun," Mattie said as we walked outside, lingering in the crisp air for only a second before approaching the shop next door. Inside, the smell of incense overwhelmed all of my senses. The whole place was lined with shelves, crystals of all different sizes and colors scattered everywhere.

"Welcome in." The owner sat behind the counter. At least I assumed he was the owner. He had long hair and half-moon spectacles pushed down the bridge of his nose. He looked exactly like the type of person who would own a crystal shop in a mountain town.

The crystals were grouped by type, and each section had a piece of paper taped to the shelf, describing what the crystal was and what it was good for.

"This is silly," I whispered.

"Fun," Mattie repeated, picking up a purple and green crystal the size of a golf ball and turning it over in her hands. "Besides, if anyone could use some positive energy right now, it's you."

"Thanks for that." I lightly shoved her, but we were both smiling. I couldn't remember the last time I'd spent a whole day with just my sister. We'd always been close, but living on opposite sides of the country meant significantly less time together.

"I'm happy you're finally out of that dark basement. I can practically see the color returning to your face," she said.

"I'm hardly down there," I insisted, even though I knew for a fact that yesterday, I only came up to the main floor once to down a slice of pizza Giles had picked up.

"Any leads?" Mattie asked, setting back down the crystal and moving on to a collection of pink ones.

"Not really," I sighed, deflated. "Hardly anyone is hiring."

"Something will happen eventually. It hasn't even been a week." Mattie offered me a sympathetic smile. "At least you're here and not stuck in your condo in Atlanta. I'm so happy I get to finally show you around and spend time with you. It seriously feels like it's been ages."

"It has been too long." Guilt crept into my voice.

Mattie had offered to buy me a plane ticket out here a number of times, but I'd always had an excuse not to come. And all of those excuses revolved around being busy with something or other at work. It was strange to think back on it. What had I thought was so important that I couldn't take time off? Clearly, I was wrong because they had let me go without a second thought. They didn't even ask me any questions about the projects that were on my plate—the same ones I thought were *so* vital—as I was on my way out the door. I had let them run my life, and to them, I was completely expendable.

"I'm glad I'm here too," I admitted. "But it's still weird to see you so at home here."

"Really?" Mattie scrunched her nose. "I'm so used to it by now."

"You're different here," I concluded. My sister had this glow about her that she'd never had before. The glow of being utterly content and happy. This town—and Giles—had brought this newfound life into her eyes that she hadn't had before.

"Different good?" she asked.

"Very good."

Her expression softened. "I hope some of that can rub off on you too. I know you're only here for now, but enjoy it."

"I am," I said, holding up a charcoal-gray crystal as if to prove my point.

"No, I mean *really* enjoy it. More than just trekking out once in a blue moon because I practically begged you."

"You didn't beg me," I said.

We continued shuffling through the shelves, reading about the different crystals.

"I saw Oliver yesterday," she offered casually.

"Oh?" I said, feigning indifference.

"Uh-huh. He asked about you."

"He did not." I set down the crystal I was examining and moved to the other side of the shop.

"He really did." Mattie followed me. "I ran into him at the lodge. He asked how you were doing."

"He was being polite," I said. But just talking about him spiked my heart rate.

"You should get his number from Giles. You're both single…new to town…" She said it in a singsong voice.

"Mattie," I hissed. "Nothing will be happening between us."

"You mean happening *again*," she corrected.

"Right, whatever. That kiss was a temporary lapse in judgment."

One I had thought about repeating many times since it happened.

Mattie smirked as if she knew exactly the thought going through my head. "Fine, whatever. I still think you should do it. Oliver screams fun. And let's face it, you could use fun."

I raised both hands. "Why does everyone keep saying that?"

"Because it's true."

Irritated, I marched away from her to a different display. People could see through me like tissue paper. I'd never realized how un-fun I was. Or at least, I hadn't cared in the past.

My fingers traced over a yellowy-white crystal on the shelf in front of me.

"Citrine," the owner said. I hadn't even heard him approach.

"Sorry." I yanked my hand away, but he shook his head.

"No, feel free to touch. That's how you transfer the energy."

"Right," I said, wanting to be polite, but also still not believing any of this in the slightest.

"You're drawn to that one?" he asked, tapping at the paper.

"Oh, I don't know. Maybe?"

He chuckled, as if sensing my skepticism. "Citrine is known as the merchant's stone. It's good for wealth and success. Some say it helps attract money and abundance."

Mattie snorted from the other side of the small store. "Of course that's the one that drew you in."

My fingers moved back to the crystal I had been originally tracing, and I closed my hand around it.

Her forehead wrinkled in confusion. "You're actually getting it?"

"Why not? I could use all the help I can get," I said, moving toward the checkout counter.

Mattie followed me, and the owner stepped back behind the counter to ring me up.

"Just this one?" he asked.

"Yep." I fished around in my purse for my wallet. Mattie stood next to me, reading the crystal display perched in front of the register.

"And this one," she said, picking up a green crystal and setting it next to the one I'd already picked out.

"What's that one for?" I asked, grabbing the small stone to examine it.

"Malachite," she said, reading off the paper next to the display. "It's supposed to absorb negative energy and help you embrace change and step out of your comfort zone."

I let out a sigh and placed it back on the counter. "Fine. I'll take both of these."

⁂

"WE'VE BEEN SHOPPING FOR HOURS, IF YOU DON'T LET ME consume a coffee and a pastry, I'm going to pass out."

I pushed open the door to the café Mattie had deemed her favorite. When I asked if there were other options in town, she'd admitted there were not. But she still insisted this would be the best regardless.

The intense aroma of coffee beans wafted through the air, and I almost moaned in pleasure. Maybe she was right, after all. The café oozed charm, with cozy armchairs and mismatched tables spread across a vintage checkered tile floor. For mid-afternoon, it was busier than I'd expected. Back in Atlanta, the crowd would have been glued to their laptops or juggling work calls, but here, people lingered over quiet conversations or lost themselves in the pages of a worn book. Small-town charm, I supposed.

Mattie and I picked up our orders before settling into one of the only empty tables in the place.

"Don't fill up on pastries. I got us a reservation at this great little Italian place. You're going to love it. It has views of the mountains and the whole place is lit by candlelight."

"I got one scone. I think I'll be okay," I said through a bite.

My scarf snagged on one of my earrings as I pulled it over my head and sat back in my chair. I hardly got settled before feeling a presence approach our table. When I glanced up,

Oliver was there, hovering. He looked infuriatingly adorable in his navy-blue Key Ridge employee jacket.

"Ladies. Fancy running into you two here," he said, his mega-watt smile directed right at me.

"Hey, Oliver," Mattie greeted.

"Hi," I said, mentally cursing myself for sounding so breathless.

"Done with lessons for the day?" Mattie asked. "You're welcome to join us."

I shot my sister a subtle glare, but she pretended to be oblivious.

He perched on the edge of the empty chair. "Appreciate the offer, but I have one more. Just needed a little pick-me-up." He held up his to-go coffee cup. "I was hoping to run into you again, Frankie, but I never seem to see you around town."

"She hasn't gotten out much," Mattie said, to which I elbowed her sharply in the rib cage. "Ouch!" she exclaimed, glaring at me.

Oliver chuckled at our exchange. "That's a shame," he said.

"I've been trying to resolve my whole unemployment predicament," I added hurriedly.

"Right." His eyes glimmered as he assessed me.

"It's a lot of work," I insisted, taking a sip of my too-hot coffee. I forced my face into one of neutrality so he wouldn't know I'd completely scalded the roof of my mouth.

"I bet," he said, checking his phone. "I've got to get going." Oliver stood and gave me a little salute before backing away toward the door. "Bye, Mattie. Bye, Frankie." He winked at only me as he said my name, and then left through the front door.

"Ugh." I slumped into my seat and stuck my tongue out,

fanning it to try and quell the burning sensation. "He's insufferable," I said, my voice sounding funny due to my tongue still sticking out.

"He's cute." Mattie sighed. Knowing her, she was already envisioning some fairy tale romance between the two of us.

"He thinks he knows me." I took another bite of my scone.

"That's the worst you can say about the guy?"

"He thinks I'm uptight."

"You *are* uptight," Mattie said easily.

I frowned. "Not all the time."

Mattie sighed. "Look, I can't force you to stop freaking out about finding a new job, but can you at least have a little fun while you're at it." She gestured at the door Oliver had walked out of. "He's cute. He's clearly flirting with you. The best way to make him think you're not uptight is to show him."

I blew on my coffee before taking another tentative sip, stewing over her words. The truth was, I *did* think Oliver was cute. And I *did* enjoy our kiss…a lot, in fact.

But even if I wanted Oliver to see me as more than some neurotic city girl, I realized that would be impossible. Because as the days here stretched on, I'd become abundantly aware that there wasn't more to me than that.

FIVE

Frankie

THE HARSH BLUE GLOW OF MY LAPTOP SCREEN REFLECTED IN my tired eyes as I scanned the qualifications of yet another job listing. Spending all this time hunched over a computer, absorbing all this artificial light would surely cause long-term damage, but I wasn't about to let that slow me down.

I had arrived in Key Ridge exactly one week ago, and I'd already applied to at least fifteen jobs. Unfortunately, the market was a bit underwhelming. There had been quite a few rounds of layoffs in my industry last year. That, mixed with a lackluster economy, meant there were plenty of qualified candidates and not a lot of open positions.

Pickings were slim, but I still hadn't expected it to be quite this lean. It didn't help that the job listing site had a banner across each job posting letting me know the exact number of applicants that had already applied. The one I had just submitted for said *over one thousand*. Confidence could only get me so far, and even I knew that was a longshot. Landing a job I was qualified for felt a lot like buying lottery tickets and hoping for a miracle.

"Knock. Knock."

I tore my headphones out of my ears and found Mattie hovering at the bottom of the basement stairs.

"You know it's not knocking if you're already in the room," I said.

"Still in a bad mood?" she asked.

Mattie had been busy working at the lodge for the past two days, so I'd hardly seen her. Apparently, even though it was toward the end of the season, they had gotten record snow this year and it would be bustling for the next few weeks until closing day.

"I'm not in a bad mood," I insisted before throwing my head back against the plush couch. "It just feels so hopeless. I'm sure there are people with a decade more experience than I have applying to these jobs. I'll never find something."

Mattie had the nerve to chuckle. "Considering you've been unemployed for all of thirty seconds, I think you should try being a little more optimistic than that."

"It's hopeless." I tipped sideways, collapsing onto a pillow nestled against the sofa.

Mattie came over and sat next to me before gently patting my back. "You've hardly left this cave in days. I think what you really need is a break."

"I can't slow down."

Mattie shook my shoulders. "Come on. Come to dinner with me. It's wine and cheese night at Marie's. Giles said he would meet me after he wraps up on the ski hill."

Marie's was the restaurant inside the lodge owned by Giles and his family, where Mattie had held their intimate rehearsal dinner. And now that they were married, I supposed Mattie owned it too.

"Fine," I huffed, taking my laptop off my flannel-clad legs and standing up to stretch.

"And you can't wear that," she said, taking in the pajamas I'd never bothered to change out of.

"I'm unemployed, not a slob," I said defensively. Did she really think I was so far gone I'd forgotten how to put on a pair of jeans and run a brush through my hair?

A phone ringing caught her attention and she pulled hers out. "It's Mom," she said.

"Don't answer—"

"Hello," she said, pressing the speaker button and holding it between the two of us. I glared down at her. Telling my parents about the abrupt change my life had taken was not on my priority list today. They'd stress and worry and ask me a million questions.

"Hi, honey." My mom's cheery voice rang through the room. "We're about to board our cruise and I wanted to call you before we got on. We'll probably be hard to reach for the next couple of weeks."

They were always going on some cruise with their friends. They had retired completely last year and were taking full advantage of all their newfound free time.

"I hope you have so much fun." Mattie waved at me before pointing at the phone. *Say something*, she mouthed.

I shook my head stubbornly.

"Have you heard from your sister?" Mom asked. "I've tried texting her a few times the past week and I haven't heard from her."

Mattie glared at me. "You know what, Mom? She's actually right here. Why don't you say hi?"

"What? She's there? In Key Ridge?"

"Frankie's in Key Ridge?" I heard my dad say in the background of the call.

Mattie pressed the mute button. "Tell them. Just get it over with."

"Fine. Whatever." I waved my hand in defeat. It wasn't like she'd given me much of a choice. They knew I wouldn't fly here on a whim and that something must be up.

"Mattie? Are you still there?"

I took the phone from my sister and unmuted the call. "Hi, it's Frankie."

"Frankie, what are you doing in Colorado?" I could hear the shock in my mom's tone.

"She's really there?" my dad asked, his voice muffled.

"Yep, I'm here." I caught Mattie's eye. It almost felt like she was enjoying this.

"Did you take time off of work?" my mom asked. The way she said it made it seem like the most far-fetched possibility. And it was. I only took vacations around the holidays and never within the first few months of a new year. That was our busy season.

"You could say that," I mumbled.

Mattie shoved my leg with her foot.

"Okay, you know what?" I sighed and drug a hand over my face. "Mom. Dad. I was laid off last week. That's why I'm here."

"Laid off?" Mom exclaimed.

"Laid off?" My dad repeated the question. He sounded a lot clearer now, like my mom had put the call on speaker and he was now hovered over the phone with her.

"That's right. I'm currently unemployed, and I needed to get away." Would saying those words ever get easier? They made me feel like a failure every single time. Even after a week, the wound still felt fresh.

"I can't believe they did that to you. You were the best that company had," my dad said gruffly.

My heart swelled a little at his words. He didn't even really understand what I did, but I appreciated the sentiment none-theless.

"They said it was a reduction in workforce. It wasn't just me. Almost everyone on my team got cut." *Almost* everyone. They'd kept on two people who were more senior than me and then another guy who'd started the same time as me. That bothered me to no end. He wasn't a hard worker, but he *was* a kiss-ass. The pitying way he'd said, "Stay in touch," while I packed my stuff made me want to wring his neck.

"Oh, sweetie, I'm so sorry." I could picture my mom's face —eyebrows wrinkled together, a look of concern in her eyes.

"It's alright. I'm already applying to other jobs. I'll find something soon." The confident statement wasn't quite how I felt, but fake it 'til you make it, right?

"Are you okay on money?" my dad asked. Of course that would be his first concern. Ever the responsible one.

"I'm fine. They gave me one month's severance, plus I have savings."

"I hate the idea of you digging into your savings," my dad said.

I rolled my eyes at Mattie, but she shrugged.

"And she can help out at the lodge while she's here," Mattie piped in.

"I'm not *that* desperate," I said, hating the idea of a handout.

"We're busy and we really could use the help." Mattie shot me a pleading look. I still couldn't tell if she was being sincere or if she just wanted me to do something other than wallow in her basement.

"Well, I think that sounds great, Frankie." My mom had switched her tone to one of encouragement instead of concern. "I'm glad you girls are spending time together.

You've got a good plan, and everything will work out, right, Ron?"

My dad grumbled something under his breath. I could practically picture my mom elbowing him in the ribs. "Right. Right," he finally said.

"We have to go, but we'll catch up soon," my mom said. "You two enjoy each other."

"Love you," Mattie said, leaning over to speak into the phone.

"Love you," I said, before hanging up.

"See, was that so bad?"

"You didn't have to ambush me like that." I tossed her phone at her and she scrambled to catch it.

"You would have put it off for way too long. Now it's over."

I had to give her that. I did tend to put off uncomfortable conversations. But she did the same thing. Truly two birds of a feather.

My parents had always been supportive without crossing into overbearing territory. They'd handled the news about as well as I'd expected them to. Still, I loathed the concern that rang through their voices. I'd always had my shit together, and floundering like this had me completely off balance.

I needed a drink. More importantly, I needed to get far away from my laptop and job applications, which were basically taunting me at this point.

"Weren't you saying something about wine and cheese?" I asked.

"And if you could move the Smith reservation to room

five and add a snowboarding lesson to their folio." Mattie pointed to the screen, but I pushed her finger away.

"I got it, I got it." I typed a few things in and dragged the reservation to a different section of the screen. This software was a breeze, especially considering Mattie had been making me work on reorganizing and finalizing reservations for the past hour.

"Wine and cheese night, my ass," I grumbled.

As soon as we'd arrived at the lodge, Mattie had conveniently remembered she needed to get some things done. And I had been conveniently dragged along to be her little helper.

Truth was, I could moan and complain all I wanted, but it was nice feeling useful after the past few days of being a recluse, stuck in that basement guest room with no real obligations. On top of that, the lodge was beautiful and cozy, just as I'd remembered it from my stay here for Mattie's wedding. The high-pitched ceilings. The massive wood-burning fireplace in the center of the lobby. The endless natural light spilling in from the windows during golden hour. It wasn't a bad place to spend time. It was easy to see how my sister had taken a few steps into this place and never left.

Mattie pulled a few pieces of paper off the printer; her eyes scanned them over before she stapled them together. "I told you, I've got a table saved for us. I just needed to finish up a few things first."

"And get free labor out of your sister."

She eyed me guiltily. "I wasn't lying when I said we were short-staffed. Besides, if you work more than twenty hours, I can add you to the payroll."

"I will not be working more than twenty hours." But even as the words left my mouth, they held little resolve. Mattie was right. Other than job searching, I didn't have a whole lot going on right now. If she wanted me to help out at the lodge, was I really going to say no in favor of wasting away all day in my shabbiest pajamas?

"Am I seeing double?" An older woman with graying hair swept into a bun wearing a worn cable-knit sweater stood at the reservation desk.

"Bev!" Mattie greeted her cheerily. "You remember my sister, Frankie. Frankie, you remember Giles's Aunt Bev."

"Of course." I smiled up at the woman.

"Your sister putting you to work already, huh?" Bev pulled down her oval-framed glasses.

I pouted and shot Mattie a look. "I was lured here under the false pretense of wine and cheese."

Bev made a tsking noise. "And now she's got you working like a dog. Sounds like Mattie."

"I'm finishing up a few things," she insisted again, placing the papers she'd printed into a folder. "Besides, Frankie wanted to help."

Bev and I exchanged a knowing look.

"Regardless if that's true or not, we're happy to have any help we can get. It's been a real challenge getting seasonal workers this year."

Even though I knew Bev had no reason to lie to me, this all still felt like some elaborate scheme my sister had concocted to make sure I didn't feel disoriented and restless with my current state.

"I'm here if you need me," I offered.

Bev tipped her head in acknowledgment. "I'm sorry about your job. That's tough," she said.

Even though I hadn't expected her to bring that up, I took the stray comment like a champ and forced myself to appear unshaken. "It's alright. Life happens."

Bev shifted her weight and the kindness in her eyes almost

made me waver. "Just because life happens doesn't mean it isn't hard. You feel what you need to feel, okay?"

Her words instantly brought heat to my eyes. It was like she knew I had fallen asleep the past two nights crying my eyes out. Change was hard for me. But change out of my control? This was really throwing me for a loop.

"Thanks, Bev."

Mattie looked between the two of us, her eyes softening before Bev gave a curt nod toward the entrance into the restaurant, Marie's. Beyond the giant fireplace at the center of the lobby, there was a floor-to-ceiling opening that led into the bustling lounge. The murmur of distant conversations and the clink of wine glasses floated all the way to the reception desk.

"If you're really serious about working here temporarily, Marie's has been absolutely slammed lately. We're getting more visitors than normal this time of year, and we just had three people quit on us to work at a new brewery in the next town over. My daughter-in-law, Erin, used to help out a lot, but with her gone, too, we're really struggling. Hell, I've even taken over running the bar most nights."

Me, a bartender? Now that was something I'd never pictured for myself. But since I wasn't in a position to say no, I said, "I'm at your service."

"Marie's? Really?" Mattie sounded nervous. "The only thing you know about bars and restaurants is how to order takeout."

"Thanks for the vote of confidence," I said dryly. "Weren't you the one who wanted me to help out?"

"I thought you'd be behind the desk." Mattie gestured to where I was currently sitting.

Bev threw a hand up. "Please. Frankie will be fine, and we need the help. I didn't know how to make a basic cocktail, and now I'm back there every night slinging drinks. It's exciting. Plus, a great way to get your mind off things."

She gave me a small wink and I smiled gratefully. Mattie was right. I had absolutely zero experience with bartending or customer service, but I could learn, right? Besides, I could only stress about job applications for so many hours of the day. I needed something else to keep me busy before I suffered from a complete mental breakdown.

"Sounds perfect," I said.

"Are you sure?" Mattie asked.

Something about the way my sister insisted I couldn't do this made me want the job that much more.

"When should I start?" I asked.

SIX

Oliver

"WANT TO GRAB HAPPY HOUR WITH ME WHEN YOU FINISH UP with this lesson?" Giles lifted the goggles away from his eyes and balanced them on his snowboard helmet.

I nodded and lifted my own goggles. "Sounds good. We just finished up our last run so I'll be done in a few."

I didn't want to ask, but part of me wondered who might be joining us at this happy hour. I hadn't had the pleasure of running into Frankie again, but even after a week, the memory of our kiss still sat heavy on my mind.

Giles headed in the direction of the employee locker room, leaving me with the two guests I had spent the entire afternoon with. They were pretty chill and in their mid-forties. Both had spent their younger years skiing and wanted to try something new. They weren't very good, but I respected the effort. A lot of people hit a certain age and decided they were done learning new skills—especially skills some might consider dangerous. But not these two. They had committed, fearlessly sending themselves down each intermediate run I'd taken them on. No matter how many times they took a tumble.

"You guys killed it," I said, holding up my fist for them each to bump.

"Thanks. You made it seem easy," Jim, the shorter of the two, said.

"Yeah." Tony laughed. He was almost as tall as I was, which was saying something, given my six-foot-three stature. "I wish I had the energy you do. You must have been doing this your whole life."

A lot of people had that misconception about me. Many people I'd met in Colorado over the years assumed I was a local and had been doing some of these sports since I could crawl. They never guessed I was from the Midwest. The most I'd done was skateboard in the old neighborhood before I picked up and moved out here. "I started when I was nineteen, so only about ten years."

"*Only about ten years,*" they repeated, looking at each other and laughing good naturedly.

"Kid, you're in the prime of your life. I hope you're enjoying it." Jim patted me on my shoulder.

Little did he know, living every day like I was checking something off an imaginary bucket list was basically my life motto.

We chatted for a bit longer before we parted ways. I'd see them back on the hill tomorrow for another lesson.

Working out here for the rest of the season was more than I could have hoped for. I'd only been here a week, but waking up within spitting distance of the ski hill and being one of the first ones out there every morning was a whole new kind of thrill.

I'd been snowboarding and teaching lessons for years, but until now, I'd always commuted from Denver, sticking to the ski resorts closer to the city. The traffic was absolutely brutal. I honestly didn't know why it had taken me years to even consider the possibility of staying out in the mountains for the season. It suited me.

"Oliver!"

A few of the guys who worked the chair lifts waved to me as they headed in the direction of town. Most of them stayed in dormitory-style accommodations right between the ski hill and Main Street. There was a time in my life when I would have enjoyed those cramped quarters and not missing out on any of the socializing. But now I found myself grateful for the solitude and space of my studio above Bev's garage.

"Hey!" I called back, waving at them.

"We're headed out tonight. There's more of a nightlife scene fifteen minutes down the highway. Want to join?" one of them asked. I couldn't for the life of me remember any of their names. But in my defense, they'd been working here since the beginning of the season and I'd just arrived.

"Thanks, but I'm good."

They kept on walking, boards in hand and playfully shoving each other, clearly pumped at the thought of a more raucous night out. They were only a few years younger than me, but the jump from early twenties to late twenties felt more substantial than I'd expected.

At times, I felt like I'd always be young at heart. But spending time with a group of twenty-one-year-olds? That made me feel ancient. I'd come here for a fresh start—or maybe to keep chasing a carefree lifestyle. Honestly, I wasn't sure what I wanted. A year ago, the idea of hitting the bars with guys like that—squeezing into places pretending to be clubs—might have sounded fun. But now? I was exhausted by the idea.

The invitation Giles had thrown me sounded a hell of a lot more my speed these days. He might be older than me, but at least we had more common ground.

The lodge loomed ahead. It was one of the only hotels that was nestled right at the base of the mountain. It reminded me of a Swiss chalet with its overhanging roof and natural wood siding. From what I understood, it had been in Giles's family for decades. Sounded like a picturesque childhood, if you asked me. Although, it wasn't like my childhood was tough to hold a candle to.

My phone vibrated in the chest pocket of my jacket. I tugged at the zipper and pulled it out, only to immediately groan when my mom's contact flashed across the screen.

Speaking of my childhood.

I had no intention of dealing with her today, so I sent the call to voicemail and put my phone back. I struggled with the zipper, and before I could even get it closed, my phone went off again.

"Damn," I muttered, irritated that my mother couldn't take a hint. But this time, my brother Nathan's name lit up the screen instead.

I hit answer. "What's up, bro?"

"Do you know that when you ignore our mother's calls, they end up going straight to me?" Impatience coursed through his voice.

I chuckled. "Thought you could field some for me, you know, since I've been taking the brunt of her love all these years."

I almost choked on the word *love*. I knew it was probably the driving force behind most of her actions, but it still left a bitter taste in my mouth.

"I don't have time to talk to her," Nathan grunted. "I'm working on a new project and she'll keep me on the phone for an hour, wondering if you're alright."

I winced. "Sorry about that."

"Yeah, well, you were always the favorite."

I exhaled slowly. There was no point in arguing that. My mother had always chosen me growing up, while our father had chosen Nathan. It was how things had always been. That divide had driven a significant wedge between Nathan and me, but we'd managed to work through our differences in recent years.

"You talk to Dad at all?" I asked. I hadn't heard from the man in forever. He'd forgotten my annual birthday call this past year, and I hadn't bothered to call him for Christmas.

"He called to ask me about an investment opportunity last month. It was a really heartfelt conversation," Nathan said sarcastically.

"Good old Dad," I said with a dry chuckle.

"Yeah, well. What else is new?" I could hear Nathan typing on the other end of the phone. "I thought things were okay with you and Mom, though."

"They're fine." And things *were* fine. Kind of.

"If they were fine, you'd take her calls."

I unhooked the chin strap of my helmet, suddenly feeling suffocated by it. "I talked to her a couple of weeks ago. And I always answer her texts…eventually."

The truth was, ever since Nathan and I had mended our relationship, all of my mother's flaws had become a hell of a lot more apparent to me. She'd always seemed so fun and lighthearted growing up. The complete opposite of my father. He and Nathan were all logic and ambition.

So our family dynamic had always been my mother and me against the two of them. I hadn't realized quite how fucked up that was until I'd finally moved out. Then our parents got divorced in the least surprising twist of the century. And now that Nathan and I were closer, it was us against our parents. The way it honestly always should have been.

I couldn't take talking to my mother lately. She was an expert at playing the martyr and guilt-tripping me over every little thing.

"You know she combusts if she doesn't talk to you a few times a week."

"I'm trying to wean her off that habit," I said dryly.

"Well, try harder. I'm sick of ignoring her calls too."

"Will do, bro." I had no intention of actually making good on that promise, but I still held out hope that she'd finally get the hint that I didn't want to talk to her right now.

"How's Key Ridge?" Nathan asked.

I sucked in a breath of the icy air, peeking back at the now-empty mountain. "Feels like I was meant to be here."

"I'm happy for you, then," he said.

"You and Charlie should come down for a weekend," I said, referring to his wife.

There was a long pause before Nathan said, "We'll see."

That was the same response I'd gotten from him the other day when we'd spoken. I was kind of surprised Nathan wasn't clamoring to visit. He hadn't been much for outdoor sports when he'd first moved to Colorado two years ago, but he'd grown to love snowboarding.

Nathan told me he had to go deal with some things before hanging up.

I stood on the walkway in front of the lodge. The one that led to the small neon open sign by Marie's. The sun had set behind the mountains, casting everything in a bluish hue. It would have been peaceful had there not been tourists packing into every restaurant and bar in sight after a long day on the slopes.

Rather than pushing open Marie's door, I bypassed it and made my way straight to Bev's house, located directly behind the lodge, and headed for the studio above the garage. I'd drop my snowboard off and change first. Another perk of staying right at the base.

Once in my apartment, I peeled off my layers and grabbed a pair of sweatpants out of my oversized duffel bag. I hadn't bothered to unpack yet. I was the type of person who could live out of a suitcase for weeks.

This job and move might have been out of the blue, but it couldn't have come at a better time. My best friend, Harrison, who I'd moved out to Colorado with, had moved out of my house to move in with his girlfriend. I hated to get all sappy, but we'd been roommates for years, and being in that place without him felt wrong.

Being on the road like this, slightly aimless, felt right. And Key Ridge was fucking perfect. If I played my cards right, maybe I'd get asked back for next season too. And then I could do something else over the summer months. I wasn't sure yet—biking, rock climbing. There were a ton of seasonal jobs in these mountain towns. Whatever I chose, going straight back to Denver after this wasn't an option.

Maybe I could even try out another state or something. The possibilities were endless. My brother was married. Harrison and his girlfriend, Lila, were attached at the hip. Everyone in my life was settling down, but that didn't mean I had to.

I was a wanderer at heart. I thrived on little responsibility and no long-term plans.

Knowing what was next was none of my business.

SEVEN

Oliver

FOUR LAUGHING CUSTOMERS SPILLED OUT OF MARIE'S AS I grabbed the door and slipped right by them. My eyes scanned the lively space. It had a long wooden table in the middle and smaller mismatched vintage tables surrounding it. The bar on one side had a neon sign above it and Bev, along with another bartender, hustled behind it, trying to catch up with drink orders.

Giles waved at me from one of the smaller tables across the bar, by the windows. I nodded in acknowledgment before striding over to him. My lips instantly curved when I saw who he was with.

"Mattie, good to see you again," I said, throwing her a smile before turning to Frankie. "Hello, Frankie. Fancy running into you at another bar."

Frankie looked up from her plate before giving me a flat, "Hey."

God, I could still remember what those lips felt like pressed against mine. Theoretically, I knew that Frankie made absolutely zero fucking sense. Career motivated was practically a con when it came to what I looked for in a woman. But I'd be lying if I said I wasn't thinking about a repeat of that kiss.

I pulled out the seat next to hers and sat down.

"How's your first week going so far?" Mattie asked, a mischievous gleam in her eyes as she glanced between her sister and me.

"Honestly, amazing." I tipped my head in Giles's direction. "I'm glad he thought of me for this gig. I couldn't think of a place I'd rather be this winter."

"I'm just happy you could make it on such short notice," Giles said, leaning into Mattie and slinging an arm around her chair.

"Trust me, there was no way I was turning this down."

"Not a lot of prior commitments and responsibilities you had to untangle yourself from?" Frankie asked in a sarcastic tone.

"Frankie, don't be rude," Mattie hissed, but I chuckled.

Frankie rolled her eyes. "I was just messing with him. Oliver and I go way back, right?"

My grin widened as I turned to take her in. "Way back," I confirmed.

I didn't even care that I was supposed to be insulted by her jabs. She was right. I went through life with a low commitment level. It wasn't like I was unreliable. I'd held plenty of steady jobs: teaching lessons at the climbing gym, working at a wilderness sports store, and a few other things depending on the season. But one *could* argue that I wasn't the most stable person around—and I was proud of that.

"How were conditions today?" Mattie asked, changing the subject.

"Pretty good," Giles said. "The powder we got last week is packed down by this point."

"I'm pumped to check out some of the backside," I said, referring to the more challenging terrain.

"We can all go together. Mattie is pretty good at this point too." Giles pointed to his wife.

Mattie held up her hands. "I don't know about that."

"What about you?" I asked, turning to Frankie. "When are we going to get you out there?"

She recoiled at the thought. "How about two days after never."

Mattie laughed. "Careful. I thought that once and now I love it."

"Didn't you also almost get yourself killed your first year learning?" Frankie retorted.

"That wasn't her fault," Giles said, his jaw clenching at the mention of whatever accident must have happened.

Before I could bug Frankie more on the subject, Bev stopped by our table and put her arm on the back of my chair. I had met her when I first arrived, and we'd run into each other a few times as I was getting to the apartment and she was leaving the house. She seemed warm and welcoming from what I could tell.

"Hey, you all have everything you need?" she asked, looking down at me and patting my shoulder.

"I just sat down," I said. "I'll head to the bar and grab a drink."

"Don't bother." She waved her hand. "I'll have someone send over a bottle of wine and another cheese platter."

"Thanks, Bev," Mattie said.

"Can I steal you two for a minute?" she asked, looking at Giles and Mattie. "That new shipment of glassware came in, and I swear it's the wrong color. I don't want the delivery guys to leave until we can confirm it."

"Oh, crap. They already messed it up once," Mattie said, getting up. "I can pull up the invoice."

Giles scooted his chair out and followed her. "We'll be a few minutes," he said. "Feel free to order whatever and don't wait on us."

Frankie sighed audibly once we were alone, which, for some reason, tickled me even more.

"Not happy with my company?" I asked.

She eyed me. "You're fine." She spread some cheese onto a cracker and stuck it in her mouth. Crumbs coated her lips and she daintily wiped them away with her napkin.

"Then what?" I propped an elbow on the table, letting my chin rest in my hand as I stared at her. "Afraid to be left alone with me? Better watch the wine or you might end up making out with me again."

"I'm having a shit week." She pointed the butter knife at me. "And that kiss was just as much you as it was me. And for your information, I've already had my one and only glass of wine for the night. I have a lot of stuff to do when I get back."

"Like what?" I pressed.

"Like apply to hundreds more jobs and watch as control of my life slowly slips through my fingertips." She frowned and stuffed another piece of cheese into her mouth.

Her dramatics made me chuckle, but when she scowled at me, I cleared my throat. "You'll find something," I said, hoping I sounded upbeat and optimistic.

"I appreciate the vote of confidence from the man who moved to a ski town late-season to work part time giving lessons," she said. Again, I should be insulted, but her playful tone only begged me to exchange more barbs with her.

"Hey, you snob," I responded, knocking her knee with

mine underneath the table. "I'll have you know, lessons are very lucrative."

"Is that right?" she asked in mock disbelief.

My grin spread ear to ear. She was impossible. I liked the way her eyes glimmered when we were sparring like this. She seemed so uptight on the outside, yet something about her made me feel like she didn't take herself too seriously. She was a riddle I hadn't quite figured out.

"Tell me," I continued. "Why was your week so bad aside from the obvious?"

She sighed, slumping her shoulders. "The obvious obviously being me losing my job."

"Obviously."

She smiled at that. "Well, let's see." She held a finger up. "To start, I haven't found a single job listing that I'm actually interested in."

My brow furrowed. "I thought you said you had dozens to apply to."

"I do."

I searched her face. The chatter in the restaurant had grown louder as the bar quickly became standing room only, but I found myself only focused on Frankie. "I don't get it," I finally said.

She sighed. "I need a job, Oliver. What's there to understand? It'd be nice if it was at a company I was interested in with a job description I found compelling, but that's not how the world works. I'll apply to everything, and I'll take whatever I can get."

I winced. "That sounds absolutely brutal. I could never do that." I couldn't relate to anything less. I'd gone out of my way to make sure every job I'd done in my adult life had been something I was passionate about.

"Some of us don't have a choice," she said, her tone more

defeated than it was a second ago. The teasing had been sucked away and replaced with some level of despair. Was that my doing?

"I didn't mean to bum you out." I stared at her, willing her to look back up at me.

"It's not you," she said in a tone that didn't convince me at all. She glanced at me and then back down at the table. "Like I said, I'm just having a hard time."

I paused, taking her in. "And being in a place as beautiful as this doesn't help?" I pointed outside the window, where the snow glowed underneath the moonlight. It was only 5:30, but it was completely dark. I loved that about the winter—the evening sky overtaking everything so early. There was something magical about a winter night.

"It's hard to focus on anything except what a failure I am, if I'm being honest," she muttered, refusing to make eye contact with me.

Damn. That tugged right at my chest. Hearing her call herself a failure gutted me. We sat in silence for a moment, the clinking of silverware echoing in my ears. Something in me desperately needed to fix the hopelessness written all over her face.

"You want to know who my brother is?" I finally asked.

That seemed to take her by surprise because she looked up at me and tilted her head. "What? Why would I care who your brother is?"

"You might have heard of him. Nathan Shaw?"

She pursed her lips. "That sounds familiar…"

"He cofounded the dating app Pulse from his college dorm room. He's worth like millions of dollars." I started to fiddle with the napkin in front of me, folding it into tiny triangles over and over again.

It took a moment, but then her eyes bulged at the revelation. I was used to that reaction. "Holy shit. I've heard of him. *That's* your brother?"

"Sure is."

"Damn," she breathed, assessing me in a whole new light. "That's…interesting."

I ignored the way she said *interesting*, as if the fact that we were somehow related was as odd as two entirely different species being connected.

"He's always been the wildly successful one. Not saying I feel like a failure or anything but…I don't know, I've definitely felt like there were times in my life when I haven't measured up."

That felt weird to share. I hated talking about feelings or anything deep. But seeing her crestfallen face had made me want to offer her some sort of crumb of empathy. I couldn't sit by and make another joke while she was clearly miserable.

We both sat in the quiet for a moment before she leaned back in her chair and folded her arms across her chest. I took a sip of water just to have something to do.

"Is he hiring?" she asked.

I nearly choked on the water sliding down my throat. I coughed a few times, a small tear forming in the corner of my eye.

She laughed at my shocked face. "Kidding," she said. "I mean, half kidding of course. I am desperate, after all."

"Damn. You're cutthroat," I said. "I just shared an intimate detail about my life, and that's all you have to say?"

A waiter interrupted us then to drop off a bottle of wine. I thanked him, but could barely take my eyes off Frankie. Her cheeks reddened as she looked out the window before sneaking a glance back at me.

When the waiter left, she said, "Sorry. I hate talking about this—about how sad my life has become. I thought I'd be celebrating a promotion right now, not starting over." Her shoulders slumped forward, as if she was trying to close in on herself.

Hell, I hated talking about stuff like this too. Wading into deeper conversational waters was never something I led the way in. I was chilling in the shallow end all day long. I just wanted to see her smile again. It was like a challenge I had to win.

"Then let's talk about something else," I said.

"Like what?"

Before answering, I poured myself a glass of wine and held up the bottle as an offering to Frankie. Her gaze dropped to her empty glass, and despite her earlier insistence she'd only have one drink, she pushed it toward me. The red wine splashed into her glass. I held up mine and, to my surprise, she clinked it without argument.

"To start, we can talk about how you really can't spend the rest of your time in Key Ridge applying to jobs. That's the most depressing thing I've ever heard."

"More depressing than an unemployed twenty-eight-year-old?" she challenged.

I leveled her with a look. "Are you kidding? An unemployed twenty-eight-year-old sounds exciting as hell."

"Maybe to someone like you," she mumbled, barely audible.

"I heard that. And I'm choosing not to take offense to your stuck-up little attitude. Just because I'm not working some corporate job does not make me worse off."

It was easy to be underestimated. I didn't have a fancy job or a college degree. Most of the time, it didn't bother me. The life I'd built kept me surrounded by like-minded people. But I wasn't completely immune to it. Plenty of dates had written me off the moment they learned that little detail, as if skipping college hadn't been a deliberate choice that I made.

"Sorry." Frankie at least had the decency to look guilty. Her life probably so heavily revolved around what someone's job title was, or where they worked. Just as she was an enigma to me, I was likely a mystery to her.

I took a sip of wine, letting it slosh around in my glass before I leaned in closer to her, doing my best to ignore her pillowy lips. "Let me help you."

Her eyes widened at that. "Help me with what? Landing a job? No offense, but I hardly—"

I held up a hand. "Let me stop you right there before you lob another mildly offensive insult in my direction. I'm not talking about your employment situation."

She set her glass down and angled her body toward mine. "Then what are you talking about?"

"I don't know. Life. Fun. Adventure. I'll help you let loose a little and not become this boring person who only cares about what title they're holding."

"I don't only care about that," she objected. But when I raised an eyebrow and dipped my chin, she snapped her mouth shut without further argument.

"Look, you said it yourself. You were planning to call it an early night, only to fill out more applications. I know we just met, and I know you're going through a bit of a crisis, but that's sad, Frankie."

"Most would argue that's actually the responsible thing to do," she pointed out.

"Well, I'm not most people. And you're telling me you can't find time in that packed schedule of yours to have a little fun?"

She didn't answer immediately, her eyes losing focus as if

weighing her options. "I don't even know how long I'll be here." The protest was weak, and I knew I almost had her.

"All the more reason to live it up while you're here," I said. "Soon enough, you'll be back at a desk, plugging away at whatever it is you do. But right now, you can spare some time and actually enjoy yourself."

She leaned back in her chair. Her eyes moved to the window, where large snowflakes now fell outside.

My body tingled with energy, waiting for her response.

Finally, she let out a sigh and said in a small voice, "Why would you want to help *me*? You don't even know me."

It was the same point she'd made at the bar the other day. But as I stared into her eyes that seemed to hold one million thoughts, I couldn't help but think that she was wrong. Or at the very least, that she would be wrong. Knowing her seemed inevitable. I could feel it in my bones.

"But I *want* to know you," I said.

Before I had my answer, Mattie and Giles returned to the table, pulling out their seats.

"Sorry about that," Mattie said, sitting down. "They were, in fact, the wrong glasses. Took a minute to sort it out with the delivery driver."

"All good now?" Frankie asked, her eyes still glued to mine.

"It's all sorted," Giles said. "We interrupt something?"

I grinned. "Nope, just talking about how Frankie and I should hang out more, since we're both new in town, after all."

The way her eyes lit up made me want to tug her seat closer to mine.

Mattie let out a small laugh. "What are you planning to do?"

"I don't know. Snowboard? Hike? The possibilities are endless," I said.

"Good luck with that." Mattie pointed at me. "Frankie isn't exactly the most athletically inclined."

"Neither are you," Frankie shot back.

Giles chuckled. "Mattie has come a long way."

"I'm not unathletic," Frankie insisted.

"Remember track and field? Sophomore year of high school."

Frankie tossed her head back and groaned at that. "That happened over ten years ago. I was doing fine until I sprained my ankle."

"*Allegedly*." Mattie raised her eyebrows before taking a sip of wine. "I still think you faked it so you could quit."

"Okay, first of all, you weren't even there when I fell, and second off—" Frankie held up another finger and launched into a prepared argument I had a feeling the two had already gone through many times in the past.

Their dynamic made me smile. I glanced over at Giles to see if he was enjoying the sibling spar as much as I was, but he ran a hand down his face. He caught my eye and gave a small shake of his head. Maybe he didn't know what to make of the two of them. He was an only child, after all. Mattie and Frankie weren't much like Nathan and me, but I could still recognize the intricacies of a sibling relationship when I saw one.

Nathan and I hadn't fought much growing up, but at the same time, we also never got along. There was an unspoken rivalry there, something put in place by our parents that we never quite understood but accepted all the same. Except it wasn't the two of us battling for the best grades or being the football star or some crap like that. We were battling lifestyles—our parents' lifestyles to be more specific. Dad had Nathan working like a dog in school, while my mother worked on crafting me to be her upbeat sidekick. Sounded fun in theory. In reality, it fucked with all of our heads.

"Where's the doctor's note, then?" Mattie demanded, breaking me from my thoughts.

"Oh my God, I didn't think I'd need to keep it for *decades*. How was I supposed to know my own sister would use this incident to question my integrity for the rest of our lives?" Frankie lightly smacked my shoulder with the back of her hand. "Back me up here."

"I mean, it sounds believable from what little I've managed to gather so far. She does seem unathletic," I added, jerking a finger in Frankie's direction.

She turned to me, mouth agape. "Hey! Who asked you anyway?"

That made me chuckle. "Prove me wrong, then. Let me take you snowboarding."

"I don't think so." But even as she folded her arms and glared at me, I could see the little crack I'd managed to form in her resolve.

Before I could press, Bev materialized at our table again. "Hey, Frankie," Bev said. "Sorry to interrupt again, but before you leave, I wanted to give you this shirt for your first shift tomorrow. Jeans are fine with it."

Frankie took the black shirt from Bev and let it unfold in front of her torso. *Marie's* was spelled in a cursive font across the chest. "Thanks," Frankie said. "I'll see you at four."

My eyebrows rose as Bev walked away. "You working here or something?" I asked.

"Apparently," Mattie said with a sigh.

Frankie rolled her eyes. "Yes, I am."

Mattie took a sip of wine, eyeing her sister warily. "Please try, and don't make Bev's life any harder, okay?"

"It's going to be fine," Giles said. "Frankie will do a good job, and Bev is drowning back there."

Frankie was about the last person I could see hustling behind a bar while simultaneously being polite to customers. But I would definitely be first in line to see it with my own eyes.

"See! Thank you, Giles." She balled up the T-shirt into her lap and rested an elbow on the table. "Besides, it's just taking orders and running food and drinks to people. How hard can it be?"

EIGHT

Frankie

"Frankie, that table still needs their drinks," Bev called, effortlessly pouring three shots of vodka with one hand while customers swarmed the bar at least three bodies deep.

"I'm going right now," I said.

Shit. What had they ordered again? I pulled out my pad of paper that was now puffy and hard to read due to the pitcher of water I'd spilled on it earlier.

This was the end of my fifth shift. At first, Bev had been quite confident I would improve. Now, I think she saw me as more of a liability and likely regretted asking for my help in the first place.

If you'd asked me last month, I'd have insisted multi-tasking was one of my strong suits, but working at Marie's had made me come to the realization that I was sorely mistaken. I couldn't take the constant onslaught of customers pulling me in every direction. "Can I get a side of fries?" "Don't forget about my espresso martini." "Another napkin when you get a chance." I couldn't think straight with all of the demands. But

I still showed up every time I was scheduled, which Bev said was better than nothing. Likely the highest praise I would get out of her until I showed some real improvement.

I found the drink order I was looking for and rushed to make it before slipping out from behind the bar and dropping it off. Another table that was finally ready to order after sitting there for fifteen minutes also flagged me down. Something else about working in a restaurant was that it was almost impossible to remember to smile and be friendly while I was also trying to feed and water these vultures. I would never take for granted the service industry again.

Once I was back behind the bar, I rang in the food order before starting to help Bev with the next rush of customers waiting to be served. Making drinks was probably the only part of the job that I enjoyed. I wasn't perfect by a long shot, but at least I had some of the simpler drinks locked down. Plus, Bev had a laminated book of drink recipes that she kept behind the bar. Sometimes if it was a guy who ordered something I wasn't familiar with, I asked them what was in it while batting my eyelashes and smiling. They never seemed to take offense to that.

Three girls all dressed in pastel puffy jackets finally made it to the front of the bar line. They all had perfect blowouts tucked underneath fuzzy hats and faces full of makeup. Had they actually gone skiing or were they just here to look cute? Honestly, a vibe I could get behind.

"What can I get you all?" I asked.

Two giggled at something the blonde had said and I tried to shove down the pang in my chest. They were about my age, and judging from the expensive outfits and manicured nails, clearly had their lives together. Alright, I had no way of knowing that *for sure*, but I could tell they weren't stressed about anything at the current moment. Meanwhile, I was here. A girl struggling to tend bar with an unsteady future. I'd already had more job application rejections than I could count over the past week. It was completely disheartening. I knew the job market wasn't great right now, but to not even be able to land a phone interview was a huge blow to my already-fragile ego.

"We'll have three palomas," the blonde in the pink coat relayed to me, hardly making eye contact.

"Great choice," I said with a forced smile.

I poured tequila into a shaker, followed by grapefruit soda, then finished making their drinks before running back to the kitchen and dropping off a few orders.

After about another forty minutes, the bar had finally quieted down a little. It was still crowded, but the rush that always happened after the ski hill closed had finally dissipated.

"You're getting better," Bev observed, wiping a few glasses and placing them behind the bar.

"That's kind of you to say, but I know you're lying."

Bev tossed her head back and laughed at that, but she didn't fight me further on it. She hadn't been kidding when she said she was basically running the restaurant now. Aside from me, there were only a few other bartenders and waiters working here still.

The bell above the door chimed. A few guys in branded Key Ridge ski hill employee jackets walked in. Lifties. A group of them almost always came in after their shifts. I saw one familiar face trailing at the back of their cluster. Even though they were all a few years younger than him, Oliver occasionally joined their group.

Oliver took off his beanie and ruffled his dark waves, before glancing my way. He winked at me, then tossed his stuff onto the table.

We'd only shared a few snippets of conversation since I started working at Marie's. I'd been so busy either here, or holed up in Mattie's basement applying to jobs, I hadn't really gotten out much. But any time Oliver popped into the bar, I could guarantee that he would take every opportunity possible to tease me about my atrocious bartending skills. And, of course, he hadn't given up on taking me snowboarding. I'd never admit this to him, but I might have relented if not just to see him more. But he'd been slammed with lessons every day, so even if I had agreed, he wouldn't have been able to take me yet. Instead, I savored the brief, flirtatious moments we shared whenever he stopped by during my shifts.

It was hard to believe we'd shared that kiss. It had been almost two weeks at this point. It was so outside of something I would typically do that I could almost convince myself it had never happened. That is, if Oliver didn't insist on reminding me of it every single chance he got.

"We can't keep meeting like this," Oliver said, stopping in front of me at the bar and propping one elbow up so he could rest his chin in his hand.

"There are other bars on Main Street, ya know?" I said, although I secretly loved his teasing. Seeing him at Marie's or around the lodge was one of the only bright spots in my life lately. I liked the little surge of butterflies that flapped around in my stomach every time he flirted with me. I enjoyed the prolonged eye contact.

"None with this level of impeccable service."

I rolled my eyes at that. He was giving me a hard time because the last two times he'd been in, I'd messed up his drink order.

"Hey, I'm getting better," I insisted. "Plus, last time you were here, it was packed. At least you got a drink."

He laughed. "You're right. I suppose I should be grateful you at least managed to shove something into my hands."

"Exactly."

Oliver smiled and shook his head. His dark hair curled up behind his ears, probably due to the wetness of the snow. "Can I get four shots of tequila please?"

"Four shots? Are you trying to wind up face down in a snow pile before eight?"

"Ha. Ha," he said dryly. "They aren't all for me."

I poured the shots and set out a tray to put them on, along with already-cut-up lime wedges and a saltshaker.

"Thanks." He slid his credit card over. "You can keep it open. I'll be back to bug you."

"Counting down the minutes," I said, unable to keep the smile from creeping across my face. Oliver's good-natured attitude was infectious. The more I got to know him, the more I realized my initial judgment call about him had been correct. He was *so* not my type. I doubted he'd ever used the word "ambition" before in his entire life. To him, this lifestyle wasn't temporary. He'd likely spend the next few decades doing exactly the same thing—jumping from place to place, working seasonal jobs. Not moving up. Staying the same.

But even knowing all that, there was something charming about him, something I found hard to resist. I could act like I didn't feel anything, but there was no denying the excited nerves that swirled in my gut every time I caught a glimpse of the guy.

The excited swirl in question abruptly stopped and my smile fell when Oliver bypassed the table of guys he'd arrived with and went straight for the table of girls I'd served palomas to earlier. They giggled at something he said as he set down the shots in front of them.

Heat pricked the back of my neck. I knew I should have looked away, but I couldn't.

I watched as he slid into the empty chair at their table and leaned into the blonde one. Suddenly, all the times he'd flirted with me felt tainted. I'd thought we had something. A mutual interest. A potential friendship. I don't know. But I thought I had been more special than a table of three random girls he'd spotted out of the corner of his eye. Seeing him wink at them made me certain I wasn't though.

Damn it.

Oliver passed out the shots and they all tipped them back. I turned away, unable to watch the scene any longer. I wasn't sure if I was more upset by the sight or the fact that I felt an inkling of jealousy right now. Oliver and I had shared all of one kiss and a few sessions of playful banter. I had absolutely no right to be feeling the way that I was right now.

But my body didn't get the memo. My pulse quickened as I busied myself tidying up behind the bar, forcing my eyes to stay trained down. I couldn't let Oliver catch me staring.

"Can I get a pitcher of beer?"

I looked up, only mildly startled, to see one of the guys that had come in earlier leaning on the bar and smiling at me. He looked young, barely twenty-one.

"Sure, can I see your ID?" I asked.

He handed it over, and I recognized it immediately as being a Florida ID. My eyes scanned to his birthday where I confirmed that he was legal, but barely.

"I'm from Florida too," I said, handing it back to him.

"No way. What part?" He stuffed the ID back into his wallet.

"Close to Orlando. You?"

"Cocoa beach," he said. "Finally came up here for college, and I'm never going back."

I nodded as if I could relate to what he was saying. While I had moved from my hometown to Atlanta, it was for a career opportunity, not because I disliked Florida. Wherever I ended up next, I certainly couldn't see myself staying in Colorado. It was too laid-back.

"What kind of pitcher?" I asked.

"Whatever's your favorite." He slouched against the bar awkwardly and smiled at me. I wanted to laugh at his sloppy attempt at flirting.

"Coming right up." I pulled a pitcher out and set it against a tap before pulling down the handle.

Foam filled the bottom. "Shit," I muttered, tilting the pitcher to try and rectify the situation. I was bad at this. Every single time I poured a beer or a pitcher, there was too much damn foam. I offered an apologetic shrug to the guy but he was staring at me with googly eyes. Somehow, I didn't think this kid would call me out on it.

"What's your name?" he asked when I set the pitcher in front of him.

Might as well play along. Usually, the lifties tipped the bare minimum, but maybe if I flirted and laughed at their jokes, I could get a few extra dollars. It wasn't like I was in desperate need of the money, but I did love a challenge.

"Frankie. What about you? I think I've seen you guys in here before."

"Kenny," he said, before crinkling his nose. "Frankie is a funny name. Short for Frank?"

I narrowed my eyes and my smile faltered. But Kenny wasn't joking. He genuinely looked perplexed.

"Um, no. It's short for Frances."

"Ohhh, right. That makes sense."

Suddenly, even fake flirting with Kenny felt exhausting.

The bar had quieted down significantly and I wanted to zone out until the end of my shift in a few hours.

"What time do you get off?" Kenny asked.

Before I could answer, Oliver slung his arm around Kenny and patted his chest a few times. Hard. He was at least a head taller than Kenny and he looked down at him before glancing back at me. "What's going on here?" he asked. "Thought you were getting a pitcher."

"I got distracted talking to Frankie." Kenny had a dumb grin on his face.

"Frankie's busy," Oliver said. His subtle change in tone caught my attention. I squinted my eyes and examined him. He still wore his signature smile, but it looked tighter somehow. His neck muscles flexed.

"I'm really not," I said. The bar was lively, but no one was currently waiting on a drink.

"What time do you get off?" Kenny tried asking again, but Oliver smacked his shoulder and forcibly turned him around.

"Alright, that's enough. Why don't you take this—" he handed Kenny the pitcher "—and head back to the table."

Kenny looked like he wanted to object but seemed to think better of it.

Oliver ran a hand through his hair before turning back to me. I scanned his face.

"That was interesting," I said.

"What do you mean?" he asked, his jaw still tight despite the smile.

"You scared off Kenny."

"Yeah, well. He's a nice kid but he can't take a hint."

His slight look of discomfort was egging me on.

"Kenny was fine," I said. "And I'm surprised you noticed anything other than the blonde in front of you." I nodded my head in the direction of the table of girls he'd done shots with.

Oliver raised his eyebrows at that. "Well, I didn't want him bothering you," he added, a line creasing his forehead.

"He wasn't," I said, only the partial truth. "Seemed like you were jealous or something." I kept my voice nonchalant, almost teasing. I was testing the waters, but I had no intention of jumping right into the deep end.

Oliver scoffed at that. "I don't do jealousy, Frankie. And was *I* really the jealous one? You seemed to be *very* aware of the table I was sitting at." I wished I could wipe that smirk clean off his face.

"It was right in front of me," I added, stuffing any defensiveness deep down. "It was impossible not to notice."

Oliver's smirk grew. "Right."

"I wasn't jealous," I insisted, narrowing my eyes.

We stared at each other for a moment, waiting to see who would break first. Finally, Oliver said, "For your information, I was just being a wingman for the rest of the guys. See?" He pointed behind him to the two tables of guys and girls who were now intermixed.

"Good for you." I tapped my fingers on the bar top. "Can I get back to work or do you want anything else?" I asked in a flat tone.

He ran his thumb and forefinger along his chin, a devilish glint in his eyes. "There is one more thing I want. You. This Friday. Seven a.m. with a snowboard strapped to your feet. I had a lesson cancel so I finally have a free day."

"Not gonna happen." I crossed my arms.

"Why?" he pressed.

"I'm busy."

He snickered at my defiance. "I know you only work nights at Marie's."

"I have jobs to apply for."

"You've been applying constantly. It's all you talk about."

I winced at that. Did he think I was boring?

"Are there really that many new applications that open on a daily basis?" he continued.

That gave me pause. I hadn't expected him to push me on this. The past few times he'd been in Marie's, he'd made the same attempt to get me out there. But he'd let me reject his previous efforts to get me on a snowboard without anything more than a fake pout. I figured he'd let me do the same this time, but there was a fire in his eyes.

"No, but—"

"And this will only be for a few hours. You can do whatever job hunting you need to do when you get home."

"I don't have a snowboard," I pointed out.

"Got you covered." He leaned over the bar to take in my full height. His eyes combing over every inch of me did ridiculous things to my imagination. I held steady though. "What are you. Five-foot-six? I can get you a board. And let me guess. Size eight for the boots?"

"Size seven," I corrected without thinking about it.

He winked. "Great. It's settled. You're coming."

I shook my head, trying to rid myself of whatever trance Oliver had me under. "I didn't say that."

"I'll have a board and boots ready at seven a.m. Lifts open an hour early on Friday for locals. It'll be perfect to get you started. It'll be fun. Ever heard of the concept?"

"I'm fun," I challenged.

"Really? Could have fooled me."

I let out a loud, exaggerated huff. "I have nothing to wear." My resolve had shattered by this point. Why shouldn't I give this a try? I was fighting it so hard, and for what? To sit alone in my sister's basement, stressing about my severe lack of prospects?

"Mattie has extra gear. I already asked her."

"What? When? You're conspiring with my sister now?"

He laughed at that, his eyes glinting. "I saw her at the lodge yesterday. Figured I'd ask."

"Uh-huh." I folded my arms across my chest, a small sign of resistance, but we both knew he'd won.

He knocked on the bar before walking backward to his table. "I'll see you Friday. Bright and early."

NINE

Oliver

"Nice outfit," I said through a chuckle.

"It was all Mattie had." Frankie glared at me while adjusting the arms of the cream snowsuit that had lines of neon color circling the elbows and knees. She looked freaking adorable.

"Sorry for wanting to look good out here," Mattie said, wearing her own emerald-green and white snowsuit.

"You can say that again." Giles grinned and ruffled her hair.

"Hey!" She swatted him away before tugging on a beanie.

Frankie sighed and eyed the board and boots in my hands. "Those for me?" she asked.

"Yep." I handed her the boots, and she took them without complaint. "You need more coffee or something?" I asked. "I was expecting about a dozen more snarky comments from you this morning."

"Wait until we're on the hill and I've fallen on my ass the first few times. You'll be begging me to shut up."

She furrowed her brow and squinted at the hill behind us.

I glanced back at it, attempting to see it through her eyes. It probably seemed pretty ominous to her, though I was so used to speeding down that steep hill that I barely gave it a second thought.

Her lack of enthusiasm only made me more determined to drag her up the mountain. I had a bit of a habit—okay, a full-blown complex—of roping people into adventures they had no interest in.

Just ask my brother, Nathan. We were never particularly close until he moved to Denver, at which point I had made it my mission to introduce him to every hobby I'd picked up since landing here. Despite his endless complaints, I took him rock climbing, hiking, snowboarding. Apparently, forcing people to do the things I enjoyed was my love language.

"Maybe you'll be a natural," Giles offered as Frankie looked warily up the hill. "Mattie picked it up pretty fast."

Frankie raised an eyebrow. "Was this before or after she wound up in the hospital?"

Giles winced and Mattie rolled her eyes. "How many times do I have to tell you, that wasn't my fault."

"We'll be on the bunny hill. Chances of hospitalization are low," I reassured Frankie. I had taught plenty of lessons over the years and so far hadn't had a single injury on my watch. Well, other than a few bruised butts. That couldn't be helped.

"But never zero," she countered.

I swiped my hand across my face, hiding my massive grin. I'd gotten to know Frankie's feisty demeanor quite well after spending almost every evening at Marie's, hoping to catch her there. Getting her to loosen up wasn't going to be easy, but hell if I wouldn't give it a fighting try.

"Are we doing this or not?" Frankie asked, lifting up the boots and waving them around, almost knocking herself right in the face.

"Careful, champ. Any injuries that happen before the hill, I cannot be held responsible for." I gave her shoulder a little shake, and Giles and Mattie laughed.

"Come on. Let's go," Frankie whined.

The slight shake in her voice told me that she was anxious. I felt a slight tug at that.

"You two go ahead." I pointed to Mattie and Giles. "Maybe we'll meet up at the base later."

"Oh, I'll definitely be stopping by before that to see Frankie fall a few times."

Frankie glared at her sister. "Wait. You're actually ditching me?"

Giles looked behind them, clearly eager to escape the beginner area.

"We can't all take over the bunny hill," Mattie said. "Oliver is going to teach you."

The sigh Frankie let out could have triggered an avalanche.

"Let's go." I waved for her to follow me, but she still stood there, hesitant.

"See ya," Mattie said as she and Giles headed to the main lift.

I turned, not waiting for Frankie to follow, and walked over to one of several outdoor benches surrounding a firepit. It wasn't turned on right now because of the early hour, but later in the day, people would be packed shoulder to shoulder around this thing.

"Come on, I won't bite," I yelled to Frankie, who was still standing there. "Unless you want me to," I added with a wink.

That seemed to finally snap her out of it. She stalked toward me and plopped down on the bench. "I don't know if this is such a good idea—hey!" She swatted my hand away, but I had already managed to pull off one of her leather boots.

"Put this on," I instructed, taking the right snowboard boot from her hand and setting it on the ground. "I can grab you another pair from the rental shop if they don't fit. They should be tight but not crushing your toes."

She looked hesitant but thankfully followed my instructions. She stuffed her foot into the bulky boot and grunted as she tried to get her heel to slide in.

"Here," I said, grabbing her waist and pulling her lightly to stand up. "Grip my arms and push."

As soon as she stood and pushed down, her foot went in easily.

"How's it feel?" I tapped the tip of her boot.

"Uncomfortable," she said.

I rolled my eyes. "It's not a tennis shoe. Are your toes cramped?"

"No," she admitted. "I can wiggle them."

"Perfect." I gave her a thumbs-up.

Once she got the other boot on and laced up, I grabbed both of our boards and headed toward the bunny hill. Frankie followed me, and when I glanced back, I could see her eyeing the small hill with apprehension. Typically, they didn't open it early like they did the main chairlift, but I'd convinced one of the guys I knew to operate it for us.

"This is a terrible idea," she said under her breath.

I chuckled and knocked on her helmet. "Relax. You're with a professional."

She narrowed her eyes and jerked away from my hand. "Somehow, not comforting."

My lower lip jutted out and I blinked down at her a few times, doing my best hurt-puppy-dog impression. That finally got her to smile and playfully shove my shoulder. It was obvious that through her tough exterior, she was all nerves. I was determined to make this fun for her.

The past couple of weeks had been a little dull, if I was being honest. Not in terms of activity, but in the sense of being alone all the time. I'd gone from living with my best friend and having a close-knit community in Denver, to being completely on my own. I could talk to anyone, strike up a conversation without effort. Casual friendships had always come easily to me, but I'd never realized how hollow they could start to feel.

Frankie was different. She felt real. It was like there was this magnetic tug that continuously pulled me into her orbit. It was why, despite not having explored many of the bars and restaurants on Main Street, I continued to go to Marie's night after night.

Without further build up, I tossed her board to the ground. "Which foot do you kick with?" I asked.

"What? Why?" Frankie looked from the board to me with pinched brows.

"Just answer the question," I said.

She pretended to step up to an invisible ball and mimed a small kick. "My right," she said.

"Perfect, that'll be your back foot then. Here—" I kneeled down and patted the front binding. "Stick your boot in."

It only took a few minutes to get Frankie strapped in and convince her to step onto the moving conveyor belt that would take us to the top of the very small, very flat bunny hill. She'd tried to convince me it might be better to practice on flat ground, but I wouldn't hear of it.

Now we were at the top, staring about 200 yards to the bottom. She looked panicked.

"Is there a way to make that belt thingy go in reverse?" she asked, her voice cracking.

"Only way down is straight," I said calmly. "It's not as bad as it looks. Watch." I started down the hill, leaning on my heels to slow myself down. "You can start with just standing up and leaning back."

It was challenging not to laugh as Frankie stood up. She kept her butt as far back as she could, but her entire torso was bent over with her hands straight out in front of her. She moved the tiniest inch forward before letting out a squeal and abruptly sitting back down.

I covered my amused expression with my mitten. "Great start."

She let out an aggravated huff. "Can you stop being so annoyingly patient?"

I shimmied forward and dropped to my knees in front of her. "What can I say? I used to teach kids. This reminds me of that."

Frankie glowered at me. "Hilarious."

My smile stretched even further as I gripped the middle of her board. "Alright. Let's try that again."

"I told you." Frankie shot me a look that was equal parts misery and blame.

The strong smell of antiseptic surrounded us while we waited in the ski hill's cramped medical room for the nurse to come take a look at Frankie's wrist.

"Mattie is never going to let me live this down," she groaned.

I ran one hand through my hair and watched as she cradled her left wrist in her right hand. The lesson hadn't lasted for much longer than an hour before Frankie had fallen forward and caught herself with her hand. Even though her cry of pain had seemed a touch dramatic, I'd still insisted on taking her to the medic to get it looked at.

"Hopefully this won't ruin your promising career as a professional snowboarder," I joked.

"Very funny," she deadpanned.

"Scootch over," I said.

The thick white paper covering the bench crinkled as I squeezed in next to her and slung my arm over her shoulders. "I still maintain you were doing okay before you fell."

She snorted and shook her head, her eyes facing the wooden door with a large anatomical chart of the human body affixed to it. Except this one was a skier, and all of the arrows pointed to the most common injuries.

"I sucked and you know it."

She *had* spent more time on her butt than riding down the mountain, but that was typical for a beginner. And even through all the complaining, I had been able to see the determination in her eyes. Like a spark that couldn't be put out. Typically, teaching beginner lessons was painfully boring. But I'd had more fun this morning than I'd had since I arrived in Key Ridge.

"I mean…I didn't say you were a natural," I said.

That got a breath of a laugh out of her.

Frankie's weight shifted slightly into me. Everything about the simple gesture grounded me in the moment. Her body pressed against mine felt like the most natural thing in the world.

I had a sneaking suspicion Frankie was exaggerating her injury. She'd been tired and cranky toward the end, and the moment I asked if she was okay after that last fall, she'd clutched her wrist delicately and gave a pitiful moan. *But* when we reached the bottom of the hill, she had picked up her snowboard with the same supposedly injured hand before I snatched it away from her.

I wouldn't press it though.

"Do you believe me now that snowboarding isn't meant for me?" she asked.

"You want to try skiing instead? I'm not as skilled of an instructor, but I can give it a try—"

"Oliver." She elbowed me in the ribs.

My arm was still draped over her shoulders. It felt heavy and I was hyperaware of it. It was probably past the point of a friendly gesture, but I couldn't get myself to pull away. It felt too good to have her tucked into me. She didn't move away either.

"Sorry if I pushed you," I finally said. "It's kind of my thing."

She tilted her head so that she could glance at me. It wasn't lost on me that our lips were only inches apart.

"Do all of your hobbies involve defying death?" she asked.

"Pretty much. What else is there?"

"I don't know. Knitting?"

The grin spread easily across my face as I continued to stare into her eyes. "Can you really picture me knitting?"

She shrugged. "Maybe."

"You'd have to teach me."

She scrunched up her cute little button nose and finally looked away. "I don't know how to knit."

That made me laugh. "Then why are you trying to force it on me?"

"I wasn't," she said defensively. "I was just offering it as an option for a more relaxed hobby that doesn't land you in the emergency room."

"I've never broken a bone," I said.

Her forehead crinkled with disbelief. "Never?"

"Never," I repeated, intentionally leaving out the time I had fallen while skateboarding when I was fourteen. Eleven stitches for a gash on my upper arm. Still had the scar to prove it.

"What are your hobbies if you don't knit?" I asked.

That question seemed to take her by surprise. "Oh, um…" Frankie thought for a moment but the silence was becoming drawn out.

"You don't have any hobbies, do you?" I asked.

Damn. When I had insisted on showing Frankie a good time while she was in town, I hadn't realized how badly she needed it.

"I have hobbies," she insisted.

"Then name one."

"What is this, a job interview?" she asked, shrugging my arm off her shoulder. I instantly felt the loss as she shifted an inch away from me.

"No, but shouldn't you be preparing anyway?"

I'd meant it as a joke but I could tell by the way Frankie stiffened that I'd said the wrong thing. The quietness in the room nearly strangled me. I slipped off the bed and moved in front of her so that I could better search her face. She was chewing on her lip, deep in thought. Her eyes stared straight through my chest.

"Hey," I said softly, reaching out my hand to brush her chin, but I retracted it once I thought better of it. "I'm sorry. I didn't mean anything by that."

She looked broken, and I fucking hated that.

"I don't have any hobbies, okay? It's pathetic and I know it. Ever since I got laid off, I've come to realize that my career was my only personality trait. I have nothing else."

"That isn't true." It couldn't be. I'd only known her since she'd been careerless, and everything about her captivated me.

"It is though. I have no outside interests. I'm not good at anything else—you've seen me bartending. And now snowboarding. That job was all I had," she insisted, absentmindedly twisting her hair.

Her distant expression made me want to pull her into a hug. Physical touch had always come easily to me, but with Frankie, it was different. Every brush of her skin against mine sent me straight back to our kiss that first night I arrived. Did she even think about it?

"Well, that's not you anymore. Use this time to get to know yourself. Try something new. I told you I'd help. Just because this didn't go to plan, doesn't mean I'm giving up on you."

Her lips twitched into a faint smile. "You still want to hang out with me after today?" she asked.

"I promise I'll pick a safer activity." I put a hand over my chest.

She studied me for a moment. I couldn't deny that her gaze on me felt good. It was no secret that I liked attention, but her attention was quickly becoming my favorite.

"What's in this for you, Oliver?"

"What do you mean? Spending time with you. Do I need an ulterior motive?"

"You must have better things to do." Her voice was soft. She did that a lot—hovered between her feisty side and a quieter, more vulnerable version of herself.

"I don't," I said.

She considered this. "How long are you even in town for?" she asked.

I shrugged. "Dunno. Lessons only go for the rest of the season and that's over in a few weeks."

"And then…"

"And then…your guess is as good as mine."

She scoffed. "How can you live like that? Floating through life without a plan?"

"How can you live a life that's so rigidly structured you forgot how to have fun?"

She winced, and I regretted my words. But she was trying to burrow into something. Something deeper than the surface, and my entire nature repelled that.

"Sorry," I muttered.

"It's okay. You're not wrong. But that doesn't mean I'm wrong either. You have to have a plan, Oliver. Goals. Things that motivate you."

It felt pointless to argue with her, but I didn't agree. My aimlessness had gotten me this far in life, and I saw no reason to change.

"Tell you what." Frankie snapped her fingers—the ones attached to her so-called injured wrist. My suspicion that she was faking it heightened even more, but I suppressed my smirk. "I'll let you continue to drag me on whatever activities you deem fun, if you let me help you come up with some goals and figure out what's next."

I folded my arms across my chest. "I don't know…"

"Oh, come on." She held her hands together and blinked up at me, the same move I'd already used on her. The fact that she actually looked excited about this struck a chord with me. "Please." She blinked again, her lips forming a pout. It took everything in me not to grab the back of her neck and haul her mouth onto mine.

"Fine," I relented. Not because I wanted Frankie to help me with some stupid two-year plan or whatever the hell it was she had in mind. But because it felt like she needed this. Needed to offer me something that she felt she was good at.

"Yay!" she clapped excitedly, and I arched an eyebrow.

"Careful. Your wrist."

"Oh." She looked guilty and instantly pulled her hands apart, cradling her wrist again. At this point, I wouldn't have been surprised if she accidently picked the wrong one.

"You know, you could have just told me you were done for the day," I said. "You didn't have to do this whole injury charade."

Before she could respond, there were two short knocks at the door and it swung open. The nurse hurried in, looking out of breath. I knew for a fact she had her hands full as the only on-site medical professional on the ski hill.

"Alright, let's see the wrist," she said, holding out her hand to Frankie. It only took her a minute of bending and assessing before she dropped it back in Frankie's lap. "Looks fine to me," she said. "Doesn't even seem swollen or sprained."

I smirked over at Frankie, but she didn't meet my eyes. "Isn't that great news? We can get you back out there."

Frankie frowned and looked pleadingly at the nurse. "Please tell this crazy man that it would be in my best interest not to go speeding down a mountain any time soon."

The nurse looked up from her tablet. "Maybe you could give it another go next season. Would be a shame for you to end up back in here."

"A shame indeed," Frankie said, shooting me a warning glare. Something told me that regardless of if she was faking this or not, I wouldn't be able to push her into giving boarding a second shot.

We left the medical room. The mountain was now crawling with tourists after the thirty minutes we'd spent inside.

"Well, Frankie. It's been a fun morning."

"Has it?"

"It has."

She barely came up to my neck and craned her head to

look up at me, shielding her eyes from the sunrays. "You're a strange guy, Oliver."

That made me chuckle. "Don't I know it."

"I guess I'll see you around."

"Sooner than you think. We've got fun to catch up on."

She snorted at that. "Alright, then. I'll start brainstorming goals for you in the meantime."

It bothered me a little that she saw me as a project. But then again, wasn't I doing the same to her? Dragging her around, trying to prove there was more to life than some stupid job?

What she didn't realize was that her plan was going to be a hell of a lot harder to pull off than mine.

TEN

Frankie

"I WAS ABLE TO IMPROVE THE COMPANY'S ROI ON AD SPEND BY nearly ten percent last quarter." I continued to list off one impressive stat after another as a middle-aged man with a sour expression nodded while writing them down.

Even though I had on a short-sleeve turtleneck sweater, I was burning up. The shirt had started to stick to my skin in the worst way, and I said a silent thank you that it was black. Even if I was sweating my ass off, the interviewer wouldn't be able to tell.

"That's impressive, Frances," he said.

I winced at the sound of my full name. Even though I had told him I go by Frankie at the beginning of the interview, he didn't seem to remember—or care.

I let it go, though, because I needed to nail this interview. It was like I had blinders on to anything else around me.

This position was far from my dream job. It was a level down in title and in pay. And to top it all off, it was located in Madison, Wisconsin. After applying to every job possible in the metro Atlanta area, I had decided to expand my search.

At this point, I was open to moving anywhere. But Wisconsin? It wasn't exactly a prime location for me. The brutal winters alone were enough to give me pause.

But times were tough and opportunities were scarce. This was my first interview beyond the basic phone screening with HR. So even though I wasn't sure I was all that interested in the job, I felt desperate—no, hungry—to move on in the process.

He asked me a few more basic questions, to which I responded with what I thought were solid answers. By the time we hung up, I felt pretty confident that I'd killed it.

I blew out a sigh of relief as I closed my laptop. Crushing interviews made me feel a little bit like myself again. I was at home in conference rooms, with a slide deck prepared and a captivated audience of my coworkers. I lived for things people dreaded, like performance reviews and presentations. It had only been a few weeks since I'd been let go, but it was like that person was already fading away.

My phone dinged.

Oliver: How's the wrist? ;)

Frankie: Excruciatingly painful, but I'll survive.

Oliver: You're so brave.

Frankie: I try.

Oliver: I have an idea for our next little funventure.

Frankie: Does it involve creating a vision board for your future? Because that sounds like fun to me.

> Oliver: Ew

"Frankie?" Mattie called out from the stairway.

"I'm done," I called back, stuffing my phone into my pocket.

"Come upstairs and hang out. Giles made some popcorn on the stove."

As she said the words, the heavenly scent of butter and salt drifted into the basement. Right on cue, my stomach rumbled.

"Coming," I shouted, heading for the stairs and rushing up them.

Mattie waited for me at the top, holding out a bowl. I took it from her and followed her through the kitchen and into the living room. Giles was already there, sprawled out on the couch, his dirty-blond hair tucked into a worn beanie.

"We just started a movie." Mattie plopped onto the couch and nestled into her husband.

My heart swelled a little at the sight as I took the open armchair. My sister had always dreamed of getting married. She had wasted so much time with her asshole ex that I used to worry she might never wake up and realize her worth. But when she'd found someone as solid as Giles to start a life with, I was thrilled. He might not be a man of many words, but he—without the tiniest, solitary doubt—loved my sister more than anything. I could see it in the way he carefully pressed her into his side.

"I don't want to interrupt your date night," I said. But my eyes were already glued to the TV as I shoved a handful of popcorn into my mouth.

"It's fine," Giles said, pressing play on whatever action-comedy movie they'd selected.

I hoped they didn't mind me crashing their little family of two. Growing up, Mattie and I had always been close. So when I got laid off and booked the ticket, overstaying my welcome hadn't even flittered through my mind. But now that I'd been here a while without an end in sight, I really should make sure I wasn't imposing. Mattie would never ask me to leave, and Giles would never ask Mattie to ask me to leave. He'd do anything for her—and that included putting up with her directionless sister.

"I'm just glad I finally got you out of that dungeon," Mattie added. "You've been down there literally all day."

"I heard lack of sunlight actually helps you find employment quicker," Giles deadpanned.

"Oh, you're making jokes now, huh?" I teased.

He chuckled and shrugged.

"I resent that comment," I added. "I get out plenty. I work at Marie's almost every night, and I went snowboarding a few days ago, thank you very much.

"And what a success that was," Mattie said, laughing.

I flexed my wrist a few times on instinct, a smile playing on my lips. Faking was such a strong word, but I had known there was nothing wrong with my wrist other than *maybe* it would be a little sore the next day. But I had been so sick of falling on my butt in front of Oliver, I had jumped at the chance to visit the medic. Perhaps I should be embarrassed that Oliver seemed to see right through me to my true motives, but I couldn't help myself. I hated being bad at things. Snowboarding was a masochist's sport anyway. Who was the first person that strapped a board to their feet and was like, *yes, this is how I want to send myself down the mountain—who cares how many times I fall?*

The movie had barely finished rolling the opening credits

when Mattie shifted on the couch to look at me. "How did the interview go?" she asked.

"I think I killed it."

"Are you interested in the job though? Didn't you say it was below what you were doing before?"

My chest burned like that was somehow a dig at me and my skills, even though she was only repeating what I had told her.

"That's the way the job market is right now," I said.

"But you shouldn't take the first thing that comes along if it's all wrong for you."

"Or I take it and then figure out a contingency plan later." I tossed another piece of popcorn into my mouth. "It's always easier to find a job when you *have* a job."

"I guess." I knew my sister, and I could hear the doubt in her voice as if she were screaming it. "I just know how hard you worked to get to where you were. I hate the thought of you backsliding."

The movie that I had honestly forgotten about paused.

"Why did you pause it?" Mattie asked.

Giles looked between the two of us. "I thought you two were talking."

"I was watching," Mattie insisted.

"Same," I agreed.

He raised a skeptical eyebrow but pressed play.

"And I'm not backsliding," I continued.

"That's what it sounds like," Mattie argued.

Giles let out an audible sigh but didn't attempt to press pause on the movie again.

"Look, I don't even know if I made it to the next step yet. At the very least, it was practice. Stop being over-bearing."

I had been waiting for Mattie to overstep like this. Just

because she had her life all figured out, she felt like she could impose some sisterly wisdom on me.

She shot me a disapproving look. "You're beating yourself up trying to find something. I want you to know that it's okay to take time for yourself."

Easy for her to say. When her life had imploded, she'd moved to Key Ridge right away and ended up falling in love and finding this whole new idyllic life. Not all of us were living in a fantasy.

"Chill, Mattie. Frankie will figure it out." Giles's words were so soft I almost didn't hear them. I flashed him a grateful smile, and he acknowledged it with a small nod.

Mattie glared between the two of us as if we had committed some sort of betrayal. "Okay, fine. I'll keep my mouth shut."

"I'm sure that resolution will last all of one day," I joked, feeling vindicated when Giles let out a small chuckle.

Mattie held up her hands in defeat. "Alright, if you two start ganging up on me, I'm moving out."

***

"Did you send that table a whiskey and Coke?" Bev asked, holding up a brown beverage in a small glass.

"Yes?" I said it like a question as I toweled off the bar. While I was getting a little bit better at making drinks and multitasking behind the bar, I think it was safe to say I was *not* meant for the service industry.

It was too damn hard.

"Taste this," Bev insisted, grabbing a straw off the bar and inserting it into the drink.

I took a sip and winced. "Yuck," I said as soon as the sharp taste of tequila mixed with Coke hit my tongue.

Bev raised an eyebrow and chuckled. "I know I haven't been bartending much longer than you have, but I can't say I've poured a lot of tequila Cokes in my time."

She was the most chill boss I'd ever had. She never berated me for making mistakes or threatened to fire me over my obvious lack of skills. She was no pushover, but she took everything in stride. It made the fact that the rest of my life wasn't going so great right now feel a little less sucky.

"My bad," I said, hurriedly grabbing a new glass and double-checking that the bottle I picked up was indeed whiskey before pouring the drink. "I'm having an off day."

Bev gave me a gentle, understanding smile, the corners of her eyes creasing a little. Bev had quickly made me feel right at home here. Even though it was Mattie who'd married into her family and not me, I still felt like she was my extended aunt or something.

Bev gave my shoulder a squeeze before dropping her hand. "Mattie told me you didn't get a job or something like that?"

"Of course she did." My stomach soured that Bev already knew about my rejection. The interview I'd spent the entire week preparing for—the only one I'd been granted since applying—had already sent me an email this morning, letting me know I wouldn't be moving on to the next round. Despite the fact that I had answered every question flawlessly, made polite small talk, and that I was overqualified for the role. None of that had been enough.

"Their loss," Bev said, taking in my forlorn expression.

I'd already spent the morning distraught and crying over this. I refused to tear up again, especially not in such a public setting. I had to keep it together.

"That's nice of you to say, but you don't even know me that well." I sounded small, but all this rejection was starting to take its toll on me. Bev's kind eyes made me feel like I could just curl up into a ball in her presence.

"I know enough," she said, leaning against the bar. "And I know what those God-awful corporations are like. Enough of them have tried to purchase this lodge over the years. It's always the same. A bunch of out-of-touch older men whose only personality trait is their career. You should wear it like a badge of honor that you don't fit in there."

I opened my mouth to protest but quickly shut it. I didn't want to see the disappointment in Bev's eyes when I explained that I, in fact, fit in perfectly with that crowd. Or at least, I used to.

"Thanks," I said instead, desperately needing this conversation to end.

"At least you're here. Key Ridge is a great place to heal and recoup."

"I do like it here," I murmured wistfully.

"Think you might stay?" Bev asked. I must have looked taken aback because Bev shook her head, laughing. "Geez, I asked if you were planning to stay and you're looking at me like it's some sort of death sentence."

"No, I'm not," I insisted, although I'm sure my expression hadn't been far off from that description.

Bev leaned a hip against the bar and crossed her arms.

Before I could say anything else, the bell above the front door chimed. Oliver waved at me before stomping some of the snow off his boots on the front door mat. Seeing him almost instantly lifted the dark cloud that had been floating around me all morning.

It had only been a few days since my snowboarding career had started and ended, and he'd come into Marie's every night for dinner or a drink. He'd sit at the bar and we'd talk a little. I was immensely grateful he was always around.

During our chats, I'd also tried to glean more information about him and his personal life, but he'd deflected every time. At first, I'd taken Oliver at face value. He was a fun-loving, good-hearted guy. But now, as we talked more, I realized he never shared anything about himself. Helping him with any sort of goal planning was going to be a lot harder than I thought it'd be.

"Look who it is," Bev said. "Our new regular."

Oliver's broad smile wavered slightly when he approached and took in my sullen expression, which made me stand up a little straighter.

"Or should I say our new *occasional* regular," Bev whispered to me, giving me a little nudge. "Funny how his visits line up exactly with your shifts every night."

"It's when he gets off work," I said, attempting not to blush at Bev's implication.

He sauntered over to the bar, shaking his navy jacket off and setting it on one of the hooks underneath the bar top. "Hey." Oliver scootched onto the barstool across from me and took off his beanie to set it on the table in front of him.

Bev passed a glance between the two of us. "Oliver. How's the snow out there?" she asked.

"Soft. Beautiful. Decadent." He flung a hand up theatrically and waved it around. "A perfect spring day."

Bev laughed. "You're always a ball of sunshine. I'll be sad to see you go when the season is over."

"I'll be sad to leave." Oliver pretended to pout.

My stomach sank a little in response. I had no reason to care that the season was winding down and Oliver would soon be on his way. Honestly, when I'd first met him, I figured I'd be the one leaving long before he did. Too bad reality had other plans in mind for me. I wasn't any closer to landing my next job than I'd been when I first got here. And now, the thought of Oliver leaving? The only positive thing in an otherwise bleak chapter in my life? Well, let's just say I didn't love the idea.

"Headed back to your house in Denver?" Bev asked.

"Nah. I've got renters in my house all year. I'll have to figure something else out."

My ears perked up at that. I knew Oliver had moved here from Denver, but a house?

"I'm sure you will." Bev gave a small nod and excused herself to check on the kitchen.

My eyebrows shot up before I could even attempt to contort my face into a neutral expression. "*You* own a house?" I asked, surprise leaking into my tone. Oliver had the whole, kid-at-heart routine down pat. Homeowner was not a phrase I had ever imagined would describe him.

He tilted his chin in my direction as if reading my mind. "Yes, I do, thank you very much. I don't appreciate how shocked you look right now. Is it so wild to think that I might be financially responsible?"

Yes.

"Of course not," I said, trying to save face. "You just never mentioned it so…I don't know. I guess you seemed more like the type that would live out of a van than a house."

He pretended to look thoughtful for a moment. "I'm going to take that as a compliment," he finally said. "But vanlife isn't for me. Not a lot of headspace for people over six foot three and I need to stretch out, ya know?" To demonstrate his point, he clasped his hands together and reached over his head, his chest puffing out in the process.

My cheeks reddened. "Sorry, right." I stuttered over my words, tearing my eyes away from his face. "Obviously you could own a house. I just never thought about it before, but it makes sense. I mean, you had to live somewhere before this, and why not a house? Honestly, I never even thought about it."

I was rambling uncontrollably, but my tangled tongue seemed to have a mind of its own. Normally, I wasn't nervous around guys, but Oliver was different. The confident—though admittedly distraught—version of myself I'd been when I first met him felt like a distant memory. It was hard to believe I'd ever had the audacity to just lean in and kiss him like I had. His self-assurance, combined with how different he was from me, was disarming. Even if I still had my successful career, I knew it wouldn't impress him in the slightest, and that thought made me uneasy. In fact, *nothing* about me could ever impress him. Now that I was aware of that, my heartrate spiked anytime I spent more than one interrupted second looking into his eyes.

"Frankie, relax." Oliver laughed softly and shook his head. "I wasn't offended. Trust me, if you ever meet my brother, you'll realize my skin is thick as shit."

"Okay," I squeaked out, cursing my voice for cracking. I knocked on the bar and nervously scanned the restaurant. "Um, so, what's for dinner tonight?" I asked him, not bothering to hand him a menu. Marie's was technically more of a lounge than a restaurant—whatever the hell that was supposed to mean—and we only served about ten items. They consisted of small plates and whole foods that had a farm-to-table feel, and most of it was vegetarian. Oliver had already tried everything at this point.

"Another kale and super grain bowl, I guess." Maybe it was my imagination, but it seemed like Oliver winced when he said it.

"I'll put it in," I said, but just then, Bev rushed behind me, holding plates and heading to the dining room.

"I got it, Frankie. I'm already running back and forth from the kitchen anyway."

"Thanks, Bev," Oliver called as she raced to a table to set down the plates of food.

His smile stayed plastered to his face. I'd grown to be slightly obsessed with the way it curled into his cheeks. Almost as if it were a smirk, but it was the most genuine thing I'd ever seen. I poured him his favorite beer and slid it across the bar.

He caught the beer and eyed my hand. "Glad to see your wrist has completely healed."

My cheeks flushed as I stopped leaning on my hands to rub the completely falsified injury. "Still a little tender."

Oliver's eyes twinkled at my obvious lie. "Is it?"

"So, about my next intro-to-fun course." I toweled off the bar, changing the subject.

"Is that what we're calling it now?" Oliver asked. "I've got it all planned out. The day after tomorrow. Bright and early."

"Can't wait," I said, not even having to feign my excitement.

"You're going to love it," he insisted.

"Am I?" I teased. I was excited at the thought of spending some more one-on-one time with Oliver. Time that didn't involve a medic room or feeling self-conscious and nervous on a ski hill.

"It's going to blow you away," he confirmed.

"Wow, confident. I like it." I winked at him, which caused his already-big smile to widen.

A new group came in and approached the bar. I held up a finger to Oliver before going over to take their order.

When I came back, Bev was already swinging by.

"Order up," Bev said, as she set a bowl in front of Oliver.

"I'll pick you up at six a.m.," he said, before picking up a fork and taking a less-than-enthusiastic bite of the kale salad.

"You have a car?" I blurted out.

He froze mid-bite before chewing slowly, squinting his eyes and giving me a strange look. He swallowed and shook his head. "Yes, Frankie. Jesus. You don't think I own a car either?"

"Sorry," I sputtered. "I just didn't picture you driving."

Now I felt like an idiot. Who didn't drive? Oliver almost felt like a character in a book to me. Like he was so far out of my typical reality, that he was almost fictional. It was hard to picture him doing normal things like driving, buying a home, going to work. But those were thoughts I really should have kept to myself.

"I drive," he promised, a small sound of disbelief escaping his throat. "I really have some ground to make up on this date to impress you, huh?"

"Date?" I choked out.

He waved a hand. "You know what I mean."

No. I absolutely *did not* know what that meant.

"I'm excited," I said, franticly needing to change the subject. "I could use the distraction."

"Job hunt not going so well?" he asked.

"You could say that." I sighed and dropped my gaze to the bar top in front of me. "I got my first rejection—well, interview rejection."

"Oh well. You'll get 'em next time."

Casual. Not a worry to be had. Exactly how I'd known he'd react.

"If there is a next time," I muttered.

Oliver sat up, reached across the bar, and ruffled my hair.

"Hey!" I jerked away.

"Don't be such a pessimist. There will absolutely be a next time, and until then, I will be dragging your ass out to have more fun because clearly, I underestimated how badly you need it."

"Fine," I breathed out, as if spending time with Oliver was a chore and not the most exciting aspect of my life as of late. "In the meantime, I'll start drafting up a ten-year plan for you to fill out. Don't think I haven't forgotten about our deal."

His smile dropped at that as he leaned away from me. "That's alright. I'm not much of a planner."

"Oh, but you will be. Trust me, a plan and goals can be so satisfying." I watched as Oliver squirmed in discomfort. "Perhaps a ten-year plan is too extreme. What about five?"

He ran a hand along his jaw. "Five months? Seems a little far out to make plans."

I let out a snort and followed it with a mock tsking sound. "Be ready, Oliver. You might have your plans for me on Monday, but I have plans for you too."

He almost looked worried, and I loved it. If he was going to push me, then I was going to push him too. Or try to, at least. Oliver was a tougher nut to crack than he seemed.

We continued making chitchat long after he finished his dinner. I'd occasionally leave him to serve drinks or see if a customer needed anything, but any free second I had, I always spent circling back to him. Oliver was nothing like the guys I'd hung out with back in Atlanta. When I used to find time to socialize, it was usually with people in similar careers as mine. They were always sizing me up, unsure if I was competition or someone suitable for companionship—never both. With Oliver, everything felt easy. Obviously, too easy. This wasn't anything that could actually go somewhere. But it was fun.

ELEVEN

Oliver

"You're killing it, man. You sure you've never boarded before?" I held out my hand for a high five, and my lesson of the day slapped it with his thick glove-covered hand.

Kevin was visiting Key Ridge from California and was easily the best person I'd taught in the few weeks since I'd been out here. He was maybe thirty-five, forty? I couldn't tell, and the fact that he was so in shape made it hard to gauge his age. His laid-back attitude gave him that youthful glow too.

"I've only ever skied, but I am pretty good at that," he admitted, pulling down his bandana.

"I know the lesson is technically over, but how about one more run?" I asked.

Kevin pulled out his phone and checked it briefly before sliding it back into his pocket. "Let's do it."

It was unusually cold today, with light snow flurries drifting down during the few afternoon runs we'd completed. Usually, days like these were reserved for late January or even February, but by March, I had come to expect blue skies and warmer temps. I'd always take fresh snow though. It extended the season and made the conditions better.

"I ski too. I've always preferred boarding though." I unstrapped my back foot and glided over to the ski lift. The mountain was crowded considering it was Sunday, but thankfully there was a second line reserved for lessons. Kevin and I moved to the front of the line, and I nodded my head in greeting to the younger guy working the lift before we were back on the chairlift and heading up the mountain.

I leaned back in the seat as the ground whizzed by below us. Everywhere I looked, skiers and boarders were catching turns or tumbling into the thick snow. I fucking loved it here. Honestly, it was kind of hard to believe I'd spent so many years in Denver when places like this were only hours away. Granted, many of them were expensive as hell, but Key Ridge had managed to maintain much of its quaintness despite the big resorts and developments coming up around it.

"Do you ski a lot out in Cali?" I asked Kevin while the lift slowly moved us up the hill.

"Not as much as I used to, but we always try to visit one new mountain every winter. The last two years, we've gone up to Canada."

I whistled. "I've been meaning to get up there."

Kevin swept his glove through the air, gesturing toward the endless expanse of snow-covered mountains stretching out before us, their peaks disappearing into the horizon. "Well, it's tough to leave when you've got all this at your back door."

"That's true," I said, breathing it all in.

Kevin was cool. Even though he was older than me, I saw a similarity in us. Hell, a new mountain every winter? Now *that* was the kind of plan I could get behind.

I had never been the kind of kid who knew what they wanted to be when they grew up. And now that I was partially grown, I still didn't have the faintest idea. Nathan was always the successful genius in the family, leaving me to be the adventurous one with the wanderlust spirit. Maybe I could drift from mountain town to mountain town. Frankie was all excited about helping me find a life plan, but maybe what was next for me was to be planless. Everyone acted like I was falling behind while they moved on with their lives, but I wasn't even thirty, for Christ's sake.

"So where are you off to next?" I asked Kevin as we neared the top of the hill.

"Who knows. We likely won't decide until next year."

"Love the spontaneity," I said.

I angled my body as we arrived at the top of the lift and leaned forward to easily exit and move out of the way of the rotating chairs. Kevin followed behind. Even though he said he'd only had one beginner lesson prior to today, I hardly believed the guy. He'd picked up everything right away and was already cruising down intermediate runs.

Although, come to think of it, that was how I had been when I first got started snowboarding. I hadn't grown up doing the activity, but I had gotten a skateboard for my tenth birthday after I'd begged my mom. I used to drag my best friend, Harrison, to the skate park two blocks away from my house. It had taken me awhile to pick it up, but I was naturally pretty good at learning a new skill. When I first came out to Colorado, I'd bought a secondhand snowboard and drove out to the mountains to give it a try. The next season, I was already trying my hand at a competition. Granted, I didn't win—not by a long shot—but I had a good time. It was actually that competition where I'd first met Giles.

"Alright, you sure you're good to go down this hill?" I asked Kevin. "If you stay to the left, it's groomed, but the right does have some moguls."

"You lead, and I'll see what I can manage," Kevin said.

I pulled down my goggles, grateful I had remembered to grab the ones for darker days. The sun was still nowhere in sight.

Cruising down the mountain, I kept my right foot forward to practice my switch riding. I did this a lot when teaching lessons—the beginner terrain wasn't very challenging for me, so it was good to practice the skill.

I kept right to hit the moguls, weaving in and out of them as I careened down the hill. There were a few spots of fresh snow that had just fallen and I let out a loud "Whoop!" as I cruised through some especially soft spots. Boarding all day every day like this was a dream—one which I absolutely did not want to wake up from.

It only took about five minutes for us to reach the bottom. I'd slowed a few times on the way down to check on Kevin, but he hadn't fallen once. He honestly barely even looked shaken anymore. Damn. He was goals. He was who I wanted to be in ten years—bumming around different mountains, learning new skills, being an all-around badass. It was comforting to see someone not conforming to the typical wife-and-kids route. Gave me hope that my current lifestyle didn't really need adjusting after all.

"You killed that." I held up a hand for another high five, and Kevin met it. We both slipped off our helmets, and I tucked mine underneath my left arm, shaking out my hair in the process.

"Thanks. Today has been epic. I'm stoked I finally feel confident on one of these things." He unstrapped his board, and I followed suit.

"You're a natural. Hey, I'm about to grab dinner in town. Would you want to—"

Before I could ask him to join me, a little girl that only

came up to my waist in a bright-pink ski jacket flung herself at Kevin. "Daddy!" she yelled excitedly.

Kevin laughed and leaned down to kiss her forehead. "Sweetie. How did you do in your lesson?"

"She did amazing. As if there was ever any doubt." A tall woman with black hair peeking out of a white knit beanie walked up to Kevin and gave him a kiss on the lips. "And how was your lesson?"

"Ollie here is the best," Kevin said. "He had me in way better shape than I ever thought I could be. We'll have to get you out there next."

"I don't think so," the woman—who I gathered must be Kevin's wife—said. She turned to me, shaking her head. "I used to love skiing, but I broke my leg a few years back. Now I'm officially retired."

"She always did like cocktails in a warm lodge more than being on the slopes anyway." Kevin looked at her with fond familiarity.

"Hey." She swatted his chest. "I was good, thank you very much."

"This is my wife, Stephanie, and daughter, Sam, by the way. This is my instructor, Ollie."

"Nice to meet you," I said, trying to hide my surprise that Kevin had this whole family. Even though I'd only met him today, this didn't fit into the vision I'd crafted of him—the vision I had already started modeling my own life after. In reality, Kevin was apparently a family man. Not at all what I saw for my future.

"Can you teach me to snowboard?" Sam asked.

I chuckled and bent down so that I was closer to her level. "I most definitely could. I bet you're a natural, just like your dad."

"Let's master skiing first," Stephanie said, smiling.

I looked down at Sam. "Maybe next year."

Her smile widened, revealing two missing top teeth.

While I hadn't spent too much time around kids, I had given my fair share of lessons to them throughout the years. While I preferred the more advanced lessons, kids always impressed me with their resiliency and lack of fear. They would truly just go shooting down the mountain without a care or a single thought toward their well-being. Meanwhile, most beginner adults completely got stuck in their own heads. Frankie's lesson came to mind…

"Thanks again. We've got to go catch our dinner reservation, but I really appreciate today."

I shook Kevin's hand and said my goodbyes, watching as he walked away with his little family.

They were cute, but I felt zero pang of longing for that dynamic. My childhood had proven to me that just because you can call it a family in name didn't mean it acted like one.

I slung my board underneath my arm and headed in the direction of my studio apartment. A hot shower to shake the internal chill that had gripped onto my bones sounded more than enticing.

"Ollie!" My name echoed along the bottom of the mountain. I whipped around to see Giles walking toward me, his own snowboard still in hand.

"Hey," I greeted him. "You trying to grab a drink?"

Did I sound too hopeful? Too desperate?

"Nah," Giles said. "I was just getting a few runs in, waiting for Mattie to finish up at the lodge. We're making dinner together since Frankie is working again."

"Sister-in-law cramping your style?" I joked.

Giles shrugged. "I think anyone in my space for an extended period of time would eat at me a little. But Frankie is trying really hard to get a job so I'm trying not to stress her out more. Plus, she works at Marie's most nights lately."

"Right, I've seen her in there." A huge understatement. I'd learned her schedule and had eaten dinner there every night she worked this week. While the food was fine—good, even—I was beyond sick of the roasted vegetables and healthy crap that was exclusively on the menu. I'd kill for a burger and fries. But any time I thought about going somewhere else—sitting alone at a table for one—I found myself wandering into Marie's yet again to sit on a barstool in front of Frankie. I'd suffer through another plate of rabbit food if it meant getting whatever free time she had in between pouring drinks.

"If you're trying to get a drink somewhere, I think some of the seasonal workers were headed to The Ridge."

I winced at the thought. I'd tried hanging out with some of those guys when I'd first gotten here, but they all made me feel ancient. Last weekend, they'd gone out for one of the guy's twenty-first birthday, and at least two people in the group had asked me to look at their fake IDs to see if they looked legit.

"I'm good," I said.

Giles chuckled. "Too young for you?" he asked knowingly.

"Is that what I seemed like to you when we met?" Giles was a little older than me, and I don't even think I was twenty when we first met.

"If anything, you seemed even more exuberant, if that's possible," he joked. "But I liked you. You weren't afraid to try anything. Plus, you had a good head on your shoulders. Responsible."

"You're probably the only person to describe me like that. Can you put in a good word with Frankie?" I wanted to take the words away the second they came out.

Giles lifted his eyebrows, but didn't necessarily look

surprised that I'd brought her up. "You're hanging out with her tomorrow, right?"

"Not like that," I said, even though he hadn't actually suggested anything. And I wasn't sure how to describe what Frankie and I were doing tomorrow. The word "date" didn't quite fit, but what other term could describe two people who had kissed, still felt a spark of attraction, and were now spending time alone together?

Giles held up his hands. "I didn't say anything."

I still felt the need to explain myself, like word vomit. "We're both new in town, we don't know many people. I just wanted to hang out and make it up to her after the snowboarding nightmare."

"I think she's half expecting that to be the surprise," Giles said. "She told Mattie yesterday that if you parked at the base of the mountain and brought out another snowboard, she was walking home."

That made me grin. "I should do that to mess with her."

"She'll like what you have planned. I'm glad you're taking her out. She needs to loosen up a little. She's constantly on her computer, obsessing over an interview or a rejection letter. It can't be healthy."

Giles had actually given me the idea of where to take Frankie.

"I'm happy to provide a distraction. It's my specialty," I said, not even kidding. That's what I'd become known for—lightening the mood with a joke when things got too serious or planning a pointless day trip to distract someone from something heavy. It was the role I'd played my entire life.

"I should go," I said, even though my only plans were to sit around alone in my apartment. "I'll let you get to your night."

We said our goodbyes, and Giles walked in the direction of his house while I turned toward my apartment.

When I strolled up the driveway to the stairs that led to my front door, Bev's garage opened. I scooted out of the way as she backed her car up.

"Want me to pick you up anything from the store?" she called.

"Nah, I'm good, thanks." I stopped at her window and leaned against my snowboard.

Bev shook her head in disapproval. "I don't know how you exercise all day and hardly eat."

I chuckled. "I eat. I just don't cook."

She brushed off my flippant response. "Fine. Whatever."

"Have a good night, Bev." I waved as she pulled out onto the street and drove away.

I took the stairs to my apartment two at a time and pushed open the door. The studio was a small square of a room, with a kitchen on one wall, a bed in the back corner, and a small living room setup taking up the rest of the space. It was cozy, though. Apparently, Mattie had lived here for a while when she'd first moved to Key Ridge. She'd joked with me that it was a rite of passage to falling in love with the town. I told her I had no intention of staying past the winter, but she'd just said, "We'll see."

I stripped off my clothes and hopped into the hot shower, cranking it up a few degrees hotter than I would normally deem tolerable. Once I'd properly seared myself, I pulled on some gray sweatpants and a worn navy-blue hoodie that said *Outdoor Adventures* on it from the wilderness store I used to work at.

The small kitchen had barely been touched since I'd moved in, but I still pulled open the fridge door as if expecting food to magically appear. It was empty, except for the random condiments in the door and the one carton of eggs I'd purchased. The thought of scrambled eggs for dinner made me gag on the patheticness more than the taste. I slammed the fridge door shut and pulled out my phone to scroll for dinner ideas.

There was a sandwich shop at the edge of town that I'd yet to try. I'd do that.

But as soon as I put on my coat and my boots, I'd already changed my mind. Because a sandwich alone was equally as sad as staying in this apartment by myself.

There was only one place I could go to feel slightly less alone right now. I hustled down the stairs, and toward the entrance to Marie's.

I was more than prepared to scarf down yet another salad just to see her.

TWELVE

Frankie

"ARE YOU FINALLY GOING TO TELL ME WHAT WE'RE DOING?" I asked, as Oliver stepped out of his SUV and slammed the door shut behind him.

"What are you doing out here?" He looked perplexed as he approached, offering a hand to help me up from the front step—the same one I'd been perched on for the past fifteen minutes. Nerves had kept me up all night and left me barely eating the day before. Spending time alone with a guy like Oliver? Definitely not something I did often. I'd felt the same jittery tension before our snowboarding lesson, and the fact that I hadn't exactly impressed him that day did little to ease my discomfort.

"Waiting for you?" It came out like a question.

He tilted his head. "I would have come and knocked on the door. I'm not a complete degenerate."

I hoped he didn't notice the slight shake of my hands as I held up my coffee mug. "I figured this way, you wouldn't have to wake Giles and Mattie. They're sleeping in today."

The three of us had gotten a little too wine drunk

yesterday—well, mostly them. Like I said, bundle of nerves over here. Mattie had noticed that so she'd broken out our favorite childhood board game and we'd all gotten way too into playing it. They had continued to play for hours after I'd gone to bed. I could hear them as I tossed and turned and stared at the ceiling.

Oliver still looked a little displeased at the fact that I was waiting outside for him, but he shook it off and placed his hand on the small of my back, leading me to his car.

"This yours?" I asked as he opened the door and I climbed into the passenger seat.

"Whose else would it be?" he asked, walking around to his side and sliding in.

The cleanliness of his car struck me immediately. I turned in my seat to look at the back, but there was no crumpled-up clothes or trash in site. It even smelled good in here. Like pine trees or something.

"Clean," I said, not even trying to hide how impressed I was.

"I like to keep things tidy," he said, buckling his seat belt. "I used to live with my best friend, Harrison, who is a total neat freak. Broke any of my messy habits right out of me."

"That's good," I said, because I couldn't think of anything more clever.

Oliver reached between us for the gear shift, and I stared his hand as he put it in drive. Was it weird that I found his hands attractive? As he put them both on the bottom of the steering wheel and I watched as they engulfed it, I realized that weird or not, I definitely found them attractive.

I tore my gaze away and stared out the window at the dark street. Why Oliver had chosen an activity that started before sunrise was beyond me, but I couldn't deny that there was something a little thrilling about being out here with him before the town stirred.

"So, this is the car," Oliver said, tapping the steering wheel. "I know you thought I was making it up, but here she is in all her glory."

"Exactly the type of car I pictured you in." It was one of those off-road SUVs that, while in great shape, was clearly at least a decade old.

Oliver laughed and snapped his gaze to mine before returning it to the road. "Hey, now. In your own words, you pictured me both houseless and unable to acquire a car."

My cheeks burned at the reminder. "Sorry about that," I mumbled.

Oliver seemed to sense my discomfort because he hit the power button on the center console. "You can control the music," he said, turning his head both directions at the stop sign before making a left turn and exiting Main Street.

Instead of looking for an aux cord or a Bluetooth connection, I went for the FM button and hit search until I found the least fuzzy station.

"A radio girl?" Oliver asked, eyebrows raised. "I'm surprised. I would have thought you'd have some carefully curated playlist to go along with every occasion."

Normally he'd be correct. But I was far too self-conscious to share any music with Oliver right now. The radio was safe. Neither of us picked it. I didn't spend hours thinking of the perfect song only to risk Oliver not liking it or pressing "skip" without a second thought. No. That was far too risky.

"I like the radio," I said, as the next song began—an old, cheesy country ballad I never would've chosen if given the option.

Oliver merged onto the highway and shifted lanes. There was almost no one else on the road.

"How far is this mystery place?" I asked, turning the heaters so that they weren't blasting directly on me. My outfit was causing me to overheat slightly. When I'd asked Oliver what I should wear, his only response was, "Something that's comfortable, warm, and that you can move in." I wasn't quite sure what to make of that, and it had me a little nervous for whatever awaited us.

"It's not far," Oliver said with a wink. He was clearly loving this air of mystery that shrouded the morning. "Any way I could convince you to give me a sip of that?" he asked, nodding toward my to-go coffee mug.

"Oh, sure." I nearly flung the mug at him, but thankfully I caught myself and handed it to him with some semblance of grace.

He smiled, unfazed as usual, and took a long sip. "Ahh." He smacked his lips and handed it back to me. "Needed that. I couldn't sleep last night."

"Same," I said. My eyes widened at the admittance. We both looked at each other, but he tore his gaze away first.

His words lingered in the air as a small explosion of fireworks went off in my gut. Had he struggled to sleep for the same reason I had? Was he nervous about today too? The thought made me want to slap myself for being so foolish—of course, Oliver wasn't nervous. Just look at him. The guy hadn't been nervous a day in his life. I was teetering on the edge of complete delusion, and I needed to snap out of it.

I couldn't sit in the silence any longer. It wasn't that it was uncomfortable—the opposite actually. It was almost *too* comfortable.

"How long have you had this car?" I asked, cringing at the lame question. He was going to think I had absolutely zero social skills.

Oliver let out a low chuckle. "You're really interested in my car, aren't you?"

"And your house," I added.

"Are you sizing up my assets? Trying to determine if I could be a good provider?"

The fireworks were now full-on blasting. It was a whole display.

"Of course not," I said hurriedly.

Had I been doing that? When I'd first met Oliver, I had been attracted to him, but I had written him off as an irresponsible man-child. One who probably didn't work hard or have any sense of obligation. And while he certainly put on a solid show of not caring, it was clear there was a lot more to him than I initially thought. In fact, he was beginning to feel like a potentially viable option.

I shook the thought from my mind. Because Oliver was definitely *not* a viable option. Even if he was the absolute perfect guy—like I had crafted him in a lab, perfect—I wasn't staying in Key Ridge, and he probably wasn't either. Ski season would be over soon, and then he'd be moving on to some other adventure. On top of that, even if our differences didn't feel *that* significant right now, they were still glaringly present. The whole "opposites attract" thing only worked in movies.

"What kind of question could I ask you right now that would make you less nervous?" he asked.

My eyes jerked to his face. He kept stealing glances at me before gluing his eyes back to the road. I thought about lying and telling him I wasn't nervous, but it felt pointless. Even though we should be nothing more than acquaintances, Oliver already seemed to know me a lot better than anyone else I'd met in recent history.

"Ask me my favorite movie," I said.

Fifteen minutes later, and one long argument about which genre was better, action or romance, Oliver pulled off the highway and into a half-full parking lot at the base of the mountain.

"What the hell is this?" I demanded. "You are not taking me snowboarding again."

Oliver tipped back his head, laughing. "Wow, you don't trust me at all."

"You said it yourself—you don't give up when it comes to dragging people on risky adventures."

He got out of the car and then rounded to my side, opening my door and holding out his hand to help me down from the SUV.

My "thank you" got caught in my throat as soon as my hand touched his. Sparks. Everywhere.

I snatched it away and dug into my coat pockets for the gloves Mattie said were there. I slipped them on, but I could still feel the ghost of Oliver's touch. His eyes glimmered as if he'd felt something, too, but he closed the door and clapped his hands together.

"Alright, let's do this," he said, moving around to the back of his car and opening the trunk. He rummaged around for a moment before producing…something. They were flat with a blue rim all the way around their long, narrow shape.

"What's that?" I asked.

Oliver's smile fell. "You've never seen a snowshoe before?"

"Wasn't a big activity growing up in Florida," I deadpanned.

He thrust the strange-looking device at me, and I took it.

"We're going on a sunrise hike to breakfast." His voice was filled with pride.

The snowshoes dangled in my hands as I assessed how

they were supposed to attach to my feet. "I like the second part of that statement," I said.

Oliver chuckled and tugged at my beanie. "The first part will be fun too. And very flat."

I turned to look at the trail entrance. It was wide, and even had a thin layer of fresh snow on it. "I do appreciate flatness."

***

Flatness my ass.

We'd been at this for thirty minutes now with no end in sight. This so-called "easy trail" was ever-so-slightly uphill. That, mixed with my out-of-shapeness and the thin mountain air, meant I was moving at a snail's pace, huffing and puffing the entire time.

Even though Oliver and I were the first car in the small parking lot when we'd arrived, three groups had passed us due to my glacial pace.

To Oliver's credit, even though he wasn't the least bit out of breath, he hung back with me without complaint. He'd only made one snide remark ten minutes ago about hoping the breakfast would still be hot when we arrived. He'd made the comment while we were walking up a small slope, and I didn't have the lung capacity to berate him for it.

"I thought these were supposed to make walking in the snow easier," I said, sucking in a breath of the cold air. It was only thirty degrees outside, but I was already roasting. As soon as the sun crested over the mountains and I started feeling the full strain of the hike, I had to shed my thick down coat and tie it around my waist.

"They do," Oliver insisted, taking a few quick steps beyond me as if to prove his point. "See? I'm practically floating."

"Oh, yeah," I wheezed. "This is a breeze."

Oliver tossed back his head and chuckled. "Not much for exercise, huh?"

"I do Pilates," I said defensively. Every Tuesday and Thursday. Which actually reminded me, I really needed to cancel that membership. It wasn't like I'd be using it any time soon, and I couldn't exactly afford to be squandering away one hundred dollars a month on a gym membership while there was still no end in sight to my unemployment.

Oliver let me walk in front of him before letting out a low whistle. "I can tell."

My eyebrows shot up as I turned around to find him smiling at me. "Like you can tell what my body looks like through all these layers."

"Maybe I've noticed before," he said, a sly grin creeping onto his face.

Heat rushed into my cheeks that had little to do with the exertion of the hike.

Oliver, seemingly oblivious to the effect he had on me, fell into step next to me. "So, no sports then?" he asked.

"What like adult intramural volleyball?" I snorted. "Hard pass."

When I glanced up at Oliver, he looked deeply offended by that. "Adult leagues are a great place to meet people, Frankie."

He had me there. Maybe I shouldn't be poking fun at any extracurricular activities when my life currently held none.

"Maybe I'll give it a try one day."

"Yeah, right," he said with a laugh. "What about high school? Did you at least play sports then?"

"Aside from my failed attempt at track and field, not really." My snowshoe hit a hidden branch, and I stumbled a little. Oliver's hands were around my waist in an instant, steadying me. "I was more into academics," I continued, stepping away from his touch. "You know, debate team, student council, those types of things."

He chuckled and shook his head. "Our paths would *not* have crossed in high school."

Oliver in high school. Without even having to ask, I was sure he was the popular, jock type. I had been popular in my own way. I hadn't had too bad of an awkward phase, and I did have friends. But all my overachieving left little time for a social life.

"Oh yeah? Not big into studies," I teased.

"Not even a little. I made sure I passed because I wanted to get the hell out of there and never think about school again, but I wouldn't say I thrived. Plus, a passing grade was necessary for sports."

"Which I take it you did in abundance."

"Yep." I could hear the smile in his voice even though my gaze was fixed on my steps. "Soccer, basketball, baseball. My dad was always irritated I couldn't commit to only one. He told me I might actually amount to being more than average if I did that. I think that just made me want to spread myself even thinner."

I winced. He'd hardly shared anything about himself, his past, or his family. Even though I wanted to know more, Oliver gave off a "ask me personal questions, and I might bolt" vibe.

"He sounds like a dick," I said.

Oliver snorted. "You have no idea. I couldn't wait to get out of that house. Moved to Colorado as soon as I graduated and never looked back."

That caught my attention. "You went to school out here?"

"Nope. Moved out here with my friend Harrison. We shared a shitty apartment and both got minimum wage jobs."

My mouth went slack at the admittance as I forced myself to take steadying breaths. Talking while trudging through the snow was proving a good distraction, but I was still basically panting. "You didn't go to college?" I asked.

Oliver turned to see my shocked expression. Instead of being offended, a laugh escaped him as he rolled his eyes. "What? You're seriously surprised that I didn't go to college? Do I seem like the type?"

"I don't know," I said, scrambling to keep up with him. It was like these snowshoes were a second skin for him.

"You thought, I—who's never had a stable job in my life, who comes out to teach snowboarding lessons on a whim, who hated school and has called your corporate career soul sucking —*went to college*?" He raised his eyebrows.

"There are lots of reasons to go to college." My tone had taken on a defensive edge.

"Yeah. To get into debt and get scammed out of a whole lot of money."

"Or to meet lifelong friends, get an education, study abroad, kickstart your career."

Oliver chuckled in a condescending way that instantly made my skin flare. "How many lifelong friends did you make in college?" he asked.

My mouth snapped shut as if he'd hurled an accusation at me. "I keep in touch with a few people."

He turned around and snapped his fingers. "Oh, and tell me about your study abroad. I'd love to hear about it."

The frustration I felt was intense—Oliver barely knew me, yet he had me so perfectly figured out that he knew I hadn't studied abroad.

"Well," I continued, ignoring the comment, "even you can't deny that it's a good place to get an education."

"There are other ways to get an education, Frankie," he

said in a low voice, dipping his chin to meet my gaze. Everything inside me went liquid. "What I'm hearing," Oliver carried on, "is that your complex with what society thinks of as success is deep rooted."

He had me there, but I still felt the need to argue. "Having goals does not mean I have a complex," I said.

"I beg to differ. Why are you so obsessed with finding a job?" he countered.

"I am not obsessed," I spat out.

"Fine. Fixated, then."

The snow crunched beneath my feet as I did my best not to fall too far behind and maintain my composure. "It's hard. There aren't a lot of options out there right now—"

"No, but *why*?" Oliver pressed. "Why do you have this deeply ingrained drive to find the next thing? The thing that will help you reach some fictitious goal that doesn't mean anything. You practically broke down when I first met you, calling yourself a failure. *Why*?"

Glaring up at him, I did my best to make myself look bigger than I felt. "I'm supposed to help *you* with *your* goals, not be challenged for mine."

"Frankie," Oliver said gently. "I was never going to let you give me goals. Especially when you can't produce one good reason for having them yourself. In fact," he gestured to me, "it seems to me like all your goals have brought you is disappointment and misery."

That stopped me right in my tracks. The words were beyond harsh but they held a grain of truth. In fact, in the small moments where I'd let my mind wander these past few weeks, I had been briefly met with the same realizations. I'd worked so hard for that company, and for what? For them to drop me like I was nothing?

"Hey."

I didn't look up but Oliver now hovered in front of me. Heat brewed beneath my eyes, and I refused to let a tear spill right now.

"Hey," he said again, even softer. "I'm sorry." He captured my chin in his thumb and forefinger, and I let him tilt my head up to meet his gaze. "That was too harsh. Fuck." He shook his head. "I don't know why I said that."

"Because it's true," I whispered. "I am miserable."

"No, you're not."

"But I am," I huffed out. "I spent years climbing and trying and only focusing on one thing. Even when they asked too much of me and I knew it, I did it without question. I figured if I worked hard enough that I'd be rewarded."

"And then they screwed you over," he said gently.

"Exactly."

Oliver sighed. "They're bastards. Greedy bastards. They don't see anyone as human beings, they only care about their bottom line and that's despicable," he said matter-of-factly. "You can't think of yourself as a failure because of this. It says nothing about who you are."

"I made that my entire personality. I let it define me. And now it's gone, and I'm worthless." I hung my head in defeat.

"No," Oliver said, more forceful than I'd ever heard him. My lip quivered at his proximity. "You. Are. Not. Worthless." He enunciated each word, his eyes darkening.

Something heavy bobbed in my throat, and I swallowed it down. While I still didn't believe him wholeheartedly, his determination had my head spinning.

When I opened my mouth to respond, Oliver stuck a finger in my face. "Don't you dare try to argue with me." The tendon in his neck pulsed ever so slightly. Intense Oliver was slightly intimidating.

I kind of liked it.

THIRTEEN

Oliver

"Now this is more like it." Frankie sipped on her coffee and did a little shimmy in her chair, a fuzzy blanket wrapped around her like a shawl.

I chuckled. "See? I told you you'd like this."

"Only this part," she corrected. "I could have done without the first portion of the morning."

It had taken us nearly two hours to get from the car to a giant yurt settled on private ranch land. Giles had mentioned that this was a popular spot for guests of the lodge, and I thought it would be the perfect excursion to take Frankie on. I hadn't quite anticipated how much she would dislike snow-shoeing, but overall, I'd say it was a win. She even stopped us at one point on the walk up here to snap a picture of the view. Maybe she wasn't hiking's biggest fan, but at least she'd stopped to appreciate it for a second.

The yurt was covered in thick rugs and had a wood-burning fireplace that heated the whole place. Less than ten tables were scattered around. There were a few other groups of two and one family in the back corner. All had passed us on the trek over here. We were the last to arrive, but thankfully, the breakfast hadn't run out. The pancakes, bacon, eggs, and coffee were still piping hot when they set plates in front of us upon our arrival. With each bite and sip of coffee, I could see the life returning to Frankie's eyes.

"At least you'll be more energized for the walk back," I said when she'd taken a particularly big bite of toast.

Her face crumpled. "Why would you bring that up right as I started relaxing?"

I burst out laughing. "Or—if you're really against the walk back—there's a shuttle that'll take us back to the parking lot."

She gasped dramatically and held her hands together in a pleading gesture. "I'm really, really, really opposed to the walk back. Please, Oliver. You can't get me all content and full in here and then force me back on that trail. That's what people call cruel and unusual punishment."

"I think they actually call it fresh air and exercise."

"Spoken like a true masochist."

"You're ridiculous," I sputtered.

"For wanting to be comfortable? Call me ridiculous all day long, because I'm not apologizing for that."

"Whatever," I said, smirking as we continued to eat.

Before getting to know Frankie, I would have considered a dislike for the outdoors a major deal-breaker in a woman. But now, I couldn't get enough of her. Challenging her beliefs and getting her to try new things was fun as hell.

"I'm having a good time," she finally admitted. "Snow-shoeing wasn't *that* bad."

I pretended to fall out of my chair in surprise.

"Hey!" she giggled, throwing her napkin at me as I righted myself. "I mean it. Thank you for dragging me on this."

"Happy to be of service."

"I can't even remember the last time I hung out with a guy

like this." Her eyes widened as if she realized how that sounded. "I just mean—"

"Haven't gone on a date in a while?" I chuckled.

"I date, okay?" Her tone did little to convince me. My face must have given away my disbelief because she folded her arms across her chest. "I do," she insisted.

I shouldn't press the subject further. I should drop it. Frankie's dating history wasn't any of my business. In fact, I couldn't care less. And yet… When was the last guy she had kissed before me? Had she kissed anyone since? My gut said that wasn't likely. I was way more social than she was and I sure hadn't. Honestly, I had no interest in seeking out other women. I'd been far too busy thinking about the girl I'd met the first night I got here…

"When was the last real date you went on?" The question toppled out of my mouth before I could snatch it back.

Her eyebrows shot up. "We're talking romantic history now?"

I tried to play it cool. "Dating falls into the category of having fun. And since I'm helping you do that right now…"

She gave a sharp laugh. "Dating? Fun? That's a good one."

"You don't think dating is fun?"

"Not the ones I've been on," she muttered, sighing. "The last guy I dated was nice enough, but our schedules never lined up. Before that, I dated some douche at work. He was cute and hard to get. I think the challenge tricked me into thinking I liked him or something. Anyway, those were both forever ago, and I've barely had so much as a second date since then."

A dating dry spell. *Interesting.*

"What about you?"

The natural progression of the conversation caught me off

guard. I liked finding out more about her. I *hated* talking about myself.

"Not much to tell. Women are great, but relationships have never been for me."

"Why's that?" she pressed.

Because I've seen firsthand what being trapped with someone you hate in a loveless marriage looks like.

"Just no interest in it," I said.

"That's not a real answer."

"Moving on." I clapped my hands together and rubbed them. "Next question."

She narrowed her eyes.

"Favorite childhood memory?" I asked.

Instead of fighting me on it, she paused to think it over. After a minute, she had a dreamy look about her. "It's not so much one memory, but a bunch of them. My mom didn't work for a few years to spend more time with me and Mattie. One summer, when I was like five and Mattie was seven, she'd decided the three of us would drive all around to check out any playgrounds we could find. She told us we were doing a survey to find the best one." She smiled, reminiscing on it. "It felt like the world was so big when we'd show up at a new one after driving for what felt like forever. When I was older, I realized the furthest we ever went was like an hour. I don't know, that was just such a fun time. Spending all summer with my sister and mom. It only got harder after that, you know? Mattie and I made different friends. My mom went back to work eventually. But that summer felt magical." She sighed. "I still love a good playground. There's one across the street from my condo, and I always think about walking over to use the swing set or something."

"Why don't you?" I asked.

She scrunched her nose. "Because I'm twenty-eight, and that would be silly."

"The only thing silly about that is denying yourself something so simple that could bring you even a flicker of joy."

She looked down at her steaming coffee. "I guess I hadn't thought about it like that," she whispered.

Damn, she was beautiful. Hair a mess from the hike. Cheeks still stained red.

"What's your favorite memory?" she asked.

Shit. Me again.

"Probably days after school spent at the skate park with Harrison," I told her. Skateboarding had been the first thing to make me feel alive, and getting out of my weird, tension-filled house was always a relief.

"You've mentioned Harrison a few times. Are you close?" she asked.

"He's like a brother to me," I said, feeling a small spasm in my chest.

Her brows drew together. "More like a brother than your actual brother?"

I ran a hand down my face. "Um, well, yeah. Nathan and I weren't the closest growing up. We're better now—a lot better, actually. But growing up, it was strained."

"Competitive?" she asked.

If the competition involved separating a family down the middle. "Um, you could say that," I said.

She carefully chewed a piece of bacon.

Despite my attempts to relax, I realized my body was taut. I forced my shoulders away from my ears, not wanting Frankie to see how uncomfortable I was discussing my family.

"Well, what's your favorite memory with your family then?" she asked slowly, as if I might spring from the table.

The simple question sank right into my gut like a lead anchor.

The thing was, a lot of memories came to mind. The diner my mom would take us to every Sunday for lunch. Watching every new season of *Survivor* and picking our favorite to win it all. When she'd sneak us away to go to a thrift store any time my dad was home and in a shitty mood—which was often.

But now those memories were tainted. Because instead of seeing any good times, all I could think about was Nathan. How left out he must have felt. I'd never realized it at the time. He'd always come across as so cold to me. But now it was so obvious in my memories how alone and alienated he must have felt. It was like getting punched in the face with it. How he'd become more quiet and withdrawn as he got older. And it was my fucking fault for not trying harder.

If there was one person I blamed more than myself, it was her. He was her son, for Christ's sake. She should have known better.

I forced out a long breath. "Next question," I said.

She opened her mouth to protest, but I kept going.

"What's your greatest ambition?" I meant it as a joke, but my tone came out a little sneering, likely because of all the thoughts coursing through my mind.

Seeing the way Frankie's face immediately fell made me feel like a fucking idiot. Greatest ambition? What the hell was I thinking? She'd just lost her job. One which was clearly very important to her. Of course, an insensitive question like that was going to hit her right in the chest.

When she didn't answer, I tried to tilt my head to force her to meet my gaze.

"Hey, I'm sorry about our conversation on the hike up. I shouldn't have pushed you like that."

"It's fine," she said in a voice that assured me it was anything except fine.

"You can help me think of some goals if you want." I kept my voice light, hoping to tempt her.

"No, it's stupid."

As ridiculous as I'd always thought all that goal-talk was, hearing her say those words nearly broke me.

"No, really. I want to hear your thoughts."

She picked at her cuticles, and just when I thought I'd have to resort to straight-up begging to get her to talk to me again, she relented. "You asked me earlier why I'm so obsessed. It feels pathetic to admit, but I honestly don't know. It's always been engrained in me that that's the way life goes. You work hard, get an education, get a good job, and life falls into place. I never even stopped to question it before."

My heart cracked.

"All I've done is question the conventional path. It's not like my life is amazing either," I said, trying to commiserate with her.

"What are you talking about? You're, like, the happiest person I've ever met."

Was I? I knew that's what was expected of me. I knew that's how I came across. But was I truly happy?

I thought I was. But then, seeing my brother get married, my best friend move in with his girlfriend, and watching my relationship with my mother become more strained—what did I really have at the end of the day? Myself. The outdoors. Sure, it was invigorating. I loved the constant adventure.

But *happy*…

What a strange word when you thought too much about it —something I rarely did. But lately, searching in Frankie's eyes had me questioning more about myself than I ever had before.

The clink of her coffee mug against the table had me refocusing on her.

"You *are* happy right?" she asked.

"Next question," I muttered.

She looked up at the ceiling in exasperation. "You can't always do that, you know? Change the subject any time I try to ask you a personal question."

"Do I?" I smiled and tilted my head, pretending I didn't know exactly what she meant. It was a side of me few people noticed, mainly because I didn't let many get close enough to see it.

"You know you do." She waved a finger at me. "Careful or I'll stop asking them altogether."

My pulse quickened. The idea should bring me comfort, but it didn't. I didn't know what I wanted, but Frankie giving up on me in even the smallest capacity wasn't it.

I laced my fingers behind my head and leaned back in my chair, attempting to gather myself. "So, about my goals."

"Forget it," she said.

I pouted. "But I was really looking forward to my fifty-year plan."

That finally got her lips to turn up. "Wow, I know you're desperate to change the subject if I've got you begging to talk about plans."

"Please. Give me direction."

She laughed at that. "You know, you might think you're above goals, but you have them too. Like getting through high school to move out here. That was a goal."

"I guess."

"And snowboarding, mountain biking, whatever the hell else you do. You intentionally learned those skills. You set a goal and you met it. Those are goals, believe it or not, Oliver."

I frowned. "I'd hardly equate picking up a snowboard to a retirement plan."

"You bought a house." She tapped her nose as if she got me. "You might want people to think you're some carefree nomad, but you're responsible. You can follow through on things."

I sighed, letting her think she had me figured out. The truth was, even though I hadn't put much thought into the things she mentioned, I had made them happen. I wasn't so much financially responsible as I was cheap. I'd always lived well below my means. Buying a house? It made sense to me. I never intended to settle there; I just figured it'd be cheaper in the short term, and I could rent it out whenever I moved on. Which, of course, I was doing now. I guess now that I thought about it, I *was* following through on a plan.

"Now what's next?" she asked.

"Next?" I repeated.

"Ski season is ending soon, meaning lessons will be over. You already told Bev you weren't going back to Denver, so what's next? Are you—are you planning to stay in Key Ridge?"

Did I detect a hint of hopefulness under Frankie's nonchalant tone? The thought of her hoping I'd stay had my ego practically bursting at the seams.

"I haven't thought about it," I admitted truthfully.

"Seriously?" She blinked a few times, as if not planning the future was a foreign concept to her. "It's only a few weeks away."

I shrugged. "Right. I have plenty of time to figure it out."

"What do you want to do?" she pressed.

I chewed on the inside of my cheek, mulling it over. "Maybe hit up a different mountain town. Maybe travel. I'm not sure. Something will work out. It always does."

She sat back in her chair. "What must it be like to have that kind of blind confidence that things will always go your way?"

"It's not blind confidence if it's always worked that way in the past."

"Let me get this straight—your only plans are to maybe drift around the state of Colorado—"

"Or another state. I heard Montana is cool."

She sighed. "What is it like in that head of yours?"

"Exhilarating?" I offered.

She picked up the maple syrup and drizzled it onto her pancakes before taking a fork and knife to them. I took a few pieces of bacon off my own plate and shoved them into my mouth.

The rest of the breakfast went by without any additional hard-hitting questions.

I made one last futile attempt to get Frankie to snowshoe back to the car, but she told me to give her the keys and she'd meet me there. The shuttle drove us the whole way. I stretched out my tired limbs next to her. Our knees bumped with each rattle of the tires against the rocky, icy service road. She kept sneaking glances at me. I met them every time, but she tore her gaze away immediately.

The drive back to her place was uneventful too. It mostly consisted of us arguing over which radio station was better. I claimed the country station was actually quite catchy, but she kept switching it back to some oldies one. Frankly, neither was great, but the argument had us both laughing.

When I finally pulled into Giles and Mattie's driveway, I didn't want the morning to be over. I figured I'd go snowboarding after I dropped her off. Since I didn't have any lessons, it was a good time to get out and do the terrain park or some of the more advanced runs. Some of the lifties had even asked if I wanted to meet up. But when I glanced over at Frankie, I realized if she asked me to do anything—watch some silly rom-com, or walk Main Street, stop by the lodge even—I'd do it. Even if that meant being under the light of her probing questions. I wasn't ready for my time with her to end. But I had already spent hours with her. I had no reason to ask for more.

Before she could open her door, I motioned for her to wait and dashed to her side. But by the time I reached the handle, she had already swung the door open.

"I was going to open it for you, you nut." I smiled, looking down at her. She was still sitting, but her legs were swung halfway out the door, making our proximity tantalizingly close. On instinct, I licked my lips as I gazed down at her. Without even realizing it, I was inching closer toward her face.

She didn't back away, and I found myself unable to resist temptation any longer. Just like muscle memory from that first night, I kissed her. It felt a hell of a lot like coming home.

Despite this being our second kiss, she moved more hesitantly this time, her mouth moving slowly over mine. It was sweet. I nipped her bottom lip and she smiled against my mouth.

After a minute, I pulled away reluctantly.

"What was that for?" she breathed.

"Because it was too hard not to."

Instead of breezing by me, she lingered there, in the passenger seat of my car. "Oliver?"

"Hmm?" I couldn't stop staring at her lips.

"You said…You said you might bounce around to different cities after this."

"Right." My head was still high from the kiss.

"Do you ever worry about it getting lonely? Living that way?" Her voice was soft.

My jaw froze for a second as my gaze drifted from her mouth to her eyes. The tendon in my neck pulsed. "No," I said plainly, hoping she'd drop this.

Instead, she gnawed at her bottom lip. "I'm kind of lonely," Frankie whispered. "It's sad, but I didn't even realize it until I came out here to stay with Mattie. Being so busy with my job meant I never noticed it, but my life was so…lacking."

My hand squeezed the top of the door. Her words were almost physically painful. Both because I fucking hated the fact that she felt lonely, and because I hated the unwanted self-reflection her words were now causing me.

Where the hell did this girl get off, being vulnerable like this? Had I given off the impression I wanted to dissect these things?

My face must have been contorted into one of aversion, because Frankie's cheeks reddened before her eyes dropped to her lap.

"Look at me. Feeling sorry for myself again."

"Hey, no self-deprecation on my watch." I tried to make my voice sound lighter than I felt. But Frankie still wore a small frown. Shit. We were rapidly wandering into uncharted territories for me. I didn't know how to help Frankie work through her crisis any more than I knew how to help myself and my own suffocated emotions.

I was the guy for a laugh. Not a shoulder to cry on.

But the last thing I could handle was how alone she looked right now. So small in front of me. Right here, yet so far. I hated it. I'd already given her so little of myself, despite the fact that she clearly wanted more. Which was maybe why I said what I said next. Something I'd barely thought. Something I never dreamed I'd say out loud.

I leaned in and pressed a soft kiss to her forehead. When I pulled back, I said, "I get lonely too."

FOURTEEN

Frankie

"I'm bored," I whined, my head draped over the arm of the chair, hair splayed out and brushing the wood floor. I had no interviews scheduled today, Oliver was busy with lessons, and for once I wasn't working at Marie's tonight. I was completely restless.

My sister sighed with contentment. "And isn't that a lovely feeling?"

I turned my head so that I could make out her right-side-up figure, curled up on the couch, pouring over a book.

My phone vibrated on the coffee table and I scrambled to a seated position, almost toppling over, before snatching it and opening the notification. I sighed in defeat when I saw that it was my mom checking in. "It's just Mom," I groaned.

"I'm sure she would be thrilled to know that's how you react when you receive her messages."

I ignored Mattie, firing off a quick response.

"We should really plan a trip down to Florida to visit them. It's been forever since we were all down there other than for Christmas," she said.

"I think the last time was when you moved out of that apartment with your shitty ex after the epic cheating scandal and stayed with them for a few weeks."

Mattie threw a pillow at my head, hitting me square in the face.

"Hey!" I yelled, tossing it back at her. She caught it.

"I can't believe you'd bring up the most humiliating time in my life." She glared at me.

I held up my hands. "What? It was literally the last time we were there together aside from Christmas. That's just a fact."

"A depressing one. And all the more reason to visit them."

"It's already April, and it's too hot in the summer," I protested. "And who knows what the vacation time will look like when I get another job."

Mattie didn't bother hiding her look of disapproval. "Fine. Good to know where your priorities are at. Hypothetical new job, number one. Quality time with family, number two."

I was about to protest, but my phone went off again. I held it up to my face without thinking. Mom again.

"You need to go put that in another room or something," Mattie said, shaking her head.

"And miss an email?" I said it as if that were the most preposterous idea she could have come up with.

I'd done a few more phone screenings this week and was waiting to hear back to see if I'd moved on. Some of the jobs I was even remotely excited about, which was an improvement from my first interview.

"The email will still be there whether you see it immediately or in a few hours."

"If I get another interview, I want to schedule it as soon as possible," I said, pulling up my email app in case I'd somehow missed a notification.

She didn't get it. She had her dream life with her dream guy. Her life was completely put together, not shattered like mine was. I was in limbo, and I was desperate to get out.

Mattie rolled her eyes. "Whatever. God forbid you relax."

"Relax? We're sitting around doing nothing. I'm crawling out of my skin."

Mattie closed her book. "It's called a day off, Frankie. I know that's a new concept for you, but most people find them enjoyable."

I sighed dramatically.

My phone dinged again, and I brought it to my face.

It wasn't an email, it was Oliver. He'd sent me a video of someone snowboarding, going off a huge jump before tumbling and sliding down the mountain. Oliver had written, *Basically you on the bunny hill.*

A smile spread over my face.

"You get an email?" Mattie asked. When I glanced up, she was staring at me.

"Oliver sent me some dumb video."

"Oh, Oliver, huh?" she asked in a knowing tone, which irritated me. Of course, I'd already debriefed her on the breakfast and the kiss we'd shared. Which I never should have done because now she was reading way too much into it.

Oliver wasn't helping her assumptions. Since then, I'd only seen him twice in passing at the lodge. Both times, he had been extremely flirty, even going so far as to walk right up to me and plant a kiss on me in front of Bev and Mattie. I had blinked at him in shock, but he'd acted like it was the most natural thing in the world. I truly did not understand the guy. He was living life by his own rule book, not caring for a moment what the typical or normal thing to do was.

"You like him. I know you do."

"He's fun," I said noncommittedly.

"I love him for you."

"He's not *for* me."

She waved off my flippant response. "You know what I mean. He's such a free spirit. *So* not the kind of guy I pictured you with."

"Because he's not the type of guy I'll end up with," I insisted, sitting up in the chair. "He's about to go live some vagabond lifestyle or something, and I'm trying—no *going* to land a job soon and I'll likely be starting over somewhere. Nothing about us is a recipe for romance. A fling, maybe, but *definitely* not a romance."

Mattie pouted. "Can you engage in my rom-com fantasies for once in your life?"

"No, because they're far-fetched, and that much daydreaming will get your head stuck in the clouds."

"You're no fun."

"Now you sound like Oliver," I muttered. "Look, just because you had the perfect movie ending where you get the guy and move to the small town, doesn't mean that's a realistic expectation to have."

"I disagree."

I made a point to turn and look out the window, informing my sister with my body language that I was no longer entertaining this conversation.

Oliver was cute, fun, and easy to be around. But he also did not take life seriously and was completely closed off. Despite constantly asking me questions and making sweeping judgments about my own life, he refused to let me in even the tiniest bit. Maybe it was a defense mechanism, but he so clearly wasn't ready for anything more than something casual and short-lived.

But maybe a fling was exactly what I needed right now. With the ski season coming to an end, and him potentially leaving soon, I'd come to the stark realization that I would be extremely disappointed if we never took things between us further. Other than trying to find a job, Oliver had infiltrated all of my free thoughts.

If he moved away or I found a job elsewhere, and we never let our flirty situationship evolve beyond a kiss, I knew deep down that I'd regret it. Now I had to figure out a way to make that clear to him without outright throwing myself at him…

A truck pulled into the driveway.

"Your husband's home," I said, my chin resting on the back of the chair.

But it wasn't just Giles that got out of the car. A figure slid out of the passenger side as well. I sat straight up when I realized that it was Oliver.

"Oliver's here," I hissed. I tried to straighten out my sweatshirt, but I knew without checking a mirror that I had the appearance of someone who had been rotting away on the couch all day.

"Do I look okay?" I asked.

She studied me. "You look like a mess, but I doubt he'll care in the slightest."

The door opened and Giles walked in first, stomping his boots on the mat before tugging them off.

"Hey, babe." Mattie beamed, and he walked straight toward her to plant a kiss on her forehead.

"Hiya." Oliver stood in the doorway, grinning.

"Oliver, what a surprise." Mattie's gaze shifted between the two of us.

"Hey," I said as nonchalantly as possible.

"Frankie, can I talk to you really quick?" He pointed outside to the porch.

"Oh, uh, yeah sure." I peeled myself from the armchair and smoothed out my sweats.

I didn't bother grabbing a coat off the front hook. The sun was beating pretty heavily down and people weren't kidding when they said it was stronger in Colorado. I barely even caught a chill in its rays.

Oliver let me go first and then stepped out onto the porch next to me, closing the door behind him.

"What's up—"

He cut off my words by dipping his head to meet mine and stealing a kiss, catching me completely off guard.

"What was that for?" I breathed when he pulled away.

His eyebrows drew together but his smile remained. "Because I wanted to."

I brushed my lips with my fingertips. They still tingled.

"Was I not supposed to do that?" he asked, tilting his head. I loved the way his dark eyes almost gleamed when they were focused on me.

"It's just—" I sucked in a breath, completely flustered. "Aren't we still in that weird phase were we're stepping on eggshells around each other? Like all awkward and uncomfortable because we're unsure of how to act because we don't know what the other is thinking and we haven't talked about anything?"

He put his hand to his chin and stroked it. "I don't feel that way around you," he said, as if it was the simplest answer in the world.

I feel that way around you, I wanted to yell. But I bit my tongue. Hadn't I been thinking a fling was exactly what I wanted? Who was I to try and dictate on what terms they happened. Just because every other guy would have been playing games right now, didn't mean that Oliver had to. He was different in every possible way, so it made sense that he wouldn't act how I expected.

"Do *you* feel that way around *me*?" he asked, his gaze carefully studying my face.

The question caused a slightly chaotic giggle to burst out of me. "What? Me? Uncomfortable? No, not at all."

He laughed, and I thought for the millionth time how jealous I was of his confidence.

"Well good, because I wanted to ask you something."

"What?" I asked hesitantly. "You have some new crazy adventure planned for us or something?"

"Kind of." He stared down at me. "I wanted to see if you were free tomorrow night."

"For some more fun therapy, or whatever it is you're calling it?" I asked.

He shrugged. "Kind of. I was just going to call it a date this time."

Heat pricked my skin. "A date," I repeated, convinced I'd misheard him, even though there was no possible way.

"Yep." He nodded slowly, raising his eyebrows.

"But, we're—but you're leaving soon. And I'm, like—" I was sputtering, unable to form a coherent sentence.

Oliver didn't seem fazed in the slightest. "I like you," he said, matter-of-factly. "And I want to take you on a real date. Sure, I could invite you on another excursion with the thinly veiled motive of spending more time with you, but I'd rather just ask you out."

"But—"

He held up his hand. "I know, I know. I'm leaving soon, you're job hunting. We have no future. Whatever. Who cares? I like you, and I know you like me. What's more fun than following through on how we feel? Not everything has to be this carefully laid-out plan with a guaranteed future. We can just have fun, Frankie. Forget about everything else."

A fling. Basically exactly what I had wanted. Every instinct I had itched to ask for rules and set guidelines on what this was. Where was this going physically? How long would we have? How deep were we getting? I forced myself to let it go, though. Those types of thoughts had no place in what he was asking.

"S-sure."

He grinned, leaning in for another kiss. It felt natural.

Which kind of freaked me out if I was being honest.

FIFTEEN

Frankie

"I'VE NEVER SEEN YOU THIS NERVOUS," MATTIE SAID FROM behind me as I franticly brushed out a curl that looked too curled.

"I am *not* nervous," I snapped, tugging at the curl more. Should I spray it with water? The last thing I wanted was for Oliver to think that I had tried for this…for this…for whatever this was. Date, I guess. But when I thought of it like that, my stomach instantly rocked with nerves.

"If you tug at that piece of hair anymore, you're going to be bald," Mattie pointed out.

"I don't want him to think I curled my hair!" I said, giving up and plugging in the flat iron.

"But you did curl your hair." Mattie looked at me like I had completely lost it.

"Yes, but I don't want *him* to know that. I want it to look effortless. Like bouncy waves I rolled out of bed with."

"As if the beauty standard for women isn't already high enough, now we have to pretend like we didn't even try while also achieving perfection?"

"Let me live," I cried, finally flattening the piece successfully with the lukewarm flat iron. Mattie was right. This was out of sorts for me. I didn't date often, but on the few occasions I had, I'd never been this much of an anxious mess.

The fact that Oliver and I had already established that we liked each other and shared more than a few kisses did little to quell my nerves. In fact, the reality that we'd already kissed left me even more nervous, because *what* was next? While everything in my body told me that I absolutely wanted this evening to progress beyond a quick peck, it didn't mean I wasn't any less in my head about it.

Oliver was like…incredibly attractive. And he was so extreme and outdoorsy and adventurous. And he was always so calm and collected and never seemed to have a care in the world. Why did he even want to hang out with me? I was an uptight mess of a human. Especially right now. At least when I had a thriving career, I could blame my bad personality on that. Now what did I have? I lived in my sister's basement and could barely get a second interview.

Mattie must have sensed the nerves radiating off me, because she finally sighed and stood up before grabbing the tops of both my arms. We were almost the exact same height, so she stood behind me and angled her body so that her face would be next to mine in the mirror. "Chill, Frankie. You've already hung out with Oliver. This will just be like that except better."

"No, this will be just like that but with the added pressure of the 'date' label being tossed onto it. What if it's, like, thirty minutes away and we're trapped in the car together and we can't think of anything to talk about? What if I'm not dressed right?" I pulled at my navy sweater to examine it. I'd paired it with light-wash jeans, hoping the look was cute and casual enough to be appropriate for anything.

Mattie rolled her eyes and squeezed my arms harder before shaking me lightly. "First off, I don't think 'trapped' is the correct verb to describe your date with a cute boy. And second, you two will fill the silence. Don't worry about it. Oliver is the least awkward person I've ever met. He's probably never met a silence he couldn't fill."

"Maybe I'll finally be his match."

"You're being ridiculous. You've spent like twenty hours this week talking to random interviewers via video chats. How can you handle all that but are falling to pieces at the thought of spending a couple of hours alone with Oliver?"

"Because Oliver is different!" I cried, pushing past her out of the bathroom and looking at my outfit in the full-length mirror for the hundredth time.

"You look amazing and tonight is going to be great," Mattie reassured me. "Stop stressing or you'll psych yourself out."

"What time is it?" I asked.

"Six fifteen," Mattie said.

"He's late," I groaned. "I can't stand it when guys are late."

"He got here fifteen minutes ago," Mattie said.

"What?" I could feel myself pale at her words. "What do you mean?" I hissed, creeping to the bottom of the stairs and straining my ears to listen. Sure enough, muffled sounds of two guys talking drifted down into the basement.

"Mattie!" I whisper-shrieked. "Why didn't you tell me he was here?"

She shrugged. "I figured I'd give you a pep talk."

"Now he'll think I take forever to get ready." I shot her an accusatory glare.

"You *do* take forever to get ready."

"He can't know that!"

"Breathe, Frankie. You're going to give yourself a heart attack."

I took a deep inhale through my nose and blew it out slowly through my mouth. Regardless of how badly I was freaking out, I needed to get it together.

"Let's go," Mattie said, gesturing for me to lead the way up the stairs.

I took the steps slowly, breathing the whole time in order to get my heart rate under control.

"The conditions were unreal this morning," I heard Oliver say.

"I can't believe we got that kind of powder this late in the season. It was incredible," Giles agreed.

"Hey," I said, walking through the kitchen and dining room to the living room, where both the guys stood.

"Hey." Oliver shot me a huge smile, which sent my stomach into a cartwheel.

Taking in Oliver made me gulp audibly. He looked good. Like *really* good. His hair was pushed back, but a few waves hung by his eyes and the ends curled up by his shirt collar. He wore a flannel button-down that made me want to tuck right into him. His jeans fit him perfectly and ended in his brown boots he always wore anytime I saw him off the ski hill.

"Sorry, I would have been up earlier, but Mattie didn't tell me you were here."

"I got distracted," Mattie said sweetly. "Silly me."

I desperately wanted to shoot her a glare but didn't want Oliver to see.

"You ready?" Oliver asked.

"Uh-huh." I walked over to him, stopping a few feet short. Was I supposed to hug him?

"Ladies first." He waved his hand in front of him.

I stepped toward the door, grabbing Mattie's green coat

off the hook and slipping it on. "See you later," I said to Giles and Mattie.

"Don't wait up," Oliver teased, winking at me.

I nudged him in the chest, and a sliver of my nerves were eased. Although a different kind of excitement brewed in my gut at the innuendo of staying out late with Oliver.

OLIVER'S IDEA FOR A DATE TURNED OUT TO BE SOME SORT OF ice sculpture park. Apparently, it closed tomorrow and he had been meaning to check it out.

We had to take a gondola up the mountain to get to it, and the ride itself displayed some of the most breathtaking views I had ever seen. My nerves hadn't completely gone away, but I was momentarily distracted as I pressed my face up to the glass and took it all in. Mountains, rolling in the distance for as far as my eyes could see. The surrealness of it all hit me on the ride up. There I was, sitting with a guy who was my opposite in so many ways, in the most picturesque setting I could ever imagine.

The layoff had felt like the worst thing imaginable, but could it have been so bad if it had led to this moment?

When we arrived at the top, Oliver placed his hand on the small of my back, letting me exit the gondola car first. It was somehow like twenty degrees colder up here, and I was grateful for the thick sweater and wool coat I'd chosen to wear.

There were a few small warming huts. One said *Tickets* above it and the others looked like food vendors. Snow sculptures and large castles were carved into the snow. Some lit up as people wandered through the mazes of structures. I was immensely grateful he hadn't picked an activity where I would likely embarrass myself within the first fifteen minutes. Walk around and marvel at intricate ice carvings? Even I was capable of that.

Oliver paid for our tickets, and I insisted on a hot chocolate from the vendor before we started walking around. He asked me to take a picture of him on top of a giant snow fort castle. I even got in a selfie with him in front of one of the snow sculptures that looked like a giant elf.

As we moved through the displays, my anxiousness had finally started to subside. Every moment with Oliver was easy. Whatever pressure I had felt about tonight was gone as soon as he slung an arm around my shoulders. While I still wasn't sure exactly what to make of us, I couldn't deny how outright good it felt to be with him.

"Admit I can plan a good date," Oliver said, smiling down at me as we walked through one of the larger light displays.

"I don't know. I kind of wish you'd taken me snowboarding again," I said.

We walked by a few other sculptures, one resembling a penguin eating an ice cream cone. "You'll never let me live that down." He chuckled.

"It's okay. I've realized you like forcing me to do things I suck at. Snowboarding. Snowshoeing. You get a thrill out of me struggling while you breeze through the activity."

"Is that what I'm doing?" he asked sarcastically. "I could have sworn I was just trying to have some fun with you."

"Fun with me or fun at my expense?" I teased.

"Can't it be both?"

I stopped when he stopped. His eyes lit up at something in the distance.

"Speaking of fun." He pointed.

I squinted to see a small ice-skating rink with people swirling around it.

"What? No way." I let out a laugh of disbelief. "I was thoroughly enjoying how chill this was."

He pouted and reached for my hand. "Come on, Frankie. Please? Ice-skating is easy. It's nothing like snowboarding."

I bit my tongue, not wanting to mention that I also had never ice-skated before. He probably thought I was the lamest excuse for a date.

"Don't tell me you've never been ice-skating either?" Oliver's eyebrows pulled together.

"I mean, growing up, we had these skating rinks made out of plastic they set out at malls in the winter. Does that count?"

Oliver gave a quick shake of his head. "Plastic? What? Absolutely not."

"I'm from Florida," I said defensively.

"Then we have a lot of catching up to do." He pulled me forward, toward the skating rink, and before I could protest further, he was shoving a pair of ice skates at me. He practically dragged me to the bench where we were supposed to take our shoes off and put on the skates. There were little cubbies underneath to store our boots.

"You can't sit still, can you?" I mumbled, but I was already putting on the skates to appease him. At this point, I was kind of convinced that he could talk me into anything. At least with this activity, the worst that could happen was falling from a standing position. There was no hurtling down a hill involved. But as I had that thought, I looked up to see another couple shakily skating around. The girl flailed her hands a few times before falling backward, right onto her butt. *Ouch*. That had to have hurt.

"I won't let you fall," he insisted.

I jerked my head around to see that he was watching me watch the couple. "I've heard that one before," I said, lacing up my second skate.

He tapped his chin, already having put his skates on. "I don't recall ever promising that you wouldn't fall snowboarding. The very nature of learning that sport involves spending a good amount of time on your butt."

"Well, I think it was heavily implied that I wouldn't get hurt."

"Oh yeah, the big wrist injury." Oliver's eyebrow raised in exaggerated skepticism. "How's that feeling? Will you ever be the same?"

"It's still sore," I insisted, but the smile I couldn't keep from spreading across my lips implied that I was completely full of shit.

"Okay. Sure." Oliver winked at me. He did that a lot. I would normally find the gesture severely sleazy. But with Oliver, it somehow made me feel special. I swear each time he directed one at me, a new swarm of butterflies was released in my stomach.

"Let's do this." He reached for my hands, and I stood shakily on the skates. Walking in them was unnatural. The blade sliced into the padded black mats that lined the path to the rink. Oliver steadied me the whole way. When we got to the entrance of the rink, he let go of my hand to lightly grip my waist.

"Alright, easy does it. No falling on my watch."

"No promises," I said, although my eyes were glued to the ice. I was determined to prove to Oliver that I wasn't completely hopeless at everything I attempted. If only he could see me in my element, back at my old job. The way I could command a room with ease. Though now that I thought about it, he probably wouldn't have been impressed in the slightest by my slideshow presentations.

"Now, start walking but drag your foot a little. So back and forth. Don't worry about gliding, keep the motions choppy at first."

"Whoa." My body jerked forward and then back as I took my first steps.

"I've got you," Oliver said, tightening his grip on me.

I found my balance and continued moving forward. Once I got over the initial weirdness of the feeling, I managed to move a few feet forward. I had roller-skated eons ago, back in elementary school. It wasn't like this was too terribly different from that. I could do this. Especially if Oliver kept his hands on me.

Oliver swung around with ease so that he was in front of me, and reached out to take both of my hands, helping me keep my balance as I gracelessly took a few strides forward.

"Did you play hockey or something?" I asked as he skated backward.

"Nope," he said, watching my feet to make sure I was getting the hang of this and not tangling them up in each other.

"Then why are you so good at this?" I asked.

He shrugged. "I don't know. It just came easy, I guess."

"You're one of those people who is obnoxiously good at everything they try, right?" I asked, letting out a frustrated huff when I clumsily almost lost my footing again.

Oliver, true to his word, took one hand away from mine and grabbed my waist, refusing to let me fall. "I *am* good at a lot of things," he admitted. "Pretty much only physical stuff, though. Sports, stuff like this. Not so much everything else."

He sounded almost self-conscious saying that, which really threw me off guard.

"So the opposite of me," I said. "I've never successfully picked up a sport in all my years trying."

That made him smile. "I had to be good at something.

Nathan was always the insanely smart one. I had to have my thing, too, or I would have felt completely inferior instead of just slightly not good enough."

"Your brother sounds like your opposite, huh?" I asked carefully.

The last time I'd tried to bring up his family, he'd changed the topic abruptly. But I was desperate to learn more about him other than the cheery, charming guy he was on the surface.

His eyes met mine before he looked away. He spun around so that he was skating in the same direction as me and held out his arm so I could thread mine through it for balance. He kept his pace slow so that I wouldn't be left behind or forced to go faster than I was comfortable with.

"Nathan and I have never been anything alike. I'm not sure if we were born that way or if it was the product of how our parents raised us…" His voice trailed off. "But you have a sister. I probably don't need to tell you about sibling rivalry."

Something about the pain in his voice told me that his childhood was likely far from the typical sibling rivalry. I decided to tread carefully so that I wouldn't scare him off.

"Mattie and I were competitive, sure. She was two grades above me and we'd compete over friends or sports. We were both on student government, but she would always be above me. I felt like I had to work twice as hard to get where she was, even though I should have recognized that she was older and it wasn't a competition." I licked my lips, glancing over to see him looking lost in thought, staring straight ahead. "But my parents always nipped any real rivalries right in the bud. They didn't want us fighting or competing. They always told us they were proud no matter what and that we should be celebrating each other instead of challenging. Of course, we were still sisters so we didn't always listen. I would still steal her clothes, and Mattie still always acted like she knew best, but at the end of the day, we knew we had each other's backs. My parents too."

I was oversharing, especially considering this was technically a first date. But this was Oliver. He'd already seen more of me than I'd let anyone see in a long time. I was desperate for him to feel comfortable enough with me to share something—*anything*—real.

"They sound great," Oliver said softly. His voice was more cautious than it normally was. I wanted to push, but I also felt like I was two questions away from him snapping out of whatever this was, cracking a joke, and skating away from me.

"Were your parents…not great?" I asked, tired of dancing around the question I was dying to know the answer to.

"Let's just say while your parents nurtured your relationship with Mattie, my parents pitted Nathan and me against each other." Oliver's eyes looked glassy.

My heart twisted at his admittance. "That's awful," I said.

Oliver blew out a pained breath. "It was just the way that they were. My dad is kind of an ass. He always only cared about work, and he saw Nathan as his prodigy or something. Nathan was basically a genius. Like, I'm not exaggerating when I tell you that he's the most logical person you'll ever meet. My dad always pushed the hell out of him."

"And you?" I choked out.

Oliver shook his head. "I never had much of a relationship with my dad."

The sounds of our skates scraping up the ice filled the air as I waited for him to continue.

"He's just… He never cared about me. Never cared what I did. My grades were never all that good, and that was all he seemed to care about. My mom was always the one cheering me on. I was grateful for it, but it made me feel…weird. She was more standoffish with Nathan and my dad. It was like it was her and me against them. I don't know. I didn't realize how not normal that was until I moved out."

"At least she supported you," I said quietly, although it seemed like they'd had some kind of unhealthy codependent thing going on when he was younger.

He rubbed his free hand along his jaw and sighed. Our pace had picked up a little. Skating was even easier when I wasn't thinking about it and was instead completely invested in whatever bits Oliver was willing to share with me.

"I don't know if she supported me or just wanted me on her side. The whole thing makes me feel weird, and now our relationship is a little tense."

"But you're close with Nathan now, right?" I asked.

"I am. I didn't know how to connect with him for years, but after he moved out here, we were finally able to talk and get to know each other without our parents breathing down our necks. I haven't really figured things out with my mom, but at least I feel like Nathan and I are in it together now. And I might just have to be okay with who she is. Maybe she isn't a perfect parent, but at least she still calls us, ya know? And it's clear she's trying harder with Nathan."

"Your dad doesn't try?" I guessed.

"He calls Nathan sometimes, but I think all of Nathan's success almost irritates him. Like he wanted him to do well, but not significantly better than him. He divorced my mom a while back—honestly, we were shocked it took them so long, but I don't think either of them wanted to deal with custody arrangements when we were younger. Anyway, I haven't talked to my dad in over a year and I couldn't care less."

"That's hard, Oliver," I said, unable to keep the thickness out of my voice.

Something about my words seemed to snap Oliver out of

his daze because he immediately shook his dark waves and threw a smile on his face. "Not as hard as ice-skating is, apparently. You look like a drunk baby giraffe out here."

My cheeks flushed instantly. Not because I was offended—I knew I sucked at this—but because of the way he so smoothly returned to his lighthearted self. It was if I had imagined him opening up a moment ago.

"I'm doing fine," I insisted. "Look." I let go of his hand for a few glides. "See?"

He tossed his head back and chuckled. "You're basically skating circles around me."

"Now back to the conversation," I continued.

His smile immediately dropped like a mask as he skated ahead of me. "You want to take a break? Get some more hot chocolate?" he asked.

"No," I said, struggling to keep up with him. "You can't run away from talking to me."

"I'm not."

But he continued to skate away from me.

Why did he have to be so impossible? Maybe I shouldn't be pushing, but he knew me by now. I wasn't carefree like him. I had been pushy with the questions the last time we'd hung out, and he should have known it'd only get worse if he asked me out on a real date. I didn't have it in me to pretend that I didn't care about who he was.

"Hey—whoa!" I had attempted to go too fast. My arms flailed as I tried to regain my balance so that I didn't plop right onto my behind. I was about to lose the battle with gravity when strong hands encircled my waist, easily steadying me.

"I've got you," Oliver whispered.

I breathed a sigh of relief as he loosened his grip, while

still maintaining contact and moving away so that he was staring down at me.

I smacked him in the chest. "You abandoned me." I glared up at him, eyes narrowed.

His eyebrows furrowed together before he let out a breath of a laugh. "I was right here."

"Don't do it again," I warned.

"Never."

We skated in silence for a bit after that. I badly wanted to ask him more, but I didn't want him to shut down on me again.

My best bet was slow and steady with him. I didn't know what we were or where this was going—likely nowhere fast. But what I did know was that I cared about Oliver. Probably more than I should. He was special. Maybe we were nothing alike, but there was nothing I wanted more right now than to understand him.

SIXTEEN

Oliver

My entire chest was on fire as I watched Frankie take off her ice skates. I had already laced up my boots and was ready to get the hell out of there. Shame had overshadowed every thought in my mind.

This date was a bad idea. I should have known that. She was under my skin, completely and effortlessly. She made me comfortable in an unfamiliar way, which had caused me to overshare—something I literally never did. Any sort of reflective, heavy conversations were my kryptonite. Somehow, Frankie had coaxed some of my deepest innermost thoughts and insecurities out of me, and now I was feeling uncomfortable as hell.

She hadn't had a bad reaction, but I also didn't stick around long enough to really *get* her reaction. I needed to take her home and try to forget some of the things I had told her that were currently whizzing around my mind. She probably thought I was some pathetic guy with mommy and daddy issues. I had wanted to impress her—show her a good time—but instead, I'd done this.

I wasn't sure if I had scared her off or scared myself off, but either way, I was trying to keep my cool until she was safely dropped off at Giles and Mattie's house.

As soon as she handed me her skates, I was already walking over to the rental hut and dropping them off with the teenaged worker.

"You ready?" I asked. "That was fun."

I could tell I was talking too fast, but my facade of normalcy was hanging on by a thread. It was all I could do to keep from cracking.

"Oliver, hold on."

Her voice sounded distant, and I slowed my pace to let her catch up. I chanced a look down at her to see her eyes wide with confusion.

"Why are you walking so fast?" Her anxious tone tugged at my chest, but I couldn't bring myself to maintain eye contact.

"Sorry." I ripped the beanie off my head to rake my hands through my hair. Heat burned through my body. It was like I was wearing my humiliation as an extra layer and it was suffocating me. "You ready to go?" I asked, a strange, fake smile glued to my face.

"Go?" Frankie repeated quietly. "We just got here."

She looked beautiful tonight. Something I regretted not telling her earlier.

"We went ice-skating, we walked around. I should get you home before you find a way to get injured." My attempt at teasing was weak, but I was fighting tooth and nail to keep it together.

Frankie's look of disappointment faded into something else—something that looked a hell of a lot like defiance. She crossed her arms over her chest and leaned against one hip, jutting out her chin to stare up at me.

"I'm hungry," she said.

"The food here probably sucks," I insisted.

"I'm starving," she repeated with added inflection. "Let's get food."

I opened and closed my mouth, unsure of what she was trying to do here. I had expected her to think I was acting a little strange but to go along with it. I had expected us to ride back down the gondola and pile into the car, where I could promptly use the radio as a distraction. I had expected to drop her off after a few more jokes. After that, I would keep my distance. I wouldn't have dinner at Marie's every night she worked, I wouldn't send her flirty text messages or steal a kiss anytime I saw her in the lodge. We had treaded into dangerous territory and I needed to get out of this emotional quicksand before it swallowed me whole.

"I need to go home," I choked out, dropping my fake niceties.

"Why?" she demanded.

I was already off, headed back to the gondola loading area. She was hot on my trail and was next to me just as the employee waved for us to board the gondola car that slowly swung around.

"What are you doing?" she asked as soon as the doors closed, sealing us inside for the ride down.

Panicking.

"Is this because of what we were talking about on the skating rink? About your parents?" she asked.

"I don't want to talk about that," I snapped, spinning around so fast she nearly collided with my chest. Neither of us had bothered to take a seat.

Her face crumpled when she met my eyes. "We can go eat somewhere else. I didn't mean to push you."

"No, we can't."

"Why not?" Her eyes narrowed and I knew there was no way she was backing down from this conversation.

"Because."

"Why?"

"Because you think I'm pathetic!" I cracked.

That caused her to reel back. "What—"

"My dad didn't love me and I have mommy issues. What kind of man am I? Who the fuck wants to hear about that?" I never, ever raised my voice and I could tell from Frankie's shocked expression that she wasn't expecting me to snap like that. "See!" I waved a hand in her direction. "It's written all over your face. You can barely stand to look at me."

I whipped around and stared out at the evening sky, the town barely visible below. I was desperate for more space than this fifty-square-foot gondola cabin allowed me.

"That's not what I was thinking." Frankie's words were frantic. "I was thinking how I wanted to learn more about you. That I want to know the things that make you up. You're more than some surface-level jock. You have so many layers. I-I just wanted to peel back one."

I kept staring straight out the window, but her words rang in my ears.

"I'm sorry I pushed you." She wrapped a cautious hand around my bicep.

Her touch made me want to melt into her, and I took a few deep breaths to calm myself. I never lost it, and I hated that she was seeing me like this. But I was miles away from my old life, and I had been out of sorts lately. Something about Frankie felt more like home than anything else I'd come into contact with lately.

"And you aren't pathetic, trust me. That's the last thing I'm thinking," she whispered, but I still couldn't turn to face her after my monumentally embarrassing outburst. "If anything, I'm thinking about what an amazing man you've turned out to be despite not having the best role models. And I'm thinking about what a good heart you have and how you take everything in stride. Ever since I met you, I've been jealous of your confidence. You're amazing, Oliver, and I want to see the whole picture, not just the highlight reel."

Her words hit me like a semi-truck. Presenting a highlight reel to people was exactly what I fucking did.

Growing up, there hadn't been space for me to be anything except happy-go-lucky. I was already a huge disappointment to my dad without even trying, and I had to win my mom over somehow. And always being in a good mood seemed to please her.

I realized it felt like a weight had been lifted off my chest —like I could finally take a deep breath. Despite how desperate I'd been not to share anything with Frankie, her seeing beneath my front was the most relief I'd felt in a long time.

I finally turned, feeling brave enough to face her. To my absolute horror, she had a single tear rolling down her cheek. My gut reaction would typically be to back away from someone crying, but instead, without thinking, I reached out and brushed it away.

She shook her head. "Look at me, crying. If anything, *I'm* the pathetic one. This whole evening, I was trying to convince you that I'm not bad at everything. I lost my job—the only thing I was good at. Now I'm wandering through life, and I can't catch my footing."

"I don't think you're pathetic," I whispered. How could she think that? She was intelligent and driven and interesting. "I've been trying to impress you since I met you," I admitted.

I brushed away another tear from her cheek, this time letting my hand linger there.

"Opening up about your past isn't a weakness. Feelings aren't flaws," she said slowly, as if scared I would bolt as soon as we got to the bottom and this gondola door swung open. "And you don't have to tell me everything in one night, but I need you to know that I want to know more about you. And I'm never judging you, okay?"

I nodded.

"I need to hear you say it."

"Okay," I said, feeling like putty in her hands.

She took a shaky breath in and my eyes scanned her every feature. I was still a little anxious about what I'd shared tonight, but her words grounded me. This wasn't the face of someone who was judging me. I had shared dark parts of myself. I had been vulnerable. And instead of cringing away, she had stepped up, wanting to see more.

"I like you," I breathed, moving my hand to grip the back of her neck.

Frankie let out a small laugh. "Even after all that?"

"*Especially* after all that." I chewed on the inside of my cheek. "Do you like *me* after all that?"

"Who said I liked you in the first place?" she asked, smiling.

That finally got a real smile to return to my face. "Shut up," I said, lightly tugging her forward to cover her mouth with mine. I wasn't sure if it was the emotional build up to it or what, but everything about the kiss was full of energy. My whole body felt like a live wire and each brush of her lips was causing a spark.

When I finally came up for air, I leaned down so that I could press my forehead against hers. "Was that romantic or messy?" I asked, which caused her to laugh again.

"Both?" She said it like a question.

My grin stretched as I pressed a kiss to her forehead. She

was real in my hands, rooting me in this moment. I never wanted to let her go.

She was so different from me, yet I'd never felt more seen by anyone. She had all these aspirations and I would always be adrift. Nothing about us was meant to be, but I couldn't help but feel like fate was telling me we were meant for *now*.

SEVENTEEN

Frankie

"So this is the place?" I asked, stepping into the tiny studio apartment.

While I'd hoped the night might lead here, I hadn't wanted to assume anything. Even though going home with a guy was something I hardly did, Oliver had a way of completely calming me down. My nerves from earlier had evaporated by this point. He'd shared more with me on this date than he ever had before. I felt like I was in—like I was in some special secret Oliver society with an ultra-exclusive membership.

"This is it." He held up his hands and spun around the small space. "Want the tour? It's a short one."

I stumbled out of my boots, my entire body buzzing with anticipation.

"This is the kitchen," he said, pointing. "And this is the living room. This is my bed. And that's basically it."

I forced my eyes not to linger on his bed as I stepped into his space, taking it in. To my extreme relief, the place was tidy. The bed was made and there was no trash lying around.

When I caught sight of a duffel bag spilling over with clothes on the bench at the end of his bed, I froze.

"Packing?" I asked, pointing to it. The last day of the season was this Saturday. I knew we hadn't exactly talked about it, but I thought for sure he'd tell me when he was leaving.

"Oh, ah." He scratched the back of his neck. "That's my bag from when I got here. I never bothered unpacking."

My eyebrows shot up. "You've been here for over three weeks."

He shrugged, giving me a sheepish grin. "I never unpack on trips."

"But…but you've done laundry, right?"

Oliver's head fell back as he laughed at my concerned expression. "Yes, Frankie. I've done laundry. I just toss it back on the bench when it's clean."

My mouth parted in shock as I walked over to the set of drawers standing next to the bed and opened one. "This is a perfectly good dresser, and it's right here. Arguably closer to the washer and dryer." I pointed to where the appliances were housed next to the bathroom. "Why can't you dump your stuff here?"

Oliver rolled his eyes, clearly amused by how appalled I was. In one fell swoop, he went to the bench, scooped his clothes up, walked over to the dresser, and dropped his stuff into the awaiting drawer. "Happy?" he asked.

"Ecstatic," I said flatly.

He grabbed me around the waist, and I looked up into his eyes. He dipped down to kiss the top of my head.

"Alright," he said, releasing me but grabbing my hand and tugging me to the kitchen. "Since I so abruptly ended our date, let me see what I have in here for food."

He gripped my waist and I let out a small squeal as he

effortlessly lifted me onto the countertop. I watched him dig around in his cabinets. Being in his space felt more intimate than I'd expected. Like I was getting some sort of behind-the-scenes peek into his life.

"So, plans," I said carefully, wanting to keep the moment light, but also desperately wanting to know more about where he'd be going next. "I haven't exactly helped you come up with any."

Oliver produced a sleeve of crackers and handed them to me. I took one and nibbled on it, trying to play it cool as I waited for his response.

"Helping me come up with a plan was always going to be a losing battle."

I swallowed and took another cracker from the sleeve. "But you said you aren't going back to Denver. You must have some idea of what you want to do next."

He shrugged. "I've reached out to a few people I know. I'm sure I'll find some gig for the summer."

The summer. He didn't have anything lined up yet. Even though I found little comfort in that, it made me feel better to know that hopefully he wasn't traipsing out of here the second his last snowboarding lesson ended. I should come right out and ask him.

"How many more lessons do you have left?" I asked.

"Why? Trying to book one more for yourself?" he teased, poking me in the ribs.

"No," I said, feeling slightly frustrated he turned every attempt at conversation into a joke. Typically, I liked that quality about him. But the fact that I couldn't even broach the subject of him leaving, or figure out where we stood, was starting to get annoying.

At this point, it was obvious to me that this was Oliver's coping mechanism. He avoided the hard stuff by constantly being the fun, chill guy. I knew he wouldn't change—not for me anyway. But some of the topics I thought were light, he still chose to avoid.

"I'll squeeze you in if you want. I promise, no more injured wrists," he continued.

"I'm good," I said.

His face fell as he noticed my annoyance. "Everything okay?" Oliver asked. His voice sounded completely different when he wasn't joking. Deeper.

"Yep." I forced a smile.

"Frankie." He tipped my chin up so that I'd be forced to look at him.

It was almost as if we were on the brink of something incredible, yet if I said even remotely the wrong thing, he'd never speak to me again.

Oliver's eyes scanned mine and his jaw clenched. "Talk to me," he whispered.

"Are you sure you want that?" I asked quietly.

That seemed to catch him off guard because he loosened his hold on my chin.

I half expected him to say that he *did* want that. To beg me to talk to him. To say something real and ask me what's going on. But Oliver being Oliver, he did none of that.

"I'm sorry," he said, his tone pained.

Suddenly, the tiles of his kitchen floor were the most fascinating thing in the world to me. My head felt heavy and the idea of meeting his eyes twisted my insides.

Oliver's fingers brushed underneath my chin. He used the tiniest bit of force to tilt my face up. While his eyes still looked dark and serious, the corner of his mouth twitched. "You can't even look at me now? Damn. I must have really messed up."

"You didn't mess up," I said.

"The fact that I can't even imagine you smiling right now

says otherwise. You're looking at me like I'm a huge disappointment, and I can't take that."

"I just…" I started before biting my lip.

Oliver moved his hand from my chin to cup my cheek. "Go on."

"I never know what to say to you. You're like my favorite person I've met since moving here. My life is completely falling apart right now, and you're the one thing keeping me from crumbling." I trembled as I continued to talk. "But I don't feel like I can say that to you. And I don't feel like I can ask you any questions about yourself or tell you anything real because you might bolt again. And I'm terrified that winter is ending, and I have no idea what that means for you. Are you leaving Key Ridge? Are you even planning on saying goodbye? But then I feel like an obsessive creep for even caring that much. I should be cool and say *see you when I see you*. Or stay in touch. But I'm not the cool girl. I'm the girl that obsesses. And right now, the idea of you leaving is all I can think about. I don't want to ruin tonight, but I can't fake some small talk or joke around with you, because it hurts too much not to know."

Oliver's hand didn't drop from my cheek like I was worried it would. Instead, his grip tightened as his fingers moved to wrap around my neck and his thumb remained on my cheek.

"You *can* talk to me, Frankie. I'm sorry I made you feel like you can't." He closed his eyes and sucked in a sharp breath. "I'm…" His words trailed off before he groaned and tipped his head back, letting out a bitter laugh in the process. "Fuck. I'm so bad at this. But you already knew that."

"I don't care if you're bad at it," I said, inching closer to him. "We don't have to have these serious, deep conversations where we dissect your past." Even as I said the words, I knew desperately that I did in fact want to do just that. "I want to know if you're leaving when the ski hill closes and your lessons are over," I finished.

There. That was a start. With Oliver, we had to start small. And small meant figuring out how soon I had to say goodbye to him. Whatever happened, I wanted to be prepared. I had grown attached to seeing him at Marie's and to our little rituals. I had become addicted to his soft kisses and the way he looked in his snowboarding jacket. Theoretically, he was a fling and this phase of my life was fleeting. But regardless, I still needed to know just how fleeting it was. I needed to prepare myself. This goodbye was going to be a lot harder than I wanted to let myself believe.

"I don't know."

His words flattened the optimistic anticipation blooming in my chest.

As if noticing my crestfallen face, Oliver gave a small shake of his head. "I've been trying nonstop to think about what's next for me." He sighed and dropped his hands from my face. "But nothing feels right. None of it feels like what I want to do."

"You just got here. Maybe you haven't stayed in Key Ridge long enough to figure out what you want your next move to be." The hopefulness in my voice made me want to puke. I wasn't the romantic in the family. That was reserved for Mattie. Right now, though, I wanted to say anything and everything that would get Oliver to consider staying. Just for a little while longer. We'd barely had any time together in the grand scheme of life.

"I don't know what I'm doing next," he finally said. "I don't know if I'm leaving… But I don't want to. Not yet."

The last words reignited the hope within me, but I didn't dare look too excited.

"Good," I said simply.

That got him to shake his head and let out a low chuckle. "That's all you have to say?"

I shrugged and put my best "unaffected look" on my face. "I think you should stay. No point in leaving if you haven't figured out what you want next. And no better person to help you figure that out than someone who obsessively plans for her future." I waved to myself.

Before I could continue on my tirade, Oliver slipped his hand around the back of my neck and pulled my face to his, kissing me. His smell always overwhelmed me anytime he was this close. I wasn't sure when I would get used to him. Butterflies still fluttered every time he touched me, and it didn't look like that would be going away any time soon.

When he pulled away after a minute, I licked my lips breathlessly. He stayed, his face hovering close to mine. He tugged a piece of hair that framed my face and shook his head.

"It's okay to just say you'll miss me, you know," he said.

I let out a surprised laugh, and he rewarded me with another kiss before pulling back.

"Don't flatter yourself," I said, not wanting to admit to myself how much truth there was in his words. I nervously leaned away from him and started to eat the crackers he'd produced from the cabinet a minute ago. "You know this is a sad excuse for a snack, right?" I held it up in disapproval.

Oliver smiled. "I don't like to keep a lot of snacks around. I'll eat them all."

No wonder he was always eating dinner at Marie's.

"The point of having snacks is to eat them, silly." I poked him in the chest, and he kissed my forehead. Just like that, the seriousness of our conversation had evaporated.

"I have to stay in shape."

"I think the insane amount of snowboarding you do has

got you covered in that department." I prodded his abs, which were rock solid.

"Hey!" He squirmed away from me.

"Don't tell me you're ticklish," I said, reaching out and pinching his side.

He swatted my hand away, laughing, before jumping toward me and tickling my sides. A squeal escaped me as I writhed on the countertop, but Oliver didn't relent.

"I give. I give," I choked out, and he finally stepped back, still hovering above me.

There was a palpable change between us as Oliver stared at me, our faces only inches apart. Everything was charged and something deep in my gut flipped.

"You're so fucking cute," he whispered while I caught my breath. I was sure my face was completely beet red at this point.

His eyes studied mine before he dipped his head and kissed me.

I lingered, savoring every second of this. I'd never been kissed the way Oliver kissed me. Both with the comfort of familiarity, as if we'd known each other for years, and the electric thrill that only came with someone new. He always touched my face and I liked how connected it made me feel to him. I craved it.

Leaning my whole body into him while still balancing on the countertop, I deepened the kiss. He brought his hand down, letting his arms cage me on either side. All I had to do was scooch a few inches forward and I'd get that contact I so desperately wanted.

When he slipped his tongue into my mouth, I decided to stop denying myself. I grabbed his arms and tugged him toward me at the same time I scooted forward on the counter-top. As soon as we made contact, I moaned into his mouth. I could feel how hard he was for me, and I wanted more. Judging from the way Oliver removed his hands from the counter to wrap them around my waist and bring me closer to him, I wasn't the only one affected by the contact.

I had been thinking about this for weeks. Maybe since I first met Oliver, if I was being honest with myself. I grasped at the bottom of his shirt and started to pull upward, revealing his abs that I wished I could spend all evening tracing.

His hands fell to the top of my ass and he squeezed. I grinded into him, eager to explore this further.

But then, as fast as we started, Oliver pulled away and gave a reluctant shake of his head. "Maybe we should slow down." His voice was gruff, as if he could barely get the words out.

"W-what?" I asked, baffled.

He was practically physically restraining himself from me and I wanted nothing more than to leap from this counter and straddle him. Slowing down was the last thing on my mind.

He dragged a hand down his face, looking completely tortured. "Because I like you," he said in a pained manner.

I snorted, those being the last words I expected to come out of his mouth right now. "Um. Yeah, that's usually a catalyst to moments like these, not a deterrent."

"Damn it," he hissed, frustration written all over his face. "It's just—I just… Fuck." He balled his fists and rubbed them against his eyes before pacing the small kitchen.

His reaction sobered my desires slightly. Rejection from Oliver had been the last thing I expected and it was hitting me hard. Sure, the date might have ended messy, but I thought we'd come to the conclusion that we wanted each other. He'd been giving me all the signals. Even now, I had no idea what the hell was going on. How could he say he liked me and then back away in the same moment?

I slid off the counter, unsure of what to do. "Should I go?" I asked, praying he'd say no.

That snapped him out of his daze. He stopped pacing, crossed back to me, and stood in front of me, taking my hands in his. "No, God, please. Don't go. That's the last thing I want."

"You're being confusing as hell right now."

"I know," he groaned.

"What's going on?" I asked softly. "Why are you pulling away right now?"

"I—I don't know. I've never done this before."

"Had sex?" I arched an eyebrow, knowing for a fact that was completely false.

"No. Not that." His eyes searched mine. "After tonight, I've shared more with you than I've shared with any other girl. I've-I've never had a real relationship. At the risk of sounding like a total loser, I've never done this with a girl I like as much as you. It feels…heavy."

His admittance sucked the air right out of my lungs.

"Heavy," I repeated.

"That sounds so fucking stupid," he grunted. "Shit. I should have kept my mouth shut."

I thought about all the times Oliver had taken a serious moment and turned it into a joke, or when we'd try to have a deeper conversation and he'd brush it off. He never seemed to feel anything beyond the surface. Somehow, even sex with me had become another extension of that.

Maybe I should have felt insulted by his hesitation to take the next step with me, or maybe I should have been worried that the moment it was over, he'd ghost me and become nothing more than a memory. But I couldn't bring myself to feel either of those things. Instead, I felt oddly privileged—

thrilled, even, that somehow, I'd gotten under his skin in a way no one else ever had.

I thought carefully about what to say next.

"I've never liked someone as much as you either," I admitted, realizing in real time that it was the truth. I'd never been excited about anyone like this before. The way he made me feel should be studied.

Instead of backing away, his gaze hardened into one of determination. "I don't want to mess anything up." He brought a hand to my cheek and traced a circle.

"Life is messy. We already established, we're messy. And that's okay," I said.

He laughed. "I never thought you'd be okay with a mess."

I put my arms around his waist, giving him a squeeze. "We don't know what's going to happen next," I murmured. "But what I do know is that I'm going to combust if you don't touch me right now."

That was all it took for his mouth to descend on mine.

This time, I could feel the difference. Any hesitation had evaporated. Instead, there was pure resolve.

He grabbed me by my ass and hoisted me up, back onto the counter. I wrapped my legs around him, impatient to finish what we'd started. As our mouths continued to move together, my body grinded against his, securing him to me. He brought a hand to the edge of my shirt, sliding it up. The feel of his warm hand against my bare skin made me gasp on contact.

The fact that he'd shared something so personal with me only made my desire for him stronger. I couldn't believe that he saw it as a weakness. To me, it made him seem real. And realness was something I had been sorely missing in my life.

I felt his smile against my mouth as he carefully traced his hand up my stomach, sliding it along the underwire of my bra before cupping one of my breasts. The relief at feeling his touch on me was both decadent and short-lived. Each little bit of progress made me want more of him.

I arched my back and he took that as an invitation to yank my shirt over my head. I followed suit and pulled his shirt up. He pulled away briefly to tug it over his head before returning his touch to my body. He broke the kiss to examine me for a moment. Him drinking me in like I was precious made me simmer under his gaze.

"Fucking perfect," he muttered, lightly grasping the edge of my bra and tugging it down to free one of my nipples.

I sucked in a breath, before he brought his lips back down to mine. As soon as he pinched my nipple, twirling it between his fingers, my eyes rolled back into my head from the pleasure.

After weeks of imagining what it would be like to finally cross that line with Oliver, to feel his touch on me without him holding back—I felt utterly undone. His touch wasn't enough. I wanted his mouth on me. I wanted *all* of him on me.

He pulled the straps of my bra down and yanked the whole thing so it now sat around my waist, leaving me bare for the taking.

And damn it, I wanted to be taken.

He pulled back to examine me again, gave a little smirk, and then dipped his head, taking one of my hard nipples into his mouth.

I moaned the second I felt his tongue and teeth pulling and teasing me. I'd never understood the sentiment that someone could pass out from pleasure, but that's about where I was currently at right now. And he hadn't even taken my pants off yet.

The thought suddenly sent a hot pulse wave through me

and I grinded against him as he flicked my nipple with his tongue before giving the other one some attention.

He had me—completely had me. I was ready to melt into a puddle right then and there, and I wouldn't even know what it felt like for him to move inside me.

I ran my shaky hand down along his abs until I reached the top of his pants and undid the button. When I fumbled with the zipper, he took over, wrenching them down easily with one swift tug, and kicking them off. I pressed my hand against the hard bulge in his boxers and was rewarded with the tiniest of bites on my breast before he pulled away and moved to my neck. He brushed his lips against my throat and then my jaw before planting a kiss on my mouth. It was both frenzied and intimate. He wasn't being rough with me, but the need was clearly there for both of us.

"I can't believe you're real," he said breathlessly, before taking one of his strong hands and stretching my leggings away from my body. I gasped as he dipped his hand below my waistband and slid a finger along me, hitting the exact spot I so desperately needed him to touch. I moved against him, driven purely by instinct at this point. He slid a finger inside me, stretching me slightly before slipping another in.

I moaned, my lips slack against his mouth as my breathing increased.

He pumped them in and out, slowly at first, but then picking up speed. I was fully convinced my body had never felt this turned on in my entire life. I was so freaking attracted to him I couldn't even contain myself. My body started to go slack as Oliver's fingers worked inside me. A feeling bloomed inside of me, growing so intense I could barely take it any longer.

"Bed," he said.

"No," I panted.

His face scrunched up in confusion and his fingers stopped moving inside me. I nearly let out a groan of protest.

"Don't stop," I whimpered.

He grinned. "I'm not taking you on a kitchen countertop, Frankie. At least not for the first time."

My insides coiled at the thought of this being a repeat occurrence.

He removed his hand from my pants. Before I could protest again, he hoisted me off the counter, my legs wrapped around his bare torso and he took a few long strides to the bed before sprawling me out on it. He fell on top of me, using his arms to pin me in and keep his weight off of me. I greedily grabbed onto the back of his neck. My entire body writhed, dying to feel him against me.

I tugged at his boxers and he chuckled.

"Take these off," I demanded when I couldn't reach my arms farther down his legs.

"Yes, ma'am," he said, pulling off his boxers and letting his full length spring free.

"And these." I pulled at my own pants before he grabbed the waistband and tugged. His biceps bulged as he ripped off my leggings in one quick motion. Now he hovered above me, both of us completely naked.

My core pulsed with need as I took in Oliver balancing above me.

"You sure about this?" he asked, his tone serious.

I traced one of his pecs, relishing the pure bliss of the moment. Nothing could beat this—the way my body hummed in the anticipation of our first time.

Oliver had been right. This *did* feel heavy.

"Oliver, I have wanted you to jump my bones since basically the first time I met you," I whispered.

He kissed my forehead before leaning up and reaching for something on his bedside table.

His fingers moved back to my slick center and he slipped his fingers in again, priming me for him. With his teeth, he ripped open a condom and rolled it over his length with his other hand.

He moved back above me.

He wasn't even inside me yet, and I was already consumed by him. His scent. His being. His everything. It had never been like this for me. Eagerly, I guided him to my entrance, treasuring every millisecond before I finally got to feel him move inside me. His tip slowly pressed into me, easing in inch by inch until he was inside me completely. My body welcomed him. Everything inside me went off like an explosion. He let out a raw, guttural moan the first time he rocked back and forth. My hips met his and the timing was delicious.

"Fuck, you feel amazing," he grunted as he slowly moved in and out of me, almost teasing me with his cock.

I met his movements with more desperation, forcing him to pick up his tempo.

The mixture of him inside me and my clit rubbing against his base had my impending orgasm flowering quickly. Maybe I should have been trying to savor this, but I couldn't stop. Instead, I arched my body up, increasing the friction between us.

He kissed me deeply, as if he was trying to burrow inside of me. I couldn't focus on one thing. The building pressure as he moved inside me. How passionate his kisses were. How my heart was about to beat out of my chest. I'd never felt this alive. Not ever. Oliver was bringing me to life when I hadn't even realized I was dead.

He thrust, deeper than I thought possible. I moaned

loudly as my nails dug into his back. We were both chasing relief.

"I don't want to come too soon," he said breathlessly, stealing a kiss, but not slowing his movements.

"I'm right there too," I barely managed to pant out.

A few more beautifully synced thrusts and we both toppled over the edge, limbs tangled in one another's.

I laid there, unable to move as he pulled out and flopped onto the bed next to me. I was floating, coming down from the high.

That was hands down the best sex of my life.

For a second, I wondered if this would be weird. Would Oliver bolt? Would he act strange toward me after all this build up in his mind?

But instead, he leaned over and planted a kiss on my forehead, then one to my lips. "I promise I'll last longer next time." He looked down at me like I was something special—like I was his.

"Me too," I breathed, tilting my head up and kissing him again.

"I like you so freaking much," he said with a huge grin, before rolling over to spoon me, my head laid against his shoulder.

It wasn't weird. Not even a little. It was perfect.

And that's what scared me the most.

EIGHTEEN

Frankie

My entire body shuddered as soon as I took a sip of the spiked hot chocolate. I clutched my to-go cup with both hands, the sleeves of my sweatshirt pulled up all the way to my fingertips.

"This is perfect," I said.

"How can you even drink that? It's too warm. I'm sweating." Mattie fanned herself as we walked carefully along the bottom of the ski hill. All of the snow had either melted or turned to slush at this point.

She had a point about the sweating. It was only forty-something degrees, but the sun beat down with a relentless intensity. I'd left my jacket inside where Mattie and I had secured a table. It was finally closing day, which everyone had neglected to inform me was basically a giant party.

"Remind me again what we're out here to watch?" I asked as I stepped over a particularly large puddle.

"The closing competition. It's for fun. All the workers pile up the snow at the bottom of the main run and make a little terrain park. They all take turns going down it and showing off. See? They're lining up over there." Mattie pointed to the base of the ski hill where a few young guys were shirtless, wearing only bathing suit bottoms and snowboard boots.

"Um. Why are they half naked?" I asked.

"Everyone wears crazy outfits. Today is just a big excuse to party. There's live music and food trucks."

"Any good bands?" I asked.

"A few smaller ones, and then The Wedding Band is playing later tonight."

"Oh, I love them," I said as Mattie linked her arm through mine and pulled me toward an area where spectators had started to gather.

I hadn't been back here since my failed attempt at snowboarding, despite Oliver begging me to give it one last try a few nights ago when I was staying over at his place. After a while, I had jokingly suggested that maybe next year, I'd give it another go. But as soon as I said it, Oliver's smile faltered. I'd meant it to be lighthearted, but the unspoken thought that crossed both our minds was impossible to ignore.

By next year, we'd likely be strangers.

"Do you see the guys?" I asked, turning to search for Oliver.

"They're probably taking practice runs or waiting at the top," Mattie said, squinting to catch sight of her husband.

We positioned ourselves toward the side of the crowd, where we had a clear visual of the course. There were a few jumps, some bars placed into the side of the snowy hill, and a few other obstacles. I tried to imagine Oliver snowboarding down. I knew he must be pretty good, but I still couldn't picture him doing all this.

There were a few snowboarders and skiers at the top of the hill. I squinted to see if I could make him out. Before I could distinguish any faces, a strong arm wrapped around my waist and I squealed on instinct. I'd recognize the feel of him anywhere.

"Oliver!" I swatted his chest, but he still had me pinned against him.

"Hi." He grinned down at me before kissing me.

My whole body warmed at his touch. Typically, I had never been one for public displays of affection. But Oliver grabbing and kissing me, without a care in the world, had an excited bubble forming in my chest that was threatening to burst.

Oliver wore a tie-dye T-shirt and black sweatpants. Something about the way his shirt strained against his bare biceps while he still had on mittens, a helmet, and snowboarding boots really did it for me.

"Nice outfit," I said.

"Wore it just for you," he replied with a wink.

"Have you seen Giles?" Mattie asked.

Oliver pointed in the direction of the hill. "He's already up top helping everyone get organized. I think we're supposed to be starting soon." He slung his arm across my shoulders and pulled me into his side as he spoke. Mattie raised an eyebrow as she took in the easy gesture.

"Shouldn't you be up there?" I asked.

"Heading up now." Oliver grinned before giving me one last squeeze and backing away. He saluted with one hand and carried his board with the other. "Wish me luck."

"Good luck!" we both called.

As Oliver disappeared into the crowd, I looked back to my sister.

"I'd yell break a leg, but that feels too on the nose for this," I said.

Mattie didn't say anything but she studied my face, clearly chewing on a thought or two.

"What?" I sighed, meeting her gaze.

She tilted her head, looking like a detective searching for clues.

"*What?*" I repeated when she continued to stare and not say anything.

"You and Oliver are really…close."

"Obviously." I rolled my eyes.

"You've spent the night there almost every night this week," she pointed out as if I didn't already know where I'd been spending my time.

"Your point?"

"I'm surprised is all."

My eyes scanned the hill, waiting to see Oliver pop up at the top in his bright shirt. "You were the one who encouraged me to have a fling," I said, glancing back at her.

She shrugged, biting her bottom lip. "I don't know. It feels like more than that. You two spend every spare minute together. And now you're sleeping together."

"Mattie," I scolded. "Not so loud." I jerked my head around but no one was looking at us or cared the slightest about our conversation. In fact, the crowd was getting quite rowdy at this point.

"Are you sure it's just a fling?" she pressed, as we both watched the first snowboarder take their place at the top of the course. I could see Giles and Oliver now, standing off to the side, waiting.

"Of course. What do you mean?" I asked.

"It's just…I've never seen you like this with a guy."

"That's because I've hardly dated," I pointed out.

"You've never really shown interest before," she agreed. "But you seem interested now."

My jaw clenched. Of course, my hopeless romantic of a sister was reading too much into the situation with Oliver. And it wasn't like I was blind to what he was doing to me. Every night, as I fell asleep wrapped in his arms, it became harder and harder to imagine letting him go. But that didn't make things between us any less temporary. We were never meant to be. He was destined for a life like this, while I was supposed to be climbing the corporate ladder in some big city. Lately, though, it was getting harder to remember that version of my future.

Oliver and I were choosing to ignore our imminent ending. For now, we were both here, and we might as well make the most of it. I still wasn't much closer to landing a job. I'd faced a few more rejections, but recently, I'd also had a couple of promising interviews that gave me at least a little hope. I had started to think that maybe fate was playing a role in all of my rejections. And even though Oliver's season as a snowboard instructor had ended, he hadn't mentioned leaving yet. He hadn't said the words outright, but I was almost certain he planned to stick around Key Ridge. At least for a little longer.

"Look, Mattie. I do like him," I said. "He's exciting to be around. I enjoy his company. But that's it. I'm leaving soon, and he probably is too. We're like two ships passing in the night."

"Really? Because to me it seems like your ships are docked in the harbor and about to settle in." She had the nerve to wink at me. "You've been obsessing about your career less and less. I've barely heard you talk about interviews all week. Do you even really want another corporate job anymore?"

"Of course I do!" My mouth fell open before I snapped it shut.

Cheers from the crowd interrupted us as the first snowboarder launched himself onto the course, hitting a jump and lifting the tip of his board.

I raised my voice to combat the noise. "I'm really excited about that position I just interviewed for in New York. It's perfect for me." I was referring to the phone screening I'd had earlier this week. The company was in demand, and I knew there would be stiff competition, but it was the first role I'd interviewed for since I got here that actually seemed like a solid move.

"Is it perfect? Or is it just available?"

Her disbelief irritated me. "It's a level up from where I was before. It's a pay raise. And I'd get to live in New York freaking City. It's a dream."

Mattie chewed on her bottom lip. I could see the flash of disappointment in her eyes. She'd always been the one that dreamed of a fairy tale ending—the one where the girl rode off into the sunset with Prince Charming. I'd been the one who dreamed of a career—of moving up the corporate ladder. I wanted the first word that people thought of when they met me to be *successful* or *ambitious*.

Mattie would give anything to see my love story unfold before her eyes. She wanted me to settle down with someone, like she had. She imagined a future where our families lived nearby, or at the very least, shared an annual tradition of taking trips together. But that wasn't the life I envisioned for myself. Marriage was never something I'd considered, let alone dreamed about.

"You're right, sorry. It sounds like an amazing opportunity," she finally said.

"It is," I insisted, ignoring the pit that had started to hollow itself inside my stomach.

"Oh look, it's Giles about to drop in." She pointed excitedly as her husband pushed forward onto the course. The whole crowd erupted in cheers. He was a bit of a town celebrity given the fact that he'd done this professionally for so many years before moving back.

Giles hit the first jump and threw a back flip like it was nothing. He landed and grinded along a pipe with ease before popping off. The crowd whistled their approval.

"Damn!" I nudged Mattie. "Did you know your husband was this good?"

She shot me a smile before turning back toward the mountain, beaming as she watched him. "Go Giles!"

I joined in her cheering as he made quick, effortless work of the rest of the course. When he got to the bottom, he stopped, spraying the slushy snow.

Mattie and I clapped and cheered along with everyone else. He unstrapped and walked over to us, tugging the bandana that covered his face down so he could walk straight to Mattie and kiss her.

"Nice one," she said, beaming up at him.

"Love you," he said back, pressing his forehead to hers.

Something inside me splintered a little watching them together. That was a new feeling. I typically loved being a fly on the wall, able to witness how absurdly in love these two were. But something about watching them now made me feel a little despondent.

"Oliver's going." Mattie caught my attention and tilted her head to the course.

I lifted my gaze to watch as Oliver waved at the crowd, lifting his arms a few times in order to pump everyone up. It worked. He tipped his board forward and dropped into the course.

He hit the first jump and my jaw nearly hit the floor when he spun in a full three-hundred-sixty-degree turn. The crowd ate it up as he moved onto one of the rails. He landed on it, but jumped off halfway, getting air and grabbing the edge of his board in the process.

"Shit, I didn't know he was that good," I hissed, looking on with awe as Oliver executed yet another trick.

When he made it to the bottom, he stopped even closer to the crowd than Giles had, spraying them with snow in the process. Instead of being annoyed, everyone cheered even louder.

He took off his board and lifted it in the air, pumping his arms a few times.

Mattie and I screamed in support as he sauntered over to us.

"Nice one, Ollie. You killed that," Giles said, holding out his fist for Oliver to bump.

"Seriously," I added. "I had no idea you could do that."

"You thought my skills were limited to what you saw those two hours we spent on the bunny hill together?" he teased, setting his board down on the snow and pulling me into his side. I loved that about him. So quick to always tether himself to me whenever we were in each other's vicinity. It made me feel wanted in ways I'd never felt before. More than just physically or sexually. Wanted in every way.

"No. I just didn't know you could do all that." I gestured to the course, where a skier was now taking a turn hitting the obstacles. "You really undersold your skills."

He chuckled and ran a hand through his tussled hair. "I didn't undersell anything. You're just not easily impressed."

"False. I was very easily impressed just now."

He smirked. "That's because the tricks I did weren't easy at all."

I shrugged and pretended to be blasé. "I mean, they were okay. Not as good as Giles but—"

A squeal escaped me as Oliver tickled my sides.

"You done talking shit?" he teased, but I couldn't even respond due to being breathless from laughter.

"You could have gone pro if you wanted to," Giles chimed in.

"I don't have the commitment," Oliver joked.

My smile faded a little at his words. Mattie clocked it immediately and tilted her head. We shared a look, but I brushed it off and returned my attention to Oliver.

It didn't matter if he couldn't commit to anything. I didn't need him to. This was only temporary and I was absolutely and completely fine with that.

***

"I can't," I insisted, shaking my head at a very excited-looking Oliver.

"You have to." He pulled on my hand and forced me to take hold of the end of the ski.

"This is going to go all over my face," I insisted, looking down at the shot glass glued to an old ski.

"It's tradition," Oliver said.

"Is it?" I looked at Mattie skeptically, but she was already holding on to the middle of the ski and shrugging her shoulders in defeat.

"I mean, people do them all the time," she admitted.

"Have you?"

Giles chuckled. "Your sister has lived here almost three years now and has never done a shotski."

"Leave it to Oliver to convince her," I mumbled, begrudgingly taking the ski.

Oliver's smile was too big to turn down. It was like telling the cutest puppy in the world that you weren't going to take them for a walk.

"Alright," Oliver called, sliding in next to me. "Pour it."

The bartender came around from behind the bar and poured a clear liquid into the glasses that I hoped was tequila, but feared was vodka.

Oliver and Giles stood at either end of the ski and crouched down so that they wouldn't tower over Mattie and me as the bartender counted down from three.

"Three, two, one," she called.

We all tipped the ski toward our mouths. The shot glass made contact with my lips, and I held my breath as I downed whatever it was. Thankfully, the pleasant taste of peppermint infiltrated my senses, and warmth flooded my chest.

"Again?" Oliver asked.

"No!" I called over the loud music.

The chairlifts had shut down, and Key Ridge Ski Resort was officially closed for the season. The crowd, and anyone skiing or boarding today, had migrated from the mountain to the party at the base of the hill. Live music blared through the speakers. We'd stayed by the stage to watch the band for a little, but the crowd had gotten too large. Even though the sun had dipped behind the mountain and there was now a definite chill in the air, people remained outside, not caring in the slightest. I suspected the layer of liquor and beer most people were wearing had something to do with it.

Oliver spun me around, pulling me toward him to dance when the band started to play a more upbeat song. I tried to remember the last time I'd had this much fun and came up completely short.

He leaned down to whisper in my ear. "You look beautiful."

My cheeks instantly flushed and I shook my head on instinct. "I look like a mess," I corrected, knowing my nose was red from the sun and my hair was starting to frizz.

"A beautiful mess," he said, before stealing a quick kiss.

My heart leapt into my throat in a sensation that could only be described as giddy.

"Get a room, you two," Mattie called, tucking her way through a group of people and joining us.

"Not a bad idea." Oliver winked down at me.

My phone vibrated in my pocket. When I pulled it out, I instantly recognized the New York area code.

"I have to take this." I barely got the words out before I was pushing past people, trying to get far away from the music so I could hear the phone call. Maybe I should let it go to voicemail. I was likely a little too buzzed to be taking a professional call right now, but I was anticipating this news way too much to not take it.

Once I was through the crowd, I sprinted for a few seconds until the loud bass of the music was just background noise. Finally, I pressed the green answer button.

"Hello, this is Frankie," I panted, before covering the speaker by my mouth and taking a few deep breaths to steady my voice.

"Frankie? This is Neil, the hiring manager for the Director of Marketing position at Weilman and Partners."

My heart went into overdrive.

"Yes, of course," I said. "How are you?"

Footsteps sounded behind me, and I whipped around to see a concerned-looking Oliver racing after me. I held my hand up to my lips and he halted, tilting his head and raising an eyebrow.

"I'm great. Listen, I really enjoyed our interview the other day, and I'd love for you to move on in the process."

Before he even finished the words, I started jumping in the air and pumping my fist in a silent celebration. A grin and an even more confused expression appeared on Oliver's face.

"That would be amazing, Neil. I'm really excited about this position."

"Perfect. Listen, I can't say too much because it's so early, but I think you'd be a great fit. You've got the exact experience we're looking for, and it's clear from talking with you that you know what initiative and hard work entails."

"I definitely do," I assured him.

"I want to be completely transparent; our hiring process is a bit extensive. We have a few interviews with the team, then an interview with executives, and a final case study presentation. We're hoping to complete the process and make an offer in four to six weeks. I know that's lengthy, but we've found it results in the best retention."

"That timeline works for me," I said, although if I was being honest, I would have said nearly any timeline worked for me. I was past the point of desperation.

"Great. I'll email you with the schedules early next week and you can select your next interview times."

"Sounds good. Thank you."

"Thanks, Frankie. I've got a good feeling about this. I'm excited for you to meet the rest of the team."

I said goodbye and hung up before reaching out and grabbing Oliver's arms. I shook them and let out an excited squeal.

His smile widened, but it didn't quite reach his eyes. "What was that all about?" he asked.

"I nailed my last interview and I just found out I'm moving along in the process. And this job is, like, perfect. More than I thought I'd ever find. It was starting to feel hopeless. I thought I might have to take an entry level somewhere or something."

"That's great," he said, tugging me toward him and giving me a hug. "Congrats, Frankie." He said the words into the top of my head.

I buried my face in his chest and lost myself for a second in how good his arms felt encircling me. When he pulled away, I stared up at him, memorizing the way the skin around his brown eyes crinkled and the way the corners of his lips always curled up.

Looking into Oliver's eyes had me falling from cloud nine where I'd just been floating. On the surface, he looked happy for me. But I knew better now. There was way more to Oliver than just the surface.

"So you like got the job or…" His words trailed off as he waited for clarification.

"No, nothing like that. Sorry, I just got excited." My voice wavered. "I still have more interviews to get through."

"It'll take a while?" Oliver confirmed, carefully brushing my cheek.

"Four to six weeks," I clarified.

He paused, his eyes scanning my face. "You'll be here at least another month?"

His words tugged at my heart. "I mean, there's no guarantee I get this job. It's so competitive and—"

"At least another month," he repeated, his eyes darkening.

"At least," I said, feeling deflated it wasn't longer. I should be glowing at the thought of landing that job, but leaving Key Ridge was the last thing I wanted to think about right now. "What about you?" I asked quietly. "The season is over and—"

"I'll be here if you are," he said, tucking a piece of hair behind my ear. The force of his gaze made me shiver, but as abruptly as it had arrived, it vanished. He threw on an easygoing smile again. "I'm going to hang around the lodge a little longer. Giles said there might be something for me to do. An old friend called me yesterday. He said I could work for him as a rafting guide this summer, but that doesn't start until June."

Even though I had every intention of getting this job and not being here come June, hearing him say it out loud hollowed out my chest. Like all of my energy was being removed all at once with an excavator.

"That's awesome." I tried to sound cheery, but the way Oliver dipped his chin to assess me told me I was likely failing.

"Is it?" he asked.

"Yep. I mean, it isn't a permanent plan or anything, but maybe you're meant to wander. Maybe that's what this season of your life is for."

I wished I could tell him to wander on over to New York, or wherever I'd end up, but I knew that was a ridiculous notion. We'd hardly started something. Plus, a guy like Oliver —all adventure and rugged and outdoorsy—being in a big city like New York? I couldn't picture it at all.

"Permanent isn't really my thing," he joked.

I laughed off his comment as we headed back to the party.

Despite the fact that I should've been celebrating the news of landing another interview, all I could focus on were his words. They weren't anything new, but twice tonight, he'd emphasized how he didn't do commitment or permanence.

I knew it made absolutely zero sense, but I found myself starting to wish that I could be his exception.

NINETEEN

Oliver

"You're thinking about staying?" my best friend, Harrison, asked through the phone.

"For a little while longer," I said.

"You were all excited about having one hundred adventures or something ridiculous like that. You're going to slow down after your first one?" His voice was gruff. I knew for a fact Harrison hated phone calls, but unfortunately for him, he was my best friend and I was a yapper. I couldn't go more than a week without calling him.

"I don't think I said *one hundred*. Besides, I've only been here a month. That's hardly any time."

"I'm surprised, I guess. You went there for the lessons, but I thought you were excited to move on after."

"I'm having fun here," I insisted. Even as I said it, the irony hit me that all I was doing tonight was sitting on my couch and eating a slice of pizza. Frankie wasn't working at Marie's tonight, so I didn't have to suffer through another dinner there.

I'd tried convincing her to come hang out with me tonight,

but she was too stressed about the job in New York. Her second interview was in the morning and she had been preparing for it nonstop.

Her commitment to getting a job far away from here didn't exactly thrill me, but who was I to say anything about that? I was, what? A fling to her? It was obvious we liked each other, but our lives weren't even close to heading in the same direction. Even though it sucked, there was no point in dwelling on it. So I chose to do what I normally did—ignore our inevitable ending and live in the moment. I refused to think about her leaving. Not yet, anyway.

There was a long pause on the other end of the line.

"Did you meet someone?" he asked.

"No," I said too quickly. How the hell could he read my mind like that?

There was a loud squeal from the background and his girlfriend Lila's voice took over. "Ollie, you met someone?"

Amusement stirred within me hearing the excitement in her tone. She was the complete opposite of my gruff, burly best friend. In fact, she was a hell of a lot more similar to me. I loved them together. They were two of my favorite people.

"Nope." I popped the p when I said it, which apparently didn't make it sound very convincing.

"Are you sure? Sticking around isn't like you," Harrison pressed.

"Come on, tell us," Lila begged. "We tell you everything. You were the first person to know when we got together."

"You sure you didn't tell Charlie first?" I teased, knowing that Lila would have told her best friend, who was also my sister-in-law, first.

"Well…" She paused. "Harrison is basically your Charlie. So you should tell us."

That made me laugh.

"Then why do you want to stay if it isn't that?" Harrison asked instead.

"I don't feel ready yet," I insisted.

"There's a girl. There's totally a girl," Lila repeated.

There *was* a girl. A girl I didn't quite know what to do about. But if I told Lila, hopeless romantic that she was, she'd insist we were meant to be and that fate had brought us together. She wouldn't see that logically, Frankie and I weren't compatible in the slightest.

"Hey." I decided a change of subject would be best at this point. "Since I'm not leaving yet, you two should come out for a camping trip."

"Yes!" Lila squealed at the same time as Harrison groaned, "Camping?"

We chatted for a while longer, ironing out the details of when they'd visit before I finally hung up. I checked the rest of the notifications on my phone. My brother, Nathan, had texted me, and I had a couple missed calls from my mom. I really didn't want to talk to her right now. Sighing, I cleared the notifications and pulled up my message thread with Frankie instead.

Oliver: Wish you were here.

Frankie: Stop distracting me.

Oliver: You should come over here for a bit. I'll help you practice your interview questions.

Frankie: Somehow, I doubt you actually will.

Oliver: Or I can at least help you decompress.

> Frankie: I'll come to you for decompressing
> after I nail this tomorrow.

> Oliver: Pleeasseee come over.

> Frankie: You're a bad influence. Turning my
> phone off now.

I STOOD FROM MY COUCH AND STARTED TO PACE. LESSONS HAD just ended and I was already bored.

Without thinking, I headed out the door to my apartment, walked the short walkway to the lodge, and stepped inside the lobby.

To my relief, Bev and Giles were both there, leaning against the front desk and chatting.

"Ollie." Giles lifted a hand in greeting as I joined them.

"What are you doing here?" Bev asked.

I shrugged. "Figured I'd come see if you need any help since lessons are over now."

Bev chuckled. "They just ended."

I shrugged. "And I'm already bored."

"Of course you are." She pointed to Marie's. "You can help out at the lounge if you want. It'll be slower now that the ski hill is closed, but the last of the seasonal workers are leaving this week, and I'd personally love to take a break from working there every night."

"You got it, boss," I said.

Giles smirked. "I think the local female clientele will go up when word gets out you're bartending here."

Bev nodded. "Tips'll go up too."

I had no experience bartending, but considering Frankie worked there, I figured I'd be fine. She was still messing up drink orders and getting flustered all these weeks later. It was honestly fucking endearing. I loved watching her during her shifts. And now I'd get a front row seat. Honestly, the only thing I really cared about right now was spending every second I could with her, so this worked out perfectly.

"I'm surprised you aren't gallivanting off to the next mountain town," Bev said.

"I've got a rafting gig lined up in June, but not a lot going on until then. Key Ridge has some awesome mountain biking trails too. I'm excited to check those out now that the snow is almost gone," I said.

"Right." Bev had a glint in her eyes. "I'm sure a certain girl has nothing to do with your desire to stay."

Giles chuckled knowingly and I smiled. "She definitely isn't a detractor."

I was hung up on the girl. What did I care if people knew? She was way out of my league and I'd proudly claim her for as long as I could.

When I'd first left Denver to move to Key Ridge, I had all these ideas for adventures. But for some reason, they didn't excite me like they used to. Sure, rafting sounded fine, but instead of giving it much thought, something else had completely taken ahold of my mind.

Frankie.

She hadn't outright asked me to stay, but it was obviously what she wanted. It almost broke me when I saw the worry in her eyes that I might be leaving before she did. It was like she wanted me to hang around to keep her company while it was convenient but wouldn't let it stop her from taking the first offer she could land.

That didn't make me feel used, though. I kind of understood it. That new job was her dream. And let's face it, I wouldn't want to be in this town without her either.

TWENTY

Frankie

———

"How did it go?" Mattie pounced on me from behind the reception desk as soon as I walked into the lodge for my evening shift at Marie's.

"Okay," I said, straightening my black shirt before tossing my wild mane into a high ponytail.

"Just okay? That's it?" she demanded, following me all the way into Marie's and spilling over the bar as I hurried to clock in.

I glanced up at her. "It went amazing, actually."

The elevens between her eyebrows immediately softened.

I'd crushed my next round with the company in New York. So much so that they said they'd get back to me this evening, rather than in the following days like I'd initially expected. I'd been blindsided by rejections before, but I had a *really* good feeling about this one. I couldn't help but feel like it was mine for the taking. It was about damn time. I'd been on the hunt for nearly a month at this point. I was past due for something to go my way.

"Thank God," Mattie breathed, placing a hand to her

forehead. "Don't scare me like that. You've been a ball of stress preparing for it. I don't think I could have handled you if it didn't go well."

"*Please.* I always have a good attitude," I said, taking clean cups out of the dishwasher tray that had been left behind the bar and stacking them up.

"Right. You had a real winning attitude when you first got here."

I scowled at that. "Hey, my life had just fallen apart."

"I guess." She waved a hand. "So you really think you'll move to New York if you get this?"

"Why not?" I shrugged. "It would be fun to try somewhere new, and it's not like I have all these roots in Atlanta. I can either sell my condo or keep renting it out. Once that's taken care of, I can just get my things, and it's like I was never there."

I hadn't realized how sad that was until the words came out of my mouth. How had I lived there for so many years and had only casual acquaintances at best? The girls I lived with had texted me once since I left just to say what a bummer it was that I was laid off. Oh, and they had asked me if their friend could move in. They direct deposited the rent money and that was it.

Damn. That really was sad.

"I guess it could be fun to visit you in New York," Mattie mused.

"We could see a Broadway play," I said.

"Try every pizza by the slice place there is," she continued.

"Go shopping."

Our eyes both sparkled at the possibilities.

"It would be fun," Mattie sighed, clearly romanticizing it all. "I mean, almost as fun as you staying here."

"And what? Be a bartender-slash-waitress the rest of my life?"

Mattie pursed her lips. "I mean, you *do* seem happier."

I glared at her.

Even though I wanted her to be wrong, she wasn't. I had a glow about me these days. I noticed it every time I passed a mirror. In a lot of ways, this was the least put together I had ever been. My hair was never straightened, my outfits were always casual, and my makeup was hardly done. But those were never the things I noticed lately. Instead, I saw my worn-in smile and the healthy flush that always graced my cheeks. I'd attributed the change to a vacation glow, but it was likely more of an Oliver glow. That boy had me off kilter in the best possible way.

"I *am* happy," I said. I wasn't blind to that fact so there was no use in denying it, but *everyone* was happy on vacation. That didn't mean they should pick up their lives and toss away their dreams to create a new reality.

"You're happy because of Oliver," Mattie said bluntly.

I threw up my hands. "Yes, Oliver is one reason, but so are you. It's been nice spending time with my only sister. And now that I'm finally free of the spell my last company had me under, I can realize how overworked I was. Being here has been the reset I needed."

"And Oliver made you realize that," she added.

"Why are you so obsessed with talking about him?" I asked, my eyes narrowed.

The door chimed and a small group walked in from the front entrance to Marie's. I waved in greeting. "Sit wherever you like. I'll be right with you."

When I turned back to Mattie, she was staring at me thoughtfully. "I'm glad you're finally having some fun. I just hope you don't forget how to have a life once you land this fancy new job."

My skin bristled. Even after all these weeks, it still bothered me when people insinuated I had no life. I didn't care if it was partially true, it raised my defenses all the same.

"I know how to have fun. Oliver isn't *making* me fun," I said. "I've done plenty over the years."

"Uh-huh." Mattie blinked at me.

"I have."

"Sure."

"Ugh!" I let out a frustrated groan. "I have! Remember that time I went to Cancún last year?"

"Wasn't that a work trip?"

"I also joined a book club right before I left Atlanta," I added.

"Were the books nonfiction?" Mattie asked.

I snapped my mouth shut. "So what if they were?"

"I'm just saying, if the book club had the words 'self-betterment' in the description, then it doesn't count as fun."

That shut me up. Because our first book was about how to get ahead in your career as a woman in a male-dominated field.

"Whatever," I muttered.

"Don't get me wrong." Mattie's tone was gentle now, as if I was a toddler she was trying to coax out of a tantrum. "I like Oliver and I'm glad you're having fun with him. I think this is probably the healthiest way you could spend your time right now. I mean, you could spend less time job hunting but—"

"How am I supposed to find another job if I'm not looking?" I interjected. "You've seen how much effort I've put into it and I've only just started making progress."

Mattie was the older sister through and through. It didn't surprise me one bit that she was so insistent that she knew what was best for me. She'd always been like this. I knew deep down she was trying to protect me, but I was perfectly capable of handling my own life.

She sighed. "You've been obsessing about your career trajectory since college. Why not take a breath and figure out what you want to do?"

"*I know what I want to do!*" I exclaimed. "I want this job."

Despite my outcry, the words held little underlying conviction. With every passing day I spent liberated from that office I'd been trapped in for years, I felt a little lighter. My head used to always be down—blindly working toward the next goal. It was nice looking up for a change instead of ahead.

I stalked off, leaving Mattie so that I could take the orders of the group that had just sat down. Throwing on a cheesy customer-service smile was definitely something I had gotten better at, but I still struggled to give all my attention to the table. After a few minutes of me asking them to repeat what they wanted, I walked back over to the bar and started making their drinks. Thankfully, Mattie had taken the hint and wandered back into the main lodge, away from Marie's.

Good.

I loved my sister more than anything, but I needed a break from her probing questions.

Before I'd finished pouring the last beer, Bev waltzed in. My eyebrows shot up when I saw that Oliver trailed behind her.

My smile grew. "Here for dinner?" I asked.

"Nope." He pinched the black shirt he had on and held it out. My eyes narrowed as I read the script font—*Marie's.*

"You're working here now?" Excitement bubbled to the surface.

"He'll be replacing me most nights." Bev patted him on

the back. "I figured it'll be less busy, and the two of you can handle tonight's shift."

"Bold statement," I said.

She laughed. "I know, but I'll be nearby if you need me."

Bev walked away, leaving me and Oliver just as another few tables walked in.

"Train me," he said with a grin. "I'm yours to mold."

"THAT'S THE WORST MARGARITA I'VE EVER HAD," I SAID, wincing as I took another sip. "It tastes like straight tequila."

Oliver rolled his eyes and took a sip before cringing as soon as he tasted it. "I guess it's a little strong."

"*Strong*? That thing could melt steel."

He tossed the rest of the drink in the sink. "Okay, let's not take it out on the new guy. I seem to remember you've had your share of drink mishaps."

"Nope. I've made every drink perfectly."

He smiled, his hand lingering close to my waist.

Even though Marie's had been relatively dead, the shift had gone by shockingly fast working with him. His stolen touches behind the bar, the flirtatious banter. It was even better joking around with him behind the bar than it was when he came in most nights for dinner.

"Was this your plan all along?" I asked. "Become a bartender?"

He swiped his hand across his chin and stared at the ceiling, pretending to mull it over. "I mean," he finally said, "I *did* surpass your skills with only one shift."

"Hey!" I swatted him with the dish towel I had in my back pocket. He wasn't far off. To no one's surprise, Oliver was infinitely better at charming the customers than I could ever be.

"Did you ever work in restaurants?" I asked.

"Never. In high school, Harrison and I usually did odd jobs on a farm nearby. Honestly, I don't think I've ever had a job that didn't entail physical labor."

"A farm boy?" I teased, poking him in the ribs. "I can picture that."

"I baled hay and everything."

"That sounds perfect for you."

He laughed. "Maybe if this doesn't work out, I can fall back on that plan."

Ever since our date, Oliver hadn't been nearly as uncomfortable sharing little tidbits about his past. He'd shared with me how strained he felt talking to his mother, and how important his still-growing relationship with his brother was. It meant the world to me that he trusted me enough to let me in.

"But seriously, speaking of plans, I have been thinking about a few things," Oliver said, eyeing my reaction.

My mouth parted in shock at his admittance. "Oliver Shaw," I said, using his full name. "Thinking about plans?" I reached up to press a hand against his forehead. "Are you feeling okay?"

He grabbed my hand, interlacing his fingers with mine and bringing them between us. "No, seriously, it's nothing huge, but I've been saving up most of the money I've earned while I'm out here."

"And..." I waited with bated breath.

He looked at the floor, almost as if he was nervous to tell me. "It's nothing big or anything, but I figured since I might be wandering for a while—rafting this summer, and then maybe mountain biking somewhere in the fall—I figured it'd be nice to have a homebase. I'm looking at buying a camper trailer. Something small I can tow with my car. That way, even if I'm moving around, I can still have somewhere that's home."

Warmth spread through me.

"Oliver, that's—"

"Stupid, I know," he joked, dropping his hand and running it along the back of his neck. "It's nothing like the goals you probably had in mind, but I figured it's a start."

"It's perfect," I said, grabbing his hand back.

He smiled, looking down at our fingers. "You think?"

The way he sought my approval made me want to burst into tears. He cared what I thought. And even though a camper trailer wasn't exactly a statement of stability, it showed that he wanted something consistent. Something that felt like home.

"I love the idea for you." I stood on my tiptoes and he met me halfway, stealing a kiss. Marie's was empty now, and we were only minutes away from closing the place down for the night.

"I wish I could see it," I murmured without thinking.

For a second, something flashed in Oliver's eyes. His neck tensed before he cleared his throat and went back to the bar. He pulled out another glass and resumed attempting to make a margarita. "Well, it's probably for the best. It'll be a small space. Barely room to cook dinner, let alone host a guest."

His subtle pull-away stung a little, but I wasn't surprised. We never talked about us. About the fact that there wouldn't be an *us* for much longer.

"It's not like you cook dinner now," I teased, attempting to lighten the mood. "I've seen your bare cabinets firsthand."

"Maybe that should be a goal of mine," he said thoughtfully, adding triple sec into the glass in front of him before pulling out a long metal spoon and stirring.

"A goal. Perfect!" I exclaimed. "We can learn to cook together."

"Sounds like fun." He winked at me. "Fun *and* a goal? Talk about killing two birds with one stone. Here—" He held out the drink he'd been working on. "Try this."

I swirled the ice in the glass before taking a tentative sip. My lips puckered immediately. "It's perfect if you're going for the record for the sourest margarita in history," I said.

Oliver tossed his head back, laughing. "Such a hater."

And just like that, everything was easy again.

TWENTY-ONE

Frankie

"No way!" My sides hurt from laughing as Oliver held up a neon-green and yellow tunic.

"I think it's your color," he insisted, holding it up to my small frame. It was about ten sizes too big.

"Put it back," I demanded, pointing at the rack of eclectic thrifted pieces. It was Key Ridge's first farmers market of the season. Main Street was closed down, and it was packed. Tents lined the streets selling fresh produce, homemade goods, and more. It was small-town charm at its best, and Oliver and I were having more than a little fun wandering into the tents.

"I think you're making a mistake," Oliver said, shaking the hanger. "Maximalism is in right now."

"Are you a fashion expert now?"

"Please, Frankie. It wants to go with you. It might never find a home if you don't take pity on it."

"Probably for the best," I said.

Oliver gasped, returning the tunic to the rack. "How could you say that in front of him?"

"Oh, it's a him now?"

"What about this?" Oliver produced a light-gray crewneck sweatshirt with Harvard stitched in burgundy writing across the front. "It reminds me of you." He held it up to my frame.

"Why? I didn't go to Harvard," I said, pushing it away.

He shrugged. "But you're smart. I bet you could've."

"I appreciate your faith in me, but I highly doubt that."

"Whatever." Oliver tossed the sweatshirt over his shoulder and walked over to the table where an older woman was taking payments.

I trailed behind him. "What are you doing?"

"Getting it for you. I like it."

Another laugh fizzed to the surface. "Fine," I said, secretly loving the idea that every time I'd wear that sweatshirt, it would make me think of Oliver. He had that way about him. Finding little inside jokes in everyday life.

He finished paying and took the brown bag. "I'll carry it for you," he said.

I tugged him over to the next stall that sold candles. I picked one up to smell it. Scents of lavender and vanilla curled around my nose.

"Here." Oliver pointed to a giant candle on display. It was bigger than my head and I doubted I could lift it. "This is perfect for Mattie and Giles. You should get it for them."

I rolled my eyes. "You're not being very helpful."

"You're the one getting distracted," he said. "Aren't we here to buy stuff to cook dinner?"

"And have fun," I added. "Who are you to hurry along my window-shopping?"

"Tent-shopping," he corrected, picking up a pine candle and sniffing it. "There are no windows."

"Semantics," I said.

We strolled down the street, my hand in his. I never imagined it could feel this natural with someone. Affection with Oliver flowed so easily, and I never grew tired of it.

"Do we need this?" he asked, pointing to a green pepper as we stopped by a produce stand.

"I don't know," I examined it. "What are we making?"

He shrugged. "Aren't they in everything?"

I tossed my head back, giggling. "This is like the blind leading the blind."

He grinned. "I'd let you lead me anywhere."

We picked out a few things, hoping some sort of tacos would be an idiot-proof enough attempt. We walked through the rest of the tents, Oliver continuing to pick up random item after random item and trying to convince me to purchase it.

After finishing up at the farmers market, we headed straight to Giles and Mattie's house.

"How was the market?" Mattie asked, peeking around from the dining room to see who was walking in. She slipped off a blazer, signaling she must have just gotten home from working at the lodge.

"Great. We got loads of stuff." I held up my paper bags in triumph. "You and Giles are in for a treat. Oliver and I are making you dinner."

"Bon appétit," Oliver said with a grin.

Mattie's face fell as she looked between the two of us in concern.

We pushed past my sister and started unpacking the groceries in the kitchen.

Mattie stood in the doorway, watching us. "Um, you really don't have to do this."

"What's going on here?" Giles asked, walking in and standing behind his wife. He wrapped his arms around her and rested his chin in the crook of her neck.

"Oliver and Frankie are making us dinner," Mattie said through a wide fake smile. "Isn't that nice?"

Oliver and I smiled at each other, taking pleasure in my sister's obvious unease.

"We aren't going to poison you," I said, taking out the bell peppers from the bag and pulling open drawers in search of a cutting board.

Giles stepped around Mattie into the kitchen and pulled open a drawer by the stove. He produced a wooden cutting board and handed it to me.

"I wanted to do something to show my appreciation for you both letting me stay here for the past month."

"I think *taking* us out to dinner would suffice," Mattie grumbled, looking over my shoulder to see what I had procured.

"Frankie and I are naturals in the kitchen," Oliver added, pulling out some more items from the bags.

"You're going to wash that, right?" Mattie squeaked when I set the peppers on the cutting board.

Oliver and I glanced at each other.

"Of course. I was about to do that," I lied, moving to the sink and rinsing off all the produce we'd picked up.

"What brought on this sudden domestication urge?" Mattie asked.

Giles had grabbed her arm, forcing her to take a few steps back from the kitchen. She still eyed us warily as if dying to intervene. As if she had any sort of culinary skills to speak of. I think I'd seen her boil water once since I'd arrived here.

"Oliver wanted to learn how to cook," I said, chopping the peppers into uneven squares.

Oliver placed a pan on the stove and turned on the gas before dropping the beef we'd purchased into the pan. "We figured it'd be fun," he said.

"So fun." Mattie looked desperate to interfere but Giles chuckled.

"It'll be fine, babe. Let them cook."

"Yeah, listen to your husband," I said, waving my knife. "Let us cook."

"I guess…I guess we'll wait in the living room?" It came out like a question.

"You two go relax," I said, shooing them away with my other hand. "We'll let you know if we need anything."

Oliver snickered next to me as he attempted to break up the ground beef with a spoon. He'd pulled up a recipe for tacos on his phone. We both peered over it to reference it. Lines formed between his eyebrows as he studied the recipe, his concentration making him look endearingly adorable.

"Do you think we'll be better at this or bartending?" he asked.

"I resent that question. I'm an excellent bartender."

He smirked, eyeing me.

Just then, the meat sizzled aggressively and he jerked away from the stove.

"Shit," he muttered before turning the heat down.

I giggled. "Off to a solid start."

"Hey, the stove is sensitive," he complained.

"Is it? You better be nice to it, then."

Oliver shook his head with laughter, and I smiled to myself as I continued chopping the rest of the produce.

"Those have to be the messiest cuts I've ever seen," he said, abandoning the meat for a moment to lean over my shoulder and examine my work.

"They're rustic cuts," I said.

"That's one way to market it."

Us moving around each other in the kitchen was borderline comical. Everything was cooking faster than we expected, and I let out a little squeal of panic whenever I walked away from something only for it to start sizzling violently.

"Everything okay in there?" Mattie called.

"Great!" we both yelled back in unison before dying in a fit of laughter.

Being with Oliver felt good.

That was the only way to describe it. He made me feel happy in a way no one else did. To think, when I'd first met him, all I could think about was how unstable he was. Now, he was basically my rock. He was becoming the person I leaned on, even more than Mattie. I genuinely loved every second we spent together, and whenever we were apart, I only thought about seeing him again

"Crap," Oliver said, eyeing the cooked meat in the pan.

"What?" I questioned as I turned off the burner for the peppers.

"The recipe said a quarter teaspoon of cayenne but I put in a quarter cup." He held up the almost empty bottle of seasoning.

I shrugged. "I'm sure it's fine."

It was *not* fine.

After we'd set the table and sat down to dinner, Giles had taken one bite of his taco before going into a coughing fit and reaching for his water.

"Spicy," Giles gasped.

Mattie slowly lowered the taco she had been about to take a bite of back to her plate, looking alarmed.

I eyed mine nervously. "It can't be that bad."

Oliver, being the only brave one, brought the taco to his mouth and took a small bite. His eyes immediately bulged before he reached for his own glass of water. "Shit," he choked out. "That's not edible."

"Oh no," I groaned, tossing my head back.

Oliver and Giles both had red faces as they continued to chug their waters. Mattie and I made eye contact before bursting out laughing.

"I think my throat has third-degree burns," Giles said.

Oliver had tears in his eyes but one look at me and Mattie and his eyes pinched together as he lost it too.

Soon, we were all cracking up over the completely ruined dinner.

"Shit, I guess you can scratch learning to cook off my goals," Oliver said, after we finally calmed down.

"Yeah, I think you might hurt someone, Ol." Giles got up and took the plates, patting him on the back as he walked them straight to the trash.

"I still had fun," I said, wiping my eye. "That was the point, right?"

"I think the point was to actually be able to eat what you made," Mattie said.

"Oh, right."

We went into another fit of giggles.

Oliver slipped his arm behind my chair, and a sense of comfort settled over me.

The four of us ended up calling out for Chinese takeout and we ate it on the floor of the living room, talking animatedly the entire time.

After dinner, Mattie switched on a movie—some horror-comedy that I would have typically never picked but Oliver was excited to watch. We sat squished together on the armchair, me in his lap and his arms wrapped around me. I dozed off halfway through, my cheeks sore from smiling.

TWENTY-TWO

Oliver

____

"Come on. It'll be fun." I placed a glass on the top of the bar and filled it with soda water before using my other hand to grab the neck of a bottle of vodka.

"It annoys me to no end that you're already so good at this." Frankie glared at the ease with which I made the drink and slid it to the woman across from me.

"Don't change the subject." I bumped my hip against hers.

"What's fun about sleeping on the ground?" she whined before reaching under the bar and grabbing a glass. She put it against the beer tap and cursed when it immediately filled up with too much foam. I chuckled, watching her. She still hadn't gotten the hang of pouring a beer. She passed it to the older man sitting at the other end of the bar.

"It's not just sleeping on the ground," I continued. "It's about being out in nature. Looking up at the stars. Taking in that crisp mountain air." I took an exaggerated breath to make my point, but immediately regretted it when the sharp smell of spilled beer hit me, making my nose crinkle in disgust.

"Camping isn't for me, okay? I'll probably get some stupid injury or get eaten by a bear or something," she said.

"I promise I will not let you get eaten by a bear." I held up three fingers on my right hand, giving her the scout's honor. "I will throw my body in front of yours if it comes to that."

"What a gallant gesture," she said, rolling her eyes but still smiling.

I clasped my hands together and held them up. "Please. I'm begging here. I don't want to spend the whole weekend without my girl."

Her eyes widened almost imperceptibly as a light blush crept across her cheeks. I knew I almost had her. After staring at me for a beat too long, she blinked rapidly a few times and turned around, pretending to get something even though no new customer had come in to order a drink.

"Fine. Don't beg. I'll go," she said.

"Yes!" I cheered, raising both arms in victory.

"What are we celebrating?" Bev asked, wheeling out a keg from the back area, the door to the kitchen swinging shut behind her. I hurried over and took the keg from her and dropped it off underneath the bar.

"Finally convinced Frankie to go camping," I said.

"Wow." Bev lifted her eyebrows, looking impressed as I installed the fresh keg. "You're going to be a mountain woman before you know it."

"Not likely," she said, folding her arms across her chest.

"Maybe you'll end up staying forever like your sister," Bev continued. "I'd be happy to give you more hours here now that you can actually make a decent drink. Well, almost."

"Ha. Ha," Frankie replied dryly. "You know I'm only here until I find a job. And I have a good feeling about my next interview."

My jaw clenched with the way she so lightly delivered

those words. Something like irritation simmered in my chest, but I swallowed it down and did my best to keep my face neutral.

I knew she wanted this job. We talked about it constantly. Hell, I even asked her practice questions last night to help her prepare for her next interview with this so-called dream job.

None of that made it any easier. Her landing this job was going from possible to probable. I could feel it.

Ever since we slept together a couple of weeks ago, we'd been even more inseparable. We spent all of our free time together. We'd even had more conversations about my family and growing up. I was trying like hell not to read too much into it, but I'd never been this close with a girl. Ever. People came in and out of my life like a revolving door—my best friend and now my brother being the main exceptions to that. It wasn't like I intentionally didn't sow deep seeds. I liked trying new things and meeting new people. Deep conversations made me irrationally anxious, so keeping it at surface level had been the perfect solution.

Until now. Until Frankie.

She'd burrowed her way right the fuck in, and now I wasn't quite sure how to let her go.

I knew I needed to. She had been very clear that her career was her dream. She belonged in some big city, climbing the corporate ladder. We were nothing alike in that regard.

By some twist of fate— either incredible or vindictive— we'd been brought together. And while I wouldn't change my time with her for anything, I was starting to resent the fact that I couldn't have her for keeps. A committed relationship had never been something that appealed to me, but now that I knew this particular girl was out of reach, it was all I could think about.

"Hello." My eyes readjusted from disassociation to see Frankie snapping her fingers at me. "Where'd you go?"

I removed any trace of distress from my face. "Sorry, I got distracted thinking about you next to me, naked, in a sleeping bag."

"Oliver," she hissed, turning to see if Bev had overheard, but she had already retreated to the other end of the bar to talk to a customer.

I shot her a wink, enjoying the pink tinge splotching her soft cheeks. Without thinking, I reached out and brushed aside the strand of hair that had fallen across her face.

She leaned into my touch, and I was sure I had the dopiest expression on my face. I would have leaned in right then and there to kiss her if my phone hadn't gone off.

I pulled it out of my back pocket and groaned when I saw my mom's number flashing across the screen.

Frankie winced when I held up the phone to her. "Going to get that?" she asked.

"I'll call her back," I muttered, stuffing the phone back into my pocket.

Frankie started stacking glasses behind the bar. I could tell she wanted to say something but was holding back.

"Say it," I said. While I still didn't love talking about heavier stuff, I had come to trust Frankie. I was a lot more open to talking things through with her—like feelings and shit. While I couldn't promise I wouldn't try and defuse the tension with the occasional joke, I'd never lose it and run away from her again. I'd at least come that far.

She looked up at me and bit her lip. "Maybe you should try talking to her. Tell her how you feel," she whispered, both of her arms resting on the bar.

"I don't know how I feel," I insisted.

She lifted an eyebrow. "You can't think of anything you'd like to say to her?"

"Not a single thing," I said, shooting her a lazy smile that I knew she saw straight through. The topic of my mother exhausted me. I'd rather pretend like everything was fine with her than actually say anything real. That had never been our relationship.

"I really think you'll feel better if you get it out," Frankie said, stepping back and picking up a glass to wipe. I noticed that about her. She always loved to be doing something. If there was a random item on the table, you could bet that Frankie would pick it up to fiddle with it. When I mentioned it to her one time, she said it helped her think.

"Get what out?" I played dumb, knowing it infuriated her.

"*It.*" She waved a hand around exasperatedly. "You know."

My grin widened. "I do know, I just love seeing the cute little lines that form between your eyebrows when you get frustrated."

Her hand flung up to her face as she smoothed out the lines in question. "You're going to give me early onset wrinkles."

"And you'll still look gorgeous," I said, backing away toward the end of the bar. "I should probably call her back before she bombards me with texts. I'll be right back."

"I'll try to manage on my own," she joked, gesturing to the near-empty space.

As soon as I walked out into the lobby, my phone rang again. I pressed the answer button and put it to my ear. "Mom," I said, hoping it didn't come out overly cold.

"Why haven't you called me back?" she demanded. "I called you three days ago. I was about to file a missing person's report."

"I've been busy."

"Too busy for your own mother?"

I sighed deeply, sinking into one of the chairs in the lobby and hanging my head back to stare at the wood-wrapped ceiling. "Did you need something?"

"I have to need something to call my son now?"

"Nope. Just wondering if you needed something." I tried to keep my voice light, but everything about our interactions annoyed the shit out of me lately.

She started yammering away about a trip she had coming up. I pretended to listen.

"Did you see the post Charlie made of her and Nathan the other day? They don't look so good. Too thin or something. Gaunt."

I snorted. "Gaunt?"

I'd seen the post. It was one of Nathan and his wife, Charlie, at the end of a hike they'd completed, looking completely normal and healthy.

"Yes. And he never smiles. I'll never understand him."

The hairs on the back of my neck bristled—like they did any time she mentioned my brother. It was like she was hoping I'd want to talk shit about him with her. Like that would somehow solidify us as the closest two in the family, pushing him out again.

"They looked fine to me."

"You really think so?"

"Yep."

After a small pause, she continued. "When are you going to come visit?" she asked, hope tainting her voice.

Guilt trickled into my veins and replaced the frustration. I had been avoiding her. Typically, I always planned a few visits throughout the year, but I hadn't been in over a year. The last time I had seen her was at Nathan's wedding months ago.

Things were already strained between the two of us. Well, at least they were strained on my side.

"Soon," I said. "Listen, I'm actually working right now. I've got to go."

"Oh. Okay," she said, her voice uncharacteristically small.

"I'll call you soon."

I hung up. I stood up to go back to the bar before giving it a second thought and sinking back down into the chair. I pulled out my phone again and called the only other family member I still had contact with.

Nathan's face appeared on my screen, mirroring my own features—but with a much more serious expression.

"Yo, brother. What's up?" I asked.

"You know I hate video calls," he grunted.

He was sitting on his couch. I could just make out the tail of Charlie's cat splayed across the back. Never would I have thought I'd live to see the day where my no-nonsense brother was curled up with a cat. I loved every minute of it.

"And you know I love seeing your face," I said with a smile.

"Lovely," he deadpanned.

"Have you talked to Mom?" I asked him. "She's driving me nuts."

"She's always driving you nuts lately," he pointed out.

"She's just…always trying to talk to me."

Nathan sighed and squeezed his eyes shut. "Look, I don't know what you want me to say. Your relationship with her is very different from mine."

"And that's exactly the problem."

I wasn't sure what I expected from this conversation with my brother. Poor communication skills was unfortunately a genetic trait in our family. Still, I itched to talk to him—to vent to the only person who might understand.

Nathan let out a gruff sigh and stood from his couch to pace. "I don't want me to be the reason there's a wedge between you two."

"It's not you," I said. "It's everything."

"And the problem is you've never spoken to her about it," Nathan said, before Charlie popped into the screen for a moment and waved at me.

"Hey, Char," I said, before Nathan's face returned to fill my screen.

"Me and you used to have our issues, too, before we worked them out," he added. "And we were only able to do that because we finally actually fucking talked to each other."

I played with a loose thread on the seat of my chair. "It feels different with her. She's supposed to be the adult."

"We're all adults now," he pointed out.

"You know what I mean."

"I'm not saying she's perfect, but she *is* our mother. And she still deigns to speak to us, which is more than I can say for our other parent."

"I don't know how you can be okay with her after how distant she always was with you growing up."

"I've made my peace with it," he insisted. "Don't let your relationship be any reflection of me."

"I guess." I let out a huff of frustration. Leave it to Nathan to always be the logical one.

"Is there anything else? Charlie and I are about to head out to dinner."

"Are you two coming camping next weekend?" I asked. "You've been skirting my invitation."

I could see Nathan's neck tense as he looked off camera, presumably to Charlie. "I haven't been skirting," he said.

"Well, you sure as hell haven't been answering. Are you in

or not? Harrison and Lila confirmed the second I asked them."

Nathan sighed and looked off camera then back at me, seemingly at a loss for words.

"Just tell him," I heard Charlie whisper off camera.

"It's too early."

"He's family."

I sat up, on high alert now. What were they talking about?

"What's going on?" I demanded.

Charlie joined Nathan on screen again, practically beaming.

"We're trying to wait to tell anyone…" Nathan started.

"We're pregnant!" Charlie announced, flailing her arms in the air.

A laugh of disbelief escaped me as I shook my head slowly. "No freaking way!"

"Way!" Charlie exclaimed, smiling.

"Congrats. I had no idea." I clutched a hand to my heart. "I'm going to be an uncle."

Nathan rolled his eyes. "Way to make it about you. And we aren't telling anyone so keep this to yourself."

"You seriously haven't told Lila?" I pressed.

Charlie looked guiltily from me to Nathan.

Nathan sighed. "She was with Lila when she took the test."

I grinned. "Of course she was."

"But no one else knows. Especially not Mom. We're waiting to tell family until after the first trimester. But as you can imagine, Charlie has been feeling pretty sick the past few weeks so a road trip out to Key Ridge and a weekend camping isn't exactly in the cards for us right now."

"Got it. Totally understand."

"I know you can't keep a secret to save your life," Nathan said. "But try to be discreet about this."

I pretended to look offended. "I'm always discreet."

"Yeah, whatever," Nathan said, smiling down at his wife.

I asked them a few more questions—mainly if they'd name their future offspring Oliver if it was a boy—before we said our goodbyes, and I hung up the phone.

When I set my phone down, I stared at in disbelief. Damn. My older brother was having a baby. He was starting this whole little family of his own. Nathan had always been such a loner I had never expected this from him.

While I felt elated for him, something sank in my gut. Marriage. Children. They had never been high on my priority list. I wasn't even entirely sure that I wanted them. But as everyone I was close to moved in those directions, I couldn't help but evaluate my own life and feel like something was missing. I loved going on adventures, seeing new things, and not having the traditional career path, but it was getting lonely.

Frankie's face flashed across my mind. How good it felt ending most days getting to see her, talk to her, hold her. How she supported my lifestyle even though she didn't understand it herself. I freaking loved being around her.

Maybe what was missing from my life wasn't more adventure.

It was someone to share it with.

TWENTY-THREE

Frankie

"Cheers to you nailing yet another interview." Mattie
held up a glass of wine and clinked it against mine.

The red blend was dry and instantly sent a buzz straight to
my head.

I'd finally had my next round of interviews with the
company in New York. While they had gone well, I had
convinced myself that I had managed to mess something up,
and I wouldn't make it to the next step. My anxiety had been
for nothing because they had called me this morning inviting
me to move on to the next round. The competition was dwin-
dling, but that just meant it was getting all the more
competitive.

When I'd told Mattie, she'd insisted on a girls' night to
celebrate. I felt a little pang of guilt knowing that I'd actually
called Oliver first and hoped to celebrate with him, but when
Mattie had mentioned going out just the two of us, I couldn't
say no. Oliver and I had been spending a lot of time together
lately, and I hadn't seen Mattie as much. If I was leaving Key
Ridge soon, that would also mean significantly less time with

my sister. I wanted to enjoy our proximity while I still had the chance.

We'd driven ten minutes to a new speakeasy bar that served overpriced cocktails in a dim setting. It was trendy and definitely had a cool vibe, but after spending so much time at Marie's, it lacked a certain charm.

"Thanks. It's still not an offer though, so let's not jinx it," I said, placing my glass in front of me.

"Having confidence isn't jinxing anything," Mattie insisted.

"Still." I knocked twice on the wooden table. "I'd rather not take any chances. I still have the case study too," I pointed out. That was about to be a shitload of work and practice presenting. I was a little irritated they weren't paying me for my work, but at the same time, in this market, I was a beggar and I couldn't afford to be a chooser.

Mattie twisted her glass of wine between her fingers and examined me. "You seem excited," she observed, almost in a surprised tone.

My eyes narrowed. "Why wouldn't I be?" I questioned.

She shrugged and took a sip. As if I was about to let that little comment slide through the cracks.

"No seriously," I pressed. "Answer the question. Why wouldn't I be excited?"

"You seem so happy here," Mattie said, like it was the most obvious thing in the world.

"I *am* happy. I've loved my time here, and spending time with you and Giles—"

"And Oliver," she finished, cutting me off.

"Right. And Oliver," I said, feeling my cheeks burning.

She sipped her wine and set it back down. "You don't meet guys like him often."

Mattie was driving me nuts lately. It was like she was

trying to leverage my feelings for Oliver to get me to stay or something. First off, I was not about to give up my career to move to a small town. And second, Oliver wasn't staying either. He'd said it himself a hundred times. He wasn't good with commitment.

"Oliver is great. Which is why I've been spending so much time with him." I leaned in. "But you know what else he is? *Supportive.*"

Mattie sighed.

"He knows how much I want this and he wants it for me too," I finished. "Besides. As soon as summer comes around, he's off to teach some whitewater rafting course or something like that. We're both moving on."

Mattie frowned. "Tragic."

I let out a frustrated huff. "It's not tragic. People meet people all the time that aren't meant to stay in their lives forever. Oliver and I are just enjoying this season together and that's it."

"Funny, I remember thinking something similar about Giles." Mattie tapped her chin.

I took another swig of my wine. Why did this feel like some sort of love intervention?

"Just because *you* moved to a small town and met your soulmate doesn't mean everyone will."

Mattie's face softened. "Frankie. I wish you could see the way he looks at you."

Goosebumps pricked my arms.

"I see how he looks at me every day," I said quietly.

"You might see it, but you're not *seeing* it," Mattie insisted. "Love is harder to find than a job."

I almost choked hearing the word "love."

"In this economy?" I arched an eyebrow. "I'm not so sure about that."

Mattie let out a groan of frustration. "You've always been so obsessed with being successful—whatever the hell that's supposed to mean anyway. You had to get the best grades, then go to the best college, then find the right job, then buy a house because renting is throwing your money away."

"It *is* throwing your money away," I interrupted.

"I've seen you more alive this past month than I have in my entire life. You never take the time to just live."

"Have you ever thought it's because I'm trying to live up to you?" I snapped.

An awkward silence fell over the table.

She opened and closed her mouth a few times. "What are you talking about?" Mattie demanded. "I've never put pressure on you. And neither have Mom or Dad."

My chest squeezed. "Maybe not intentionally, but you were always perfect, Mattie. In high school, all the boys wanted to date you. You barely studied and always got good grades. Then you got that amazing job right out of college without even trying."

"I try," she insisted, leaning in.

"Not as hard as me." Tears pricked my eyes and I willed them to retreat back into my body. I refused to cry at happy hour. "Even this life you built here. When everything you had in Florida fell apart—and I'm sorry about that, I know how much that sucked for you—but even then, you moved here and met the love of your life. I'm not the one things come easy for. I'm the one that tries so painfully hard it's pathetic. I'm not about to give up when I'm on the cusp of making it."

Mattie squeezed her eyes shut, shaking her head. "You think *I'm* the perfect one? That's how I've always seen *you*. You always got the better grades, had the better style, got the higher-paying job. You were better with money—smarter." She waved her hand in the air. "And you're wrong, I do try. I try a lot. Especially before I moved out here and finally decided to start appreciating my life."

I sniffled and wiped at my eye.

"And second of all," she continued. "There's no making it when you don't have an end goal in mind. You're on this treadmill set at this insane incline, going nowhere. What you want will always be out of reach because you don't know what it is." Her eyes softened and she reached over to gently grab my arm. "Success is a word made up to make us feel like we're failing. So take this job if you want to take this job. Move to New York if it's what you really want. All I'm saying is that I've known you my entire life and I've never seen you laugh the way I've seen you laugh lately. I wish you'd take a second to think about what that means before you go off sprinting in the wrong direction."

Mattie's words sent my mind spinning. I felt lightheaded.

My first instinct was to deflect—to tell her that she was way off base and if I could actually land this job, it would be the best thing that could happen to me. The words twisted on my tongue. They were so mangled I couldn't get them out.

"I'm laughing because of Oliver. He doesn't take anything seriously," I said finally. "And I seem happy because I've never had a break before."

"Life shouldn't be about tiny little breaks where you find happiness. The happy part should be the whole thing—or at least the vast majority of it. Trust me, I learned that the hard way."

I snorted, thinking about where her life had almost landed her before she wound up here—the happiest I'd ever seen her. I remembered thinking when she was with her douchey ex, living so close to where we'd grown up, that there was so much more for her. I'd tried gently nudging her in different directions, but she'd always insisted she was happy. Was that what was happening now? Could Mattie see my life better than I could? Did she have that sisterly intuition that was screaming at her that I was making some sort of mistake?

I attempted to shake the doubt from my mind. "I don't know what you want me to say. I want this job, Mattie. I'm so close to finally landing something, and I'm going to see it through."

Mattie smiled, but the light didn't touch her eyes. "Then I can't wait to celebrate when you finally land it."

Her words didn't help the pit that had formed in my stomach. It wasn't lost on me that all I wanted in that moment was to call Oliver, fall into his arms, and let him hold me until I felt whole again.

I was in dangerous territory.

Oliver was like this beautiful mountain lake that I'd seen while driving. I'd pulled over to take a quick dip. Except that dip was a little too luxurious and now I couldn't quite imagine getting out and back into my car.

Was it nice? Sure.

But the reality was, I was going to get pulled under if I stayed in for too long. I would drown in how good it felt and never resurface again.

I had to do something about this. Putting any distance between the two of us felt impossible, but since I needed to let him go eventually, I might as well start peeling away now.

TWENTY-FOUR

Oliver

____

"Here's a sleeping bag, a sleeping pad—" I continued to rummage through the bins of camping equipment that Bev had given me from her garage. She'd said we were welcome to any of it. I already had my own gear, but Frankie had nothing, and neither did Harrison or Lila, who were arriving later today.

"What about a tent?" Frankie asked. She was lounging on the loveseat in the living room corner of my small studio. I'd been trying to build up her excitement for this camping trip for days, but she still wasn't fully convinced.

I, on the other hand, was pumped. I wanted nothing more than to be out in nature with her, sitting by a bonfire with our friends, not thinking at all about what was next and just being with each other. There would be no cell reception so she'd finally be forced to take a break from preparing for interviews for this supposed dream job of hers. If you asked me, it was freaking ridiculous to put a potential candidate through this many hoops just to decide if you wanted to hire them or not.

Frankie had already killed three rounds of interviews; they should have known what they had by now.

"My tent is pretty small, but we should both be able to squeeze into it." I grinned up at her, but it faltered when I found her frowning back at me. "What?" I questioned.

"I don't know if that's a good idea," she said. "I mean, your best friend and his girlfriend are coming up. I would totally get if you didn't want to say that we're together—or whatever it is that we are. It's so confusing, and they're only here for a few days."

My smile remained frozen to my face, but I could feel the vein in my neck start to bulge. "Frankie, you're overthinking this," I said carefully, because like hell was I letting her sleep anywhere except for my tent. She'd be lucky if I didn't squeeze her into my sleeping bag.

"It's confusing," she insisted.

I stood up slowly, dropping my smile and raising an eyebrow. "Confusing? What are you talking about? No, it's not."

I mean, I guess it kind of was. I was confused as hell. I'd never felt this way in my entire life, yet we were only temporary. Everything in me was screaming to fight for whatever this was, but every logical thing in my brain was telling me we weren't meant to be. Actually, come to think of it, "confusing" about summed it up.

"Look," she said in a gentle tone I kind of hated—like she was bracing to let me down or something. "There will be a group of us. It's not like it's some romantic getaway, just the two of us. We can keep it casual in front of your friends. Mattie and Giles have an extra tent I can borrow. I'll just use that one. It isn't a big deal."

I opened my mouth to protest again, but she shuffled off the couch and cut me off.

"I don't want to have to explain myself to your friends, okay?" She let out an exhausted-sounding sigh, and I fought the urge to pull her into me. "They'll ask questions that I don't feel like answering. I'd rather get to know them in a chill environment—without any pressure."

If she knew Harrison, she would know that he'd be as likely to interrogate her as a monk that took a vow of silence. He was not the chatty type, nor would he ever stick his nose in anyone's business.

I didn't say that, though. Something felt off about today. In fact, something had felt off for the past couple of days. She'd made a few excuses not to hang out. I knew she was stressed about getting this job, but I also knew how fucking prepared she was. There was no way she needed as much alone time as she'd insisted on, but I wasn't about to call her out on that. I didn't beg people to spend time with me, and I wasn't about to start now.

"Okay, we'll play it by ear." I gave my best noncommittal answer.

I wouldn't push her on it right now, but I would figure something out. She'd be in my tent tonight, that was for damn sure. And this weird energy she'd been giving me this week? Yeah, that needed to go right the hell away. I only had a limited time left with her, and I wanted it to be amazing. Not stifled and awkward.

I went to her and bent down to place a kiss on the top of her head. "Harrison and Lila will be here any minute. We were going to grab lunch and pack up the car. Do you want to stay here or should we pick you up—"

"I'll drive up with Mattie and Giles," she said, waving her hand as if it were no big deal. As if she wasn't painfully, achingly slicing my chest open with a dull butterknife. "See you up there," she said cheerfully, taking the sleeping bag and headlamp I'd set aside for her. She gathered them up in her arms so that I could barely see her face over the gear.

I sighed. "Put that down. I can at least bring your stuff, can't I?"

"Oh." She dropped the things before looking back at me. At least there was finally a hint of guilt in her expression. "Yeah, I guess that would make sense. Thank you." She backed away, waving awkwardly. "Bye."

"See ya," I said, cocking my head and giving her a look that I hoped said "We will definitely be discussing your bizarre behavior later."

Frankie let out a nervous laugh before gulping and scurrying out my front door.

Yeah, no. We would *definitely* be figuring this out later.

"AND THEN SHE SAYS WE SHOULD SLEEP IN DIFFERENT TENTS." I said that last part like even the idea repulsed me, which to be fair, it did.

"Separate tents? Why? That seems so random." Lila leaned forward from the back seat, hanging on my every word.

Harrison, meanwhile, let out a grunt of disapproval and pinched the bridge of his nose. "Maybe we shouldn't be discussing this. She clearly didn't want us to know you two were together," he said.

I scoffed and Lila snorted. "What? Like I'm not going to tell my best friend about the girl I'm seeing?"

Lila squealed. "Oh, so you're *seeing her* now?"

"As if that isn't the vaguest fucking term ever," Harrison grumbled.

"It's more than he's ever said before." Lila reached out

and tugged on his bun, which got his lips to quirk up as he turned to look at her. My tenseness softened a little at the sweet gesture. Harrison and I had been best friends for basically our entire lives and he'd never let anyone in the way he'd let Lila in. It still caught me by surprise seeing how comfortable the two of them were together. An added bonus was that Lila was basically the female version of me. We'd already been friends before she and Harrison got together. She was peppy and always down for something new. She got Harrison ever so slightly out of his shell, which was a huge bonus for me. I'd been trying to get the guy to loosen up since high school to no avail.

"I like her," I admitted, tightening my grip on the steering wheel as we took another hairpin turn up the side of the mountain. "I mean, obviously we can't be anything serious, but…"

My words trailed off—because but *what? But* maybe we could stay friends? *But* she'd had some profound effect on me and changed me forever? I was probably playing with fire here, but fuck it. I was ready to get burned.

Harrison shot me a disapproving look. "Shouldn't we respect what she asked and not talk about this? She didn't want to sleep in the same tent so you wouldn't have to explain your relationship status, and here you are, spilling every detail ten seconds into this drive."

I made eye contact with Lila in the rearview mirror, and we both smirked at each other.

"She's just getting her first lesson in Ollie one-oh-one. That being that he can absolutely not keep his mouth shut," she said.

Harrison sighed. "Fair."

"Hey, I can keep my mouth shut when it matters."

"Can you?" Harrison challenged.

"Definitely," I insisted, although I hoped he didn't come through with a plethora of examples proving me wrong.

Finally, after a beat of silence, he said, "I'm glad you met someone."

My eyebrows shot up, shocked to hear quite possibly the most sentimental thing that had ever come out of my best friend. "As you can see, it's not exactly straightforward," I said.

He shrugged. "Still. You care. That's a start."

The words of the person who knew me better than anyone twisted inside my chest. If he could tell this was real, then there was no doubt that it was. Or at least it was real on *my* end. But fuck, what did that even mean? Likely nothing good, considering we were on a countdown toward ending and she was already pulling away from me.

If there was one thing about me, though, it was that I was going to take life by the balls and savor every moment. So if my gut was right and she *was* trying to pull away, I wasn't about to let her do that without a fight.

"Okay, okay. Enough obsessing about me and my situationship. How are you two?" I asked.

Harrison turned and glanced back toward Lila, whose eyes lit up.

"We're good," she said.

"Fucking fantastic," Harrison added, flashing a rare smile.

"Even without me in Denver?" I asked, feigning a pout.

"You're missed daily," Lila said.

"It's all we ever talk about."

"I knew my absence would hit you hard," I said, pretending to be distraught. "Don't worry, maybe I'll find time to head back to the city for a week or two before my next gig starts. You have room, right?"

Harrison's smile fell. "It's a small house," he mumbled, to which I laughed.

Lila giggled. "We always have room for you, Ollie."

My chest swelled. Home wasn't a place; it was a feeling. I felt it right now sitting with my best friend and his person. And fuck me if I also didn't feel it anytime I was with Frankie.

Eagerness electrified my body as every mile swept by and I was closer to being in the same vicinity as her again.

TWENTY-FIVE

Frankie

"What do I do with this pole?" I held up the long stick that kept collapsing and let out a frustrated huff. "It won't stay straight."

"It will if you use it right," Mattie insisted.

She and Giles had already assembled their tent with ease, while I was left struggling to get mine to cooperate.

The campsite was made for groups so it was large. It was grassy and overlooked the mountains; some in the distance still had snow on the peaks. There were grills and firepits. It was still early in the season so only one other group of a few girls was here. We'd said friendly hellos when we'd first pulled in.

Mattie, Giles, and I had beaten Oliver's car, although they probably weren't too far behind us.

"I'm doing everything in my power to make it bend like you said and I swear it's broken," I insisted.

Giles let out a clipped breath. "I've used that tent a thousand times. I can promise you, it's user error."

I narrowed my eyes. "I don't appreciate your insinuation. I'm very capable of figuring things out."

"Just not this?" Mattie challenged.

"It's broken," I insisted, waving it around.

Giles sighed and stood up from his crouched position where he was nailing a stake into the ground to secure their tent. He brushed off his pants and sauntered toward me. He took the offending pole in question from my hands and made a quick snapping motion. The pole's pieces came together so that it was in one long, uninterrupted line.

"Give me the tent." He held out his hand. "You thread it through the top."

"I almost had it," I said, fighting back a laugh. I knew I was bad at this, but I was also just as stubborn as I was indoorsy. Admitting I couldn't do something was hard for me, even if it was so obviously true.

"Let Giles make your tent and you can help me with the sleeping pads." Mattie waved me over, and I left her husband to finish assembling my tent.

I hated the idea of sleeping on the ground like this. Honestly, I was kind of kicking myself for insisting I'd sleep on my own. All I really wanted was to be next to Oliver. Especially with the threat of a bear or some wild animal ripping me to shreds out here.

"What's up with that?" Mattie whispered once I was by their tent.

"It really wasn't working—"

"Not that," she hissed. "The fact that you're setting up your own tent. Why aren't you sharing with Oliver? Are you two fighting? You've been sleeping at our house a lot this week—"

"We aren't fighting," I interrupted.

Guilt trickled in. I *was* pushing him away and it was obvious to everyone around me. Including him. I had seen it in the look he gave me when I left his apartment this morning.

Not wanting him to tell his friends about me was the lamest excuse in the book. The worst part of it was that none of it was making me feel any better. Every night I spent away from him left me feeling achingly empty, and this weekend was about to be no different.

"Then what's going on?" Mattie pressed.

"I'm probably going to get that job," I blurted out. Normally, I wouldn't say that out loud, but I could feel it with every fiber of my being. When you knew something was going well, you knew, and I just had that feeling. The hiring manager had even let it slip this week that I was their favorite candidate. It was almost like it was mine to lose.

"Okay," she said flatly, waiting for me to continue.

"If I spend more time with him, I'll get more attached and where is the benefit in that? It's just going to make the inevitable harder."

Mattie scowled before rolling her eyes, making her thoughts on my handling of this situation very clear. "Then why don't you cut him off now? Stop talking to him if you're so worried about that."

"No," I said, gulping audibly. I hated the sound of that. It wasn't even bearable.

Mattie shook her head. "Then what's the alternative? This weird limbo where you push him away but still stay just within reach? That sounds cruel, especially if you haven't told him that's what's going on, which, judging by your guilt-ridden face, you haven't."

My eyes cast down to the deflated orange sleeping pad. "I know," I whispered.

Mattie stood up and brushed away a few small pebbles that were stuck to the knees of her leggings. "Stop being a jerk. Either let him go now, or enjoy him while he's here. Don't have one foot out the door already." She snapped her fingers, and I glanced up. "Or, even better idea, you could stop lying to yourself and realize that you're falling for this guy. Hard."

I narrowed my eyes. "Not helping."

She shrugged and backed away toward her husband, who was almost done assembling the tent in a matter of minutes. "Just because it's not what you want to hear, doesn't mean it's not helpful."

My cheeks burned as I was left there to blow up the three sleeping pads by myself. She was right, of course, but that didn't make it easier to hear. I was being selfish. Especially considering I was the one always encouraging Oliver to talk to me—to get past the surface level. Now here I was, closing off. It wasn't fair.

Thinking about his face from this morning, when I'd asked him not to tell his friends about us, made me queasy. He'd mentioned how excited he was for me to meet them multiple times. It was like bursting a bubble.

Before I could dwell on it too much, another car pulled into our camping site.

Nerves flew around my stomach as Oliver stepped out of the driver side door and lifted his arms overhead to stretch. His long-sleeve T-shirt rode up slightly, revealing his lower abs. The same ones I had traced in bed. Running up to him and throwing my arms around his neck sounded like the most natural thing in the world. Instead, I sat frozen.

The other passengers spilled out of the car.

First was a serious-looking guy covered in tattoos with dark features and his hair pulled back into a bun. Harrison was exactly how Oliver had described him. A girl in a bright pink and orange fleece pullover popped out of the back seat. Her rust-colored hair spilled over her back, and she wore the most approachable smile. She must be Lila.

"Hi," Mattie said cheerfully before she, Lila, Harrison, and Giles went into a flurry of greetings and introductions.

Oliver hung back, scanning the campsite before his eyes fell to mine. He shot me a questioning smile, like he still wasn't sure where we stood. I scrambled up and approached the group.

"This is my sister, Frankie," Mattie said, saving me from having to introduce myself.

"Hi," I greeted.

"Hi," Lila beamed. "We've heard so much—"

"It's great to meet you," Harrison interrupted, pulling his girlfriend in close to him.

Lila glanced from him back to me. "Oh, right, yes. So nice to meet you."

"Hey," Oliver said, lifting an eyebrow at me.

"Hi." I gave an awkward wave like I hadn't just woken up in his bed this morning with our naked limbs entangled.

He smirked and gave a small eye roll while shaking his head. He clapped his hands and moved back to his car, popping open the trunk and handing Harrison a bin of supplies.

I thought about approaching him, saying something to break this building tension. But when Lila started asking Mattie and me a million different questions, I chose to instead use my conversation with her as a welcome distraction.

Breathing in the crisp spring air while gazing at the mountains in the distance might have been the most peaceful moment I'd ever experienced. I'd never given meditation a try, but this had to be what all the hype was about.

I sat in my camping chair that Oliver had brought for me

and nestled into the fleece blanket I'd brought from my bedroom. The guys were cooking food on the charcoal grills, laughing at something Oliver had said.

The girls were gathered around the firepit. We were waiting until dark to actually start a bonfire. Lila was sharing a story about the last time she'd camped. She'd been convinced she saw a bear and had crept out of her tent in the morning armed with bear spray only to have nearly blinded her best friend, Charlie, who had left her tent to use the bathroom.

Lila was warm and friendly and I already loved being around her even though I'd just met her.

"Hey, Mattie? Would you mind getting the buns and the condiments out of the cooler?" Giles called.

"On it," my sister shouted back before getting up and walking over to the car.

"This is so great," Lila said, scootching her camping chair so that it was closer to mine. "We don't get out this far into the mountains as much as I'd like."

"It's beautiful out here," I murmured. "I grew up in Florida, and we don't have views like these."

"Is that where you live now or…" Lila asked.

"Well, I was in Atlanta until…" I let out a sigh, hating to admit that I was currently unemployed. "I got laid off recently. I hadn't gotten to spend much time with my sister lately so I just up and left, and I've been here ever since. The whole thing was kind of spontaneous. *So* not typically what I would do, but I needed to get out of there."

Lila winced. "I'm sorry to hear that. It's hard losing a job."

"Even harder finding one," I joked.

Her eyes narrowed as if she were calculating something. "What did you say you do?"

"I am—well, was—in marketing. Used to be the Director of Marketing."

Lila gasped. "Wait, really? This is, like, fate or something. Any chance you'd be interested in joining a women-owned start-up?"

I furrowed my brows. "What?"

She laughed. "Oh shoot, let me explain. I own a women's meetup network with my best friend. It's called ConnectHer. We're popular in Denver and a few other markets, and we're growing fast. We're hoping to be completely national by the end of the year. We're looking for a Chief Marketing Officer right now. Obviously, you'd have to interview with Charlie and me, but I have a good feeling about this. We've been struggling to find a good fit."

"Wow," I said. "That's totally unexpected."

"Now, the pay isn't amazing, of course. We try to be as competitive as we can, but we're still a start-up after all. But the benefits are great, and I promise it's the most fun you'll ever have at work. We have a Denver office but are totally open to remote employees."

I had been pulling teeth to find decent jobs to apply to and here Lila was, presenting me with this opportunity. It was completely unexpected.

But a start-up? I had never gone that direction because I didn't like the uncertainty of it all. An older company might not be exciting or have innovative ideas, but they were usually secure. And they paid more. It would look better on a résumé.

I sucked in a breath through my nose. "Look, that sounds amazing," I said. "But I'm actually really close to the final stages of another opportunity. It's kind of like my dream job."

Lila's smile fell a little. "That's amazing. I totally understand. It was just a thought. I mean, of course you're close to landing something, you seem great."

Lila hardly knew me, but she seemed like the type of person to instantly see the best in everyone.

"I'm sorry," I offered. "Maybe if it doesn't work out."

"Totally," she said. "I can give you my number and you can let me know if anything changes."

"I will," I said, smiling at her offer.

"Oliver!" A loud feminine squeal caused us both to spin around in our chairs to see the source of the noise.

"Elise!" Oliver called back, before a short blonde with two braids launched herself at him.

Immediate heat boiled in my chest and rose to my face as the two started talking excitedly. I couldn't help but notice that she kept placing a hand on his chest.

Oliver appeared to introduce her to the others at the grill. I strained my ears and thought I heard the word "coworker."

"Wonder who that is," Lila said.

I met her eyes only to find her looking at me knowingly.

Shit. I probably had jealously written all over my face.

"Oh, uh. I'm not sure." I forced my tone into a nonchalant one, even though I was feeling all sorts of uncomfortable and insecure.

The girl wore hiking pants and a vest. She looked like she'd been raised in the wilderness, camping or whatever. And on top of that, she was stunning. I could see her perfectly symmetrical features all the way from over here.

"Hey!" Mattie called to us. "Come over here and meet Elise." My sister had a wicked smile on her face as if she knew every single thought that was flying around in my head.

I reluctantly got up and walked over to them with Lila. Crap. For someone that usually had my shit together, I felt like an absolute mess.

"Hey." I waved awkwardly just as Oliver tossed his head back with laughter at something Elise said. Had I ever made him laugh like that? The envious thought planted like a weed in my mind.

"Nice to meet you all," Elise said. "Ollie and I used to work at the same outdoor equipment store."

"How is the old place?" Oliver asked.

"I left a few weeks after you did. Jay asked if I would come on as a tour guide for the new whitewater rafting company he just joined."

My heart squeezed as Oliver's eyes widened. "He asked me too. I'm headed there in a couple of weeks."

Elise shoved his chest. "No way! I'm so pumped now!"

I threaded my hands together as my gaze rose, immediately catching my sister's questioning eyes. I gave her my best "mind your own business" glare before returning my attention to Oliver's apparently favorite person in the world. The way his gaze lit up when he looked at her made me want to throw up. Everything that I was not, she surely was. She looked like she knew how to set up a tent. She also looked like she could competently get down the hill on a snowboard without incident.

Oliver's eyes finally landed on mine, and I gave him the biggest smile I could muster. He narrowed his eyes and tilted his head. He looked confused. I didn't blame him. We hadn't left things in the best place this morning, and now here I was, looking about as comfortable as a deer in the headlights of a massive truck.

"Do you all want to head out on a sunset hike after you eat?" Elise asked.

There were some grumblings of agreements among the group.

Oliver walked over to me before leaning down to whisper in my ear, "Hey, everything okay?"

"Everything's great," I forced out. "I set up my own tent."

The lines between his brows formed as he looked at the tent, then back to me. "I think you mean Giles set up your tent. But listen, about that——"

"Oliver, let me show you my new setup!" We both looked up to see Elise waving him over to her site.

Oliver sighed and stepped away from me. "I'll be right back."

"No rush," I said, as my insides turned.

I watched as he walked over to the girl that was a way better fit for him in every imaginable way.

TWENTY-SIX

Oliver

"Frankie doesn't seem like your type," Lila said in a low voice so that only I could hear.

The two of us were toward the front of the hiking group, behind Elise and her friends. Giles had stayed back at camp with Mattie and Harrison was trailing the back of the group with Frankie.

My heart swelled a little knowing my best friend and my girl—hell, I was still going to call her that even if it wasn't exactly accurate—were getting along.

"She's career driven, motivated, intelligent. She also looks about as out of place out here as Harrison does." We both glanced over our shoulders to see the two of them helping each other over a particularly muddy log, Frankie scrunching her nose in the process.

My lips tugged up at the sight. She was so damn cute.

"Harrison is my best friend," I pointed out. "We've made it work despite his aversion to activities."

"I guess." Lila considered this. "I never pictured you with

someone like that. Don't get me wrong, she seems lovely and smart. I'm just surprised is all."

"Well, I never thought you, Ms. Sunshine herself, would end up with my grumpy ass of a best friend, but here you two are."

Lila smiled. "Yeah, here we are."

"Oliver, when did you say you were leaving for the white-water rafting training course?" Elise asked from in front of us.

"Probably in a few weeks. What about you?" I called. I was trying to get excited about the idea, especially since I'd found out Elise would be there too. I'd always gotten along well with her. She was a blast.

"I might head out there earlier. Do you remember my girl-friend, Jules?"

"Of course," I said. A group of us had gone boarding together a few times.

"She's going to be a guide, too, but we wanted to rent a van for a week before it starts. Just for fun to see the area and get an idea for vanlife. We might want to try it out after the rafting season is over."

"That's awesome. You two will love that. You used to always talk about living in a van."

"I know." Elise beamed. "I'm so excited."

She turned and resumed her conversation with her friends as Lila and I fell a few steps behind.

"You know Frankie is totally jealous of Elise, right?" Lila asked.

My eyebrows shot into my hairline. I snuck a glance back at Frankie but she was too far behind to see.

"I don't think so. She doesn't seem like the jealous type," I insisted.

Lila let out a breathless laugh. "Her face was bright pink

when she introduced herself earlier. She was totally eyeing Elise up like competition."

"That's ridiculous." Although I'd be lying if I said the thought didn't give me a twinge of satisfaction. Hearing earlier that she hadn't wanted to claim me or for me to claim her, stung like hell.

"Elise is totally textbook your type," Lila said.

"Except for the obvious fact that she has a girlfriend." I chuckled and shook my head.

"Frankie doesn't know that," Lila pointed out. "To her, Elise looks like some outdoorsy, adventure babe who you're about to go work with for a few months. I bet she's freaking out."

I thought about reversing the situation. If some guy in a suit showed up in Key Ridge who used to work with Frankie and talked about moving to New York, I'd sure as hell be seeing red. As irrational as that was, it was the truth. But a New York guy in a suit would be perfect for her. Not like me.

"I'll clear things up with her."

Lila snorted. "Yeah, you seem to be in a rush to do just that."

I shrugged. "Maybe I want her to feel a tiny bit of what it could be like to lose me."

Lila cringed. "That's not healthy."

"Hey, don't judge me. It's not my fault the best relationship I've ever been in also happens to be the most complicated one."

"Relationship is a strong word—"

"Whatever," I cut her off.

"If you really like her so much, you should tell her."

"I have."

"No, I mean like *really* tell her. Tell her you don't want it to be temporary."

"But I do," I lied.

"You don't," she said. "I knew it as soon as you started going on and on about her on the drive up. That's not the Oliver I know. You're flustered and you don't know what to do about it."

I stepped over a large tree root, before bringing my eyes back to the horizon. "She's kind of like…the right person at the wrong time," I said. "Except instead of that, she's the *wrong* person at the *right* time. The two of us are nothing alike and want different things, yet we happened to end up in Key Ridge at the exact same time, causing this little glitch in the universe."

"If she was so wrong for you, then you wouldn't be strung out like this." Lila's words got choppier as we made it to an uphill portion of the hike.

I wondered how Frankie was doing trailing behind. I'd thought a few times of joining her in the back, but I couldn't handle a rejection from her right now. I figured she needed some space and I'd give it to her. For now.

"I know you're right in theory," I started, "but it's her dream job. There is nothing keeping her from chasing that, just like there isn't anything that could get me to move to New York." I laughed at even the idea. "How fucking crazy would that be? Could you even imagine me there?"

Lila sighed dreamily. "Sounds like an adventure."

Unease stirred inside me as I took in her words. She was serious. *Me?* In a big city like that?

"I would be bored out of my mind," I said.

Lila snorted. "Right, because that's what everyone always says about New York. How boring it is."

I glared at her. "You know what I mean."

"I'm just saying, love is a pretty big adventure. One you probably don't want to cut short."

My first instinct was to scoff. "Love? I never said anything about that."

She had the nerve to smile. "I know, but you also wouldn't be obsessing this much if it wasn't love, or something close to it."

"You're way off." I threw my hand in the air and waved off her comment.

"If you say so," she singsonged.

I pulled my water bottle out of my backpack and squeezed it lightly in her direction. Water spewed out of the top and landed on her arm.

"Hey!" She looked at me with mock horror before laughing. "You're so immature."

Before she could reach for her own bottle, I took off running.

"Get back here!" she yelled.

I slid in between Elise and her friends and sprinted a few feet up the trail, running more from her words than Lila's retaliation efforts.

Love was big. Love was heavy. It wasn't a word I had ever used before. Not when it came to a romantic partner. I wasn't even sure I knew what it meant. Did I love Frankie? The idea seemed insane.

I mean, did I love spending time with her? Obviously. Did I think about her when she wasn't around? Of course. Was I dreading our time together ending more than I've ever dreaded anything in my entire life? Abso-fucking-lutely.

But that wasn't love.

Right?

TWENTY-SEVEN

Frankie

I DOUBLED OVER, GASPING FOR BREATH FOR WHAT FELT LIKE the ninetieth time this hike. We'd started this as a group but everyone was out of sight by this point. Everyone aside from Harrison. I'd tried to force him to go on ahead, but he wouldn't hear of it.

"I hate hiking," he'd said, waving off my comment as if it were ridiculous.

The rest of the group had been twenty feet in front of us for a while. Then it was thirty, then forty. Now they were out of sight.

Oliver was definitely at the front, arm in arm with Elise. The thought made me more nauseous than the hike. I grabbed my water bottle and took another sip.

"We'll still get there before sunset," Harrison said, squinting toward the direction of the end of the hike.

"Thank God. I was so worried," I said, still bent over.

The corner of his mouth lifted. "It'll be worth it at the end. At least, that's what Lila always says."

"She seems like a glass-half-full type of gal." I straightened up and took one big inhale through my nose before starting on the hike again.

"She definitely is." Harrison was gruff and covered in tattoos. It would be a lie to say I hadn't been intimidated by him at first. But the way he watched Lila, always making sure she was okay and not overexerting herself, the way he couldn't stop his eyes from lighting up anytime he looked at her or anytime her name was brought up—it immediately made me feel comfortable around him.

I was still confused as hell about how this was Oliver's best friend though. The two couldn't be any more different.

"She and Oliver probably have a lot in common," I said.

"They're exhausting together," Harrison admitted. "I finally got a break when he left for Key Ridge." Even as he said those words, it was obvious he missed his friend.

"I can imagine that," I joked, then quickly backtracked. "I mean, it's not like I know him that well or anything. He just seems like the type."

Harrison and I made brief eye contact before I ripped my gaze away to focus on my feet. The view at the end better be worth it because my only view going up was the ground. If I looked up for even a second, I stumbled.

"Look." Harrison let out a sigh. "I'm going to be straight with you. Oliver told us everything."

That halted me in my tracks.

"What?" I asked shakily.

"He told us that you two have been hanging out and that he likes you. He said you wanted to keep it a secret, but you should know that Oliver cannot keep a secret to save his life."

I gripped my backpack straps, feeling silly and unsure of what to say next. Of course it had been a stupid suggestion. I should have realized that as soon as I said it, but once it was out, I couldn't take it back.

"I feel like an idiot," I admitted.

Harrison didn't look apologetic, he simply shook his head. "Don't. Oliver isn't the best communicator. I'm not surprised he'd land himself in a situation like this."

"But *I'm* supposed to be the good communicator." I tilted my head back and groaned. "This is probably the worst first impression I could possibly make."

Harrison shrugged. "I like you so far."

"You do?" I asked skeptically.

He'd been hanging back with me on the hike, but we'd mostly walked in silence. He wasn't much of a talker, and I wasn't much of a pusher. If someone wanted silence, who was I to deny them that?

"You're relaxed. You aren't trying to be anyone but yourself. Oliver brings around a lot of girls." He winced as soon as he saw me cringe at his words. "Shit, forget I said that. My only point is, let's just say I've seen my fair share of girls who've tried to fake an interest to get his attention. Pretend to be this bubbly girl that loves to snowboard or rock climb. It gets old."

I blew out a breath. "He took me snowboarding and I pretended my wrist injury was worse than it was just to get off the mountain and stop falling on my ass."

To my genuine shock, Harrison let out a low chuckle. "See? I like that. That's the kind of shit I would do."

"Well, I probably ruined it all. I've been acting like a weirdo all week, and now he's up at the front talking to his dream girl."

Harrison squinted. "Who? Elise?"

I nodded. "She's stunning and perfect for him." I waved my hands in the air, not even caring that I sounded insecure. "They're about to go work at the same place all summer. It's practically destiny."

Harrison paused before staring up ahead. "I don't know about all that. What I do know, is he wouldn't stop talking about you the entire drive up here."

"Probably about what a basket case I am."

"Maybe a little," he admitted, stuffing his hands into his pockets. "But it was mostly about how he needed things to stop being weird between the two of you. You've got him majorly stressed out. I've never seen him like that."

We walked in silence for a bit before Harrison continued.

"We've been best friends for almost our entire lives. The way he grew up…he didn't exactly have a lot of people in his corner."

"I know," I whispered. "He told me about his parents—what it was like growing up with them."

Harrison's eyes widened a little at that. "He never talks to anyone about his parents." He sighed before continuing. "He might try to come across as this chill guy who doesn't have a care in the world, but he's the most loyal person I've ever met. You can always count on him when it matters. Don't let his act fool you."

"I don't," I said, meaning it. Oliver was a lot more to me than some free spirit.

Guilt twisted inside my stomach. I hadn't wanted to make him stressed out about us. This was all wrong. We should be savoring our short time together. He should be the one back here, giving me a hard time while I struggled on this hike. We should be cuddled up by the fire together later tonight. I'd gone and messed it all up.

Our hiking boots hitting the dirt path was the only sound other than the distant chatter of the hikers in front of us.

"Do you think I'm too late to fix it?" I asked quietly.

"I think as far as Oliver is concerned, you'd probably never be too late to fix it."

"We did it," I gasped when we reached the clearing.

The rest of the group stood with their backs to us, looking out at the vast view. The sun was only inches from poking itself behind the tallest mountain range.

"Nice," Harrison said. "I knew we'd make it."

"Did you?" Oliver's voice startled me as he stood from a nearby rock at the end of the trail and walked toward us. "Because I was five minutes away from heading back there and making sure one of you didn't get attacked by a mountain lion or something."

"We did our best," I said, breathless from the hike and also from Oliver looking down at me with those piercing dark-brown eyes.

"Let the record show I could have gone a smidge faster," Harrison said, backing away from us toward Lila and the rest of the group.

"Traitor," I called after him.

He smiled before he turned and wrapped an arm around Lila's shoulders.

Oliver watched his best friend retreat before returning his gaze to me. "You two seemed to have gotten along okay."

"Yeah. We did," I panted, wanting nothing more than to wrap my arms around him and breathe everything about him in. But a divide existed between us. One of my own making.

"Can we talk?" he asked, his expression unsure but inviting all the same.

"Please," I said.

He loosely grabbed my hand and tugged me along next to him. We walked away from everyone else to the other side of the ledge. A fallen log lay facing the view like a bench. We sat on it, and he faced me instead of the beautiful view.

"Why are you trying to avoid me?" he asked.

Goosebumps pricked along my neck. "Getting straight into it, huh?"

"Aren't you the one who says I need to do that more?"

"Right, of course." Nerves bundled inside me, and I ran my hands along my leggings to calm them.

"Look at me," he whispered.

When I met his eyes, they were staring at me intently.

"I'm sorry. This is such a mess." I offered him a weak smile. "I guess I started to panic."

His eyes widened. "Because of me?"

"Kind of?" I inhaled, letting the chill in the air ground me. "I like you, Oliver."

"I like you too," he said, not missing a beat and causing fireworks to go off in my stomach as a result.

"And we're both leaving soon—I mean, assuming I get this job—"

"You'll get it," he interrupted.

"It's confusing," I blurted out. "I know this is temporary and nothing about us makes any sense, but all I can think about lately is how sad it's going to be to say goodbye to you. And I don't know, I guess that freaked me out. I didn't want to get any more attached than I already was."

"So you stepped away," he finished, blowing out a breath.

"Yes," I admitted.

"Well, I'm going to be blunt. That sucked."

"For me too," I added hurriedly. "I've been miserable all week. Then on this trip, all I want to do is be close to you. But seeing you with Elise and how perfect you two would probably be together stung. It's such a reminder that we don't fit at all."

His eyebrows scrunched together. "Elise?"

"Yes, she's like the female you." My eyes dropped to my hands but jerked up again at the sound of Oliver's laughter.

"Lila was right," he muttered.

"What?" I croaked out.

He shook his head. "She said you were jealous. I told her there was no way."

"Jealous is a strong word," I said, even though that was the exact emotion I was feeling earlier today.

His fingers grazed my chin before he forced me to tilt my face up again. "Elise is just a friend."

"For now."

"I think her girlfriend would beg to disagree with you on that."

My lips formed a soft "O." "Girlfriend?"

"They've been dating a few years now."

"Oh." I felt even stupider than I had before.

"And you seriously think I would flirt with some girl right in front of you?" He narrowed his eyes, looking disgusted at the thought.

I shrugged helplessly. "We've never defined anything or set labels or—"

"We might be confusing, but we're sure as hell exclusive, I can tell you that much," he said forcefully.

His words made me snap my mouth shut, and I instantly melted.

"And what makes you think I want the female version of me, huh?" he asked.

"So they can keep up with you."

"You're wrong. All I want is you."

My heart raced as he leaned into me.

"I like dragging you on things you don't want to go on. I like that you challenge me in ways that have nothing to do with my physical ability. I've genuinely loved every second we've spent together, and they still aren't enough."

I tried to mentally ignore his use of the big "L" word, but my heart couldn't seem to let it go.

"Can we stop being weird with each other?" he begged. "I'm sorry that I can't offer you more than right now. Trust me, the past few weeks I've been wishing that I was some hedge-fund, Wall-Street-type guy who could just move with you to New York and get some job and fit right in. But that's not me. You'd never ask me to change, just like I'd never want you to change. We might not have forever, but can we stop wasting the time that we do have?"

His words simultaneously excited me and broke my heart. They were the best things he could have said in the moment, yet part of me still wished he could come up with some grand plan. Some miracle that would allow us to be together despite every obstacle in our way.

"What do you say?" he pleaded.

"I say, I'm done pushing you away."

His mouth covered mine in an instant. His lips were warm and inviting against mine. I hated that I'd tried to deny myself this. With my career-obsessed self, maybe I wouldn't get another feeling like this for a very long time. Oliver was special.

We rejoined the rest of the group and watched the sun disappear behind the mountains, resulting in an explosion of color. Oliver pulled me into him and held me close the entire time.

The hike back down wasn't quite as strenuous as the hike up. Oliver stuck with me the whole way, making sure my headlamp was attached properly and forcing me to grab his arm so that I didn't trip over anything.

"You really are terrible at this," he said with a laugh when we finally reached the bottom, at least fifteen minutes behind everyone else. They'd already formed a circle around a crackling fire and I could see marshmallows being passed around.

"You know what I'm not terrible at? Sitting my ass around a fire."

Oliver grinned and planted a kiss on top of my head.

When I went to go find my camping chair, he stopped me and sat down in his before pulling me into his lap.

"You're not getting away from me the rest of the weekend," he said into my hair.

"Get a room, you two," Mattie said, smiling at me when I looked up at her. She was sitting next to Giles, leaning into him.

"How about a tent?" Oliver asked.

I chuckled and swatted his chest.

This felt so unbelievably right.

"Looks like you set up that extra tent for no reason," Oliver said to Giles, wrapping his arms around my waist and hugging me to him.

"I helped set it up," I insisted.

"No, she didn't," Giles said, and we all laughed.

Lila launched into a story about the last time she and Harrison had gone on a hike when they were stuck together in Greece. I listened, captivated.

"I love this," Oliver whispered into my ear so that only I could hear. There he went again. Tossing out that "L" word so casually.

"You were right about camping," I said.

"Oh? Say that again."

I giggled as he pinched my side. "You were right. I'm glad I came."

"Now we just have to sit out here for an appropriate amount of time before we can go back to the tent. It'll be chilly tonight, but if we strip naked and get into the same sleeping bag, we should stay warm."

"Huh, that sounds convenient for you," I teased, turning my face so that I could see the playful glint in his eyes.

"Well, I am the expert. You really shouldn't argue with me."

"It's not like we can do anything with everyone's tents right here," I whispered.

He lifted a finger. "I put our tent at the far end of the site, by the river. Wanted to make sure we had a little privacy."

I looked to where he pointed, and he was right. The tent was all by itself.

"Why'd you put it all the way over there when we weren't even planning to share?"

He let out a snort at that. "Please, Frankie, give me some credit. I was never going to let you sleep on your own."

I rolled my eyes but my smile widened.

The rest of the evening wound down and soon we were all headed to our designated tents.

The hike and the emotional warfare I'd been having with myself had me absolutely exhausted.

Oliver led me to the tent, my fingers threaded loosely in his. I hadn't had anything to drink tonight, but I felt buzzed. High on life, or whatever the saying was. I could do this every weekend with him. Getting lost in a new place. Seeing the beauty of nature. I had been all wrong about camping.

The evening got even better when we climbed into the tent and Oliver's wandering hands slowly traced circles all over my body.

When he kissed my stomach, I gasped, wanting more. Never would I have thought that I'd want to sleep with a man on the ground, but Oliver made this feel like the most comfortable thing in the world. Happiness didn't even begin to cover it.

We continued exploring each other, slowly stripping ourselves of our layers in the process. When he finally slid inside me and started moving, my hips eagerly went up to meet his. It felt familiar. It felt whole. I had to bite back my moans of pleasure as I wrapped both of my legs around his waist.

I'd never get sick of this—that I was sure of.

After we both tumbled into our shared ecstasy, Oliver rolled over and tucked me into his side. Everything surrounding us was cold, but he was warm as I nestled into his body.

Perfect.

The only word I could think of.

Perfect… and momentary.

Despite the bliss I was in, a hot tear formed in the corner of my eye as Oliver pressed his face against the top of my head and we both drifted off to sleep.

TWENTY-EIGHT

Oliver

"You sure you don't want to come?" I batted my eyelashes.

Frankie let out a loud, exaggerated laugh. "Me? Rock climbing? I can't think of anything more disastrous sounding."

"Come on, it's not that hard. I could show you how it's done."

Bev, who was making a whiskey and Coke next to Frankie, looked between the two of us, amused. "I can give you the rest of the night off if you want," she said. "It's pretty slow."

Frankie's ears perked up at that. "If you're serious, that would be great. I'm supposed to hear back about that job any minute now and I'm freaking out. It's all I'm thinking about."

"She can only have the rest of the day off if she comes climbing with me," I insisted.

Frankie's hopeful look fell. "Not happening."

I grinned. "It was worth a shot."

Bev chuckled at our exchange. "Why don't you close out that table over there and call it a day."

"Thanks, Bev." Frankie looked at her gratefully.

"And it's been fun having you around. We'll miss you when you inevitably land that job," she added, causing my skin to bristle even though I knew it was true.

"Don't jinx me," Frankie demanded before pointing at the bar. "Knock wood right now."

Bev shook her head but tapped on the bar a few times to appease her.

"You're going to get it," I said, hoping I sounded casual and not bitter about the whole situation.

"I know." She smiled to herself before taking off for the back corner to ask the only remaining table in Marie's if they needed anything.

The thing about the inevitable was that even though you knew it was coming—could prepare for it even—it didn't make anything easier.

Frankie had stopped being weird with me since the camping trip. The past week had been fucking perfect. We'd gone hiking, slowly but surely. We'd had a few shifts together at Marie's full of laughter as we both tried to learn to make new drinks. We'd even tried cooking a meal together again and had managed not to burn down my apartment. I wouldn't trade those moments for anything, but damn if they didn't make this countdown as painful as it could possibly be.

My friend Jay had already told me I could head to the rafting base camp whenever I wanted. Tours wouldn't start for a few more weeks, but he'd said I could help out with training. I was stalling though. I planned to be in Key Ridge precisely one day longer than Frankie would be—whenever that was. I wouldn't leave her, and I didn't want to be here for any amount of time that she was gone. It hurt too much to think about.

My phone buzzed in my pocket. I pulled it out to see my

mother's name flashing across the screen. I hit the green button and held it up to my ear.

"I'm busy right now, Mom. Can I call you back?"

"Too busy for your only mother?"

I let out a gruff sigh, and Frankie raised an eyebrow at me as she slipped back behind the bar.

"I'm meeting a friend in a few minutes."

"Of course." She couldn't keep the hurt out of her voice. "I just got off the phone with your brother. Can you believe Charlie's pregnant? I was trying to do the math from the wedding and it's a close one. He told me he told you first. I can't believe you didn't say anything."

I pinched the bridge of my nose. "It wasn't my news to tell," I said.

"Still, I'm the mother. The grandmother. Someone should have told me."

"He just told you," I said slowly, hoping she'd recognize how ridiculous she was being.

"Well, I'd be lying if I said I wasn't hurt."

"I hope you didn't say that to Nathan."

"Of course not. I'm telling you. We're different."

"We're not though."

Frankie met my eyes and gave me a sympathetic frown.

"Look, I've got to go."

"Wait!" she cried. "Have you bought tickets to come visit yet?"

"I'm starting a new job, Mom. It'll have to wait. I'll call you back."

I hung up before she could say anything else.

"A bit cold," Frankie said, and I cringed.

"You should hear the other end of the conversation. She's impossible."

"But she loves you," Frankie pointed out.

"She drives me insane."

"I still think you should talk to her. Maybe you can work through your childhood and get to a better place—"

I interrupted her by reaching over the bar and grabbing her neck, pulling her to me for a quick kiss. "Got to run. I'll talk to you later, okay?"

"Okay." I could see the disapproval written all over her face. Here I was, yet again, running from a conversation. Frankie didn't understand how maddening my mother could be. She wouldn't take any responsibility for driving a wedge between Nathan and me. I would rather not deal with it. Maybe pushing her away wasn't healthy, but it was easy.

MY ARM FLEXED AS MY FINGERS HELD ON TO THE SMALL HOLE on the side of the rock. I was only about six feet in the air, but it always felt higher without a rope.

"To your right," Giles called from underneath me.

"Got it," I said, moving my hand to the hold he was calling out. The weight of my bottom half moved too far away from the rock's edge, and I felt myself slipping.

"Shit," I mumbled, two seconds before I let myself drop onto the mat we'd set up below.

"That was a good path," Giles said, smacking my shoulder. "I think if you had caught your foot at the same time you moved holds, you would have gotten there easily."

"Next time," I said, flexing my fingers and pulling off my helmet. "Let me give my hands a break."

Giles nodded. "Man, it's good to be out here like this. I don't have anyone else that likes doing this stuff with me."

"Let's get as many sessions in as we can," I said.

"Can't believe you're leaving soon. It's been great having

you. You seriously have to come back at the beginning of next season."

"I'll be here if you'll have me," I said with a grin. It felt like someone else was making the plans. Mentally, I knew future me would be excited to return to Key Ridge for next winter season, but present me couldn't look past the immediate future.

Giles seemed to sense my shift in thought because he paused before saying, "Mattie thinks Frankie is making a mistake. Leaving."

My eyebrows pinched together. "A mistake? It's her dream job."

Giles shrugged. "I only know what Mattie tells me. She seems convinced Frankie doesn't really want this."

"Well, that's for Frankie to figure out," I said, feeling defensive over her. She'd worked her ass off for this.

"That's what I told her," Giles insisted. "I don't have siblings, so I don't get their dynamic."

I thought about my own dynamic with Nathan. How we'd never seen eye to eye growing up. And now, even though he was my total opposite, I tried to reserve any judgment for him and chalk it up to our differences. Just because the way he walked through life wasn't like me, didn't mean it was any better or worse. That had taken a couple of decades to figure out, but now that we both had come to that understanding, we were better off for it.

I placed my helmet back on my head and pulled the straps of my climbing gloves tighter. I positioned myself to try the climb again, wanting to escape this conversation with Giles.

His motive for telling me Mattie's thoughts about Frankie probably came from a good place, but the thought was fucking with my head.

I placed one hand into the first crevice and hoisted myself up the rock face.

There was no way Frankie was making a mistake. She was so sure of herself—always. She wasn't the type to get sucked into the small-town charm and end up staying for good. That wasn't her. And it wasn't me either, for that matter.

My body hugged the boulder as I swung my left foot up to propel myself a few feet higher.

If Frankie told me she wanted to stay, would that change things for me?

The thought nagged at me as I navigated a particularly challenging part of the rock face with very small handholds.

"Careful. That's a hard line," I heard Giles call from below me.

It wouldn't change things for me. She was great, but I wasn't ready to settle down. One girl, one job, one place? That wasn't for me.

A loud crack sounded above me. I barely heard Giles yell, "Watch out!" before my gaze jerked up and a large rock came hurling at my head. It knocked my helmet clean off.

Shit. Had I not strapped that?

Another rock came barreling at me. I let go of the wall to fall back and try to avoid it but it still cracked me right on the side of the head. I barely had time to register the pain before my back hit the hard ground, only partially covered by the mat since I'd fallen so far backward.

"Shit, Oliver. Are you okay?"

I went to give Giles a thumbs-up, but black dots rimmed my vision and I couldn't quite get the signal from my brain to my hand.

The last thing I saw was his face hovering over mine before everything went dark.

TWENTY-NINE

Frankie

My heart skittered in my chest as my sweaty palm held tightly onto my phone.

"I want to thank you for your patience and your persistence once again. We know our hiring process is rigid, but that's why we only hire the best of the best. I really think we found that in you, Frankie."

I held my breath, wishing he would spit out the words already.

"Which is why we're thrilled to extend you an offer for the position of Director of Marketing."

Silently, I pumped my fist in the air. "That's amazing news," I said as relief rushed through my veins and I paced the lobby of the lodge. I had been about to leave Marie's and head straight for the comfort of my bed when I'd gotten the call.

The alert of another incoming call sounded. I pulled my phone away to see Mattie's name flashing across the screen. I sent it to voicemail and put the phone back to my ear.

"I know it's soon, but we'd really like you to start at the beginning of next week."

Everything inside of me sank. That was the original time-frame they'd given me, but I thought with how long they'd taken to make a decision, maybe they'd push it back a week or two.

"Next week," I repeated.

"We can push it if you really can't make that work, but we already have trainings in place for other new hires and it would be the best logistically."

I squeezed my eyes shut and swallowed back the anxiety that swelled in my chest.

"Next week is fine. I'm excited to start."

My phone buzzed again and I pressed the send to voice-mail button without looking at the caller.

"Great. I know you don't live in New York currently, but we can set you up in a hotel for a couple of weeks while you find something more permanent. It'll all be in the official offer letter from HR. But you can call me directly if you need anything."

"Thanks, Neil. I'm so excited to join the team."

As he went over salary, benefits, and what I could expect for my first week, I tried my hardest to focus on what should be the best news I'd received in a long time. Despite my best efforts, my mind kept glazing over. The triumphant feeling of finally landing the job that had once seemed so elusive had already begun to fade.

"That's everything. Once again, we're thrilled to have you on the team."

"Me too," I said as brightly as possible.

"We'll see you soon."

We said our goodbyes and I hung up the call.

Next week?

I could hardly believe it.

Next week at this time, I'd be in New York, likely sitting in a cubicle watching some HR training video and looking at spreadsheets. Maybe I'd pass by a window at lunch, see the warm weather outside, and just be forced to imagine what the sun's rays might feel like while being trapped in some heavily air-conditioned office.

It hit me like a ton of bricks how much I'd taken the past couple of months for granted. At first, I hadn't been able to shake the feeling of failure. Then I was consumed by job hunting. Even now that I had started enjoying myself more, it still felt fake—like a summer vacation destined to end too soon. It made it difficult to be one hundred percent present.

Before I could dwell on it anymore, Mattie came flying through the entrance to the lodge. Her eyes searched the room in a panic before they landed on me.

I raced to her, dread crashing into me as I took in her rattled expression.

"Mattie? What's wrong?"

She waved for me to follow her. "You need to come now. There's been an accident."

My tears had dried, leaving streaks along my cheeks by the time I was allowed to see him. They'd done an MRI and were adamant that only family could visit.

Giles had called me Oliver's girlfriend and insisted I be let through. It made me sad to think that would be the only time I'd be called Oliver's girlfriend by anyone.

The nurses hadn't seemed particularly sympathetic to my situation, but they eventually ushered me out of the waiting room. The steady beeping of machines and the quiet murmur of families huddled in rooms filled the hallway as I followed her. We eventually turned right, and she gestured toward a door left slightly ajar.

I gasped when I saw him, hooked up to a few machines and a large stitched-up gash along his hairline.

He was still smiling. Of course he was. It was Oliver.

"Hey, fancy meeting you here," he said, far too cheerily.

Which, of course, caused me to immediately burst into tears.

His smile faltered. "It's okay. I'm okay. Come here." He sat up and patted the hospital bed next to him.

"You really scared me," I choked out, joining him on the cramped bed.

"I didn't mean to." He pressed a kiss to my forehead. It wasn't lost on me that I should be the one comforting him right now, and not the other way around.

I leaned back to examine the gnarly gash on his forehead. "Why weren't you wearing a helmet?" I demanded, feeling irrationally irritated that he could be so irresponsible. This wasn't like him. He might prefer his sports more on the extreme side, but I'd never known him not to take the proper precautions.

"I was," he insisted, but looked down sheepishly when I leveled him with a glare. "I mean, I forgot to strap it, but it was technically on."

"How could you forget to strap it? You're always doing crazy shit like this. You know how important a helmet is."

His grin turned goofy as he tilted his head to examine me. "You're really lecturing me right now?"

"Yes!" I got up and circled his hospital bed, waving my arms in the air like a madwoman. "You're about to go teach a whitewater rafting course. You can't do shit like forget to strap a helmet. What is wrong with you? That's so dangerous. Ugh, I'm so mad I can't even think straight."

My heart pounded as fresh tears threatened to burst free from my eyes at any moment. Oliver was invincible. Lying in a hospital bed was not anywhere I ever expected to see him, and I hated it so much. I felt powerless.

"Hey. Hey. Hey," he cooed, reaching out and gently wrapping a hand around my forearm, halting my haphazard steps. I jerked my gaze to his, and his eyes softened. "I'm sorry, okay? I know I scared you."

I let out a frustrated sigh. "Do you know how terrifying it was having Mattie show up at the lodge to tell me you were in an accident?"

"Pretty scary, I can imagine."

"No, you probably can't."

"Yes, I can," he pressed, rubbing his hands up and down my arms. "I'd feel the same way if someone told me you were in the hospital."

"Oh," I breathed. Jitters ran through me at his admission, but I forced my expression to remain stern.

He raked a hand through his hair, careful to avoid his fresh stiches. "Look. It was dumb. I know it was. I don't make mistakes like that. But I was distracted."

"Distracted?" I perched on the edge of his bed. A faint beeping sound came from one of the machines he was plugged into. Why was he plugged in to so many machines?

"I…I was thinking about you," he admitted.

"About me?" I asked in disbelief.

"Yeah." His eyes dropped to his hands. "It's stupid, but Giles was talking about you leaving and all of a sudden it was all I could focus on."

The words about accepting my new job lodged in my

throat. Even though I knew that he knew they were coming, sharing them now felt so wrong and gross.

Instead of saying anything, I took one of his hands in mine, letting it ground me.

"I seriously don't know why I was so distracted," he continued, the frustration evident in his voice. "I never get like that climbing. I'm always in the moment, and I'm always careful. I guess our looming expiration date was weighing on me more than I realized."

"Me too," I said. Not only had it been weighing on me, but my mind was nearly crushed with how much the topic preoccupied my every thought.

"But that's no excuse." He smiled up at me. "I won't let it happen again, but it's pretty easy to get distracted when thinking about you."

I let out a small laugh. He could never be serious, even for a second.

"I like you a lot, Frankie," he said.

"I like you a lot, too, Oliver." I squeezed his hand. "Now don't scare me like that again, okay?"

WHILE I DESPERATELY WANTED TO TAKE OLIVER HOME WITH me that night and spend hours curled up in his arms, assuring myself that he was indeed fine, the doctors insisted on keeping him overnight for observation. They said that because of the size of his head injury, and the fact that he had been unconscious for nearly five minutes, they wanted to rule out anything more serious.

It felt awful leaving him there, but he really did seem fine. The doctors had assured us it was just for an abundance of caution.

Still, instead of going back to Mattie and Giles's, I went to Oliver's apartment. All I wanted was to curl up in one of his sweatshirts and sleep in his bed, surrounded by his smell.

Mattie wouldn't hear of me being alone, so she stayed there too.

I had a hard time focusing on anything except getting back to him, so she put on a movie to distract me. It was a pointless effort. Oliver's large frame in the hospital bed was all that I could see.

When I wasn't consumed with worrying about him, my thoughts turned to my new job. I hadn't even worked up the courage to tell Mattie yet—Oliver was the first person I wanted to share the news with. I knew he'd be happy for me, but it also marked the end of us. It made everything feel more real—more final.

Eventually, I fell asleep with my thoughts still spinning.

Finally, when my alarm went off at seven a.m., I ripped away the covers. Giles was supposed to pick us both up and I wanted to be ready the instant he arrived. Mattie was still passed out on the couch, so I jostled her awake.

"Wake up. Is he almost here?"

Mattie groaned and stretched, before turning over and picking up her phone to check. "He's on his way."

I didn't bother with makeup or brushing my hair before I rushed to the entryway and pulled on my shoes. I flung open the door and almost collided with Giles, who held a brown bag and a tray of to-go coffees.

"Ready?" he asked, but I was already brushing by him.

"He's going to be okay, Frankie," Mattie called, still slipping on her tennis shoes and scrambling down the stairs behind me. "They would have called if anything happened overnight."

"I'll feel better when I see him," I said, pulling open the door to Giles's truck and climbing into the back seat.

Mattie slid into the passenger side. Giles handed us both a coffee.

"Donut?" he offered, holding out the brown paper bag to me.

"I can't eat right now." My foot tapped furiously against the floor as Giles maneuvered the car off of Main Street and to the highway.

"I'm sorry," Giles mumbled, shaking his head. "We should have been more careful."

"This isn't your fault," I said. "Accidents happen, and Oliver was the one who was distracted."

"Still, I was there, I should have—"

"Hey," Mattie said sternly, grabbing his shoulder and squeezing. "It isn't your fault."

The next few minutes passed in silence as we drove the remaining distance to the only major hospital within a twenty-mile radius.

When Giles pulled into the hospital entrance, he went straight to the main entry of the massive building. He placed a hand on the passenger seat headrest, turning his body toward me. "You go ahead, Frankie. We'll find parking."

"Thanks." I barely got out the words before I was out of the truck, walking hurriedly toward the automatic doors that led to the entrance of the emergency room. I already knew which room he was in, so I bypassed the check-in counter and walked straight back. Visiting hours had started, but I still made sure to avoid any nurses or doctors on my way, unwilling to be stopped for anything.

When I rounded the corner to his room, an immediate wave of relief blasted through me. He was already up, alert, and speaking with an older nurse who reminded me of my grandma.

"You take it easy," she said, smiling and dropping off his breakfast tray. "Be more careful so I don't see you in here again."

"Of course, Irene." He winked at me when he noticed me hovering in the doorway. "You won't catch me back here, I can promise you that."

"Good." She walked toward the door and gave me a small nod when she noticed me. "You make sure that one wears a helmet from now on."

"I definitely will," I assured her.

She patted me on the shoulder and walked out of the room.

Oliver sighed dramatically. "I've told them all a million times that I was, in fact, wearing a helmet, it just slipped off. No one believes me."

"It does seem like a lie you would tell to make yourself seem more careful."

"Giles can corroborate my story."

I drank in the sight of him, my night of restless sleep catching up with me now that I could see he was completely fine.

"The tests all went well? The doctors aren't concerned about anything?" I asked, eyeing the styrofoam cup of black coffee in front of Oliver. I'd left the one Giles had given me in the car. I'd hardly been able to drink it with the nerves churning around in my stomach.

Oliver followed my gaze and picked up the cup of coffee to hand it to me. I gratefully took a sip. Too hot, and had that distinct burnt taste, but it still roused my senses.

"Nothing they're concerned about. They said I should be out of here in a few hours."

"Thank God." I took the seat next to his bed and spilled into it, reaching out and grabbing his forearm to tether myself to him.

Oliver looked at our point of contact, a grin forming on his lips. "Thanks for coming," he said.

My forehead wrinkled. "I would have stayed here all night if they would have let me. I slept like shit because—"

"Because I wasn't there," Oliver finished, flashing me his teeth.

I squeezed his arm. "Something like that."

"Well don't you worry," he continued. "Tonight, we'll be back in my bed—or yours, if you prefer—and the doctors gave me the all clear on any extracurricular activities, especially those that can be done in the bedroom. In fact, he encouraged them. Said they would help with the healing process."

"Oliver!" I scolded, shaking my head.

Maybe it should feel strange sitting with a guy I was only casually dating in the hospital, but it didn't. Nothing felt weird with Oliver.

I chewed the inside of my cheek before finally spitting out the words I had been dreading. "I got the job. Found out yesterday."

Oliver's eyes widened and he sat up in bed. His smile never faltered, but I noticed the vein bulge slightly in his neck. The same way it always did when he tensed. It was so rare, but I'd come to recognize it.

"Of course you did! Congrats, Frankie." He grabbed my hand and tugged me toward him, wrapping me in a hug.

"I've been waiting to hear back for so long, it's surreal to finally have a start date and everything."

His grip tightened around me and my heart cracked a little. "When is it?"

"Next week."

He pulled away to cup my face before brushing his lips to mine. "I'm so fucking proud of you."

That familiar burn of tears roared at the back of my eyelids. One escaped before I could stop it.

Oliver's eyebrows pinched together as he brushed my cheek with his thumb. "No crying on my watch. This is amazing news."

I let out a shaky breath. "I'm happy." I sounded like I was trying to convince myself.

"You look it," Oliver said with mock seriousness.

"Shut up." I tried to pull away, but his gentle grasp held me in place.

"What's going on in that head of yours?" he asked.

I sucked in a breath through my nose, trying to sort through my thoughts like I was rifling through a jumbled file cabinet. "I'm happy I got it," I repeated. "I'm-I'm excited about the fresh start in New York."

"Then why the tears?" he asked.

"I guess I'm just mourning this." I waved my hand between the two of us. "This tiny little taste of whatever this was. Dinners with you at Marie's. You trying to drag me on some outdoorsy adventure I'm bound to be terrible at. Learning something new together—we haven't even conquered cooking yet."

"The last dish was almost edible," he said.

That made me laugh through my tears. "Being close to my sister too," I continued. "Having coffee with her every morning and seeing her whenever I want. It's stupid, but I never realized how incredible all the little things could be."

Oliver wiped away another tear. "That isn't stupid at all. I've thoroughly enjoyed experiencing all those things with you too. And hey, we still have another week of it. Don't go saying your goodbyes to me already."

I sniffed and leaned into his hand, letting him tangle his fingers in my wild, bedhead-riddled hair. "I know. It's just bittersweet." Even as I said the words, all I tasted was the bitterness.

Oliver offered me a lazy grin. "Why waste energy on feeling the weight of an ending when we should be celebrating what a ride it was?"

That was such an Oliver answer. I forced myself to nod in agreement, but the casual way he delivered those words stung a little.

This was all expected. Me getting a job. Him heading off to another adventure. Everything was right with the world. Yet I found my own personal universe thrown completely out of orbit.

Logically, I knew that Oliver was never going to make some grand gesture, like begging me to come with him. And logically, I knew I'd have no business exploring a life like that. However, the irrational, subconscious parts of me that I'd been working overtime to quell desperately wanted Oliver to make a move. Say *something*. Say that he couldn't imagine letting me go. Or say that he didn't have the answers, but we'd figure it out together. I secretly wanted him to tell me that losing me wasn't an option.

Finally, I said, "Who knows? Maybe you could swing by New York sometime. I could show you around."

Oliver's face fell, and my stomach dipped when I saw the pained expression twisting his features.

"Probably best to remember this as it is now. The perfect, fleeting moment in time."

I bit down hard on my lip and forced my gaze not to drop. Something like embarrassment ate away at my gut. Here I was, fantasizing about him not letting me go. Meanwhile, he was all too fine with never seeing me again. It wasn't like he hadn't been up front about who he was. He wasn't a long-term type of guy.

It didn't matter if I had fallen for him. This was ending in the way it was always supposed to. I couldn't wish for a rule change this late in the game.

Oliver's eyes scanned mine. "Frankie…" But his words trailed off to nothing as his eyes jerked to the doorway. I turned.

An older woman with dark hair pulled back into a braid entered the room. Her features were dark and her eyes all too familiar.

"Mom?" Oliver questioned.

I sprang from his bed and took a step back.

"Are you alright? The doctors wouldn't tell me anything." Her voice shook as she walked into the room.

Oliver sprang up from where he sat perched on the hospital bed, the thing in his arm monitoring something pulling taut as a result. "What are you doing here?" he demanded, clearly in shock.

I winced, feeling guilty. This was definitely my fault.

"Nathan told me, and I caught a flight late last night. I spent the night in the Denver airport, and flew straight here."

Oliver groaned. "How did Nathan know? I haven't called anyone." He pulled his hand from his face and turned to look back at me.

"I texted Lila," I offered. "I thought Harrison would want to know. He must have told Nathan."

Oliver let out a jagged sigh before opening his arms and giving his distraught-looking mother a hug. He still towered over her, but she was tall. Maybe five foot ten.

He held my gaze and I tried to pour every little bit of "I'm sorry" into my eyes. He gave me a small smile, and I chose to believe that meant he'd already forgiven me.

"I can't believe you didn't call me yourself. My son is in the hospital and I had to hear it secondhand."

"I didn't tell anyone because I'm fine," he insisted. "I'll be out of here soon. You shouldn't have wasted your airline miles."

Hurt splashed across her face and despite what I knew, I felt bad for her. She obviously wasn't perfect, but it was clear she loved her son.

"I'm going to give you two some privacy," I said, backing away toward the door.

"Wait," she called, extending her hand. "I'm Gina."

"Frankie," I said, shaking it.

She raised her eyebrows and glanced between Oliver and me.

"I'll call you later," Oliver said evenly, before I slid out into the hallway.

I felt guilty as I rushed back to the waiting room to find Mattie and Giles. Oliver would now be forced to spend some unexpected time with his mom because of me. I hadn't anticipated that result when I'd sent Lila a text about the accident.

A part of me thought this might be for the best. The two of them needed to talk.

Oliver might be an expert at avoiding tough conversations, but it seemed one had finally caught up to him.

THIRTY

Oliver

I LET MY MOTHER BERATE ME FOR NOT CALLING HER UNTIL A doctor thankfully released me a couple of hours after she arrived.

She'd driven me back to Key Ridge in my car, which Frankie and Mattie had dropped off earlier. The ride was quiet after I'd lied and told her I needed to rest. In reality, I'd pressed my face against the cool glass, shut my eyes, and let my thoughts spin.

Thankfully, it was slow season so Bev was able to put my mom up in a room at the lodge. I'd tried to pay, but Bev had insisted that family stayed free.

Now I was back in my apartment, showering the hospital feel off of me that was somehow simultaneously sterile and grimy all at once. My mom was getting settled in her room, and she was insistent that I show her around Key Ridge.

Seeing her show up to my hospital room in a panic had made me feel a little bad. She looked small and alone. We used to be so close. Now I'd put this distance between us. It was like I'd thought that the further I pushed her away, the better I'd feel.

But I didn't feel better. I felt gross. Ashamed. Talking never came easily with my mother. Growing up, activities had been her love language. I used to cherish that time. It made me feel special.

I'd just finished getting dressed when a knock sounded at the door.

"Shit," I muttered, knowing without checking that it was my mom.

I'd told her I'd meet her in the lobby in an hour but she hadn't listened. I was positive she'd asked Bev where I was staying and walked straight on over here.

"What happened to meeting in the lobby?" I asked, pulling open the front door.

My mom's smile fell for a moment before she put it back on. She brushed by me and into my space. "Excuse me for wanting to see where my son has been staying."

"Not much to see." I held up my hands and spun around, emphasizing the tininess of the space.

"It's adorable," she cooed, walking around. "Perfect for a short stay."

"Yep."

"How's your head?" She picked up a couch pillow and fluffed it before placing it back.

"Fine."

"Are you sure, because I can sleep here if you want. I don't mind a couch."

"I'll be fine," I insisted curtly.

She raised her thin brows. "Are you sure? Because—"

"Yes." My tone was even sharper this time.

My mom took a step back as if I'd physically slapped her or something. She cleared her throat before shaking her head.

"I'm not understanding all this hostility." I could hear the hurt in her voice, masked by frustration.

"Come on. I'm not being hostile." My head fell back with impatience. "Weren't we going to check out the town?" I asked, walking to the door and holding it open.

Ignoring my mother's phone calls were one thing. Having her standing in my space, openly addressing the cold way I had been treating her was another thing entirely. I couldn't take this. Especially not the day after a head injury.

"I don't want to cramp your style," she whispered, walking past me and reaching out to pat my chest. It was a clear sign of defeat. "Maybe I'll eat at the hotel and get some sleep. It's been a long day."

I squeezed my eyes shut. "No, Ma. Don't do that."

Her eyes searched my face. I wondered what they found there.

"I know when I'm not wanted," she said.

"I want you here," I insisted, although I knew my complicated feelings were displaying anything except that notion.

She shook her head. "Doesn't feel like it."

My gut churned when I saw the tears forming in her eyes.

"You never take my calls anymore," she continued. "Your visits are growing scarcer and scarcer. I'm not stupid, Ollie. I know you're pushing me away."

I sighed deeply and reached out to grab her arm, keeping her from stepping out the door. My avoidance tactics could only get me so far, and I was clearly at the end of my rope here. I needed to speak my truth as best as I could.

"Can you sit down for a minute?" I asked, walking over to the small kitchen table and pulling out a seat. I sat and waited for her. Thankfully, my mom obliged without resistance, shutting the front door and joining me at the table.

"What's going on with you, Oliver?" she finally asked.

Anxiousness coiled in my chest as I prepared to finally let the spring loose.

"First off, I'm sorry I've been ignoring you."

"I knew it."

"It's because I don't know how to talk to you—to clear the air."

She opened her mouth to speak, but she seemed to think better of it. For the first time, I wondered if she'd been expecting this conversation.

"I think you know that Nathan and I have grown close the past couple of years. Closer than we've ever been."

"Right," she said softly.

"Well, it's bringing up a lot of shit from growing up, and I don't really know how to handle it, if I'm being honest."

She stared at the ground, rendered speechless. I knew I needed to continue but the feeling in my gut begged me to stop. I took in another deep breath.

"You put too much on me, Mom. All those years of acting like it was us against Nathan and Dad…it wasn't right. I didn't know how to be close to my brother—I felt like I couldn't be. It was like being close to him was betraying you in some way. Do you know how fucked up that is for a kid to feel?"

She met my gaze briefly before jerking her eyes back to the floor. I half expected her to deny it, but she didn't. Instead, she finally whispered, "I'm so sorry for that."

It was like those words opened a floodgate.

"How could you treat him like that?" I demanded. "You ignored him, treated him like he wasn't even your son. Even now, whenever we talk, I hear the way you subtly throw digs at him. He's your *son*. He deserves better."

"I know."

"And I deserved better too. I should never have been your emotional support child, or whatever the hell I was."

She clasped and unclasped her hands. The silence was enormous. I thought I might suffocate in it, but at least I'd finally said *something*. Maybe not in the most eloquent way, but I'd gotten the words out.

"Your father and I weren't always…we weren't always like the way you knew us to be."

My eyebrows drew together. My mother *never* talked about my father and vice versa. Growing up, I hardly saw them interact. They didn't even share a bedroom. I'd realized that when I was in sixth grade.

"We met when I was young. He was older, successful. He was quiet, but I was enamored with him. Thought my flirty ways were getting under his skin, I don't know." She shook her head. "It was never supposed to be a forever thing. We had a short fling, that was all. He was too different from me. He was cold and calculated. In the short time we spent together, I realized he didn't want to change. He didn't think my free spirit was charming, he thought it was irritating. We didn't work. After we parted ways, I—I realized I was pregnant with Nathan."

My eyes widened. She'd never told me this.

"I knew I wanted to keep him the second I found out. Your father…he insisted I marry him. Perhaps I hadn't learned all my lessons at the time because I agreed. I thought it was romantic in a way. He was so harsh, but he was stepping up and doing the right thing. I thought we might be a real family. But walking down that aisle and signing the papers was the only thing he ever did right by me."

"Mom…"

"I had a hard time after Nathan was born. I wasn't feeling like myself. I was stuck at home a lot. It was hard. Nathan was the spitting image of your father. He took an interest in Nathan the way he never did me. Wanted to set him up for all these classes at a young age. Had all these grand plans. It felt like he was turning him into a mini him, and I felt all alone."

Tears welled in her eyes. "I know how wrong it seems. I was his mother. I should have stepped in. Should have bonded more. But I felt so alone. So empty."

She smiled sadly. "Then you came along. The day you were born, your father was on a work trip he'd insisted he couldn't miss. Your grandmother watched Nathan while I went to the hospital by myself. You were like this ray of sunshine immediately. Some women would have mourned the fact that their husband was thousands of miles away during the birth of their second child, but I rejoiced that it was just me and you."

She opened and closed her mouth, searching for the right words. "The older you two got... I knew it was wrong, but when I looked at Nathan all I saw was your father. I couldn't separate the two."

"He needed you. You knew how Dad was."

"I know, and I regret it. But at the time, I convinced myself I saw the same judgment and hatred in Nathan's eyes that I saw in your father's. I clung to you instead. My little sunshine."

I let her words sink in. They made sense in a way. I knew she thought Nathan and my father were cut from the same cloth. For years, I'd thought that too.

Nathan had been forced into that, though. Sure, he'd always been the logical one. He was never going to be naturally warm, and he'd always be a touch socially awkward no matter what. But it hurt to think that the coldness he'd developed was partially because he'd felt ostracized. If I had been left to be raised by my father, I doubted I would have turned out the way that I had.

I sighed and ran a hand through my hair.

"I'm trying to make things right with Nathan. I know I'm probably too late, but I'm trying," she added quietly.

"I know," I said, crossing my arms in front of me and taking in my mother.

For all her faults, she wasn't a bad person. She might have made a lot of mistakes, but hearing her side of things made me falter. Being stuck in a relationship with someone who made you feel that small…it couldn't have been easy. I knew how harsh Dad could be. He'd never cared for me. I'd grown to accept it, but it had never been easy growing up.

"Why did you stay with him?" I asked, struggling not to fantasize about what a childhood could have been like without my mother underneath his thumb.

"He would never agree to a divorce; said it was too messy. I had no savings of my own. I didn't know what to do…"

My heart broke a little for her. I knew she'd lost her parents when she was young. The only grandparents I'd ever known were my dad's parents, and they had always been harsh with my mother. They treated her like she wasn't good enough for their son.

"Hey." I reached over and set a hand on her forearm. "You were young. I get that. It must have been hard."

She looked down at the point of contact I offered her. "I regret everything with Nathan." She sniffled. "I saw a safe haven in you. Someone to finally be on my side. I should never have pitted you two against each other. I didn't even realize that's what I was doing. When Nathan said he was moving to Denver, I prayed that would be the moment you two finally grew close. There was nothing I wanted more in this life than to see the two of you get along…be the family I never gave you."

My mom had pressured him to stay with me back then, so I knew there was truth to her words.

"I'm glad I have Nathan now," I said. "I needed him."

She sniffled loudly and squeezed her eyes shut. "And I'll never stop trying to be better. I'm sorry if I can be judgmental toward him sometimes. It's just that I still struggle so much to understand him. I know that's my fault, though," she finished quietly.

I sighed and leaned forward. Nothing was fixed. It wasn't some magical conversation that wrapped all of the hurt into a neat bag and tied it off with a bow. But it was a start.

"Well, we can all try to be better," I said.

"I hope you can forgive me one day." A ghost of a smile drifted across her face before she finally met my eyes.

My shoulders sagged. I hadn't even realized how tight they'd been.

We talked for a little while longer, and she shared things with me I hadn't expected. She told me that all she wanted was to be a better mother to Nathan and me, to make up for the things she felt she'd missed. She was so determined for us all to be a family, especially now that Nathan and Charlie were expecting a baby. Despite the anxiety I'd had about this conversation, I could feel the sincerity in her words. There was no pretense, no effort to win me over. She was being real. It was a step in the right direction.

After what must have been hours, we had moved on from more serious topics to lighter ones, and I actually started to enjoy my mother's company again. I found myself grateful she was here.

"So." A mischievous glint formed in her eyes before she asked, "Who's Frankie?"

A strangled laugh escaped my throat. "Really? Subtle change of topic, Mom."

Her smile grew. "What? I couldn't help but notice the

beautiful woman at your bedside today was definitely not a nurse or a doctor."

"She's just a girl," I said, making the understatement of a lifetime. "A girl who's leaving soon. We both are. I'm headed out of Key Ridge next week."

"Ahh." Recognition flashed across her face. "Well, you've always been an adventurous soul. I thought maybe…the way you were looking at her." She offered me a shrug. "It seemed different."

My chest tightened, suddenly choked with the desire to go straight to Frankie and wrap her in my arms.

"She is different."

My mother nodded. "If my story can teach you anything, it's that you shouldn't change for anyone. If it's right, it'll all work out. You shouldn't have to force it."

Her words hit harder than she probably realized. Because I'd have to change a hell of a lot to work out with Frankie. We weren't meant to be in any sense of the word. We were temporary, just like my mother and father should have been.

But if that was all true, then why did everything feel so wrong?

***

"AND OVER THERE IS THE SKI HILL." I POINTED TO THE NOW-green mountain. There were still patches of snow here and there but it was almost completely dried up at this point. "You sure you don't want to get out there?" I joked, nudging my mom.

She laughed, her arm hooked in mine. "Please, I haven't skied in decades."

I smirked and shook my head. We'd already walked all around Main Street. My mom had popped into a few of the shops to get a few souvenirs—mostly baby clothes for Nathan and Charlie.

It felt good to spend this time with her, unburdened by some of the things that had been weighing so heavily on me. She seemed lighter too.

Things between us weren't shiny and new, but at least we'd popped out some of the dents. It helped that I knew how badly she wanted to make things better with Nathan. She was actually headed back to Denver tomorrow to spend time with him and Charlie. She was glowing at the thought of her first grandchild. My family was fractured, but that didn't mean it couldn't be mended. A patch on a hole was better than throwing the whole boat away.

"Dinner?" my mom asked. "I'm starving."

"Sure." I checked my phone to confirm Frankie had gotten my text. "Let's go."

We walked toward the Italian restaurant in town, one of the nicer establishments. It always had a line and smelled amazing.

Everything in me settled as soon as I caught sight of Frankie standing out front. Her hands were stuffed into a lightweight windbreaker as she looked up and down the sidewalk.

"Hey!" I called.

As soon as her eyes met mine, warmth spread through my chest. Damn, I loved that feeling.

"Thanks for meeting us." I wrapped my arms around her, sealing her to me in a hug.

"How are you feeling?" she asked, and gave a small wave to my mom. "Hi again, Mrs. Shaw."

"Gina," she corrected.

"I'm feeling fine. Good as new. Think I'll go mountain biking tomorrow," I said with a stretch.

"*Oliver*," my mother and Frankie hissed in unison.

I chuckled and let them think I was joking. In reality, the possibility of me hitting the trails in the morning was very real.

I held open the door to the cozy family-owned place as the only two women in my life walked through. The aromas of garlic and fresh bread hit us instantly.

"I'm surprised you didn't want to take her to Marie's." Frankie pulled off her coat as we waited for the host to seat us.

"I don't really like the food there," I said nonchalantly.

Frankie's eyebrows furrowed as she gaped at me. "You've eaten dinner there like four times a week since you got here."

"Because *you* worked there four times a week," I pointed out.

She blinked a few times. "You—you seriously don't like the food? Like at all?"

I bent over to plant a kiss on her forehead. "I like *you*." When I pulled back, I noticed my mom watching our exchange.

We were seated and ordered quickly. My stomach growled in anticipation. I'd only had the shitty hospital food to eat since yesterday.

As we ate our meals and fell into easy conversation, everything about the evening felt warm, like slipping into something comfortable. As I listened to my mom ask Frankie about herself, I couldn't help but feel at ease—like I could finally breathe again.

When my mom went to the bathroom, Frankie leaned in to whisper, "Things seem better between the two of you."

"We talked," I admitted.

"I'm proud of you." She squeezed my thigh, and all felt right in the world for a moment.

It was easy to trick my brain into thinking this was the first of many times the three of us would share a meal. That I wasn't about to say goodbye to her in less than a week's time. It was hard not to picture Frankie coming home with me for the holidays or spending our next birthdays together. How could this feel so fucking *right*?

When she'd asked me about visiting her in New York, it had pained me to say no, but I couldn't do it. As hard as a clean break would be for the two of us, continuing to talk from opposite sides of the country would be even harder. Letting myself see her knowing it was just for a short visit? That would be too cruel. What we had here was special— once in a lifetime. It was best to leave it at that.

After dinner, we said our goodbyes outside.

I gave Frankie a hug and whispered in her ear, "Can I come pick you up after I walk my mom home?"

She melted into me. "Please."

I stared as she walked the short block back to Mattie and Giles's house, not looking away until I saw her turn onto their street.

"She's great," my mom said.

"She is."

"Different than you," she added, no doubt thinking about how often Frankie had mentioned her new job over dinner. "But that isn't a bad thing."

I let out a sound of disbelief as we waited at a crosswalk. "Not a bad thing? You just went over recounting the tales of how disastrous you and Dad were. How I should never let anyone change me."

"Does she *want* to change you?"

My mouth snapped shut at that. Thoughts scurried through my brain. Frankie had tried to help me make plans, to get me to talk about my feelings and my past. It was all to help me, not to change me. In fact, I hadn't felt so seen and accepted by someone in…in I didn't know how long. No one had ever made me feel the way that she did.

"No," I finally said. "She doesn't want me to change."

"That right there is special."

"But I don't want her to change either," I said hollowly.

We turned down the street the lodge was located on. When we got to the front entrance, I gave my mom a hug good night.

She pulled away and squeezed my arms. "Oliver, I love you."

"Love you too."

"And I want to see you happy," she continued.

"Ma," I groaned, dragging a hand over my face. All I wanted to do was rush back to collect Frankie in my arms. I wasn't ready for any more talks tonight.

"Listen." She pointed a finger at my chest, eyes determined. When I didn't interrupt again, she continued. "I guess maybe moving on to the next thing will be what brings you happiness. But I can't help feeling that if you're always searching—always on the move—you might miss out on what truly matters. In the end, you could find yourself disappointed. Don't let your need to live a full life make you miss out on what could be the most fulfilling adventure yet."

THIRTY-ONE

Frankie

The day after tomorrow.

That was the end of my sentence here in Key Ridge.

I could hardly believe it. As much as I wanted to pretend it wasn't happening, my ticket was booked and I was already packed. Maybe packing days ahead of my departure was a bit excessive, but hey, I hadn't changed *that* much during my time here.

In less than forty-eight hours, I would be on a plane to Atlanta. I'd stop by my condo to get anything I'd need. Then it was off to New York to start my new career—or life, really. Funny, it didn't feel like much of a life. But it would be, right? It had to be.

I tossed my waves up into a messy bun before tugging on an oversized fleece I'd borrowed from Mattie. Something like homesickness washed over me as I toyed with the soft green collar. My sister would be sad to see me go, but she definitely wouldn't be upset about the fact that I could no longer raid her closet on a daily basis.

Before I walked out of the bedroom I'd hardly spent time

in lately, I paused in the doorway to take it in for a second. It was funny how sentimental big changes could make you. This was just my sister's guest bedroom, but when I looked at the worn quilt and the ancient wood side tables, all I could see was how relieved I'd been to rest my head here when I'd first gotten here. It had been a safety net amidst the unraveling of my life.

I sprinted up the basement stairs and through the house, stalling to say a quick goodbye to Giles and Mattie, who were curled up on the couch watching a movie, before stepping outside. The front porch light switched on even though the sun hadn't completely set yet. I hugged my arms around me. It was the warmest night I could remember since arriving here. But the crispness of the mountain air still hovered.

Taking a deep breath in, I perched on the front step, waiting for Oliver to pick me up.

He'd dropped his mom off at the airport earlier, and while we'd still managed to see each other plenty during her short visit, I was excited to have him all to myself tonight and tomorrow. While it was clear his relationship with his mom was still strained, and of course they'd bickered a little, I could sense a grain of relief in his demeanor. He was different. Released. When I told him again how proud of him I was for talking it out with her, he'd said he wasn't sure if he could have done it without me. I flushed at the memory. That alone filled me with more pride than landing any job ever could.

Headlights shone into the driveway, and I leapt up. Oliver jumped out of the car as soon as it was in park. I crashed into him. He laced his arms around me, holding me tightly as I inhaled the scent that clung to his sweatshirt.

"How many times do I have to tell you? I'll come to the door." Oliver pulled back a little, taking me in.

"I like waiting outside." I stood on my tiptoes and pressed a kiss to his lips.

We got into his car. I immediately went for the radio, turning it to one of the only two stations that came through. Our windows were both rolled down, the wind snaking through the car as he drove us down a few different residential streets.

The song playing in the background wasn't one I particularly liked, yet it fit the moment perfectly. I pulled out my phone to write it down. I needed mementos to bottle this feeling.

When Oliver pulled up to a park in front of a rather large playground, I turned to him with raised eyebrows. "A park?" I questioned.

"Yep." He smiled, looking pleased with himself, before hopping out of the driver's seat and jogging around to my side to open my door.

He took my hand and led me up a short sidewalk to the empty, colorful jungle gym.

"Swings," he said proudly. "You said you liked them, right?"

I barely remembered the time I'd told him I sometimes thought about swinging in the park across the street from my old condo. "We're too old." Even as I said it, I climbed onto the swing, my smile huge.

Oliver waved his arms around at the empty park. "Good thing there's no one around to see."

"I can't believe you remembered."

He dipped his chin. "Frankie, give me a little credit."

I gave him more credit than he could ever know. He was unique. Not to mention kind, thoughtful, genuine, and loyal.

I should have said all that to him, but instead, I focused ahead and started to rock back and forth on the swing, my legs kicking beneath me. The clouds from earlier in the day had cleared, leaving a bright orange and pink sunset in the distance. Soon, stars would start to poke out. It felt like a little Colorado gift for one of my last nights here.

I looked over to Oliver, who was swinging next to me now, a huge grin plastered to his face.

"How could we ever be too old for this?" he called.

Laughing, I tossed my head back, appreciating how uninhibited I felt any time he was around. Would I dare go to a playground and swing by myself in New York? Oliver made me feel brave enough to try anything. I hoped even a fraction of his boldness had rubbed off on me.

After a few more minutes, I let my feet graze the ground, abruptly halting the swing's momentum. I came to a stop, swaying back and forth. I turned toward him.

He stared at me instead of ahead. When I caught his gaze, he winked before leaning back in the swing, pumping aggressively, and launching himself off it. He landed a perfect backflip.

"Show off," I said.

He walked toward me and grabbed both chains of my swing in his hands, caging me in. "I've got to impress you somehow."

"You impress me all the time."

Something flashed in his eyes. He cleared his throat. "I wanted to thank you again. For spending time with my mom. I know it must have been awkward, but it really helped having you there."

"You don't need to thank me for that." I watched him closely, catching a fleeting glimpse of the uncertain side of him that I only saw on rare occasions. "I'm glad I got to meet her."

He smiled. "Me too."

Silence stretched between us, the weight of our separation hanging in the air. I was trying to ignore it—to be present, here in this moment—but it was all I could think about.

"So…" I started. "Any plans for after rafting? Going to try a new city this fall? I have to make sure you've got some sort of direction now that we're parting ways."

While I hated the idea of thinking about the future, I felt desperate to know where he'd be. To gather any information possible about what his future might look like. His future without me.

He paused, licking his lips before glancing down at the mulched ground. "It's hard to think beyond tomorrow, if I'm being honest."

"Same," I said weakly.

His words stabbed right into my heart. The tension building inside me threatened to burst free, but I attempted to force myself to remain positive and carefree.

"I wish you could take me rafting," I offered with a small smile.

He barked out a laugh. "I think I would be overly concerned for your safety."

"You could take me on an easy river."

"An easy river," he repeated with a chuckle. "Sure, pop on down, and I'll take you."

"And after that, you could come to New York and we could go to the top of the Statue of Liberty."

"Or walk across the Brooklyn Bridge," he added.

We were lying to ourselves. Oliver wasn't coming to New York any more than I was going to meet up with him to go rafting. We were pretending—imagining our lives as if this weren't goodbye.

Suddenly, the forced jokes were too much for me to

handle. The sadness that they weren't true broke the dam inside me, and tears flowed freely from my eyes.

"Why is this so hard?" I choked out. My sobs became more forceful as I wiped my eyes on one of my sleeves.

Oliver released the chains of my swing and clutched me to him, lifting me off the seat. He pressed his face into the top of my head. Everything in me felt like I was going to be physically ill. I had never had a relationship serious enough to be well-versed in breakups, but this felt abnormally difficult. How could it hurt so much that I could barely breathe?

"Why does it have to be like this?" I asked. "How am I supposed to leave you behind?"

"I like you more than I ever thought possible," he murmured into my hair. He sighed deeply before pulling back to stare into my eyes. "I've never cared about a girl the way that I care about you." He pressed his lips to both of my cheeks, kissing the tracks of my tears. "But you're headed to New York and you're going to kill this new job. I wish—" He let out a sharp exhale. "I wish that I could be the type of guy that gets you in the end. The one with a buttoned-up job and a college degree. But I don't deserve you, I never did. I don't belong in New York, just like you don't belong here."

His words were like a knife slicing right into my chest and turning slowly. Everything around us faded into the background. There was only me and Oliver.

"This isn't fair," I whispered.

My whole life, I'd been on this hamster wheel, honed in on a single direction. Now that I had veered slightly off course, getting back on track felt nearly impossible. How was I supposed to turn and walk away from him? He'd changed my life for the better. He made me happy—being here in this town made me happy.

But how could I stay? How could I give it all up?

"Frankie," he whispered, his eyes scanning mine as if in pain. "Trust me, if I could, I'd be yours. No question about it. But you're bigger than me. You're meant for more."

That made me cry harder.

"Hey," he said gently, but when I pulled away to look at him, I saw that his eyes were wet too. "No crying, okay? Tomorrow is our last day together and I want to see your smile so much it's permanently ingrained in my brain."

I sniffled.

"Okay?"

"Okay," I said.

"Now come on." He jerked his head toward the rest of the playground. "When else are we going to get to play on one of these things without any judgy mothers staring us down?"

We were off, climbing on monkey bars and sliding down slides. Only Oliver could have me smiling so much it hurt, while simultaneously still feeling the dry, cracked tears on my cheeks.

Was this what love felt like? It had to be.

Ever since his accident, when I'd seen him all vulnerable in that hospital bed, I was pretty sure it was love. Now I was certain.

Those three little words swam around inside my mouth—like they could gush out at any second, but I held them back. They'd only cause more pain. I couldn't tell him I loved him right before we said goodbye. It wasn't even the fact that I was worried he might not say them back. It was the fact that if I said them, I was worried I might never be able to let him go.

THIRTY-TWO

Oliver

"You had to outdo yourself, huh?" Frankie asked as we piled into the small cart set into a metal track.

Lately, our relationship had revolved heavily around healing, support, and letting each other in. But that wasn't where it had started. It had all started with fun. And what better way to end our time together than barreling down on a mountain coaster on a beautiful spring day?

"I figured I wouldn't be cruel and force you to do a physical activity on your last day here."

She sat between my legs, and I squeezed her tight as we fastened our seatbelts.

"I'm worried I might go into adrenaline withdrawal without you checking up on me," she said.

The employee ran through a few safety instructions before sending us down the hill. Frankie squealed almost immediately as our speed increased and the trees whizzed by us.

"Press the brakes!" she demanded. "This is too fast!"

"Life is too short for brakes!" I yelled, laughing as gusts of air breezed against our faces, whipping our hair back.

As we rode down the mountain, I felt more alive than ever. Not because of the rush or the speed, but because of the way my knees were firmly locked around Frankie's hips. With our countdown reduced from days to hours, I made every excuse to touch her and have her as close to me as possible. Tomorrow was going to absolutely gut me, and I knew Frankie wasn't fairing much better. But true to her word, she'd kept up a genuine smile nearly all day.

If I was being honest with myself, I was kind of worried how I was going to handle tonight. The last time I'd get to hold her in bed. The last time I'd hear her soft breathing next to my ear as she fell asleep right before I did. I shook the thought from my mind and focused instead on the beautiful scenery surrounding us and Frankie's delighted laughs.

My chest swelled when we got to the bottom and she begged to go again.

There was a lightness about her that wasn't there when she'd first arrived in Key Ridge, and I couldn't help but feel a sense of pride in playing a small part in the change in her. She'd changed me, too, of course. Despite this thing between us being temporary, her impact on me was permanent.

The only problem was that after our goodbye, I wasn't so sure what I was supposed to do with this newfound reflection of myself.

We rode down a couple more times. The last time, she went solo and slowed down so much, I ended up riding her tail. When I called out to remind her that she had nothing to be scared of, she turned and yelled back, "It's not about being scared, it's about enjoying the view!"

Damn it if that didn't make me even more obsessed with her than I already was.

After the rides were over and we got back into my car, I grabbed her hand and brought it to my lips, kissing it.

"Thanks for today. It was perfect," she said, looking beautiful with her hair wild and going in every direction.

"Can I drive you to the airport tomorrow?" The question fell from my lips, and I regretted it as soon as I saw her smile fade.

"That might be too hard, I think."

Her answer killed me, but I understood it all the same. It was going to be hard regardless of when the final goodbye happened. That still didn't stop me from wanting to drag out every moment with her—steal every last second like it was all I had.

I put the car into reverse and pulled away from the lot at the base of the mountain coaster.

"What would we do right now if we were the most carefree people in the world?" I asked her, rolling down both of our windows.

She squinted into the distance before offering, "Ice cream?"

"Ice cream it is."

LATER THAT NIGHT, I HELD HER IN MY ARMS, TIGHTER THAN I ever had before. My mind raced relentlessly.

First, it replayed every memory Frankie and I had made together in our short time here. From that first kiss at the bar, to her failed attempt at snowboarding, to sleeping in a tent underneath the stars together.

I had imagined Key Ridge would be an unforgettable experience filled with incredible outdoor activities and one extreme sport after another. Reflecting back on it all, it would have been nothing without her.

My thoughts drifted to her in New York. Wearing some

business-casual outfit and holding a to-go coffee mug as she raced to her new office. It was a side of Frankie I had never known, but that was the real her, apparently. She'd go on to have this perfect life that had nothing to do with me. She'd go apartment hunting. She'd find her new favorite restaurant. She'd meet new people. She'd *date*. I grimaced at the thought. She was still wrapped in my arms, and I still found myself being preemptively jealous of the next guy who would get to hold her like this.

She was *my* fucking girl.

Letting her go would be the hardest thing I'd ever done. My mind was starting to grow blank—forgetting every reason we couldn't be together. Was changing for a girl really the end of the world?

I attempted to picture myself in New York, showing up in a polo and khakis to an interview for some entry-level office job that I likely wouldn't land due to lack of experience. My entire being repelled that idea. But an idea my body found even more objectionable was never holding Frankie again.

I was in love with this girl.

There was no use in trying to deny the fact, especially within my own brain. Even though I had zero experience when it came to these things, I knew she was everything. Love wasn't something you could block out. Maybe I wouldn't say it out loud, but it was there.

What was that old saying? If you loved something, let it go.

And unfortunately, I loved Frankie so much that I would indeed be letting her go tomorrow.

THE DRIVE BACK TO HER SISTER'S HOUSE THE NEXT MORNING was quiet. Our fingers were loosely threaded together, resting in my lap. I kept sneaking glances at her, only to find her staring at me each time.

She was right not to let me drive her to the airport. This alone was already too difficult.

The goodbye had to happen sometime.

As we pulled into the driveway, every muscle in my body seized. This was it. As much as I'd tried to put this moment out of my mind, it was here. Throughout my life, I'd always managed to plaster on a smile no matter what—in awkward times, hard times, sad times, you name it. Making light of a situation was how I'd dealt with every problem.

So when we both got out of the car and slammed our doors shut, I was surprised to find that the corners of my lips were the heaviest they'd ever been. My forehead was tensed and my jaw clenched. I was fighting back emotion, and I couldn't even fake a smile if I wanted to.

It was taking everything in me to hold it together right now. I wanted to so badly for Frankie's sake.

When she came around the car to give me a hug, a few tears had escaped her eyes. I reached for her and held her to me like my life depended on it.

"Thank you for everything," she whispered.

I wanted to laugh, but I couldn't quite bring myself to. *Her* thanking *me*? Everything she'd given to me was far more than what I'd offered her.

"Miss you already," I said against the top of her head.

"Same." Her hands gripped the back of my shirt, and I never wanted to let go. Wetness formed in the corners of my eyes, and I begged the tears not to fall. I wasn't someone who cried, but I had never had to say goodbye to the girl I was in love with before. This shit wasn't for the weak.

The sound of the screen door opening caused me to look up.

"There you are. It's almost time to go…" Mattie's words trailed off as she caught sight of the both of us still in an embrace. "Sorry, I'll give you two a minute." She hurried back inside, the sound of the door swinging shut behind her.

"I guess this is it," Frankie said, looking up at me with wet eyes.

"Go knock 'em dead in New York."

"And you be safe out there rafting," she said, digging a finger into my chest. "No helmet mishaps again, got it?"

"Yes, boss," I said before dipping down and capturing her mouth with mine. My lips moved softly over hers, tracing every detail. When she pulled away, everything in me protested. No matter how long we stood out there, I knew the kiss would never be enough.

Then I let her walk away from me.

"Bye, Oliver." She gave me a wave, backing away toward the front door to the house.

"Bye, Frankie," I said, forcing myself to open the door to my car and climb in. My hand clenched around the gear shift as I put the car in reverse, actively making myself leave.

I rolled down the window to catch one more glimpse of what surely must be the most beautiful woman on the planet. She stood on the front porch, her body leaning against the door she had propped open. I backed out of the driveway, hardly taking my eyes off her.

With one last wave, I drove away from her, my eyes glued to the rearview mirror as I watched her grow smaller and smaller.

It wasn't lost on me that she didn't go inside until I turned off the street and was completely out of sight.

THIRTY-THREE

Frankie

My chest heaved with another sob as Bev wrapped me in her arms.

"Oh, dear, don't cry," she said, patting my back.

"Thank you for everything," I said. "For the kind advice. And for giving me a job even though I have no business being a bartender."

Bev chuckled and pulled away from me. She had stopped by the house to say goodbye to me. We were standing in the driveway along with Giles and Mattie.

"I'm going to miss you. Marie's was better off with you working there. I don't care how many incorrect drinks you made."

"That's nice of you to say, but I think the customers would disagree," Mattie said.

"Hey." I glared at my sister. "Be nice to me. This is an emotional goodbye."

Mattie's face was red too. We'd already had a nice little cry session as we'd packed my suitcases into her car. Being physically close to my sister during this time had been such a gift. I hadn't realized how badly I missed her until I was in her orbit.

"You guys will visit, right?" I asked, stepping over to Giles and giving him a short embrace.

"Definitely," he said. "Just let us know when you get settled." He gave me a few short pats on the back. "And you get back here too. Seriously, whenever you want, even if it's just for the weekend."

"Wow, you aren't sick of me?" I joked, stepping away from him.

He shrugged, smirking. "I mean, I didn't say come back for another *extended* visit, but…"

"I promise I have no plans to live in your basement again any time soon," I assured him.

With my last goodbyes being said, I had no choice but to climb into the passenger seat of Mattie's car. Part of me wished it was Oliver's car, but the intense ache in my chest assured me that I had made the right call not letting him drive me. I could barely think about him without completely breaking down.

Mattie got into the car and pulled away from the house. I watched it dreamily through the window, giving one last wave to Giles and Bev, who remained in the driveway.

"This is so much harder than I thought it'd be," I said, as she pulled away from her street and onto the main road.

"It doesn't have to be." Mattie glanced over at me. "You don't have to go."

Her simple sentence set me off once again. Waterworks flowed from my eyes. I opened the glovebox in search of a tissue only to find a crumpled brown napkin. I took it and blew my nose into the rough material.

"Why would you say that right now?" I wailed.

To Mattie's credit, she didn't back down. "Because it

doesn't have to be like this. I know not every decision in life is going to be the easy one, but don't you think chasing your dream shouldn't be this hard?"

"It's hard because of *him*," I said, knowing she'd know what I meant.

"Which is why I think you're going in the wrong direction."

"I can't believe you're trying to talk me into not going *on the way* to the airport."

I could hardly believe the gall of my sister. Didn't she know the kind of internal warfare I was already facing? The last thing I needed was for her to pile on the doubt too.

"I think you're making a mistake," she said.

"I can't upturn my life for some guy! Who do you think I am?"

"It's not for *some* guy, it's for your happiness!"

I blew my nose loudly and my body heaved again. I couldn't hold it in any longer. "I love him," I blurted out.

Mattie's mouth fell open, and she looked from me back to the road. "Oh my God. Frankie, what? Are you serious? Did you tell him?"

I shook my head. "That would just make things worse."

"He needs to know."

"I think he already does," I admitted. While we hadn't exchanged the words, actions spoke louder. The care with which we treated each other—the pain in our goodbye. It could only mean one thing.

Mattie let out a loud huff. "I can't believe you're about to get on a plane and leave without telling him that."

"What good would it do?"

"Ugh!" Mattie drug a hand over her face. "You have no idea how badly I want to turn this car around and drive you straight to him."

"It's already over," I said, the words hollow. "Once I get to New York, this wound, or whatever it is, will slowly start to heal. I'll kick ass at my new job and all will be right with the world."

Mattie sighed. "I really doubt that." Her voice was defeated, but I couldn't let her doubt infiltrate my mind. I needed to get on that flight.

This whole experience was like ripping off a Band-Aid. The sting would linger, but it would only get better the faster I did it.

When we finally pulled up to the airport, my sister wordlessly got out of the car and walked to the trunk before opening it. I pulled out my luggage and slung my backpack around my shoulders.

"Don't be upset with me," I said, a new set of tears threatening to be released as I gave my sister a hug goodbye. I knew I'd see her and that we'd talk, but it wouldn't be the same. Having her close again had been so comforting. I'd cherish this time forever.

"I'm not upset." Judging from the deep frown on her face, I wasn't sure I believed her. "I just want you to be happy."

"I will be." I squeezed her arms and tried to believe the words as I said them.

"I love you," she said. "Text me when you land."

I watched her get into the car and pull away, sticking her hand out the window and waving until she was out of sight.

I pulled in a slow breath and exhaled. This was it. The moment my next chapter started.

As I entered the airport and checked my bags, no feeling of excitement or anticipation crept in.

There was only emptiness.

THE GROUND SHRANK AS IT ROLLED BY UNDERNEATH THE airplane.

When the flight attendant stopped by and asked me if I wanted anything to drink, I half contemplated getting a glass of wine to numb myself but then decided that would just make the whole situation even sadder. Instead, I sipped on a ginger ale, praying the bubbles would settle the queasiness that still brewed in my gut.

I hadn't been on a plane since the day I'd gotten laid off. I'd felt so small and scared for what was next back then. I'd felt worthless.

When had that all changed?

Part of me thought it might have been the moment I'd first met Oliver. Even before I knew he would be someone significant. Bantering with him at that bar was the first time I'd felt even a crumb of pleasure. And then our first kiss…

Ugh, why did flying make me feel so reflective? If I started to think about Oliver again, I'd definitely start crying, and my eyes were still swollen from this morning.

Even as I tried to stop the floodgates of memories, they started to play like a compilation of our greatest hits.

From the moment I met him, Oliver had challenged me to live a life worth remembering. Every interaction we'd shared had changed me for the better. It was the kind of connection that only came around once in a lifetime, I was sure of it.

Despite the tears bubbling to the surface, the tightness in my chest loosened at the memory of us snowshoeing together. How patient he'd been despite how obviously out of shape I was. He had a knack for turning the things I dreaded into something worthwhile.

Pretty soon, I caught myself fantasizing about the future. But in my fantasy, there was no small New York apartment. There was no drinks with coworkers or a big promotion at work. Instead, I saw myself laughing over a picnic with Oliver. I saw us hiking, him always trailing behind to stay next to me. I saw us getting dinner with Mattie and Giles and Bev. I imagined myself going back to Denver with him and finally meeting his brother.

It all filled me with such an overwhelming sense of peace that I nearly jolted straight out of my seat at the realization.

I was in love with Oliver.

That wasn't just going to go away. He had somehow become the most important thing in my life.

As the miles grew alarmingly fast between us, I started to panic.

What the hell was I giving up? The man of my dreams for a *job*? The thought made me shudder. What was I doing? Forcing misery on myself to complete some preconceived notion I had of my future? It was pure stupidity and denial.

My dream had changed.

I didn't actually *want* this job, I'd just wanted to get it. To assure myself that I was still worthy. Now that I had it? I couldn't think of anything worse.

Mattie was right. I was making a mistake. A colossal one. The pain would never ease because this wasn't the path I was supposed to be on.

I belonged with Oliver. I wasn't entirely sure what that meant or where it would lead me. All I knew was that being with him was where I needed to be.

THIRTY-FOUR

Oliver

I stuffed the last of my T-shirts into my duffel, forcing the zipper shut. All of my stuff had been packed up in a matter of minutes. The small studio apartment I had found so homey at first now felt stifling.

As soon as I'd driven away from Frankie, I'd come back here and paced for an hour straight. The energy coursing through my body urged me to chase after her. I had to actively keep moving to stop myself from rushing to her before her flight took off.

What the hell was wrong with me? I had no big master plan.

She was gone. I had to accept it. Simple as that.

Except there was nothing simple about it. My brain had gone into overdrive, thinking about nothing except her. It was pure torture at this point.

As soon as I'd gotten back to the apartment, I realized there was no way I could stay.

Originally, I'd told Bev I'd work one last shift at Marie's, but I honestly thought being back at that bar without Frankie would kill me. Shame ate at me that I'd have to bail on my commitment, but I wasn't strong enough to fake it. Plus, a grown man crying behind the bar because he'd let the girl he loved get away? Talk about pathetic. Bev would likely send me packing anyway if she had to witness that.

I strode out of the apartment, not bothering to linger and give it a final look. All the happiness I'd had inside it was already gone. Vanished, just like that.

Closing the door behind me, I locked it before stuffing the key underneath the welcome mat at the top of the staircase.

Dread consumed me as I walked down the stairs and tossed my bags into my car. I could only hope this feeling would ease slightly as I put Key Ridge behind me.

The lodge loomed in front of me as I debated a quick and easy escape. Even as I thought it, I knew I couldn't do it. Bev and Giles had done so much for me in my short time here, and I wanted to say my goodbyes and apologize to Bev for bailing a day early.

As soon as I walked into the lodge, a tension grew. This place held only fond memories for me, yet I was itching to leave the instant I caught sight of the entrance to Marie's out of the corner of my eye. Thankfully, Bev was at the front desk so I wouldn't have to torture myself with going in there right now.

She lifted her eyes from the computer in front of her and took me in. Recognition flashed across her face instantly. "You're heading out." She didn't ask it, she said it matter-of-factly.

Wincing, I propped up an elbow on the desk, resting my head against my hand. "I have to."

She sighed, looking at me with warmth I didn't feel like I deserved right now. "I figured you might say that. Too bad, I was looking forward to spending one last evening with you."

"I'm sorry about that. Hopefully the bar won't be too slammed."

She waved off my apology. "Don't worry about it. It's been dead this past week. I'll manage."

I still felt like shit, though. When had I become someone so fragile I would bail on my commitments when things got hard?

"I wanted to say goodbye."

She walked around from behind the desk and gave me a quick hug, patting me on the shoulder as she pulled away. "It was absolutely a pleasure having you, Oliver. You're welcome back any time."

"Maybe next winter," I offered, although this pain was still too raw to consider returning to Key Ridge.

"You leaving, man?"

I turned to see Giles and Mattie walking into the lodge. Mattie's face was bright red and her eyes were swollen. Shit. She looked about as good as I felt.

"Yeah," I said. "Just making the rounds."

Giles walked over and clasped my hand and we gave each other a brief one-armed hug.

When I went to offer Mattie a hug, she glared at me.

"Um, bye?" I offered, wary to go in for a hug.

As fast as the glare arrived, it crumpled and a few tears streamed down her face. Damn, the resemblance between her and Frankie was obvious right now. It killed me.

"This is all wrong," she said.

Giles let out a long sigh. "Mattie, don't."

"No," she said, shaking her head. "This sucks. You two are so hellbent on following these ideals you've made up in your mind, you're blinding yourselves. You're giving up the only thing that matters."

Now I wanted to bolt. She was talking about Frankie and

me, and I didn't know what to say. I was trying to do the right thing by her, but this whole situation was so far out of my league. I had no idea what the hell I was doing. All I knew was that doing what was best for Frankie was the most important thing.

"She loves you, did you know that?" Mattie sniffed.

My ears perked up. "What did you say?" I demanded.

"Mattie, that isn't yours to share," Giles said, rubbing his jaw and looking between the two of us.

I barely heard him. All of the wind had been knocked out of me.

"She told me she loved you but she wouldn't tell you because she didn't want to make this worse." Mattie flung her arms out in frustration. "How stupid is that? You two are clearly miserable and fighting some internal war against yourselves. How can you both be so dumb?"

"I—I…can't be the kind of guy she needs," I stuttered, still in shock.

She loved me? She'd actually said that?

"Says who?" Mattie's eyes narrowed. "When you have to actively fight this hard to be away from someone, that *means* something."

Everything started clicking into place. It was like slow motion and the speed of light all at once.

Frankie loved me. Probably not nearly as much as I loved her, but it was a start. I had this all wrong.

You didn't let go of the ones you loved. You showed up over and over again, even when they didn't ask you to.

What the hell was wrong with me? I didn't have any ties. I was going off to be a rafting guide, for Christ's sake. And then in a few more months, I'd be on to something else temporary. I had no ties holding me in place.

Well, except for one.

At some point, Frankie had tied a string right around my heart—the kind that couldn't be severed. As I stood here, that string was getting pulled more taut by the second.

No wonder I was in so much fucking pain.

"I think I have to go," I said, my voice rising.

Mattie scanned my face as Giles's eyes widened.

Bev let out a low chuckle. "Seems like some sense is finally getting knocked into you," she said.

I reached out, gripping Mattie's shoulders. "What's her flight info?" I asked.

She smiled broadly. "You mean it? You're really going after her?"

"What's her flight?" I demanded again, panicking I had already let so much time pass.

Mattie checked the time on the clock against the wall.

"She'll be landing in Denver in the next twenty minutes or so, but she's got a layover."

"There's another flight to Denver that leaves in an hour," Bev chimed in, typing on the lodge's computer. "I don't know if you can make it, but…"

I was already sprinting for the door.

I heard yells of, "Go get her!" at my back.

Who the fuck cared if she was meant for some hotshot job in New York? I was wrong when I said I didn't belong in a big city. I belonged where she was. I was aimless and she was my direction. If she didn't want me to follow her to New York, then she'd have to tell me herself. Because I wasn't going anywhere without her.

I wasn't about to let Frankie get away like some sort of coward. I had been running from what was real my entire life.

This time, I wasn't going to let the realest thing that had ever happened to me slip through my fingers.

THIRTY-FIVE

Frankie

My foot tapped incessantly against the marble-tiled floor.

We'd had to wait on the tarmac for over an hour, and I'd almost suffocated being stuck inside that hot plane. The moment I'd gotten off my flight, I'd made a beeline for the ticketing counter. Apparently, everyone going to Atlanta had some dire need to speak with a customer service representative, because the line was still ten people deep.

I'd tried calling Oliver, but it had gone straight to voicemail. I anxiously scanned my phone. There was only one more flight back to Key Ridge tonight, and I had to be on it. I didn't even care that my luggage would still be routed to Atlanta; I'd get it later. All I knew was that Oliver was supposed to leave in the morning, and I couldn't let that happen without baring my soul to him. I hoped it was enough.

I had to tell him I was in love with him.

Maybe not taking this job was about to be the craziest, most irresponsible move I'd ever made. Maybe chasing a guy was completely delusional. The only thing I was certain of was that ever since I'd come to this decision, I hadn't stopped smiling. Joy radiated from me, the kind that I'd expected but had never appeared when I'd accepted that so-called dream job.

I felt free—free to run into his arms. Now I had to hope they'd still be open for me. Part of me was nervous. This was Oliver, after all. Allergic to commitment, hater of deep conversations, carefree Oliver. But underneath my nerves, I knew how he felt about me.

I'd be yours if I could.

Oliver had never said he hadn't wanted me for keeps. He just wasn't meant for the life I thought I'd wanted to live. A life I had now realized I didn't want either. It couldn't bring me the happiness I'd found in Key Ridge. I could confidently return to him now, excited to start the next chapter, whatever that may be. I had absolutely none of it figured out, but I didn't care. He was all I wanted. We'd figure the rest out together.

The line remained stalled as I anxiously checked the time on my phone. I couldn't miss this flight back to Key Ridge. I thought about calling Oliver again, but I wanted the big grand gesture. His face when he saw me knocking at his apartment door? It was too good to pass up.

I was barely aware of someone yelling something in the distance as I peeked around to watch in agony as the elderly woman at the front of the line fished around for something in her purse.

Then I heard it. The faint sound of my name. It couldn't be though…

I jerked my head around and nearly choked on a laugh.

Oliver was sprinting down the moving walkway, dodging people and waving frantically with a huge grin on his face. "Frankie!" he called again.

The entire terminal was staring at him at this point, but he didn't seem to care. Of course he didn't.

His hair hung in his face and his eyes were brighter than I'd seen them in days.

I gasped and brought a hand to my mouth, leaving the line and jogging toward him. He caught me in his arms as I wrapped my hands around his neck. He kissed me and I wanted to sob with relief.

"What are you doing here?" I asked when we broke free.

"Getting the girl," he said, tucking a piece of hair behind my ear.

His words nearly caused my heart to explode.

"I can't believe you're here," I said, brushing my fingertips along his jawline.

"Well," he said, squeezing his arm even tighter around my waist, "it was brought to my attention that you might be in love with me, and I thought it would be a shame to let you get on this flight without telling you that I'm in love with you too."

"Y-you are?" I blinked the tears from my eyes.

"Very much." His dark eyes searched mine.

I kissed him again, still not believing this was real life. Maybe Mattie had been right all along. Life could be a fairy tale, and this was mine.

When we finally parted, he raised an eyebrow and tilted his head.

"What?" My forehead crinkled.

"Don't you have something to say to me?" he probed.

Thoughts whizzed through my mind. I had about a million things I wanted to say to him, but where to start?

He gave a dramatic sigh. "I know that you told Mattie you were in love with me and all. And, of course, she told me. But —now this is just me personally— I think it would mean a hell of a lot more coming from your mouth. You know what I mean?"

I giggled, my cheeks tight from smiling. "I love you, Oliver."

"Ugh," he groaned, dipping his head to kiss me again. "That sounds so fucking good coming out of your mouth."

"I wanted to tell you, but I thought I was being selfish," I admitted.

"Never hold back from me again, okay?" he said, forcing a stern voice that didn't sound at all natural coming from his lips. "That was my thing, and you broke me of it. No more secrets, got it?"

"Got it." I nodded.

His arms were the only thing keeping me tethered to the ground.

He took a piece of my hair and tangled it in his fingers. "I'm sorry I let you go. I thought that I couldn't be the kind of guy you need, but I realized, the kind of guy you need is someone who's going to show up. Someone who will put you first. I thought I didn't have it in me, but you made me realize that I do. I don't care if it's New York or the middle of fucking nowhere. I want to be around you always. Adventure will come no matter what, but it's not going to be worth living if you aren't there."

His words were even more than I had been hoping to hear. He was thinking about coming with me to New York? Even though I had already mentally turned away from that path, just the fact that he was willing to follow me there meant the world.

"I'm not going to New York," I said, smiling.

His eyebrows drew together. "What are you talking about?"

I pointed to the line behind me. "I was waiting to get a

flight back to Key Ridge. To tell you that my dreams have changed. I think they did a while ago, but I was too scared to admit it to myself."

He looked at the line and then back at me, comprehension spreading across his face.

"That job isn't important to me. You showed me what living could really be like. And I want that. With you. I don't care what we do—stay in Key Ridge, try something else. Whatever it is, it sounds like the most exciting thing in the world, and I can't wait to experience it with you."

"Are you joking?" he said, shaking his head slowly.

"Nope."

"You have no idea how happy that just made me," he said before his mouth covered mine again.

After a minute, when we came up for air, I started laughing.

"Look what you did," I said. "You did exactly what you said you would—showed me how fun life could be. You got to me."

"Yeah, I did," he said proudly.

I shook my head, still smiling. "You even left me without a plan. And even after all these weeks, I never did manage to help you find any of your own."

Oliver's gaze stayed fixed on me, as if I were the only person in existence. "*You're* my plan, Frankie. You're all my plans."

Epilogue

OLIVER

"GOT EVERYTHING PACKED?" FRANKIE ASKED AS SHE LUGGED A bag into the back seat of my car.

"Yep," I said, stuffing a duffel bag along with a ton of loose items into the trunk.

She rolled her eyes at my mess.

Spending all of my time around her had changed me in so many ways, yet when it came to the small stuff, it seemed I would be this way forever.

She pinched a pair of my socks between her fingers. "Are these clean at least?"

"Of course, babe," I said, dipping down to kiss the top of her head. "I'm not *that* bad."

"I'm buying you a new duffel," she insisted.

We moved to the front seats. I slammed my door shut before buckling my seat belt.

"My duffel is fine," I said.

She laughed and stretched out in the passenger seat. "Clearly not. You're busting out of it every time. You should be a pro at packing by now, considering you've been living out of that thing for months."

"I'll figure something out eventually," I said. "Maybe whenever we get settled."

"I'm not worried about it." She beamed at me—fucking *beamed* at me.

I'd never get sick of this. To think, there was a time I was worried I wouldn't be enough for her. Now she looked at me like I hung the stars. I ruffled her hair before placing my hand on the back of her headrest and turning my head to reverse the car out of the driveway.

"Wait!" Mattie called, sprinting down the porch stairs, waving a sweatshirt. "You forgot this in the laundry pile."

Frankie rolled down her window and snatched it. "Thanks."

"See you in a few weeks," Mattie said, still panting from her short burst of exercise.

"See you," Frankie said. "And I promise, we'll find somewhere more permanent to stay that's not your basement."

"No, stay." Mattie pouted. "August flew by, I mean it. You can stay as long as you want."

"I think Giles might prefer his privacy," Frankie said.

I'd prefer my privacy too. The basement room had been fine, but I was definitely looking forward to having a place of our own.

I'd joked about buying us a camper, but while Frankie seemed excited about that idea when it was just for me, she hadn't been too keen on it for us as a couple.

We pulled away, heading straight for Denver. The summer heat had finally faded as September brought the promise of fall with it. Pretty soon, winter would be here. I could practically sniff it in the air. I was looking forward to teaching snowboarding lessons for the entire winter season this year in Key Ridge.

The summer had been a blur of smiles and laughter and lazy nights spent wrapped around each other. After I'd made my grand gesture at the airport, Frankie had turned down that job in New York, almost having an anxiety attack in the process. But after she'd dropped the news and hung up the call, she'd giggled maniacally and jumped up and down. I was kind of worried I'd created a monster.

Instead of heading straight back to Key Ridge, I'd bought a flight to Atlanta instead so that Frankie could officially leave that phase of her life behind. She showed me around the city and we spent a few nights in her condo, slowly selling things online as she realized she didn't really like anything she owned. Her roommates were less than welcoming; they had their noses stuck in the air the whole time.

"You turned down a job for a *guy*?" one had said.

"You're moving to the middle of nowhere?" the other asked.

Frankie barely gave either of them the time of day, choosing to spend all her time frolicking around the city with me instead. She'd said it was funny how she'd had more fun with me in a few days in that city than she had in all the years she'd lived there. Seeing something through the lens of being stupid in love did that to you, I guess.

It also made me even more sure that even if I had followed her to New York, we would have been just fine too. Having a partner like her completely balanced my life in every way.

When we'd gathered all her stuff and caught a flight back to Key Ridge, Mattie's squeal had nearly broken the sound barrier.

At first, I had thought I would bail on the rafting gig, but

Jay had said Frankie was more than welcome to come and stay in a cabin. She could help out with meals and the place had internet. Driving down there had cemented for me that this had been the best decision. Arriving there with her hand in mine felt like winning the lottery. The summer that had started to dim, once again shone with possibility now that she was by my side.

The summer months went by fast. While I guided rafting tours, she spent days enjoying the weather or casually job hunting, trying to decide what she might want to do next. She'd completely freed herself of any prior preconceived ideas she'd had about what her career should look like, and only searched for things she thought might add value to her life.

Being a rafting guide had been fun—up until mid-July, that is. I had finally convinced Frankie to go on one of the tours with me. During an especially violent wave, she got knocked in, nearly giving me a fucking heart attack. Thankfully, she'd remembered everything I taught her and we were able to get her back inside the raft without further incident. When we got back to land, she even had a glint in her eye and said it was fun. I, however, was permanently scarred and refused to let her go again. I couldn't handle it.

Funny, I used to be the king of pushing people to their limits. Now I was acutely aware of just how fragile Frankie was at any given moment. Maybe I wouldn't be attempting to convince her to give snowboarding another try this winter after all. I'd feel much better if I knew she was safe and cozy in front of a fireplace somewhere.

"You sure Charlie and Nathan won't mind us staying there? It's so weird. It's like she's my new boss, and I'm staying in her guest bedroom. I barely know her."

Funny enough, Frankie had gotten back in touch with

Lila. Apparently, what Lila had said about the job at her start-up had really stuck with her. She ended up interviewing remotely and landing it. Now we were headed to Denver for a couple of weeks so she could onboard in person and get to know the team. I was pumped to be back in town for a bit to spend more time with Harrison and my brother.

"It'll be fine. She's excited to get to know you better. Nathan's excited too."

I glanced over to find her leveling me with a look. "He did not say that."

I chuckled and stared straight out at the road ahead of us.

Nathan, in fact, had *not* said that, but that was just Nathan. He had, however, insisted we stay with them when I had mentioned getting a hotel—something that had surprised even me. My brother was growing softer by the second. Perhaps it was the fact that my niece would be here in a couple of months.

Even my mom had up and decided to move to Denver on a whim last month. She'd said she wanted to be near Nathan in case he needed her help. I wasn't sure how thrilled Nathan was with that idea, but it meant a lot that she was trying. We might not be the most functional family, but we were a family, nonetheless.

I reached over and squeezed Frankie's hand. "Love you," I said.

"Love you too," she replied, smiling. "What was that for?"

I shrugged. "Because I'm so fucking happy."

She scooted over to nestle her head on my shoulder as we set off on the hours-long drive. The road ahead looked pretty damn great, both literally and figuratively.

I'd never not feel like the luckiest man in the world that she had chosen me. The twist of fate that had landed us both in the same town at the same time must have been the universe screaming at us that we were soulmates.

No one got me the way she did, and I knew she felt the same.

Everything about us was meant to be.

The End

Thank You for reading
Meant for Now! As an indie author,
I appreciate your support so much.
If you enjoyed it, please take a few
moments to leave a review!

Haven't read Giles and Mattie's story yet?
Key Ridge *is available to read now!*

Keep reading for a sneak peek of…

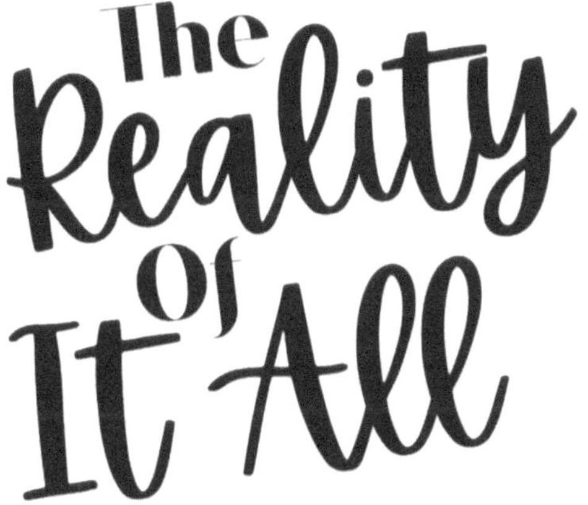

*A reality TV romance ft. a writer stuck in her own head
and a washed up actor with a bad reputation…*

The Reality of It All

"Calla, you almost ready?"

I tore my gaze away from my reflection to find Brady hovering in the door of my suite.

"Um, can I have a few more minutes?"

"Of course." He flashed a reassuring smile that did little to settle the queasy feeling in my stomach. "I'll knock again in five, but then we really have to go." His tan hair flopped forward as he raised a walkie-talkie to his mouth. "Number two needs five more minutes. I repeat. Number two needs five more minutes."

The way he so effortlessly reduced me to a number made me wince. Brady seemed nice for someone who worked in reality television, but then again, I was completely oblivious to this world. Anyone who knew me would never have said I was the kind of person to do this sort of thing. They'd all have insisted that quiet, shy Calla did not have the right personality for TV.

I looked back at myself in the mirror, taking in my bright blue eyes, now lined with soft brown liner. Rosy blush dotted both of my cheeks, and my raven hair was styled in a long braid. The hair and makeup team had begged me to wear my hair down in loose, long waves, but I'd insisted on wearing it pulled back. The makeup already felt like a lot. This was a writing competition, after all; it wasn't like I was going on *The Bachelor*.

Smoothing one of my eyebrows, I continued to inspect myself. I had never felt self-conscious before now, but I had also never experienced the stress of considering what the general public might think of me. People were harsh and cruel, and I feared I would be no match for their scrutiny. Sure, I was pretty, but not in the way that caused people to stop and stare. Everything about me was intentionally understated, just how I liked it.

This was a writing competition, I reminded myself again. For authors. How many people would even watch? And if anyone did, surely they'd care more about my talent than the way I looked.

Calla Scott, budding novelist from Chicago, arriving for her chance to compete on The Next Great American Classic.

The whole idea was unfathomable. When my sister, Piper, had applied for me, I'd told her she was being utterly ridiculous. Then, when the call came announcing that I'd been selected, apprehension had smacked me in the face.

Of course, I'd declined. I had already sold my first novel two years before. Sure, there had been a bit of a publishing delay, and now I had terrible writer's block, but I'd still sold it. I hadn't written anything new since the accident, but I found it hard to fathom that a show could help with that.

But Piper had begged me, with tears in her eyes. She'd said I was fading into nothing right in front of her. I believe her exact words had been something along the lines of, *your numbness is sucking the life out of me.*

So, because I loved my sister, and not because I thought this experience would have some profound effect on me, I'd agreed.

Another knock.

"Calla. It's time."

Standing from the vanity, I tugged on the hem of my most comfortable sweater, ensuring it lay smooth. It was my favorite and made me feel like a writer whenever I put it on, which is why I'd found it so strange earlier when the producer had begged me to change. What said 'writer' more than a cable-knit sweater? It was even weirder when they'd strongly suggested I wear a dress. Why would I wear a fancy gown to pitch book ideas? Surely the other contestants would be wearing similar things.

"Let's do this," I said, with more confidence than I felt.

"That's the spirit."

Brady ushered me through the door of my room, and I found myself face to face with a mounted deer head. It stared right into my soul before I tore my eyes away and continued down the hall. The whole thing was being filmed at a remote lodge in Montana. It seemed a bit random, but when I'd asked, Brady had mentioned something about a state tax credit and budget restrictions.

"Don't get overwhelmed, but you'll be meeting a lot of people when we first get down there. We've split everyone into two groups. You'll meet one set first, and then we'll bring the others in."

I practically had to jog to keep up with his hurried pace.

"I'll put you in one of the side rooms we use for interviews and knock when it's time for your big entrance.

"The sound guy will come in and get you all mic'd up. Remember, any time you're in the lodge, there will be hidden cameras recording you. It's vitally important that you don't remove your mic during filming, and you stay in the designated rooms. You remember which ones those are, right?"

He'd provided me with a map yesterday that labeled all of the areas of the lodge that we'd have access to. I thought back to that, recalling most of the information. My head spun trying to process it all. I was surprised to learn they'd be filming us even during our downtime. Wouldn't people just be tuning in for the competition aspect? Maybe they thought there would be drama among the contestants. They certainly wouldn't be getting that from me. Confrontation gave me hives.

Brady stopped abruptly at a wooden door in the middle of the hallway. I recognized it instantly as the room where we'd filmed my introduction interview. They had peppered me with question after question about my "sob story," as the producers had so eloquently called it. I had tried to limit the information I'd shared with them as much as possible. The last thing I wanted was for people to root for me because they felt sorry for me.

"Okay, here we are." He ushered me inside. "Our sound guy will be here in a moment, then someone will come get you when we're ready."

I nodded.

Brady sighed. "You know you'll actually have to speak once you get out there, right?"

"Of course," I said hollowly. Piper had made me promise to make an effort, but my heart wasn't in this at all. I suddenly felt desperate to be back home in the comfort of my small apartment.

"Good luck." Brady squeezed my arm and closed the door, sealing me inside the windowless room; one which had most likely been a closet before they decided to film in here.

Tears welled up at the corners of my eyes and an overwhelming sense of feeling out of place washed over me. In the past two years since the accident, this was the farthest I'd ventured from home. I already missed my mother, whom I spoke to almost daily. And I missed Piper, who, despite being single and having better things to do, always dropped in to check on me every Friday. She knew weekends hit me the hardest.

I was still afraid that coming here had been a mistake, but I pulled my shoulders back and drew in a deep breath.

I'd promised Piper I would give this a fair shot.

Plus, I couldn't hide forever.

Twenty minutes later, a microphone hung around my neck, connected to a wire around my waist. I'd been given very strict instructions not to remove the mic under any circumstances; the sound guy had basically put the fear of God in me.

The door opened, revealing Shay.

Shay was the other producer—or handler, as they called themselves. She and Brady oversaw the contestants. They ensured we were in the right place at the right time, and had conducted our original interviews. Shay was maybe forty, with a cropped hairstyle and a stern look about her. While Brady at least pretended to be empathetic and kind, Shay's eyes held no warmth.

When I arrived from the airport two days ago, she had immediately taken me to be interviewed. I had begged for a shower and a nap and she had begrudgingly agreed, complaining the entire time that we'd be behind schedule. After that, I was definitely on her bad side.

"Let's go." She waved me out of the room.

I followed, not wanting to give her any more reasons to dislike me.

She pointed down the hall. "Follow this to the main lounge. The other contestants will trickle in slowly. Introduce yourself as they come. The host will join you all shortly. Whatever you do, do not leave the lounge until instructed to do so."

I nodded, even though she wasn't looking at me.

"Got it?" she barked.

"Got it," I squeaked.

"Don't forget your voice. This is a TV show."

"I won't," I insisted.

Following her direction, I took tentative steps toward the space where the hallway opened up into a room. Beyond the arch were high, vaulted ceilings. Cameras were likely embedded in every wooden beam. Brady had told me to pretend they didn't exist.

The hallway shrank before me. Five more steps and I'd be there. No turning back now.

Four.

Three.

Two.

One.

The room was a grand, open space, with several couches and chairs arranged around a massive stone fireplace. Walls of large windows on both sides of the room let in the afternoon sunlight. Before I could take in anything more, someone let out a loud squeal. A short blonde I hadn't noticed at first came ambling toward me.

"Hi, I'm Trace. It's so nice to meet you."

She opened her arms and heat pricked the back of my neck. I was decidedly not a hugger. But I had already anticipated this would happen today, so I braced myself and returned the quick hug.

"I'm Calla. It's nice to meet you."

"Where are you from?" she asked, still hovering close to me.

"Chicago. What about you?"

"Nashville."

My shoulders sagged with relief as I took in the genuine warmth in her expression. At least not everyone on this show would be cutthroat.

Trace looked like sunshine would, if it were a person. She wore a short pink dress, cowboy boots, and a hat. She was adorable, but also not what I was expecting from an author. Then I felt like a jerk for making any type of assumption simply based on what she was wearing.

"Cute dress," I said. "That color is great on you."

"Thank you. I spent hours picking it out." She beamed at me. "I love your sweater. It's so cozy."

"Thanks." I blushed and played with the hole in my right sleeve. Maybe I should have dressed up more for this after all.

"This is a little nerve-wracking, right?" she said in her subtle Southern drawl.

"I'm so glad you said that." I was only five feet six inches, but I had at least four inches on Trace.

"I was a bundle of nerves last night. Could hardly sleep."

"Me either," I admitted. "Every time I rolled over to check the time, only fifteen minutes had passed."

"It was the absolute worst, and they took my phone so I couldn't even distract myself," she said, before asking me more about Chicago and my flight in.

I answered her questions, grateful to find such a friendly ally so early on. Maybe Piper was right and this experience would be good for me.

"And this lodge is stunning," Trace continued. "I can't believe we get to stay here."

"The views are breathtaking," I said, staring out the enormous floor-to-ceiling windows. Rolling plains stretched out away from us until they dissolved into mountains in the distance. I had never been this far west before, and I doubted I'd ever get sick of staring at that view.

"I wonder where we'll all be recording," Trace said, peering down the hall.

"Recording?" Confusion knit my brow. "Like cameras? I'm pretty sure they're all hidden."

"No silly. *Recording equipment.*"

Her emphasis did not help my comprehension.

"Like laptops and notebooks? I'm sure they'll provide us something to write with."

"What do you—"

She stopped talking as we both turned our heads to see a stunning, tall, tanned woman saunter into the room. She wore a black dress with cutouts that instantly made me feel all kinds of inferior. Apparently, I was the dowdiest writer they could find in the continental US.

Trace raced over to hug the new arrival while I hung back and waved, hoping to excuse myself from the obligatory interaction.

"I'm Sofia." She grabbed my shoulders before giving me two air kisses on either cheek.

"Calla," I said.

"This place is adorable." Sofia waved her arms and walked around the room as if already starring in her own personal fashion show.

"Where are you from?" Trace asked.

"I'm in Miami right now."

"Oh, it's beautiful there!" Trace exclaimed.

"It is," Sofia said, turning her face and pursing her lips, almost as if to give the hidden cameras her best angles. She didn't bother asking us any questions. Trace snuck a smile at me and winked.

"So, what do all y'all do for work?" Trace asked.

"I'm a full-time model," Sofia said with a bored tone.

"Wow," Trace gushed. "That's awesome. I'm just a wait-ress. . . Well, you know, at least until I make it big. What about you, Calla?"

I did not want to admit the reality—that I'd been living off the modest advance for my first novel, but had recently depleted it, plunging myself into a mild financial crisis.

"Um, I'm between things right now," I said.

Trace nudged me. "I get it. All of us hanging in the balance until we become superstars."

"Wait, what?" The word superstar felt like an odd choice to describe a successful author.

My question hung in the air unanswered as another new arrival walked into the lounge.

A girl dressed in a flowing, all-white two-piece set waltzed in, her long black hair in braids that hung almost to her waist. "Hey everyone," she called out. "I'm Rachel," she greeted us, and in return, we all introduced ourselves.

I was beyond grateful she offered us each an outstretched hand instead of trying to pull us in for hugs.

"You're stunning," Trace said. I couldn't help but notice Sofia eyeing Rachel up and down, sussing out the competition.

Brady stood in the entrance to the hallway. "Ladies, you're doing great. If you could just migrate over to the couch by the fireplace and continue chatting for a few minutes, the host will be in shortly."

"Thanks, Brady!" Trace called.

"Calla, right?" Rachel asked, as we all followed Brady's instructions and made ourselves comfortable by the fire.

I nodded before remembering I needed to speak more. "Right."

"You seem nervous," she observed.

"Do I?"

"You're balling up your fists so tight in your sweater, I'm worried you might rip it," she pointed out.

I immediately released my hands. "I guess I am a little nervous. And right now, I'm wishing I hadn't worn this stupid sweater."

Rachel shrugged. "I was thinking how jealous I was of your outfit. You look comfortable."

I stifled a groan. "You are not jealous. I look like I'm headed to the grocery store. Meanwhile, you literally look flawless." I gestured at her.

"Thanks." She tugged at the white fabric. "I wasn't sure what to wear. They gave us no indication of what the first day would entail."

"I know. I tried to get something out of Brady, but he gave me nothing," I said as we all leaned forward in our seats. "They tried to get me to change into a dress. Like, for what?"

"Same!" Rachel exclaimed. "I didn't want to, just in case there was some kind of surprise competition. I need to move." She gave Sofia's skintight dress a once-over.

Sofia giggled. "Move? All I cared about was looking as hot as possible."

Rachel shot me a look with raised eyebrows, and I tilted my head. What kind of writing competition would involve that much movement? I looked over at Trace, who now also appeared perplexed.

"What's all y'all's favorite genre?" she asked after a moment of silence.

"Probably romance or fantasy?" I responded quickly.

She gave me a funny look. "I meant music, silly."

"Oh." It was a strange question, but I suppose it was nice to get to know these women. We'd be spending the next few weeks together, after all. "I guess I listen to mostly folk, indie-type music."

"R&B for sure," Rachel said.

"Pop," Sofia said. "I'll listen to anything that's Top Forty."

"How fun. We're all different." Trace clapped her hands in excitement. "I only sing country."

"Wow, you sing?" I turned toward her. "I'm totally tone-deaf. I'd love to hear you sometime."

Trace's mouth dropped open and she whipped her head around, looking at us all. "What do you mean you're tone-deaf?"

"Same here," Rachel agreed. "Can't carry a tune to save my life."

"I'm not that bad. I can act a little, too," Sofia said.

Trace looked between us all "Are you. . . are you not all here to sing? I'm so confused."

"Sing?" Rachel balked. "I'm a dancer."

I snorted. "I can't do either." Puzzle pieces flew through my mind, but I couldn't connect them. "Uh, I'm a writer."

"Then why are you on a singing competition?" Trace asked, bewildered.

"I'm not," I said, panic rising in my chest. *What the hell was going on?* "I'm here for a writing competition."

Rachel snorted. "I don't know what you're all talking about, but I'm here to dance."

We all looked at each other, wild-eyed, before turning to Sofia.

She gave a dismissive flick of her wrist. "What? I'm just here to get famous."

Ice ran down my spine. Something was seriously wrong.

About the Author

Allison Speka aims to bring a refreshing blend of passion and authenticity to her writing. A self-proclaimed romance aficionado, Allison has been lost in the pages of love stories since she discovered the genre. She met her partner in Chicago before they both picked up and moved to Colorado six years ago.

Follow her journey!
    TikTok: @AllisonSpeka
    Instagram: @AllisonSpeka

Trip Switch: A hopeless romantic, a grumpy tattoo artist, and the dream vacation their stuck on alone together…

Love Linked: A grumpy millionaire boss, forbidden workplace romance.

Comfort Zoned: A romance about finding yourself and stepping outside of your comfort zone.

Settle Up: A friends to lovers, aspiring rockstar romance.

Key Ridge: A small town, haters-to-lovers, snowboarding romance.

www.ingramcontent.com/pod-product-compliance
Lightning Source LLC
Chambersburg PA
CBHW020230010826

48973CB00006B/1457